Edwina Currie is a [...]d for fourteen years was the Conservative MP for Derbyshire South. Born in Liverpool, she was educated at St Anne's College, Oxford and the London School of Economics. The author of three bestselling novels, *A Parliamentary Affair*, *A Woman's Place* and *She's Leaving Home*, she is also a successful broadcaster. She has homes in France and London.

Also by Edwina Currie:

Fiction
A Parliamentary Affair
A Woman's Place
She's Leaving Home

Non-fiction
Life Lines: Politics and Health 1986–88
What Women Want
Three Line Quips

EDWINA CURRIE

The Ambassador

WARNER BOOKS

A *Warner* Book

First published in Great Britain in 1999
by Little, Brown and Company
This edition published by Warner Books in 2000

The author gratefully acknowledges permission to quote from the following:
An Intimate History of Humanity by Theodore Zeldin. © 1994, Theodore
Zeldin. Reprinted by permission of Sinclair-Stevenson
Darwin Revisited. © *Economist*, London (30 August 1997)
Candide by Voltaire. © 1990, Roger Pearson. Reprinted from Voltaire's
Candide and Other Stories translated by Roger Pearson (Oxford World's
Classics, 1990) by permission of Oxford University Press
The Troubled Helix eds. Theresa Marteau and Martin Richard. Extract by
Marcus Pembrey. © 1996, Theresa Marteau and Martin Richard. Reprinted
by permission of Cambridge University Press

A CIP catalogue record for this book is available from the British Library.

ISBN 0 7515 2849 8

Typeset in Melior by M Rules
Printed and bound in Great Britain by Clays Ltd, St Ives plc

Warner Books
A Division of
Little, Brown and Company (UK)
Brettenham House
Lancaster Place
London WC2E 7EN

The Ambassador

'What we make of other people, and what we see in the mirror when we look at ourselves, depends on what we know of the world, what we believe to be possible, what memories we have, and whether our loyalties are to the past, the present or the future.'

An Intimate History of Humanity, Theodore Zeldin

'Do you think,' said Candide, 'that men have always massacred each other the way they do now? That they've always been liars, cheats, traitors, ingrates, brigands? That they've always been feeble, fickle, envious, gluttonous, drunken, avaricious, ambitious, bloodthirsty, slanderous, debauched, fanatical, hypocritical, and stupid?'

'Do you think,' said Martin, 'that hawks have always eaten pigeons when they find them?'

'Yes, no doubt,' said Candide.

'Well then,' said Martin, 'if hawks have always had the same character, why do you expect men to have changed theirs?'

'Oh!' said Candide, 'there's a big difference, because free will . . .' Arguing thus the while, they came to Bordeaux.

Candide, Voltaire, translated by Roger Pearson

'No parents in that future time will have a right to burden society with a malformed or a mentally incompetent child. Just as every child must have the right to full educational opportunity and a sound nutrition, so every child has the inalienable right to a sound heritage.'

Bentley Glass, President of the American Association for the Advancement of Science, December 1970

'There are two types of gene therapy: tricky and very tricky.'

Marcus Pembrey, Mothercare Unit of Clinical Genetics, Institute of Child Health, London in *The Troubled Helix*, ed Theresa Marteau and Martin Richards

'Never underestimate the propensity of scientists to treat people as mere objects under observation, or of governments to make a hash of trying to be clever.'

The Economist, August 30 1997

Chapter One

The United States Ambassador, His Excellency the Honourable Lambert W. Strether, known as 'Bill', leaned cautiously over the rail of the old liner *King William V.* He ran his fingers through his thick fair hair and whistled softly to himself. Below, for twenty decks, the white bows curved away to the waterline. His stomach muscles tightened in excitement as he braced himself against the ship's motion, and tried to take in the remarkable scenes on the quay.

Between the vessel and the slimy stones of the jetty the swell was green and sludgy; that must have been done artificially. A sulphurous odour of rotten vegetation arose from the water, the like of which he had not smelled since his boyhood, but it brought wistful pleasure rather than distaste. The attention to detail was astonishing – tufts of grass straggled in corners and by one wall rose-bay willow-herb had been planted, its pink flowers nodding gently. The wheels of horse-drawn wagons clattered over the cobblestones – how clever of the harbour authority to reconstruct them. A band of buskers in shabby bowler hats played nostalgic snatches of Beatles'

songs. Best of all, one large dray, its sides lettered in
Gothic script, was pulled by live shire horses, colossal
beasts with flaring nostrils and ribbon-plaited manes
whose flanks steamed in the morning sun. Yet this was a
real working harbour. Not Disney, not virtual reality.
Liverpool: as authentic as could be found in modern
Britain.

The dockside bustled with figures in old-fashioned
denim dungarees, with bales and bags on their shoulders,
who shouted raucously at each other and to the passengers and welcome parties. The porters were small, dark,
wiry men with stout backs and broad-brimmed felt hats,
their faces turned protectively away from the glare. Some
had hand trolleys on which trunks and cases were piled
in unsteady ziggurats; to keep the tottering heaps upright
on that uneven surface took some skill, Strether noted
admiringly. It would have been much easier to unload
baggage by underground conveyor as was usual, but
much less fun. The port, he supposed, was maintained in
all its historical accuracy not only as an extraordinary
tourist attraction but as a make-work project. The
Europeans took such matters seriously. He must be careful, when commenting to new acquaintances, not to
sound patronising.

The liner rocked gently as hawsers were flung across
the gap and hitched to squat metal capstans. Bill Strether,
a creature of the prairies, had not found his sea legs
during the voyage; his knuckles whitened as he steadied
himself. Below his eye-level black cameras at roof height
swivelled, watching everyone with impartial passivity.
And it was so noisy! The air echoed with cries, klaxons,
tooting trombones and the clang of horses' hooves. A
sudden blast from the ship's hooter made him jump,

along with a bilious churn of the diesel engines in its bowels; though these, he had deduced on the way over, were also fake. The ship must be fuel cell driven: that stood to reason.

The *King William V* was, by any assessment, a marvel. Its very slowness (sixty hours to cross the Atlantic) had given him the chance to adjust to his sudden transplantation so far from home. To accustom himself to his new role would take far longer. It had also been useful to cram some of the mounds of briefing – mostly old technology, on paper, for security – handed over by the President a week earlier. Had he flown in, the forty-minute Mach 3 flight would surely have left him disoriented and queasy. No wonder air passengers were demanding that the journey be extended to an hour to allow time at least for a meal.

By contrast the liner offered the ultimate in traditional luxury travelling of a kind that had otherwise vanished. He had indulged himself with hours of sleep under deckside awnings, a massage with aromatherapy, and chaste dancing with a score of escorts into the small hours. And the menu! What stupendous dishes, a mixture of cuisines from throughout the globe. He had especially relished the vintage Scottish and Danish wines, and the fine mango and paw-paw specialities of Kent, the Garden of England. Definitely the way to go: he was arriving fresh, invigorated and ready to be dazzled by whatever he found.

Bill Strether had not expected to be an ambassador. He had merely raised the largest sums in the Midwest for James Kennedy's election appeal, as local chairman. That had been eighteen months ago. He had wanted to see James in office, as his Kennedy grandfather and great-grandfather had been before him. When the contest was successfully over, Bill – 'good ol' Bill', as he liked to be referred to – would have retired, content, to obscurity in Colorado. He was not a politician and had no desire to be one. In the headiest days of the campaign, while he slapped backs at fundraising dinners and rode in caval- cades with his candidate, he'd had no inkling that some day the motorcade might be for himself. He still had that to look forward to, when he would be chauffeured in a century-old Volkswagen-Royce to present his credentials. An exception had been graciously made for him to use a petrol-fuelled car. The King of England and Prince Marius would be first, then later in Brussels he would meet Herr Friedrich Lammas, President of the European Union, head of the free world.

On the rail Bill Strether's hands felt clammy. The clean life he'd always led, out in the clear high air of his native state, had been a poor preparation for what lay ahead. Paradoxically, what had counted most in Washington was that his personal file was a blank. He'd done well in ranching, that was true. He was liked and trusted by everyone who had done business with him, and was proud of his reputation as a shrewd and fair man. He'd never done a dirty deal as far as he knew, and would have tried to make amends had anyone so accused him. For a moment he wished he had not been so cussedly upright, for it was precisely this blamelessness that had brought him thousands of kilometres to Europe on a bright spring morning.

He had not been President Kennedy's first choice of ambassador: certainly not, he an unknown with crow's- feet etched on his face by the sun. But one by one, as men and women of greater distinction and deserts had been paraded before Congress, each had dropped out. Hostile and capricious questioning was an ingrained habit in vetting committees. The first nominee had been promptly arraigned on a sexual-harassment suit by two former women staff. Similar accusations by an hermaphrodite swiftly dispatched Ms Harriman. Another had allegedly made disparaging remarks about Native Americans while a student. The next, Clifford Vidal *was* a Native American, and gay to boot: several pluses there, Strether reckoned, but after the second day's interrogation he'd withdrawn in floods of tears. A year later the President had stormed about the Oval Office in fury as his ninth nomination collapsed, and in pique threatened to leave vacant the post of Ambassador in London.

At that point he had called his distant Colorado state chairman Lambert Strether, who had set foot in Washington but twice in his career and whose private life was exemplary – about whom, indeed, nothing whatever could be dredged up. Even as a single man, a widower, he had been either celibate or at least utterly discreet, and there were no vengeful children to disgrace him. The cattleman had dutifully put himself straight on the next eastbound plane. Congress had tired of the game and the appointment had been confirmed without further ado.

The turn of events bemused but scared Strether. He was willing with all his heart to serve his country. That much was easy to promise; it would have taken more nerve to deny a desperate President his request. Nor did the task itself seem beyond him; though duly modest, Strether did not entirely picture himself as a common man. He would be one of a team of ambassadors to the European Union and could call on advice from colleagues in the former capitals of Europe – Berlin, Prague, St Petersburg and, still paramount, Brussels. Fast trains could speed him between one and another in less than an hour. For a man whose nearest stamping ground had been Denver, the names alone made his pulse race.

He did wonder, however, about the limitations of his role, now that America was no longer able to tell either Europe or China what to do. Both had become larger, more powerful and wealthier than his own nation, even counting Canada and those less salubrious partners to the south. It was not surprising, therefore, that his instructions were to be the acceptable, affable public face of the United States, Europe's most important and ancient ally. An air of genuine innocence would be an asset. It might be useful also in the more private tasks assigned to him by the White House.

For America's Commander-in-Chief had a secret agenda for him.

'Cigar?' The President had poured two bourbons with ice, then smiled conspiratorially as he unlocked a plain wooden box covered in peeling gold stickers. Behind him the USA, Canadian, Mexican and Panamanian flags were draped in dusty splendour. Beyond the tall window the noon light blazed mercilessly. It was siesta; the streets were quiet.

Strether shook his head. 'Thank you, no, sir. I wouldn't know what to do with one.'

The President's youthful face vanished behind a cloud of smoke through which his teeth gleamed. 'Never tried one? Don't let the First Lady see me – or the police – but I confess these are still one of the great presidential privileges. Rescued from a strongroom in Cuba. I had to get the smoke alarms switched off specially.' He puffed happily for a moment, lifted his long legs and perched his boots on the desk. His head bobbed briefly behind a transparent presentation clock, a mounted miniature NASA rocket, a gold-plated powerbook. He lifted the cockpit off the rocket to use as an ashtray and poked the air with his cigar.

'Now, Ambassador. To business. Europe. You'll love it, all our Foreign Service staff do. Can't get them home when their time's up – they say serving in Lima after London is impossible. So be warned.'

Strether made non-committal noises. The silent circular rhythms of the clock were mesmerising; the white-painted office with its ventilators off was stuffy.

The President swung his legs off the desk and concentrated. 'What we want to know, Ambassador, is what the hell's going on over there? It's supposed to be such a humdinger, a great success story. Population is bigger than ours plus the Japs' put together, and gross national income more than twice the USA's. A big player, and a highly advanced society, as you'll see for yourself. But something's wrong. We get sporadic reports of demonstrations. And there's more. For example: who the devil are the boat people who keep getting washed up in Florida and elsewhere?'

Strether blinked. 'Boat people?'

'Yeah, we've kept it out of the news. Or where it's leaked out locally, we've hinted they were illegal immigrants – nobody cares about *them*. The latest group washed up in the Gulf of Mexico last month. About twenty men and a couple of females in a leaky old tub. Some had odd tattoos on their thumbs. The strange thing was they were incoherent – babbling rubbish, not making any sense. Some died within a few days though physically they'd seemed in fair shape. The previous batch all died within a few weeks of arrival. When we made discreet inquiries to Brussels, we got a bland assurance that there were no problems, and that these people could be returned at any time.'

'Are we sure they're Europeans?' Strether asked, for want of anything more profound to offer. This was news to him. 'I mean, if they were Spanish-speakers . . .'

'No, they were Europeans for sure. From various regions, though mostly they communicated in English. English-English, if you see what I mean. And some had papers. But what beats me is this: why would anybody want to escape Europe, let alone by such dangerous means? And what in heaven's name is wrong with them?'

'Is it catching, sir?' Strether asked anxiously.

'No, no, not as far as we can tell. Though we kept them in isolation, of course. And tests are being run. But so far, no answers. It's been going on a year or so now, apparently; since before my time.' There was a pause; the tobacco fumes formed themselves into an opaque blue haze a metre above the desk. With that mop of golden hair and his smooth-shaven cheeks the President seemed to emerge from a heavenly cloud. His boyish good looks had been a significant factor in his victory.

An idea occurred to the new Ambassador. 'What age did you say they were?'

The President consulted his powerbook. 'Ah, smart thinking. Yes, they were young. Well, under forty. The mystery may well have some link with the demography of Europe, if that's what you have in mind. That is *most* unusual. The Europeans will tell you that first they sorted deaths from the environment – cholera, typhoid and such. Then the infections of childhood like scarlet fever and polio, so by a century ago the average infant could expect to reach its eightieth birthday. A higher life expectancy than in the US, it has to be confessed – but those countries had socialised medicine, and we didn't. So: more recently, everyone's concentrated on the ageing process. And, by and large, cracked it.'

'Alzheimer's, arthritis, osteoporosis, prostate cancer, strokes, poor circulation: that sort of thing?' Strether supplied.

'Right. You and I will never suffer from them. Nor our wives – oh, I'm sorry, Strether, I didn't mean that.'

'She was a Christian Scientist,' Strether replied, with dignity. He was used to such unintentionally cruel remarks. When transfusions had become necessary, she had refused. The death, the loss, still hurt deep inside; time had not lessened it. What remained, too, was a dark loneliness, a need for companionship that had never been filled. He sighed. 'To be frank, sir, I think she'd had enough. Despite the improvements in treatment, it's still pretty savage. And expensive.'

The President paused sympathetically and sipped his drink. 'The Europeans will regard that attitude as strange, I guess. They provide most of those life services free, plus nursing-home care, though God knows how they can afford it. One big distinction between us and the Europeans – they regularly spend half their national income through the state and don't bat an eyelid over it. They don't see the loss of liberty that entails. Here, Congress rightly limits us to no more than one dollar in three. The result's an explosion in the numbers of old people over there. And they're *healthy*. Boy! More than

half the European population is over fifty and a full quarter of the workforce is over seventy. No wonder they've
abolished age discrimination. Be careful: it's even forbidden to say jokingly of someone that he's past it.'

'I'll take that on board, sir.' Strether's head was beginning to ache in the airless heat. Outside, he could hear
faint rumbles as traffic began to move again. A child
laughed somewhere in the building.

'You'll meet a lot of octogenarians. In high places, too.
They're running the show, especially behind the scenes.
Some of the top ranks in the European civil service were
born back in the days of President Clinton. The second
one – Chelsea, I mean.'

'They don't see this as an issue?' Strether was puzzled.

'No, they don't. They have huge private pension and
insurance funds. Vast operations, billions upon billions.
The old are not a problem – the opposite, in fact: they
have enormous spending power. Clout, in other words.
We never got anywhere near that. Makes me as President
distinctly envious, when we're still tinkering with
Medicare. So why would young people want to escape
this earthly paradise?'

'Maybe *that*'s why, sir. With the top jobs blocked, it
won't feel like paradise to them,' Strether ventured.

'You could be right. But aged leaders, of whom you'll
meet a lot, are nothing new in Europe. The British had
Gladstone and Churchill as Prime Ministers in their
eighties. The Russians had a procession of them, like
Yeltsin, well past his prime. The Chinese too: in imperial
and Communist days alike, geriatrics ruled. Funny how
these ancients clung to power just as their empires were
heading for collapse, isn't it?'

'D'you think that's likely to happen, sir? There's been talk,' Strether asked quickly.

The President snorted. 'There's been talk of the European Union breaking up since the day it was founded. That's over a hundred and fifty years ago. It's a helluva long time since the Scandinavians seceded, then saw sense and came back. They quickly discovered which side their *smörgåsbord*'s buttered. On the other hand, if there were tensions, if the Union began to split, or weaken: east-west, or north-south . . .'

Strether waited. Kennedy waved a hand, vaguely. 'Not a matter for my newest ambassador. I don't need you or anyone to start intriguing. But it must be obvious. If the Union weakened, then *this* Union could be the gainer. I wouldn't object to the USA being leader of the free world once more, as we used to be.'

Strether felt himself utterly out of his depth. He examined the carpet for a moment. 'I guess I'm going to find daily life quite a shock there.'

'No doubt about that.' The President aimed at the ceiling and blew a perfect smoke ring. It shimmered briefly above his head like a halo before slowly dissipating. 'We still have a lot in common. Genetically we're pretty much the same stock. But you'll find them a godless bunch, by and large, compared with Americans. Here, we believe in God and we attend divine service at least once a week, mostly. Officially they're the same, but in truth the majority in western Europe are atheists or agnostics – or claim to be – and only ten per cent go to church. It makes a difference.'

'It means they have no worries about playing God. The genetics programme.' Strether shuffled his feet unhappily.

'Precisely. Americans take a – a more *fundamentalist*

view. We are Christian conservatives: and, may I add, I am proud to be counted in that number.' The President's chin went up. Then he shrugged. 'To be honest, they suffered a lot more from the mid-twenties explosions. Much nearer than us. We only got the tail-end of that man-made mayhem. They were breathing, eating and sleeping under a radioactive cloud. Perhaps if we'd seen the same genetic damage, we'd have made similar laws.'

Coming from the President of the United States that was remarkably tolerant, Strether noted. Opinions on the matter were usually expressed with far greater ferocity. A thought occurred to him. 'Say, were these – ah, refugees – copies?'

'We're trying to find out.' The President tapped the dying cigar into his makeshift ashtray and examined its ash regretfully. 'Look, Strether, I don't like the idea any more than you do. It gives me the shivers. But what you got to get into your head is that copies are people. You can't tell by looking at them – no outward signs, no labelling. Though, incidentally, if you use the term "clone" anywhere in Europe you'll get a smack in the mouth. And everybody will deny they exist. The term is "NT" – nuclear transplant. Because that's how they're made.'

Strether nodded glumly. 'NT' it would have to be. 'It'll be difficult, sir,' he mumbled.

The President wagged a finger. 'For God's sake, don't forget it. We can't afford any undiplomatic incidents. Keep this in mind: these people have the same manners, the same looks, and the same rights as everyone else. What happened at the point of conception – if, indeed, they were conceived at all – isn't branded into their foreheads. Those stories about how they have no fingerprints? Absolute balls. No way of distinguishing them.'

'That's why it's banned in the US,' Strether murmured.

'It's been banned from federal funds, yes, since nineteen ninety-seven, but that's not the only reason.'

'Sir?'

The President grinned. 'At college I took a double semester's credit on medical ethics. The moment I got here I called for the secret files. You know cloning was legal in various states for a while? Then it went bottoms-up in California, before you and I were born. A group of militant homosexuals had wormed their way into the top laboratories. They had a mission to prove that they were normal; the plan was that the more people there were like them, the less they'd be seen as freaks. The parents had no idea. But a gay lifestyle doesn't involve loads of babies. A generation later, when the fertility rate in that state dropped to almost zero somebody got suspicious. They'd screwed up the gene bank good and proper. The whole operation was shut down and Congress passed the fiftieth amendment.'

'It's illegal to play with genes in America.'

'Exactly. Our pastors and preachers act as guardians; we politicians take the path of least resistance. But in Europe, the practice is widespread. For them, it's the logical next step of medical science. And they, believe it or not, see it as progress.'

'We use it in cattle. Have done for ages.'

'And it works. *That's* the problem.' The President stubbed out his cigar and drained his glass. The child's laughter was more insistent, and closer now. 'Extra intelligence, resistance to disease, stamina, wisdom, all at the push of a laboratory button. Master-race stuff, may the dear Lord preserve us. You will find it – interesting.'

Strether raised the remains of his bourbon in a toast. 'I

will pledge to do my best, sir.' The two men rose, the President wafting away the tell-tale pungency with a sheepish grin. Strether hesitated. 'One more thing, sir. I can't exactly ask them to their faces. But will the senior people I meet – the Prime Minister, the head of the civil service, people like that – will they be clones ?'

The President frowned. Swiftly Strether corrected himself. 'I mean – ah – NTs.'

'Yep.' James Kennedy responded brusquely, for it was seldom admitted in polite company. He moved towards the door, hand outstretched. 'Just about every one of them; at least, the members of what they call the upper castes. Your maid and chauffeur will probably be, well, like us. But whatever happens, you treat 'em with the deference they deserve. Make sure of it.'

Strether swallowed. 'Even the King?'

'Especially the King. Who in his right mind would do a thankless job like that, unless he was bred to it? Ambassador, stop worrying. You'll do your country proud. Don't forget to pack your auto-translator: you'll need it. And come back when it's all over: Colorado will be waiting.'

At that point the door flew open. A small boy stood boldly in a purple tracksuit, his azure eyes and white-blond hair proclaiming his paternity. He raised his head and sniffed suspiciously.

'Daddy, you've been smoking,' the child announced severely. 'What are we to do with you?'

Strether could still feel that firm handshake, still see his President's clear eyes and pearly teeth. The child's confidence and looks had also touched his heart: that dynasty would continue. Dozens more questions had whirled in his mind, but the opportunity had gone. The answers would have to be found on this side of the ocean.

And maybe other gaps could be filled. It was three years since his wife had died, but longer than that since she had fallen sick. The ache in his breast did not disturb him much in Colorado where her presence was almost tangible, surrounded as he was by her Navajo artefacts, her furniture and pictures, her favourite books. He had not been tempted as he danced on the ship, but the pretty women had been a reminder. In Europe he would face many strange offerings. Perhaps a man could respond. If he wanted to, if the need was there. And it was.

A steward approached, his uniform crisp and starched, gold braid on each epaulette. Out of the corner of his eye, Strether noticed that the movement was tracked by an on-shore camera. He felt an urge to wave, to announce his arrival.

'Your Excellency, welcome to Europe. On behalf of the staff and crew of the *King William V*, thank you for voyaging with us. We hope we'll see you again. Your limousine has arrived on the dockside. Will you come this way, sir?'

Chapter Two

'Strictly speaking, Ambassador, you're accredited to the Court of St James's. Hope it doesn't feel too odd to be coming to Buckingham Palace first.' The Lord Chamberlain snickered, in a way that told Strether this was a standard jest.

'We do still have St James's,' the old man went on. 'For proclamations of a new sovereign and such. But mostly it's used for commercial purposes. Business lunches, company training conferences and the like. It has to earn its keep.'

Strether kept a tactful silence. His escort, Sir John Lanscombe, was tall and narrow-framed. He stepped as if his joints were stiff; he must have been over eighty. Above the black tail-coat and starched white tie the Adam's apple bobbed painfully up and down as if searching for a hearty meal. The mouth was thin-lipped, the eyes pale blue and fringed with sandy lashes, but the pate was fashionably bald. The style was patrician, ascetic, as if self-discipline had been elevated to a primary virtue. Strether sucked in his paunch and pulled back his own shoulders. The surveillance cameras would notice any laxity; he was not yet used to their ubiquitous presence. He might be broader-beamed than the Lord Chamberlain but he was not ashamed of his appearance, even if the court dress and sash of office felt a little silly.

'This way. This is the Throne Room. Now, do you have your letters patent? The King and Prince Marius will be with you in a few moments. As the representative of a foreign power, Ambassador, you may bow if you wish, but you're not one of his subjects so it is up to you. And you can stay for lunch? Excellent.'

Strether was left alone. He gazed around. It had been brave of the British to leave Buckingham Palace intact, marooned along with Clarence House, Lancaster House and other fine buildings on an island out in the enlarged Thames. The Mall ended abruptly in a small dock at which the Royal Barge was moored. A single Tudor Beefeater looking hot in cherry velvet marched slowly around the Victoria Memorial, picking up bits of litter, while guards in striped pantaloons and burnished breastplates lounged sleepily at the gates. The desalination plant, hidden behind a gold-painted trellis topped with crowns and powered by solar panels, provided fresh water for the properties and for the lavish fountains and fish-filled lakes in the gardens. The turrets and chimneys of the palaces were duplicated by their reflections in the river's glassy surface. Strether could see at once, however, that the cost of removing such magnificence to higher ground would have been prohibitive.

His brief tour had shown him that most of the principal State Rooms were on the first floor, approached up a double curved staircase which, he had been languidly informed, had been remodelled for King George IV, almost three hundred years earlier, at a cost of £3,900.

Old pounds, that was. His brain struggled to reconvert first into dollars then euros and gave up. From the thickness of the gilding on the curlicued balustrade and everywhere else he looked – he dared not touch – it must have been an enormous sum for its day. He could not help noticing that the chairs in the Green Drawing Room were a mite threadbare, but they were probably three hundred years old too, owned by a Royal Family that had been strapped for cash for generations.

The room he found himself in was as magnificent as any he had ever seen; the grandeur took his breath away. No Las Vegas imitation could compete. Gold and red, purple and white, imperial colours, gleamed everywhere. The wallpaper was of red watered silk, the curtains, two metres or more high, with braided pelmets, of crimson velvet trimmed in purple. His feet sank into a patterned carpet laid on a wood floor polished to a high sheen, which creaked as he walked. Above his head seven chandeliers sparkled; in the ceiling frieze he could make out the symbols of what once had been the United Kingdom – the harp, lion, the leek and the thistle. Under a richly carved canopy, heavy with more velvet, stood two thrones on a dais, their backs embroidered with the 'WVIR' and 'P' of King William VI and his queen, Patricia.

The English (though not the Scots) had decided they liked their monarchy, despite oscillations of opinion over the century. Strether managed to identify the initials on the backs of the other chairs: EIIR must be Queen Elizabeth II, who died in – when was it? – 2030 at the age of 105, her son Charles having predeceased her. So there was no chair for Charles III. The line had passed to his son William V (after whom the liner had been named), who abdicated during the middle years' uprising: by then he had become a nervous recluse who had never enjoyed his regal status and was, the history books implied, glad to go. His daughter Anne II took over at the Restoration and did an excellent job of re-establishing support for royalty as an institution. She retired in favour of her son, Prince Mark, who died tragically in an accident before he could be crowned. Thus from his accession in 2090, and for the first time in living memory, the nation had a young king, Anne's grandson William VI. The monarch was about thirty.

'Good morning, good morning!' A stocky man in a simple blue tunic and trousers hurried in. He was fresh-faced, sandy-haired, with the prominent Windsor nose. 'I'm so sorry to have kept you waiting. Do pull up a chair.'

Strether was taken aback. This was the King? He had expected a much grander entry. The monarch's unassuming manner was infectious, however, so he shook the hand that was offered and decided to dispense with the bow. The envelope with its crest of the Office of the President of the United States of America was duly presented.

Behind the King entered a slim, taller man, a little older, dark-haired and sallow-complexioned with a cool, intelligent expression. He, too, wore the day suit of tunic and narrow trousers but with a more military cut. The newcomer glided smoothly to position chairs – thrones, Strether realised wildly, as he seated himself gingerly on the edge of one – until the trio was comfortably intimate, knees almost touching.

'Oh, sorry, I forgot. This is Prince Marius Vronsky. He's my cousin, and representative here of the other crowned heads of Europe. And an elected member of the House of

Lords, of which he's far too proud. But mostly he's my friend.' Strether and the Prince shook hands and eyed each other. A door opened and a maid entered with coffee on a tray. Marius brought a small table and helped her to pour.

'So! Welcome to the European Union,' the King continued. 'Been over here before, have you?'

'No, not at all, sir,' Strether answered. 'Not seen that much of my own country either, to tell you the truth. I was a rancher, out west.'

'Like in the old movies. Did you ride a horse?'

'Oh, yes, I was brought up on them. Mostly we ranch with microlites and trail bikes, but there's something special about a horse. They're cheaper, and environmentally friendlier. And you can talk to them, and they don't answer back.'

'Helps if you have to go find a lost dogie, yeah?' The King's eyes were shining. A smile played on Marius's lips.

'We don't lose 'em, sir. Every beast is microchipped at birth and we can track 'em by satellite. But, yes, we do have to go dig 'em out of odd places sometimes.'

'Your life sounds much more entertaining than mine,' the King replied wistfully. 'Still, I'm born to it. I ride for ceremonial occasions; the tourists love to see me. I think that's the main justification of my existence, really.'

Born to it. Strether swallowed. The President had said the King must be – born to it. No, bred to it. The King was the first of those – what was it? – *NTs* – he had met up close. The first, at any rate, of whom he had been aware. Though maybe the Lord Chamberlain was too. How could you tell? Of course, such people appeared on US television and he had seen documentaries on how it was done, but never before had he breathed the same air as one. He studied the young face thrust eagerly so near to his, and began a rambling saga of a night lost on the prairie to give himself time to think.

Absolute prejudice dominated discussion at home about these matters. Wild and frightening tales circulated, designed to bolster the prohibition against such practices. Yet the King looked perfectly normal. Everything moved and functioned precisely as it was supposed to: the blue eyes shone, the skin creased convincingly, the hair was evidently not retouched, though trimmed close to the scalp. An earring gleamed discreetly in one ear. The front teeth were capped, but that was common enough among public figures. He bore a strong resemblance to Diana, Princess of Wales, his great-great-grandmother, but that, too, could have been engineered. It could all have been false; it could all have been real. How was a newcomer to know?

Strether faltered. It dawned on him that he had expected NTs to be more android in appearance, with some tell-tale indication of their origin. The image in his mind was of a manufactured human. He wrestled inwardly and spun out his story as the King peppered him with questions. This youth was something made, manipulated – a Frankenstein's monster. Strether realised he had been convinced (if subconsciously) that such creatures must have a mark to give them away. Nothing as crude as a piece of metal protruding from their necks, or extra nostrils or deformed earlobes. But something, surely. The President had said not. It was a shock to realise that the President must be correct. With no signs, that made it harder. Strether bit his lip.

Prince Marius had been observing him. 'Ambassador,

if you are new to our continent perhaps you will do me
the honour of allowing me to show you around?' The
slight accent betrayed that English was not his first language. Another NT, probably. His hair and eyes were
dark: not, then, the same genetic material as the King,
despite the description 'cousin'.

'That'd be kind of you,' Strether accepted gratefully.
'I'd like to see – everything, I guess.'

'Well, we'll fix that,' the Prince replied. He turned to
the King. 'Our other guests should have arrived. Perhaps,
now that the official business is done, we can move to the
Music Room? I ordered lunch to be set out there. It's so
much cosier than the State Dining Room, don't you
agree?'

It had been done so elegantly. Strether felt checked
over, categorised and made welcome all at once, through
a faultless performance that must have been repeated
many times. The Prince's invitation must mean he had
passed muster. Still, he felt uneasy.

Obediently Strether followed as the King, still talking
animatedly, led the way through great carved doors, some
of which needed both hands tugging hard to open.
Marius brought up the rear. Strether had expected uni-
formed flunkeys, but apart from the maid who had served
coffee no servants were in sight. Evidence abounded that
cleaning staff were also in short supply: a large cobweb
hung from a chandelier in the State Dining Room and
gobbets of dust disturbed by their passage skittered away
into corners. While the opulence was overwhelming,
Strether wondered whether the King and his wife didn't
live quietly upstairs in a modest apartment.

As if reading his mind, Marius remarked, 'Not the most practical house these days, I'm afraid. His Majesty is determined to keep it up, though. His grandmother, the former Queen, held court in a detached property near Hampstead, but it wasn't the same.'

Strether remembered the open space of his own ranch-house, its extended glass wall giving breathtaking views over a lake, the brown hills hazy in the distance. That was far more to his taste than this endless red plush, the tatty edges, the faint mustiness in every corner.

'We get an annual grant from the European Union,' Marius was continuing. 'Then the President, Herr Lammas, can make use of the state apartments when he's in London. He brings his entire household and the palace gets a thorough spring-clean! But he prefers to stay at the Dorchester. Here we are.'

They had entered a sumptuous blue room with marble pillars, its ceiling the most flamboyantly decorated yet. Exquisite pieces of blue and gold china – Meissen? Sèvres? Strether didn't know – adorned every flat surface, most of which were also marble, but aquamarine in colour. Instinctively he held his hands at his sides to avoid knocking anything priceless to perdition. He did recognise Shakespeare in bas relief at one end, and paused in awe before double-life size portraits of the King's ancestors.

'The Georges were hideous,' the King commented, 'and several of my ancestors carried the haemophilia gene. And porphyria. So much misery – changed the course of history, too. Poor Tsar Nicholas! I'd far rather live now, when we can eliminate defects. Wouldn't you?'

There must be an etiquette, Strether brooded. At home the subject was taboo; whenever it was raised, it provoked

fierce controversy. The careers of prominent politicians
who had dared to suggest genetic therapy might have its
virtues had been destroyed overnight. Instead, dwarfs
could still be seen on the streets of Denver, or children
with ill-repaired hare lips or those bulbous foreheads that
had appeared during the 2020s. Playing around with
genes was anathema, even where the benefits were obvious and easily obtainable. Not that the corrective surgery
wasn't on tap, but without publicly-funded medicine it
wasn't much use, not for the poor.

Marius had gone ahead and flung open a door into a
room with a floor-to-ceiling bow window: the Music
Room where, legend had it, Princess Diana had learned to
tap-dance. The view out of the window was of the tran-
quil Thames, which was close to its widest at this point.
The floor was a delicate circular marquetry of black,
browns and tans; the massive columns supporting the
cupola were of black marble, which shimmered in the
light reflected from the water. The effect was to enhance
the isolation of the palace from the bustling metropolis a
few kilometres to the north. A table had been set for
lunch; a single footman in a white jacket held a tray of
drinks.

Four men, the Lord Chamberlain and three others,
glasses in hand and smartly attired in well-cut tunics,
some with ribbons of office at their throats, acknowledged their entrance. Another man in army khaki stood
slightly to one side. The King leapt forward eagerly to
make introductions.

'Do you know Sir Lyndon Everidge, our Prime
Minister? And this is Maxwell Packer, one of our media
tycoons and a great supporter of the monarchy. Our
friend from the military is Mike Thompson, my attaché.

And lastly, this splendid chap is Sir Robin Butler-
Armstrong, the Perm Sec. That stands for Permanent
Secretary – he'll be around years after the rest of us have
come and gone. He is head of the civil service in London.'

'Which means he runs everything, along with his
mates in Brussels and Frankfurt,' added Sir Lyndon, as he
greeted the Ambassador. The Prime Minister was a squat,
solidly built man with thick jowls and piercing eyes;
about seventy years old, Strether judged, but vigorous,
almost bullock-like in presence. His suit was made from
a shiny metalloid fabric that hissed as he moved, as if
hinting at its wearer's slippery character.

The civil servant bowed slightly. He was older than the
Prime Minister and quite similar in appearance to the
Lord Chamberlain. Startled, Strether saw how a desired
(perhaps, fashionable) genetic pattern could begin to
make too many men look like brothers. But the Prime
Minister was of different stock – or, since his eyes were
exactly the same light colour as Sir Robin's, was he?
Strether began to feel confused. He knew he must stop
himself dwelling on the issue, or he would lose track of
what they were saying – and of the job in hand.

The attaché was the tallest, a rugged, muscular figure,
with regular features and a calm, disciplined manner. He
appeared to regard himself as a lower rank than the
others, and busied himself rather as Marius had, moving
chairs and ensuring that the King and the geriatric Lord
Chamberlain had everything they wanted. The strong,
silent type, Strether reckoned, as he concentrated on the
others.

The media owner had a knowing, sardonic air. He was
trim, of medium height with long-lashed dark eyes, not
dissimilar to Marius's. Maybe there was some eastern

European blood in both. Packer seemed not to blink at all, but gazed coolly from King to Ambassador and back again without a word. Strether immediately resolved to guard his tongue in the man's presence. The camera on the opposite wall had already registered their arrival and was swivelling silently from one to another. Strether wondered crossly who was looking at them, and whether anyone in Europe was guaranteed privacy if even the King was not.

The eight men settled themselves at the white-clothed table where they were served by the sole footman and the maid. In deference to himself as guest, Strether noted, the wines were Californian, though modern taste would have condemned the climate as too hot to compete with the world's finest. He'd have preferred a cold beer.

Maxwell Packer was speaking, with a faintly colonial twang. 'Don't take any notice of them, Ambassador, when they talk like that. They all went to the same school. They've been plotting how to run Europe since they learned to walk.'

'Call me Bill,' Strether invited diffidently. 'It is my name. Lambert William Strether. The Fourth. But Bill for short.'

'Ignore Max, Strether,' the Prime Minister responded. 'He may be half-Australian, but he went to our school too, though he was in the class of seventy-eight whereas I was there in forty-nine and our Perm Sec, who knocks everyone into a cocked hat age-wise, stalked the famous corridors in thirty-five or thereabouts.'

'Which school is that?' Strether inquired, his mouth full of oat bread. The starter was smoked farmed tuna, which tasted cheap; the menu card offered a choice of main course, kangaroo, shark or the vegetarian dish, roast truffles, all local produce. At home he could live for ever on beef – or lamb, at a push – but both had long since disappeared from European menus, to the grief of American and antipodean exporters.

'ÉNA, of course,' the King answered. 'I refused to go, and fortunately my grandmother was indulgent. What do I need to know about administration? Not my role – it's theirs. A rough Scottish upbringing suited me. I'm one of the few people in Britain allowed a hunting licence to keep down the deer, and it wouldn't be much use if I couldn't shoot.' Strether was looking blank. The King took pity. 'ÉNA. The school. *The* school. It's French. The École Nationale d'Administration. Oh, you explain it, Marius.'

'Set up in nineteen forty-five by General de Gaulle,' the Prince took up the line. 'It started as a university in France for administrators and politicians. All parties. That's why the French were so dominant at the start of the European Union; you could say that the Énarques were the driving force behind the whole achievement. Students from other countries attend also. Anyway, it's now the supreme academy for everyone who counts throughout Europe. If you're not a graduate, you'll find it much harder to get to the top. And if you do –'

'You'll float up there effortlessly!' the King finished. Strether could see that Sir Robin was not amused, while the Prime Minister regarded the exchange with more indulgence. Maxwell Packer was laughing softly and crumbling a bread-roll without eating it, as if he had heard the joke many times. Opposite Strether Prince Marius half smiled.

'So how influential is it? For example, how many people round this table went to ÉNA, are – what did you

say? – Énarques?' Strether asked. He struggled to pro-
nounce it as they had – *Ayna. Aynark.*

Five hands went up. The King, the attaché and
Strether were the odd men out. The officer shrugged.
'Sandhurst. And Oxford, I'm afraid.' He said no more.

'Bit like the playing fields of Eton, I fear.' Marius
caught Strether's eye. 'But in reality ÉNA is superb. We've
tried setting up rival establishments elsewhere; there's
an annexe in my home town of Budapest, and the LSE up
in Hemel Hempstead. The press have their own college,
but still the most ambitious families like Maxwell's send
their offspring to ÉNA. The network of contacts, the
intense training – ideally suited to the gifted students
selected to go there – makes the place invaluable. Max is
absolutely correct. ÉNA's contribution is not merely a
matter of past glories. It's still the driving force behind the
Union. Even more so, these days.'

'We are governed by an Énarchy, you might say,'
Packer murmured mischievously. 'Everything's decided
behind closed doors. Even what I can broadcast.'

There was a split second's hiatus. Strether saw Sir
Robin cast the newsman a sharp glance. It seemed to contain a mixture of annoyance and warning.

The conversation had moved on. Behind them river boats
plied for trade, their occupants sheathed against the
midday sun by full-sleeved shirts, Hong Kong straw hats
and wrap-around sunglasses. Tourists trained vids on the
palaces and craned to peek through the windows. A pink-
eyed seagull cried and flapped at the glass before
wheeling away. The boats' wash made a soft plopping
sound against the palace wall beneath the bay window.

At last Strether felt able to put down his fork. The kangaroo was supposed to taste like venison, but it was too bland and stringy, as if from overbred rather than wild stock. The staff cleared plates and brought exotic fruits and water ices. A delightful Estonian port began to circulate. Sir Robin dabbed his mouth with his folded napkin.

'This house' – his beautifully manicured hands and pale eyes directed Strether's gaze to the rococo ceiling, the exquisite chandeliers – 'is probably older than anything you've been in before, isn't it? It was built around 1702, we believe, and acquired by King George III as a family home. It became known as the Queen's House. At that date your country was still a collection of unattached colonies.'

'He wasn't mad, you know,' the King said quickly. 'Not that one. He's the King George you Americans are supposed to hate. But there was nothing he could do.'

'Quite,' said Sir Robin. 'Once the colonies knew their own strength, it was obvious that they would break away from the mother country. Such a pity.'

Strether gaped. They were talking about the crises of history as if they had happened yesterday, as if barely a moment ago the personages involved had walked out and slammed the nearest door: the echoes still floated in the air. American habits were exactly the opposite. Whatever had occurred fifty years or more before was ignored or ridiculed. As for household or personal items, everything more than two summers old was thrown out and replaced. It had always been thus. To do so was patriotic, providing jobs for American workers. Here, they seemed to prefer old things. He shifted his weight on the creaky antique chair and, to reassure himself, reached for a ready-peel baby pineapple.

'They kept rebuilding the house so they never had a chance to enjoy it,' the King added. 'The first monarch to live here was Queen Victoria.' His lips were smeared with fluorescent water-ice: children's food. But, then, he was the host. 'D'you know, during the interregnum it was used as a twilight home. And down in the basement was the Metropolitan Police's arsenal. The crumblies wouldn't have slept so sound in their cots had they seen the flame-throwers and bombs a few metres below!'

'A bad time,' the Prime Minister growled. His face had darkened; he seemed to have taken offence at the King's jocular reference to the aged. Strether was reminded of the President's caution about age discrimination. The port was passed swiftly around. 'Thank heaven the voters saw sense. Here, and in much of the rest of the Union.'

'And now we have more crowned heads than at any time since the Union's establishment.' Maxwell Packer smiled at the young King. 'Isn't that right, sir?'

'Well, we're useful, that's what it is, for the tourists, and ceremonial. I'm a fine figure on a horse, I told you. We don't complain, we're punctual, and we take a lovely photograph. Plus we've learned our lesson and we don't cause trouble. How on earth do you manage, Strether?'

Strether spoke carefully. 'The same way they do in France and Denmark. They elect their king for seven years like us, with many of the powers that medieval monarchs had. Only ours is called a president. Checks and balances, for sure, to keep any excesses at bay. If he's capable, he'll be re-elected. Or she. Then that's it. So the country can't be saddled with an absolute disaster.'

'*We* haven't had any absolute disasters,' the King objected. 'Anyway, I can't actually *do* anything. It's down to Parliament for local questions, or Brussels for economics and stuff. Frankfurt for the money. Honestly, Strether, both the PM here and Prince Marius in the House of Lords have more clout than me. I can't even vote.'

'It doesn't seem to bother you,' Strether ventured, 'that so little is decided in London. I mean, we Americans have had our battles over states' rights, but you seem to have conceded far more to the – ah – the centre than we have.'

'That's an outdated debate.' Sir Robin frowned. 'Fact is, Britain was becoming a very insignificant place. On the fringes of the continent, isolated. Our culture was in danger of dying out. Our youngsters were leaving in droves for the richer shores of the mainland. Anyway, people eventually got fed up, always being left out.'

'Or, if you can't beat 'em, join 'em,' the King added joyously. 'So for the last eighty years my country – sorry, region – has given up any fantasy about independence and opted instead to be committed to the Union. Like your Rhode Island or Louisiana. And far better we are for it.'

'Absolutely.' The Prime Minister nodded vigorously. 'And, Strether, we do bloody well out of it. Vast chunks of subsidy. Plus we practically run the place, you know. We provide many of the Union's civil servants. Most senior officers of the European Armed Forces are from England – like Thompson here – and Scotland, and we train the lot at Sandhurst. The combined forces command uses English. So if they have to attack the Chinks, they'll do it yelling, "God for England, Harry and St George!"' He laughed uproariously at his own witticism, jowls wobbling.

'Rubbish.' The newsman rose good-humouredly to the

bait. 'Anglophile nonsense, Strether. Fortunately most of
the regular soldiers are German, though I shouldn't repeat
that outside. And the Turks and Bosnians are fine, when
we can get them off their prayer mats.'

'You see the dilemmas?' The Prime Minister grinned at
Strether and spread his hands. 'Your Union in America,
Ambassador, has sixty states with two languages. Ours
has forty-two former countries, forty-six regions, thirty-
five languages. Thank heaven for auto-translators, though
I loathe 'em. But Sir Robin is right. It works, somehow.
Probably because of ÉNA. We're prosperous beyond our
imaginings; safe, with the Army securely in place at the
frontier, where it belongs. And, whatever our distinguished newshound here implies, with English as the
lingua franca.'

Maxwell Packer tapped his nose. 'I publish in whatever language will sell. But in the Union we had a
communications problem, and an obvious solution. With
thirty-five languages the cost of translation was astro-
nomical, Strether. Even so, that left out many regional
dialects, like Catalan and Breton.' ('And Welsh,' the King
interjected.) 'That was before those dreadful auto-
translators. My father was in Brussels at the time. He told
me interpreters seeking a bonus could halt proceedings at
the drop of a hat by downing headphones. Then meetings
had to be chaired by the Dutch, who understood everybody. So official translations were eventually limited to
languages spoken in more than one region. Hence
English, yes. But also German. And, when anyone can
remember it, French.'

Language ability would have been high on the list
when their parents selected their infant genes. It dawned
on Strether that, with the exception of himself, the entire

conversation could have been conducted as easily by the others in several living languages. And possibly in dead ones such as Serbo-Croat and Greek as well.

'Nor should you assume, though I say it with respect in the King's house, that it is the King's English that is commonly taught.' Packer continued easily. 'As a practitioner I should know. The classic syntax of Milton and Shakespeare, the cadences of Dr Johnson, the novelistic style of the cult authoress Catherine Cookson have been obliterated. Modern English owes more, Ambassador, to your American-English, through the influence of Hollywood, civil aviation and Microsoft.'

The Prime Minister scooped himself another portion of dessert. 'I still say we should have made learning Chinese compulsory. China may not be hostile indefinitely. You've got to think ahead. Our grandchildren may bless us for it one day.'

'So what about you, Strether?' the King asked. 'How does it feel, coming from a small country?'

Strether's mouth opened and shut. 'What do you mean, sir?'

'Oh, well, not *small*, exactly. But not big, either. Smaller than us – the European Union. Russia alone is the world's largest region, larger than China. I may not be bred for my brains, but I know that much. That makes Europe the biggest. Doesn't it? And China's second. You're third. A third-world country.' He tittered.

There was an embarrassed silence. The water-ice must have had alcohol in it; the King's cheeks were flushed. 'I suppose that's right,' Strether said doubtfully. 'We've had to come to terms with that. But, you know, when you sit in the middle of that huge continent as I've done most of my life, you don't see it that way. It's only when you're brought face to face with the – ah – true size and power of Europe, that it dawns on you.'

'That was always the intention,' Sir Robin said softly. 'The founding fathers – ours, I mean, not yours – were determined to set up an empire to rival the Americans'. And, eventually, to outdo and eclipse you. Which we have.'

'Don't let it bother you, Strether,' Maxwell Packer intervened smoothly. 'We will stay friends. Hands across the Atlantic. The Special Relationship. And remember, we are in the front line against the Chinese, not you. It's our troops who protect the liberties of the free world now. Though you're always welcome to join in.'

Strether felt extremely uncomfortable and was conscious of having been put in his place. A career diplomat would have known what to say next; instead, he reached for his coffee and made a play of stirring it.

The elderly Lord Chamberlain appeared to be dozing. From time to time the officer prodded him gently upright, but otherwise seemed to have no role, though he was listening with quiet interest. Prince Marius also had said little. Strether caught his eye. Perhaps in response, Marius sat forward and made to change the subject by turning to the Permanent Secretary.

'How are the plans for the Celebration going? You're on the Committee, aren't you?'

'For my sins, yes.' Sir Robin readily took centre stage. For Strether's benefit, he added, 'The Great Celebration, to which you, Ambassador, will be invited as a most honoured guest.' He sighed. 'It will be a busy year for firework manufacturers with the end-of-the-century commemorations. And next month, I suppose, one cannot avoid observing the anniversary of the signing of the

Treaty of Rome, but every year Europe Day drives me straight to my Prozac.'

He warmed to his theme. 'Europe Day will be a mere rehearsal for the events on New Year's Eve. The Tower of Babel writ large, with chaos thrown in. You wouldn't believe such sensitivities still existed, or such puerilities. We are to have days on end of Latvian folk-dancing, Israeli transvestite popstars, Russian opera, Scandinavian plays – Strindberg *and* Ibsen, in Swedish. The Tibetan monastery in Scotland is putting on a day-long display of chanting. The Ukrainians are running a camel hunt. The Irish are reviving *Riverdance*, though they've forgotten the steps. The Venetians want a gondola race simultaneously up the Rhine, Thames, Seine and Oder tracked by the Astra 42 satellite. The Square Mile here in London is to have a four-week lottery game in which the winner breaks a bank. The only ones making any sense are the Saxon-Germans and French. The Saxons are offering an AleFest in every major city throughout the Union with free beer, while the French –'

'– will do a cook-in in each region, with free perfume samples for every lady from sixteen to ninety-six!' Maxwell Packer finished. 'Well, why not? The French have always adored *la différence*. They like to give pleasure.'

'Not lost our quintessential characters, as you see,' the Prime Minister pointed out. He drained his glass. 'That's why ÉNA has become so important. The top boys and girls can talk to each other and get things done, while the ordinary mortals indulge themselves with folk-dancing. And we politicians rant, rave and exercise our modest influence through local assemblies weighted down with tradition. The House of Commons, I mean. To which, with apologies, sir, I must now return.'

Chairs were scraped back. The King rushed over to the door, heaved it open and could be heard calling to staff that the meal was finished. The Lord Chamberlain was awoken and helped to his feet. Hands were shaken once more, courtesies and compliments exchanged. The Prime Minister hurried off, followed at a more dignified pace by the two older men. The King and the attaché disappeared through another door. Packer seemed to know his bearings and slipped away. The soulless cameras followed his passage and paused as if bereft. Strether was left in the capable hands of Prince Marius, who walked him slowly through another set of fine rooms and back to the front courtyard.

'Well, Strether, I hope you found that enjoyable.' On his own Marius seemed larger, more dominant. It took some skill to wax and wane like that, always to fit in.

'Bill,' Strether said resignedly. 'Call me Bill. Yes, it was fascinating.'

The Prince chuckled. 'I'm sorry. We don't use the given name here except for close intimates. It's not polite. They are treating you with due decorum, in fact – going quite far in using your surname.'

'Oh? I don't get it.'

The two men strolled towards the gates, avoiding the fierce sun wherever possible. The embassy water-bus was waiting, lolling gently on the tide. The Thames sparkled invitingly; a cormorant on a post flexed black wings then suddenly lifted and dived, surfacing with a wriggling angel-fish in its beak. On the far shore the queue for the afternoon's palace tour chattered excitedly. The Swiss Guards ceased to lounge at their approach and presented arms. Marius saluted.

'The surname is used between those who went to school together. It's the custom in Europe, implies they've known each other since childhood, which, in the case of upper castes, is likely to be true. But I'll call you Bill, if you prefer. And I'm Marius.'

'Thanks. And thanks for looking after me, Marius, I appreciate it. Say, did you mean it when you said you'd show me around?'

'I'd be delighted. What would you like to see? Parliament, certainly. That will be arranged. The underground cities: yes, I know you have them, but nothing like ours. Global warming has changed everything drastically, you know. And you must inspect the troops at the front — Maxwell was right to mention that. Then how about leisure? You are not married, no? You can come with me to the Toy Shop, if you like.'

Strether allowed himself a quick smile. 'Thanks for thinking of that. I'd like to get to know — I mean, I think it's time . . .' He stopped, embarrassed, but the younger man patted his arm.

'Understood. I've read your file, naturally. We have some charming women over here. When you are in Brussels for Europe Day in May I will take you to our gentlemen's club, the Forum. Now, have I missed anything important?'

Strether shuffled his feet. 'I'd like to see . . .' He hesitated. 'Sorry. It's difficult.'

Marius turned his back on the impassive guardsmen and spoke low. 'You'd like to see the laboratories, is that it? You want to know about our genetic programme?'

Strether nodded dumbly. He was conscious of blushing furiously. Marius laid a hand on his shoulder. 'Not open to the public, as you'd expect, but you'd be a privileged visitor. Leave it to me. But be warned. It can be quite a shock when you go there.'

'Yes, I guess so. There are so many questions I want to ask. Will that be allowed?'

'You can ask me. After your visit, preferably. I will try to be straightforward with you, my dear Bill, but just remember this. We in Europe are certain its activities are central to our well-being. Essential, indeed. We regard ourselves as in many ways far ahead of America, you know. Go with an open mind, and don't be alarmed at what you see.'

They parted cordially and Strether settled into the water-bus. The Prince had declined the offer of a lift and was now hailing a water-taxi heading in the opposite direction. Strether envied the easy style of the young aristocrat: he seemed so comfortable, in contrast to the clumsy American who was painfully aware of how inadequate was the show he made in such sophisticated company.

But perhaps he should not have revealed that he had heard of the Toy Shop. Nor hinted that his curiosity might overcome any moral scruples, should the chance arise to visit. What he had had in mind, when the fair sex was mentioned, was not a lady who earned a living at it. Marius had spoken of charming women in Europe; those he had seen so far, though few to talk to, had impressed him mightily with their poise and grace.

Maybe it was only a matter of sending out the right signals when the moment arrived. And being watchful, ready. Like those damned cameras, whose eyes seemed to follow him wherever he happened to go.

Chapter Three

'You would think' – Lisa Pasteur grunted to herself – 'that with all the advances' – gasp – 'available to modern science' – heave – 'at the end of the twenty-first century,' – *pant* – 'we might have found some better way' – *oh, Lord* – 'of staying fit' – puff – 'without so much bloody *effort.*'

The rowing machine pinged. The six minutes were up. The drag on the flywheel slackened as the machine's androgynous voice sighed encouragingly: 'Well done, Lisa. You were within three per cent of your score two days ago.'

Lisa pushed back a lock of dark hair that had escaped from the sweat-band and wiped her brow on her forearm. She bowed her head till her pulse stopped racing, then reached for a capsule of isotonic concentrate. The chilled drink tasted both salty and sweet and made her grimace.

Time for a tone-up of her upper arms. Lying back on a bench, feet placed firmly on the ground, she swung the batons in tidy arcs over her head, twenty, forty times. Her shoulder muscles were protesting too early; the weights

seemed heavier than usual. Still muttering crossly, she
switched to the lateral-pull machine, seated herself
squarely and reached upwards. At the first tug her spine
jarred and she stopped dead. *Darn it.*

Perspiration beaded on her forehead and on the backs
of her hands. In the training shoes, her toes wriggled
stickily. The new non-metalloid leotard clung to her ribcage, showing off in silver and lilac stripes the womanly
outlines of a flat stomach and curved hips. She chided
herself for the momentary weakness that had allowed her
to purchase the idiotic outfit. Self-coloured cotton was
definitely more sensible.

Around her other lithe figures paused with words of
sympathy. The sessions for the obese came later; experience had taught that both groups were happier if kept
apart. The spring sunlight streamed through the sky-
lights. Perhaps she should have gone for a run instead. As
she stretched and towelled off, the wall computer offered
the results of her monthly blood test. A pinprick at the
start of the session was sufficient. *Cancerous cells, nil.
Pre-cancerous cells, below normal levels.* Okay.
Cholesterol: 4.2 mmol/litre. No risk of heart disease there.
Haemoglobin, 14. Excellent, almost athlete standard.
*Thyroid function: satisfactory. Serum prolactin: 470 mu/l,
serum FSH 3.8, LH 6.1.* Consistent with pre-menstrual
state. *Prostaglandins, gamma linoleic acid (GLA): normal.
Leucocyte count, high.* Could that mean a mild respira-
tory infection?

Her back had ceased to twinge, but a bout of water
relaxation would help. Medication would sort out both
the PMT and the possible cold, but she would rather not
take it. What was the point in introducing enhanced disease resistance into the genes then bludgeoning the

system with chemicals? Instead she headed for the flo-
tation tank: on a quiet afternoon in the gym she would
have it to herself. As she entered, soft neon lights began
to glow in ever-changing colours and Mozart's flute and
harp concerto filled the cubicle.

She felt unusually tense. Even on her back, with
warm, viscous liquid lapping against her thighs and rose
perfume in the ionised air about her face, conflicting
thoughts jostled in her mind.

Thirty-four. Quite young; below the average age for marriage, and still with years to go before the average age of
first conception. With hormone therapy, indeed, she could
conceive any time up to her eighties. Strictly speaking,
there were no limits; it was a matter of personal preference.
The biological clock could be altered, suppressed or postponed at will. At any age eggs could be surgically removed
and united with the designated sperm *in vitro*. Or ready-
made fertilised cells, already inspected, might be selected
from the bank. Motherhood could be bought off the shelf.
But instinctively Lisa sensed that none of these advanced
alternatives would do. The niggling desire for her own
genetic baby had crept to the surface. It was as impossible
to ignore, as much a *part* of her now, as the shape of her
own breasts bobbing in the scented water.

The conception would be done under a microscope, of
course. And once the embryo was created, the best that
modern medicine could offer would swing into action. A
surrogacy could be arranged, though a laboratory pregnancy was by far the safest. Since she was an NT and
must protect herself, and her child, giving birth the old
way was to be avoided. But she wanted her *own* baby,
flesh of her flesh, bone of her bone. That much was un-
deniable, and had been for more than a year.

What was lacking was the man to share the partner-ship. And the joys, and horrors, of parenting.

The problem wasn't sex, as such. The division between sex and childbearing was complete. The physical act had few undesirable consequences: except, unavoidably, that the unwary fell in love as ever, and could be betrayed or abandoned, their emotions in shreds. Nothing new about that; human nature did not alter. The other risks were few. Sexually transmitted diseases had been eradicated, first by vaccination then by genetic manipulation, though new bugs were an ever-present feature; nature was always, infuriatingly, one step ahead. Both men and women enjoyed casual liaisons and professed to suffer no damage. Lisa did not care for such lack of commitment and chose not to sleep around. She was not averse to a fling, but she had never learned to value sexual gratification for its own sake. She preferred to know the name of a partner whose hair she might find on her pillow in the morning.

What about the possibility of bearing a child without a partner? Artificial insemination was commonplace for professional women like herself, but its clinical heart-lessness did not appeal. Nor did the murkier and mainly illegal processes that could reproduce a human replica from a scrap of one's skin. So strong were the prejudices against such deviancy, indeed, that Lisa had not considered it for a moment. Such action required a misapplication of the genetic programmes on which she worked, to which she had devoted her life. She would not dream of doing that, for purely selfish purposes. And if she were found out, it would probably cost her her job.

It was far better to stay within society's norms. Marriage had been through a bad patch until the turn of the century, as feminist theory conspired to make men expendable. Then the disaster of that movement's long tail of detritus, sole-parent families – mostly women, mostly poor, their children distressed and at serious disadvantage – had at last hit home with policy-makers. The rejection of 'independence' in favour of 'interdependence' had been hesitant to begin with and had provoked furious debate. But women, Lisa reflected, had wished to have it all, and hormone therapy made that easy. Now monogamous marriage was celebrated as the best environment for both adults and children, and was encouraged by tax incentives, fashion and example.

She should be setting that example. The accepted pattern was a career lasting fifteen or twenty years, then wedlock and children. So she was right to be thinking about it, if a trifle early. A combination of family life and work was entirely acceptable for both partners, provided that neither parent was ever completely absent. That pattern, repeated research showed, was healthy both mentally and emotionally. The offspring were serene and comfortable individuals, able to accept responsibility and with high social skills. If this fomented laziness, especially among the highest castes, it could be countered by dosing the embryos with a dash of extra ambition. Her own parents had requested it for their children, which was why she occasionally felt driven, as in the gym. Beneath, though, was the growing realisation that she had begun to yearn for a settled homelife. The troubling questions were, How? and, Who with?

He had to be kind, but not necessarily handsome – appearance was so much a matter of transient taste, and as a scientist she prided herself on deeper values. Intelligent, certainly, though perhaps not in her own field: nightly conversations about her research would probably irritate rather than stimulate her. Older, possibly: a father figure had intense appeal. Mostly, it was his character that counted. And how much she meant to him, how much he cared, and how capable he was of telling her.

No man lingered round the corner. Nobody available, and suitable. Nobody terribly interesting, to tell the truth. Once, she had thought so, but the two of them had been too young and had drifted apart. The taste of love had lingered. She knew, or felt she knew, what love was about. The prospect did not frighten her, but it was daunting. And it was not the only worry she faced.

Her project at the genetic laboratory had reached a crucial stage. Within weeks she should discover why that chromosome kept breaking down, and set in train the arduous business of elimination. It galled her that mistakes had recently entered her realm with such regularity. Others might call her a perfectionist, but to Lisa it was a simple matter of scientific competence and control. To maintain the highest standards, everyone in the chain had to be devoted to the programme and respect its disciplines. Anything else was perverse and counter-productive. One might almost think that somebody *wanted* human chromosome 21 to keep breaking: somebody further up the line, faceless and nameless, who dealt with the early foetal material before it came anywhere near her own dispassionate investigations.

One thing was quite obvious: whoever it was, he (or she) was playing a dangerous game. Someone, perhaps, with an unfortunate taste for the macabre.

*

St Martin's-in-the-Fields was deserted, as he knew it would be. At this time, early in the year, there were no festivals, no particular reasons to attend and thank God, though the blossom and the glory of early spring never failed to make his heart dance.

Mike Thompson slipped into a pew, knelt briefly then sat, hands clasped in his lap. The carved angels looked down mutely on a solidly built man in faded khaki drill, his face weather-beaten, his blue eyes deep-set, with that ruggedness Strether had noted at the palace. In the stillness of the afternoon, shafts of sunlight slanted from the church's windows high above the oak gallery. The tips of ancient gilded plasterwork on the ceiling glowed as the light slowly shifted. Dust motes hung in the air.

He had sung here, in the choir, as a small boy. It was more common then, and quite acceptable, for the military to be believers. The third generation of NTs had only just made their appearance; older manners still predominated. Remembrance Sunday had not been abolished till 2070, ostensibly on the grounds that it had become obsolete. But the year before young Michael, then aged eleven, had sung 'Onward Christian Soldiers' with gusto in a church over half full. Indeed, he could still recall the words of 'Abide With Me'. Perhaps the dislike of commemorating the dead of forgotten European conflicts was understandable; the bones of the First and Second World Wars mouldered in neglected cemeteries while the interregnum and even the Restoration were passing from living memory. The change, however, probably had more to do with the accession of the Russians to the Union in 2060 and the atheistic opinions of the newly elected Vice President, who claimed his ancestry back to Stalin.

Abide with me; fast falls the eventide;

The darkness deepens; Lord, with me abide . . .

The soldiers' hymn. He hummed it under his breath, loath to disturb the peaceful stillness. *I fear no foe with thee at hand to bless: Ills have no weight, and tears no bitterness.* Sung on battlefields from time immemorial before facing the bullets; and at the end of a day, as the bloodied remains were collected and prepared for burial. *Where is death's sting? Where, grave, thy victory?* Superstition, much of it. Both sides calling on their God for protection, and professing to believe in the same deity. Each man asking for personal protection that day, and for his comrades and loved ones. *I triumph still –.* Wishful thinking, of that he was convinced. No God of any value would take sides: the battles were of mankind's own creation.

– if thou abide with me.

Yet the superstitions of the prayerful were irrelevant. The shallow simplicity of their belief did not rule out a superior power. If such a being existed, most soldiers would rather have it content than displeased. Thompson was bred, he had been told, with specially sharpened spatial and numeric abilities to broaden his martial range. His father, a renowned four-star general, had also requested psychological insight and man-management skills for his son, for whom he had great plans. Thompson suspected that his slowish progress up the promotion ladder – he had barely been gazetted as Brigadier at the age of forty, and had only just made it to Lieutenant-Colonel – might have made the old man impatient, had he lived to see it. The General had not approved of that International Studies degree at Oxford, either: idleness, he had called it. His son's appointment as an aide to King William might have impressed him, though he would have spotted that palace duty could be mind-numbingly tedious. The father's death when his son was at Sandhurst had freed the young man to grow at his own pace. None the less, it was at moments like this that Thompson was grateful for his traditional Christian upbringing.

Officially the Union was still God-fearing though its citizens were more than lax in attendance, in contrast to the durable fundamentalist revival in the USA. In Britain most churches had closed and had been converted into housing or mini-malls. Even the latter-day arrivals in Europe, Sikhs and Moslems, bewailed their vanishing congregations, while European Judaism was confined to a few squabbling suburbs in Golders Green, Tel Aviv and Jerusalem.

As for Christianity, Serbian and Russian Orthodox observance had replaced Roman Catholicism as stylish among the glitterati. The Church of England had wilted under the burden of maintenance of its great cathedrals. One Archbishop of Canterbury had hit on an answer. It had been decided to save the jewel of the Anglican rite, Westminster Abbey, by dividing up the days of the week. An auction was held and sealed bids invited (the Catholics held aloof from what they regarded as a disreputable exercise). The results might have been foreseen. Night after night the ancient stones rang to the sounds of strange music, wails and caterwauls from New Age cults and the like, while an astonished public crept in to watch. That was why Mike Thompson preferred St Martin's: he was alone, but still the church preserved an atmosphere of sanctity. The same could no longer be said of the Abbey.

Rationalise as one might, it was still helpful to believe,

particularly in an occupation which required him to carry a laser gun at all times. In his jacket pocket lay his new orders, folded. He was doubly thankful; they would take him out of the palace frying pan (though that was unfair, the King was a kind and undemanding master), but at least, not into the fire. It was not North Africa, this time. The climate change which had wreaked havoc on Mediterranean vineyards had rendered the Magreb virtually uninhabitable. The sub-Saharan region had become a furnace in which nothing could survive outdoors at noon longer than twenty minutes. Why anyone should bother to fight over its empty wastes was beyond him; but they did, and had to be kept at bay.

Asia was not much better, but he was familiar with it. A command there was no picnic, especially if the Chinese decided to cut up rough. If he were to meet his Maker, Mike Thompson's main reaction would be polite curiosity. Until then, he professed the religion of his forefathers. Especially just before his second posting to Outer Mongolia.

In life, in death, O Lord, abide with me . . .

The television studio was, to Princess Io's surprise, no more than a black-painted box hardly large enough for herself, the interviewer and the paraphernalia of camera, video and sound equipment. In deference to her royal status and her age, the lights had been dimmed slightly but still they burned and made her skin itch. Maybe her son Marius had been right: he had recommended refusing this interview. But it was her favourite fibre optic channel and her favourite star, 'Flash' Harry Docherty. And she was flattered to have been asked. So why not? Why shouldn't an elderly Princess, who passed far too many days bored to stupefaction, have her moment on the air-waves?

A flicker of disappointment nagged at her. Flash Harry was shorter and portlier than she had imagined and far less respectful of her than he should have been. He sat hunched, drumming his fingers, eyes half closed while his face was powdered. He was taking no notice of her whatsoever, despite her foray at a few words of genteel conversation. When the makeup girl had finished he began tapping buttons on his powerbook, presumably to check his notes.

A voice in the darkness called out that they were ready. The Princess smoothed her cream silk-and-linen tunic with the tiny pearl embroidery, and tweaked her skirt. Her legs were still shapely and she crossed them neatly at the ankles, before realising that the camera would show only her head and shoulders. She sat up, hands folded in her lap, and allowed that enigmatic little smile her friends said was her hallmark to play about her exquisitely crimsoned lips.

'Well, hi to you all!' Flash Harry leaned roguishly into the camera. To the Princess it was disconcerting: she half-expected a cheering audience somewhere to shout 'HI, HARRY!' back. They did, when the programme was broadcast.

'Today we gotta special guest. Princess Io.' He pronounced it with emphasis – 'I-O' to rhyme with Hi-ho, as if she had been named for a song in an ancient Disney cartoon. 'Born in Japan, the great-granddaughter of the last Japanese Emperor. When the Chinese invaded, she fled with her parents. Picture if you will, leddies and gennlemen, this tiny child – nine years old, terrified and clinging to her mother – brought out of the land of her fathers to an alien world. Ours.'

That was not quite accurate: Io sniffed impatiently. The invasion had certainly taken place in 2022 when she was young, and, temporarily, the family had thought it wise to move. But they had returned. It was not until her twenties that she had left for good. And then it had been for freedom from her family, and for romance.

Flash Harry turned to her. 'Princess, welcome.' His eyes burned with sincerity. They were so blue they must be coloured contact lenses. He didn't look like an NT. 'It must have been a very traumatic event for you, Princess, to see your country overrun in that way? You, a small girl, forced to leave your homeland?'

The Princess inclined her head with the utmost delicacy. 'Indeed it was. Dreadful. And to know that we could never go back . . .' She sighed and lowered her eyes. It was a supremely Japanese gesture, so much in contrast to the arrogant glares of China's leaders to which news-watching westerners were accustomed.

'Right. You must feel anxious still for your own country, Princess. Japanese culture is in danger of disappearing altogether, isn't it?'

'One country, two systems, they say.' The Princess gave a diplomatic flutter of the eyelids. 'One does not know how far to trust their intentions. The Chinese are remarkable people. They say they are keen to develop the economic strength of the Japanese islands, but they do not understand that business success comes from the liberty to make decisions without the state setting obstacles at every step.'

Flash Harry cleared his throat. This might be a bit esoteric for him, the Princess reflected. She waved a beringed hand dismissively. 'I have lived in the West for over sixty years, Mr Docherty. I married a Hungarian prince, may his soul rest in peace. My children are second cousins to dear King William. I have established my home here and been made to feel so welcome. I love the European Union, and would not go back.'

That was more like it. The pucker on Flash Harry's brow vanished and was replaced with a broad grin, as if she had paid him a personal compliment. 'Well, Princess, that's what we like to hear. And your family was born in Britain too.'

'Not quite. My younger children, yes. Prince Marius was born in Budapest. We left when Hungary voted to become a republic, otherwise he would be king there now. But, like myself, he has opted for the modern world, not the world as we might wish it to be. His service as an elected member of the House of Lords here in London gives me great pride.' She smiled sweetly.

They spoke of how much had changed in her lifetime – the weather, the disappearance of traffic jams, new-fangled gadgets such as the vidphone and self-wash laundry unknown in her youth. The studio clock showed that the allotted seven minutes were nearly up. 'Princess, you know we ask our guests to choose a favourite piece of music and a favourite book,' Flash Harry said. He was looking relieved: the thinking part of the interview was over. He gazed at her intently. 'What are your choices, ma'am?'

'Mr Docherty, that was so difficult,' Princess Io cooed. 'I like all music. But the concerto for bamboo pipes and zithers by the renowned Japanese composer Michiko Hirano would give me great pleasure, and for my book, the collected works of Kazuo Ishiguro. You know he wrote in English, of course?'

It gave her great and wicked pleasure to see the blank expression on Flash Harry's face. There was no *of course* about it: he hadn't the faintest idea what she was talking about. The courtesies were concluded and she was invited to remain in her seat until the recording was finished.

'That's it, we have a clear,' came an authoritative voice from the darkness. Another anonymous hand touched her arm and led her to the side. Flash Harry nodded a curt 'Thanks, Princess, 'bye,' before rummaging for his powerbook. He had already wiped from his limited brain the Princess's details and was immediately engaged in absorbing the bare facts about his next distinguished interviewee, who was waiting in the wings and fiddling nervously with his necktie.

It had not been an uplifting experience, the Princess confided later to her son. What she did not tell him, however, was her horror as she watched herself that evening from the comfort of her boudoir.

She looked old. She *was* old, but that was not itself a nuisance. Not normally. Her body was in fair condition: it has never been denied whatever care and treatment it required. She had never abused it with alcohol, tobacco or psychotropic drugs. Her clothes emphasised her bird-like fragility; her hair was as black and glossy as in her youth. And she had prided herself that her most recent face-lift, at the age of seventy-five, would last her till her natural end.

But the face looked haggard and wizened. The eyes sagged. Turkey skin disfigured the chin-line. On her fine bone structure the result was appalling, a stark contrast to the featureless inscrutability she had cultivated both as a princess and as an oriental.

As the programme credits rolled to the sound of enthusiastic applause from the mystery audience, the Princess reached for the vidphone. She might not be able to exchange her birth certificate, but she could tackle its unwanted outcome, and at once.

The office of Rottweiler Security Services, situated in the heart of political London, was busy. On the wall the big vidscreen zizzed, untuned. A radio crackled; a voice could be heard, gruff and staccato, barking out orders in a drill room nearby. Mugs of instant coffee steamed untouched as Captain Wilt Finkelstein stood scratching his head.

For all that he cultivated the style and manners of a New York police chief (which, in another incarnation, Finkelstein was convinced he had been), he was purebred Essex Man, born Charlie Cooper. He had retired from the Met with a medal, a pension and a bullet-hole in his groin. Active service, despite the bulging holster on his hip, was out of the question. The Met, however, looked after its own. What the public services could not provide was the fiefdom of private security firms. The best and biggest was Rottweiler, known for the splendid beast's head on its leather jackets and for the uniformly stolid appearance of their guards. RSS operatives had a reputation as hard men who fulfilled orders efficiently and without haggling, a necessary consideration for the government contracts in which it specialised. Its chief executive, a former Met commander, was delighted to ensure that heroes such as Cooper/Finkelstein could continue in lucrative and respectable employment.

The door crashed open. In came the colleague

Finkelstein thought of as his sidekick, Dave 'Dozy' Kowalsky. His real surname was Manningham-Buller, but the two men had agreed that it did not have quite the right ring. The adoption of another, harmless identity was quite common when men joined RSS. Kowalsky was carrying a chipped china plate piled high with pastries.

'I shouldn't,' Finkelstein muttered, as he helped himself. 'I'm not an NT, you know. My doctor says if I carry on like this my arteries will fur up, and it's a bypass next. Maybe even a new heart.'

'Sod it.' Kowalsky was already chewing. 'We need the energy. And we're both in our prime.' Since both men's bellies sagged over their belts, that was not strictly true.

'I won't be if the big jobs keep coming in at this rate.' Finkelstein indicated the electronic telefax machine. 'Where do they think we're going to get the staff? Protecting Parliament from outside is one thing. Uniforms, laser weapons, shoulders back: we're used to that. Putting our men on the inside needs a different type altogether. Undercover, they say. I don't like it. What for?'

Kowalsky wiped his chin with the back of his hand. 'I shouldn't bother your head about it, Wilt,' he advised. 'Ours not to reason why. They pay the bills, we do the contract. Maybe recruit a couple of smart girls, yeah? Kit 'em out in posh tunics from Harrods. Then they'll look the part, blend into the background with all them MPs.'

Finkelstein glowered. 'We'll lose 'em. They'll want to become MPs themselves. Or marry one. Lord knows what they see in politicians – must be the whiff of power. They don't get no prettier.' He paused. 'And what about this? New American Ambassador. Got to keep an eye on him too.'

Kowalsky peered over his shoulder at the photograph

and DNA details. 'No problem.' He shrugged. 'Standard stuff, that. Nothing he'll get up to that we won't know about. And the automatic eyes keep most things in sight. Those cameras give me the creeps, so God knows what effect they have on the criminal fraternity.'

'The eyes are the main reason for the fall in recorded crime as you well know, which is why you and me have reason to be grateful for these security jobs.' Finkelstein was permitted by his rank to be portentous.

'But Jeez, Wilt, d'you think anybody ever actually checks out the stuff we dig up?'

'Nah,' his captain agreed. 'You're right. It's for show, and to keep the natives docile. Mostly, you an' me, we're wasting our time. So let's get on with it, shall we?'

The dark-skinned man backed away, his face working. Outside the sun blazed; in the dank hospital, the air hung chill with death.

He waved helplessly at the flies that buzzed over the corpse. Already the orderly was disconnecting the drip lines; what remained on the stained bed was a disintegrating collection of organic molecules, not a human being.

Yet this had been his friend, someone he had learned to trust, to care about. That had been against the odds; for a prison official to befriend an inmate was most unusual, and probably forbidden. Even here in Kashi, on the edge of the unknown, somewhere between the borders of the enlarged Union and the vast brooding might of China.

Not that he, Ranjit Singh Mahwala, was the usual run of warder, any more than the dead man was a typical convict. His friend had been a cool, dedicated man, a political prisoner, who had lifted the lids on Ranjit's eyes and guided him as to the true nature of the programme, the Union, and what its leaders were attempting to do. Those discussions, under cover of prisoner re-education, had been a revelation. Answers had been summoned for many of the tangled dilemmas in the Sikh's brain: not least, the white child borne by his brother's wife, and the pinch of green powder that was added to every prisoner's daily diet.

And then this man, with his tattooed thumb, his whimsical smile and his passion for truth, had sickened; here in the desert steppes the latest medical science did not reach, though genuine efforts had been made. But saving a lifer was hardly a top priority. Only one blood transfusion had been sanctioned by the Minister and it had been insufficient. Ranjit suspected that the prisoner's name was significant. He was obviously a high-bred NT and had once, he told Ranjit, been in government himself. They were probably happy to see him dead.

Who would mourn? Not the hospital staff. Not the other guards. Indeed, he would have to hide his own grief. He was surprised he felt so bitter, both over the loss and the discoveries, those insights he had gained in recent months from the dead man.

The corpse was being stripped. In the grey indoor light it lay waxy and limp. At the small of the back was the partly healed scar, a purple crescent, over the kidney area. That had been the cause of it. And Ranjit was certain no permission had been given.

Suddenly a terrible misery flooded his soul. If he returned to duty and carried on as before, he would be perpetuating the system that had given rise to such wrong-doing. He was a trained soldier, allocated to the furthermost ends of the Union's empire; he had believed implicitly in his role as a peace-keeper. Attending to the prison had not been in his original brief, but the shortage of staff willing to serve in this godforsaken spot had required it. So he had obeyed orders, as he always did.

Not any more.

A blindness seized him: a fury, a self-hatred and loathing the like of which he had never before experienced. With a choked cry he fled from the ward and, once outside, climbed into his hoverjeep and shoved it roughly into gear. It rose, shivered, and flew off, leaving a cloud of dusty particles in its wake.

And when he saw the wall ahead of him, he did not waver or turn aside, but opened the throttle as full as it would go, and prayed for forgiveness.

Lisa woke with a start, her eyes staring from their sockets, her heart pounding. What was that?

In the distance the faint unearthly scream lingered, the echo of a ghostly cry from somewhere across the ether.

Or perhaps it had been only in her mind.

She let her body flop back, quivering all over. The sheets were limp with sweat; she must have been tossing hotly for ages. She scrabbled to retain the distorted visions that, seconds before, had seethed in her head, but they were like dew in the dawn, barely visible and insubstantial, and slowly vanished.

A child; a baby. Nothing so strange about that. She had dreamed about babies before, and had tended to dismiss them as waking fantasies. But this baby had been beautiful: to begin with, at least. Fat and gurgly, with a toothless, gummy pink mouth and bright clear eyes. It had lifted its arms to her and gurgled, begging to be cuddled.

But as she had bent to kiss it, the baby had changed. The skin had broken and cracked, like old parchment. The eyes had filmed over; the mouth had become slack, with jagged teeth that brought up weals on its thin lips. The little hand, formerly so plump and innocent, had twisted into a set of claws. The child had become a monster.

With a sob Lisa flung herself back into the pillows, face down. What had awakened her had no reality; it had stemmed from what used to be called a nightmare. It was solely her imagination. Such a thing had never happened. Nor could it, not these days.

Never.

Chapter Four

Strether was settling in. He was becoming used to European manners, so much less effusive than Stateside, to the diminished size of helpings on his plate, to the ever-present security cameras, and to paperwork which, despite modern technology, threatened daily to over-whelm him. He suspected that it was provided to keep him busy, and thus trapped where his staff could contain him. It succeeded too well.

Yet the polite young employees at the embassy, all American nationals, were delightful. He wished he might get to know them a little better. Most were of an age to be the sons and daughters he had never had, and he felt comfortable with them. In a crisis they could be useful. He sensed that he could trust them absolutely, a feeling evinced by no European he had met so far.

As the staffer put the coffee tray on his desk Strether looked up and smiled. 'Yes, Matt?'

Matt Brewer, Harvard and Princeton, Rhodes scholar and college football star, was the same height as his chief but around twenty-five years younger and much fitter. Strether had instantly liked the youthful career officer with the trim American crew-cut, the jutting jaw and earnest manner.

'Sir. I just wondered. It's Friday. Some of the Chancery guys have tickets for the games this afternoon at White City. We were thinking. Would you like to join us?'

Strether grinned. 'That's kind of you.' He indicated the folders. 'I don't need much excuse. Shifting paper mountains was never my favourite occupation.'

'In that case, sir . . . Well, you've not seen much of the city yet, have you? I was planning before the match to visit the Portobello Road mall. The travel shop there has great offers. And I have to make our monthly trip to the recycling centre.'

'Sure. So what time are you leaving?'

'About eleven, sir.'

Strether checked the digital timepiece. 'Fine. Meet you downstairs in half an hour.'

It was a balmy day. In the square outside trees were heavy with leaf and in full bloom, with drifts of pink blossom in the gutters. The temperature was already 25°C. Overhead a 'copter bus whirred, spanking smart in its red Virgin livery. A fastjet vapour trail described a feathery arc in the sky. Above the electric hum of traffic, songbirds were chirruping loudly. A flock of rooks, disturbed by a tooting horn, rose angrily from the treetops, then, grumbling and squawking, flapped back on to their shambolic nests.

A woman teetered by in a tightly cut tunic and hot pants with a befrizzed dog on a lead. As the animal moved to relieve itself, she nudged it to the pavement's edge with her toe. Beneath its haunches the dog drain opened automatically. Before it closed again the animal's

backside was sprayed with a mildly antiseptic deodorant.
The dog wagged its tail, wriggled its bottom and, with its
mistress, trotted on.

Strether stood on the embassy steps. 'Take the car or
public transport?'

'Let's take the tube,' Matt answered. He held a carrier
bag in which rustled bulky foil-wrapped packages. 'They
prefer it here – when in Rome. You'll have many occasions to travel in style, sir, but you should see how
ordinary Europeans live.'

The two began to stroll towards Highgate tube
entrance. The embassy had had to be moved, like every
other important edifice in London (with the exception of
the royal palaces) as the waters rose, to higher ground
beyond Regent's Park, near Hampstead Heath. The
Thames barrage had been dismantled, once it could no
longer cope with neap tides; that was around the year
2050, two decades beyond its expected lifespan. From
then on, the risks of remaining in central London for
those with a choice were simply too great.

The Northern tube line, the deepest, was abandoned
without regret. Other sections of the underground railway
liable to flooding were strengthened and pumps installed.
A huge suspension bridge from Holborn Circus to
Bermondsey, the Blair Memorial, opened on the cente-
nary of the birth of the former European President.
Otherwise, the cellars of Dickens's London were left to
night-dwellers and shadowy unfortunates.

In effect the capital had become two cities separated by
a river a kilometre wide at Greenwich. The political and
business communities had shifted *in toto* fifteen kilometres north, using Union grants to take their façades with
them. The produce markets had been relocated sub-surface

and were linked to docks and freight terminals by sterile conveyor. The opportunity had also been taken to abolish the Zoo. But while a time traveller would have recognised many familiar landmarks, he might have been disorientated by strange juxtapositions: the Bank of England faced Big Ben, Covent Garden nestled around Nelson's column, and Westminster Abbey had been turned on its axis at the suggestion of the owners of Harrods – who had made a mighty contribution to the expense – to give their shoppers next door a better view.

Strether was struck by how clean the streets were. Hologram hoardings were neat, their messages witty and vivid. Verges were tidy, drains free of detritus. Street signs and lamps in blue and gold, the Union colours, were elegantly designed, with not a broken fixture in sight. He was still disturbed by the tiny cameras slung from every other post and puzzled, not for the first time, about what they might be looking for.

But it was impossible to feel down at heart. Trees at every five paces had primroses and hyacinths flourishing at their base – untouched by any vandalism, he noted with pleasure. He had expected the original London plane trees, whose peeling bark could survive in smoke, but was delighted at the more exotic varieties relishing the cleaner atmosphere, with glorious aromatic foliage in red and yellow. They were also value for money. It was cheaper to perfume the air by natural means than the old way via gratings at street corners. And more reliable, since operatives were forever forgetting to replace the empty capsules; and, during the interregnum, terrorists had filled every capsule in Milan, Luxembourg, London and other Union cities with artificial skunk smell, which put thousands in hospital. A safer alternative had been sought, and the gratings sealed.

London had once had a reputation as a dirty city. It had ranked with Naples, Marseilles or Moscow as a place of broken pavements, boarded-up shops, beggars with aggressive dogs, battered car lots masquerading as car parks, foul public conveniences, endless graffiti, red-light areas where wan-faced child prostitutes hovered, overflowing rubbish bins, smashed syringes, dead cats, live rats and a slatternly population that did not care or notice. 'Inner city' had then meant crime and squalor, especially at night, rather than entertainment, the avant-garde, glamour. The law-abiding moved out, the poorest were worst hit. Similar problems had afflicted American cities, such as New York and Chicago. Strether liked historical novels and had recently finished a bloodcurdling effort entitled *Bonfire of the Vanities* set in a gruesomely unrecognisable New York of the 1980s. Of course, it was fiction; he doubted that such an exaggerated picture could ever have been true.

He could have believed it of London, a century earlier, but not today. Buckingham Palace might be shabby, but money was obviously being spent to keep the public environment in a most attractive condition. Since voters' moods were influenced by their daily observations, the aim must be to keep them satisfied. As Strether moved with his young companion through the busy hum of the modern city, he saw that misery and filth, or hopelessness, were virtually impossible to imagine. The citizenry had a lot to be thankful for, and probably knew it.

As they turned a corner, a camera swivelled to follow them. Strether paused and pointed at it.

'Matt, what in the devil's name is that for?'

Matt looked around. 'What, sir?'

'The camera. They're everywhere. Who's watching us, and why?'

The lens was black and remote, hunched on its high lamp-post like a hungry crow. It stared straight down at them and had ceased moving when they halted.

'Oh, those. You stop noticing after a while. Security. To keep the streets free from crime.' Matt Brewer began to walk on, with the Ambassador trailing slightly and glancing back over his shoulder.

'That sounds like a slogan, Matt,' Strether admonished. 'If it's just for crime, why are they everywhere? Even inside Buckingham Palace? Dammit, they were gawping while we had lunch. Even there.'

'I don't know, sir.' Matt sounded unhappy. 'I've never been inside the Palace so I can't comment. Been meaning to go on the tour but haven't had time.'

'It must take an army, to keep an eye on everyone,' Strether mused, falling into step again. 'One helluva job, that. A whole industry of watchers. Then what do they do with the information?'

Matt shrugged. 'It doesn't seem to bother the locals, sir. They don't even notice and they never object. And it does seem effective – there *is* almost no street crime. The answer to any questions we've raised is, that those who have nothing to hide have nothing to fear.'

Strether grunted. 'Sounds like another slogan. But the guys behind the cameras: they're hidden, aren't they? What are they up to? What have *they* got to fear? It's so darned sinister. Why aren't there any identifications on the equipment, or explanations, or apologies? The only place which seems to be free of them is the public toilets.'

'And that's because of a specific Act of Parliament. To protect gays.'

'Really?' Strether raised an eyebrow.

'Non-discrimination codes of the Union. It used to be

common practice to entrap men when they were . . .
cottaging, I think it's called. But that was made illegal
years ago. I guess if we wanted an entirely private conversation, sir, that's where we'd have to go.' Matt stared
straight ahead, but Strether could see that the young man
was discomforted and as baffled as himself.

The two walked on in pensive silence to the entrance
to the tube.

The travelator slid them down into a noisier world: the
low curved ceilings bounced back scraps of conversation,
the click of entry machines, the clump of footwear even
on the sound-absorbing floor, along with the hiss and
whine of trains arriving and doors opening. Both men
used their swipe cards to gain access to the passenger
hall and entered their destination on a request board. In
an instant a mild female voice told them to go to platform
four where their unit would be arriving shortly.

Even at mid-morning the station was crowded. By far
the largest group of travellers was elderly, some on sticks
but most hale and hearty and talking loudly to each other.
Later, at rush-hour, the station would be packed, even
with a speedy service that cleared platforms every half-
minute. Outdated work habits still survived. Despite the
freedom to network from home, many employees preferred to travel to central units. Diurnal bio-rhythms were
well attested, but their persistence was a surprise. Maybe
mankind was simply a more gregarious species than early
analysts had understood.

The younger passengers, Strether saw, were serious
but not morose. Many were reading, their powerbooks
opened in one hand or on laps, pixels winking. One or

two were concentrating hard and tapping in information. A man nearby prodded his screen with an electronic pen, cursed softly and chewed a finger. Several were absorbed by the output from their cordless music plugs, nodding and swaying with faraway expressions. One woman cradled a dog in her smartly dressed arms and was cooing to it. Strether, closer now, noticed it was one of the new three-eared breeds and turned away in distaste.

Everyone looked healthy, though many were overweight. He pulled in his stomach, then forgot and relaxed. Idly he began to categorise the passengers. First the older men and women, none bowed and not particularly frail, third-agers out for a treat, or possibly part-time workers. There was a sprinkling of operatives, mostly in dungarees, many with that stocky build and swarthy skin he had noted first in Liverpool. Few carried powerbooks; those without music plugs appeared bored. Elegant females such as the dog owner turned and twisted to catch a glimpse of themselves, or watched the hologram adverts, mesmerised. Young functionaries in dark tunic suits stood purposefully with a hint of impatience; Matt Brewer could easily be one of these, an office holder with a good salary, excellent prospects and every hope of living to 120. A group of chattering foreigners surrounded their guide, from a Chinese genetic group but more likely Indonesian or Singaporean: to his shame, Strether could not tell. And odder figures caught his eye: a pair of gaudy hermaphrodites, leaning sleepily on each other, presumably heading home after a night's work, unmolested and ignored. And three burly men, heads shaved and red-necked, who stood with feet turned out to accommodate massive thighs and whose navy fatigues proclaimed their attachment to the Rottweiler Security Company.

He commented briefly to Matt on the natural courtesy on display. When travellers brushed against each other, smiles would be exchanged or apologies or a soft word. Despite the Rottweilers, the sequined hermaphrodites and the twittering oldsters, this was self-evidently an orderly, gracious society.

The train arrived. The dog woman stepped on without waiting for passengers to alight, but she was the only one who did. In a moment the carriage had filled and the doors sighed shut. The ceiling ads briefly held Strether's attention: back pain and ear-wax were on the increase in London, it seemed, while the unreconstructed aged were warned to take their daily tablets against Alzheimer's: 'Don't go dotty – take Izzy's Interferon today!' A buxom lovely told the world, 'I'm Ulrika, call me' and gave a vidphone number, 00 44 SEXYHOTFORU. A jolly giant wreathed in smiles urged the consumption of Schmeckel's low-cholesterol bratwurst: 'Eat as much as you like – I do!' A clinic trumpeted: 'Your choice of face! In and out in half an hour! Pout like Pamela, lips like –'

Matt nudged his boss. 'We're here. Notting Hill Gate. Doesn't take long.'

They emerged into a bustling scene. Following a public campaign, nearby Kensington Gardens with its exquisite Dianist chapel had been protected by flood defences and pumps in subterranean caverns. Further north these were supplemented by efficient auxiliaries in the old catacombs beneath what had been Kensal Green cemetery and was now the New White City Stadium. As a result the Kensal and Kilburn areas were regarded as risk-free

and had risen dramatically in value; the antique shops of
Portobello Road, in a frosted-glass mall, flourished anew.

'Where first?'

'Travel shop, if you don't mind, sir.'

The shop front was covered in stickers advertising
trips on the Maglev to Malta and Cyprus for 59.99 euros,
with an optional stopover in Corsica. The spectacular
view from the Mediterranean bridges was rumoured to be
worth the trip alone. Egypt was a day trip for 99 euros,
with duty-free vouchers and a Mummy Death Experience
thrown in. A week at the North or South Pole, with or
without penguins, could be had for 259 euros, not far
short of the price of safaris to Disney's Atlantic Trench
Undersea World or Attenborough Enterprises' Jurassic
Park, out in Korea. But Matt had a glint in his eye as he
presented his swipe card. A camera bobbed above their
heads. The door opened.

'What are you after?' Strether hissed.

'The trip of the century. Or so it's been billed. New
Year's Day 2100.'

The assistant was elderly and grizzled; probably came
cheap, Strether suspected, if he were already a pensioner
from a previous job. Or two, or three.

'Can I help you, gentlemen?'

Matt sat at the desk and pointed at a hologram on the
wall. Strether began to chuckle and clapped his staffer on
the shoulder. 'I might have known.'

'That one. It was advertised on CNN last night. I tried
vidphoning but you were jammed. Are there still seats
available?'

'Let me see.' The assistant pushed buttons on his console. 'Well, they're running an extra flight due to the
extraordinary demand. You're in luck. How many places?'

'Just one. At a thousand euros a kilo, it's all I can afford.'

'Right. How many kilos, then?'

'Well, I weigh about eighty. Have to allow for my clothes and a bag, I suppose. Is eighty-five cutting it too fine?'

The assistant appraised him carefully. 'You could lose a couple beforehand to make sure,' he remarked helpfully. 'I'll put you down for eighty-five. Excess baggage will be left on the tarmac. A deposit is payable now and you can pay the rest in instalments, with everything due six weeks before the event. Would you like insurance?'

Matt handed over his swipe card and offered his palm for DNA sweat analysis to confirm his identity. 'What happens if I can't go? Is the money refundable?'

The assistant laughed indulgently. 'My *dear* young man, by the time we get close to the date your ticket will be worth ten times what you've paid for it. We don't run trips to the moon every day, you know. They drive us travel agents mad, what with passengers who can't make their weight limit or who insist on bringing children or pets or who we can't find suits to fit. The tantrums in the departure lounge! You'll need a full printout from your doctor before I can confirm this, Mr Brewer, and I will have to check any criminal and mental illness records.'

As he spoke he was tapping into the computer. 'Load of nonsense, these safety rules. There aren't any bugs out there for you to bring back: the place is sterile, for heaven's sake. You won't exactly be bouncing around on the surface stark naked. The moon's just a chilly theme park staffed by robots. In my view – and I've only been in this agency twenty years since I retired – the Transport Commissioners should pay more attention to what goes on in the skies *below* the stratosphere, never mind above it. Right, here's your provisional booking.'

Matt took the laminated card and looked at it, though he knew it was unreadable by human eyes. He sighed happily. 'I'm going to the moon. Golly.' He turned to Strether. 'You ever been, sir?'

'No,' his boss growled in mock ferocity. 'Don't fancy it either. That's a young man's caper. We oldies prefer to gaze at the heavenly bodies from *terra firma*. Heck, Matt, I had a twinge or two on my sea voyage to get here. If there's anything swaying under me, I'd rather it was a horse, not half a dozen Lockheed X-33 aerospike engines.'

'I went in 2090, coronation year,' the old man reminisced. 'We get concessionary fares, of course. Quite an experience, though I wouldn't want to repeat it. Thank heavens they've abandoned those foolish ideas about holidays on Mars. It's fine for the fanatics, but I have to run a commercial operation. Such an inhospitable dump, Mars, and two weeks travelling there, and back. No sick bags – they don't work in zero gravity, so use your imagination. Total familiarity with other passengers' nasty little habits. Everything passing through a tube – and they pinch. Ouch! Not a luxury trip. Who the heck would want to go if they didn't have to? Nobody, that's who.'

'Next century, maybe,' Matt ventured.

The assistant sniffed. 'I've handled travel arrangements for research scientists required to do a tour of duty at the Mars station. They hate it, I can tell you. It's about as nice as a week outdoors in aboriginal Borneo. And I don't recommend that, either.'

The two Americans rose and left, Matt clutching his ticket, a dazed look on his face. Outside, his carrier bag reminded him of other tasks. The young man squared his shoulders. 'Sorry, sir. The recycling shed. This way.'

The blue filters overhead cut the power of the sun's rays and lent an almost ethereal feel to the mall, as if it were situated in the lower reaches of some delicate Botticelli heaven. Muzak floated over their heads. Even the cameras were painted pale blue and silver, reflecting the mellow light. The business of shopping was designed to be a delightful pastime, which helped explain why, despite vidphones and electronic catalogues, individuals chose to come in large numbers, to bring their families, meet their friends and spend the whole day over it.

Strether and Matt left the upper levels, found the escalator down and descended five floors, until they were around forty metres underground.

The light here was dimmer. Matt turned a corner. As they pushed open the big door they were assailed by mega-music: crashing metallic thunder that rattled their ear-drums and set their teeth on edge. There was no point in shouting. Matt darted about until he found the proprietor, a big, pale-faced bear of a man with frizzy grey hair tied in a topknot. Then he waved his arms vigorously to gain his attention. At last the man noticed his visitors, and turned down the volume.

The underground warehouse was cavernous, its walls lined with metal cupboards, some half closed, others without doors, spewing out a disorderly jumble of parts, keyboards, wiring, computer towers, white, black, beige, translucent and psychedelically coloured. On the floors were heaps of broken items: bits of monitors and screens in one corner, printers elsewhere, circuit boards, loudspeakers, cooling fans. A mini-mountain of joysticks testified to aeons wasted in playing outdated games. Dustbins carried smaller parts in slightly better condition, presumably awaiting recycling. Strether could see floppy-disk drives, modems, diskettes in all sizes. An ancient supermarket trolley held copper wire, another a stack of shiny aluminium disk hard drives. In a plastic tray hundreds of tiny squares identified themselves as Intel Pentium chips. A shrink-wrapped pallet of inter-faxes had been half stripped. On a workshop bench lay an ancient Apple Mac, its innards spilled out, a light wink-ing on a console board. Above on the wall was a sign:

Welcome to the Chip Shop!
Where all good computers go to die.

The bear ambled over and offered a grubby paw. 'Hi. Wotcha brought?'

Matt opened his package. 'Three empty toners and a broken hologram screen.'

The man examined them cursorily. 'Five euros the lot.'

'Fine. I wasn't expecting anything. Just like to ensure they're safely disposed of.'

'Put it in the charity box?' the bear asked hopefully. Matt nodded. The man grinned and rubbed his greasy palm over his hair. 'Yeah. Thanks. There's still lead in them screens, you know. Don't want to see them end up in landfill.'

Strether picked his way cautiously among the debris. 'Where do you get this stuff?' he inquired. 'And what do you do with it?'

The proprietor prodded Matt. 'Concerned citizens bring it in; we get it by the pantechnicon from IBM and

other big corporations. Over forty million computers are
retired every year, you know, in Europe alone. Plus users
like the banks and the NHS. One of our jobs – and we're
bonded to do it – is to clean out confidential info before
we recycle. Don't want your DNA details ending up in
anyone else's printout, do we?'

'Dismantling must be a big task,' Strether ventured.

The man laughed. 'Nope. All you need to disassemble
a computer are a Phillips screwdriver and the floor.
Everything comes apart with screws: they're required to
by law, better than the old hermetic seals, which didn't
separate. But we use the floor when we have to.'

With a sudden movement he picked up the Apple Mac
chassis and swung it heavily down on to the concrete.
The cover splintered and cracked. Strether winced. The
bear chuckled. 'You can't break it – it's already broken.
Worth about five cents a kilo like that, but there's money
to be made if we dismantle.' He turned to one of the scrap
heaps. 'We're non-profit. Got everything here. This is a
400-megabyte C80 251. Used to be the industry standard.
Now it's almost worthless except as scrap. Alas, poor
Yorick.' He moved to another bin. 'Slow modems. These
are 2400-baud. No use here, but they like 'em in Guyana
where the phone lines can't handle high bandwidth.
We'll fix up the machines with a Union grant then the
Red Cross'll ship 'em.'

'Amazing,' Strether murmured.

'And these.' He indicated the silvery Intel processors.
'Last forever, they do. Computers don't die, they become
obsolete. Not because the hardware don't work – some of
these are fifty years old, recycled a dozen times.
Integrated circuits turn up here, still functional, beautifully made. But the configurations can't cope with the

new software they bring in every year. That's why they do
it, see? The more programmes, the more so-called consumer choice, the slower your machine works. So you
have to upgrade to get back to the speed you want.' He
slurred *so-called* with a curl of his lip. 'Then it starts all
over again. I found a refurbished Compaq Contura 420
the other day dating from 2015 and it was fabulous, still
working. But where'd you find software for it? Nowhere.
Deleted. Patents self-destruct every ten years. Bloody
racket, if you ask me. The government oughta do something about it.'

'It's been a problem since the things were invented,'
Matt agreed. He bent and retrieved a sliver of the Apple
Mac.

'Huh!' the man snorted. 'When petrol cars first became
popular, manufacturers ignored safety rules to sell more
cars. Once buyers insisted, cars got safer. They could do
the same thing with PCs, hardware and software. Insist on
durability. Make simple options available. But they don't.'

The man suddenly lost interest and turned up the
music once more. The Americans beat a retreat.

They re-emerged into the hazy light at ground level near
a clutch of open stalls.

'The flea market,' Matt said. 'Don't you just love this
stuff?'

The two men lingered at a bookstall. 'I wish they still
made these,' Strether remarked as he picked up paper-
backs with lurid covers. 'Sure, I can download anything I
want on my powerbook or on the wall-screen at home.
Multi-media, pot-boilers, thrillers, films, holograms,
music, live theatre broadcasts, the lot. I like novels read

to me by audiobook if I'm feeling idle. But to curl up with the real thing – to turn the crumbly paper pages in your hands. That's something special.'

'With respect, sir, you're betraying your age,' Matt teased. He moved on to the next stall. 'Wow! I haven't seen these except in museums. D'you remember them?'

Strether allowed himself to sound mildly offended. 'I'm not *that* ancient, Matt.' He picked up the black plastic headgear and twisted it about. Then he lifted it to fit his eyes and loosely fastened the strap while the stall-holder, a stout woman, looked indulgently on.

'Here,' she said. 'It's got new batteries. You press this switch.'

Strether yelped as the internal image flashed on. 'Hey! I'm being attacked by tigers! Get 'em off me!' He danced about, tugging at the straps. The stallholder cackled as passers-by turned in curiosity. She began to rummage for the hand console. 'Where did I put it? Then you can fire a rifle and kill them.' But Strether had torn off the helmet, and stood panting and red-faced.

'Virtual reality! Huh. You can see why *that* was a passing fad. Not a nice sensation at all.'

'Yeah, well,' the woman shrugged, 'they were all the rage for a while. I sell 'em for only ten euros complete with new batteries. The kids like 'em. Addle your brains after a while, though. That's why they never caught on.'

'The cinema's coming out.' Matt pointed. 'They've had a retrospective this week. Early films. I might catch it with the guys after the game.'

Strether was still panting slightly. He smoothed down his hair, then stopped. 'Boy, their customers seem to have had a wild time. What's on?'

'I don't know exactly, sir. Let's ask.'

The two men mingled with a substantial crowd, who were tumbling out of several exits. Mostly young, they were laughing uproariously and clinging to each other as they wiped blood and gore from their clothes. One young woman, her entire head a bloody mess, stood shaking helplessly with giggles as her friends tried to clean her up.

'What was it? Oh, *Pulp Fiction* – supposed to be Tarantino's masterpiece,' volunteered a boy. His face was disfigured by a bullet-hole through the cheek, which oozed wetly on to his tunic.

'And you – what did you see?' Strether addressed an older woman whose clothes were flecked with green slime.

'What was it, darling?' She turned to her companion. 'Oh yes, *Alien*. Monsters from outer space. God, this stuff's disgusting – it really stinks.' She scrabbled at the mucus with a paper tissue. Others nearby moved away, their noses twitching.

Behind came a youth whose face was blotched red. His eyebrows had disappeared and his hair was badly singed. The smell of scorching hovered about him. To Strether's inquiry he muttered, '*Gone with the Wind*. Silly story, but the Atlanta scenes were terrific. 'Scuse me.'

The last cinema-goers to emerge stood shaking sodden clothes and pulling pieces of seaweed out of their hair and mouths. They, too, were laughing and holding on to each other in their merriment. One girl spat a seashell into her hand. '*Titanic*. Fantastic movie. God, I think I actually drowned in there.'

Yet as Strether and Matt watched, the apparitions slowly dried up. The gore, the slime, the water, the bullet hole evaporated before their eyes, leaving not a mark or stain. The burned boy stood quietly as his skin returned

to normal, the singed hair miraculously restored. The
smell lingered; then he rubbed his chin, smiled and was
gone, with, Strether thought, a touch of relief. He
watched as the seashell in the girl's cupped palm disappeared, molecule by molecule. It took about a minute to
vanish entirely. The girl sighed. 'That was lovely. Pity
it's all an illusion.'

'The wetties,' Matt murmured. 'Brilliant invention. So
much better than the feelies they had in Grandad's day.'

'Available on vid, now, aren't they?' Strether commented.

'Yeah, but much more fun going with your mates,
trying to see who can dodge the muck. The vids are best
for romance and porn, to be honest. To be watched in
private.' He glanced at his boss and coloured. 'Sir.'

By the time they had lunched and taken the walkolator,
large numbers of people were heading in the same direction. It was Friday afternoon: the bulk of the population
had finished work until Tuesday. A twenty-five hour
week standardised throughout the Union was sufficient
to combine high productivity through sustained skills
with an optimum level of job creation. In America the
government was not allowed, by the constitutional
amendment of 2015, to interfere with working hours. In
Europe that, along with many other aspects of life, was
regulated with great determination. It made Strether
obscurely uneasy. Perhaps those cameras were checking
that citizens did not work longer than their quota. It
would be virtually impossible, if the camera operators
were efficient, to operate a black market, to avoid taxes, to
indulge in illicit liaisons. Was that what the surveillance

was for? Who decided? Who controlled it? And who controlled the controllers?

The stadium roof soared over their heads, its aluminium alloy struts glinting in the sun. Watch-towers at
each corner contained shadowy figures – Rottweiler
guards, Strether guessed, shading his eyes against the
sun. Yet no police appeared to be on patrol. Perhaps,
given the complaisant nature of the spectators he had
seen so far, crowd trouble was not a problem.

The stadium capacity was over eighty thousand. Its
sides curved ovoid and soared over their heads. Strether
noted that, as in America, the seats were of extra width to
accommodate the larger body. The term 'obese' was
frowned on as excessively judgmental and, under codes on
both sides of the Atlantic, discrimination was outlawed.
One stand in particular was advertised as suitable for those
weighing over 150 kilos – almost as much as Matt and
himself put together. Since one adult in three in Europe,
and one in two in the US, could now expect to reach such
a body weight, that made commercial sense. It also made
Strether feel almost puny by comparison with the massive
girths and spreading thighs waddling in on all sides.

The man to his right was mountainous by any standard. He was accompanied by a short, dumpy woman
and two roly-poly children. On one arm the man carried
a basket from which spilled out packets of food, while the
other cradled a metre-deep tub of buttered popcorn. His
wife was similarly encumbered. As they sat down the
entire row of seats creaked and sagged.

'Hi!' He nodded to Strether. 'Should be quite a bust-up
this afternoon. Name's Fred.'

'Bill,' Strether returned. The man was struggling with
his belongings. 'Can I hold something for you?'

'Nah, thanks. This lot's not for me – the kids get hungry. Who d'you support?'

'Nobody, exactly. I'm new here. American.'

'Yeah, your accent. Crystal Palace, the home team, are pretty fair. They'll beat Chelsea. Then there's the Villa A side – I reckon they should murder Liverpool. The basketball at the interval – try the Brixton Babes. Dunno about the women's matches, though. Got some new talent there.'

'I think we should have mixed teams,' his wife butted in. 'Don't hold with this single-sex rubbish. Why should I have to sit through two twenty-minute premier division games till it's our turn?'

'You should count yourself lucky,' her partner retorted rudely. His fist was deep in the popcorn; his jowls glistened with butter. 'Those matches used to be forty-five minutes each way, plus a break in the middle. You'd have had to wait three and a half hours.'

Several members of the embassy's staff had appeared, checked their tickets and found their seats in the row beyond Matt. Vendors moved along the wide terraces selling team favours, programmes, snacks, drinks, betting slips. More could be ordered by pressing buttons on the console embedded in the seat arm. On an impulse, Strether stopped a vendor and, on the basis of Fred's tips, bet ten euros on the outcome of the first two matches.

His new acquaintance leaned alarmingly towards him and spoke out of the corner of his mouth. 'I shan't bother watching the wimmin,' he confided. 'I'll go down inside the stand for the hologram of gladiators and lions. Blood and guts. That'll suit me. I like to see a geezer with his arm torn off.'

He smacked his lips. To Strether's eyes he looked as if

he would have relished tearing off the limb with his own teeth. And eaten it. Given his own queasy entanglement with rampaging wildlife on the virtual-reality toy, the Ambassador declined the invitation to do likewise.

To much fanfare the first teams ran out on to the pitch. There were seven players on each side, a far easier number for fans to follow than under the old rules, Fred informed him. And the intense competition to get into these smaller teams had sharpened up players' performances on and off the pitch. In quieter moments Strether's podgy companion waxed lyrical about other recent improvements. Modern footballers were exponents of speedy acceleration but had poor stamina, so shorter games had become popular; the whole of the two main games, along with advertising, would fit neatly into an hour's viewing that night. That had been the brainwave of Mr Maxwell Packer, the media tycoon Strether had met at the Palace, who was much praised for his intelligent appreciation of audience requirements.

Fred and his family entered fully into the spirit of the sport, roaring encouragements and insults, punching fists in the air as play ebbed and flowed. A disputed free kick had Fred on his feet, the row of seats see-sawing behind his vast posterior. Nor was he mollified by the instant replay on the giant screen opposite. With a furious expletive he pulled out the complaints box from the seat arm, entered his swipe card and recorded a string of reasons as to why the electronic referee should be emasculated. Yet his fury had a synthetic feel: Strether understood that it was style without substance. The man and his family, like the rest of the crowd, were far too good-natured to be threatening. Perhaps, he caught himself thinking, it had been bred into them.

At the interval between the first two games Strether saw his chance. He accepted the offer of a handful of crumbs from the bottom of Fred's grease-smeared tub as the man ordered another.

'You and your family,' Strether remarked. 'You do seem to be having a great day.'

'Yeah, it's not a bad life,' Fred agreed. He licked his sausage-like fingers. 'Me and the missus, we've been married twelve year. The kids, Jockey and Pony – me other hobby's following the horses – they're ten and six.'

'Fred.' His wife dug him in the ribs. Her elbow seemed to disappear into the mountain of flesh. 'The foreign gentleman doesn't want to listen to your rubbish. Belt up.'

'No, no,' Strether demurred. 'I am interested. I was married myself, once. No kids. You should be proud of your family.'

'Yeah, we are. Especially our Pony. He's an NT,' Fred smirked.

'Oh? And why is that?'

'Well, we can afford it now, see. I gotta better job with Walls Ice Cream. I test new products. Heh! Heh!'

The children looked alike, though the younger one was slimmer than his sibling. Fred explained, 'We modified the fat gene. He'll be able to eat more for ever without getting as big as his Mom and me. Jammy bugger.'

Strether felt his mouth drop open and quickly shut it. On his left, Matt was engrossed in a mild sporting dispute with a colleague so could not come to his rescue. 'I see,' Strether said. 'I'm intrigued, Fred. Did you have to pay?'

'A bit,' the man admitted. He had opened a double packet of chocolate chip cookies, which he rammed between the folds of his thighs, alternately cramming biscuits and popcorn into the sticky cavern of his mouth.

It did not stop him talking. 'But we're on a scheme, see. We get our optional health care half price. Great employer, Walls.'

'You didn't think of spending the money on anything else?'

'Nah. We got everything we want, the missus and me. Nice house, all paid for. Had to work hard for it: I used to do a thirty-five-hour week. Not any more.'

'Do you take an interest in politics?' Strether ventured. He felt manipulative, probing in this manner, but his companion seemed amiable enough. Matt had been correct: there would be lots of occasions to mix with the élites, the Énarques, but not so many to meet an average family.

'Not a lot. We vote, like. Gotta do our duty. Even so, I don't bother every time. Not unless it's something important.'

'What was the last thing you voted on?'

Fred screwed up his face. 'Mayor of London, I think,' he answered. 'I voted for the geezer offering free tickets to the Internationals. He won, but we heard no more about it.'

'The Prime Minister vetoed it,' his wife reminded him. 'Them NTs always get their own way in the end.'

'Doesn't that bother you?' Strether asked quickly.

'Nah,' Fred answered again. His cheerful face broke into a wide grin. 'They look after their business and I look after mine. I ain't got much to complain about, an' that's the truth of it: as long as my kids can grow up okay, and the wife's willing, and the gee-gees run fast once in a while. I'd like to see my grandchildren some day. They'll all be NTs, I hope. Then I'll die a happy man.'

The new teams were on the pitch. Fred broke off the conversation and began to howl abuse at one particular opponent. To Strether's untutored eye, the players looked identical to the previous teams apart from the differently coloured strip. He nudged Fred and remarked on the similarity.

'Yeah, well,' Fred shrugged, 'don't you do that in the States? They're NTs too. The finest quality. That one' – he pointed – 'he's Maradona. Supposed to be, anyway. That one's Pele. Fancy footwork but a bit slow. I prefer the Italian types meself.'

'Gimme Cantona every time,' his wife said, rolling her eyes.

'When you think about it – and I don't much – I reckon we're sitting pretty,' Fred added. 'Got our pick. The best in the world. The best ever. Gawd, look at that. Pass it! *Go on, you stupid tosser!*' He half rose then slumped as a penalty was declared. He prodded Strether's arm. 'If you don't have this in the States, no wonder you've slipped behind. Sounds a bit backward to me. *Yes!*' The penalty had been saved.

Suddenly there was a commotion three rows in front, on the other side of the gangway. Two Rottweilers marched down the steps, batons in hand. In a trice they had lifted a middle-aged man in a grey tunic suit bodily out of his seat and frogmarched him, arms bent painfully behind his back, up and along the terrace to the nearest exit. Strether saw the man's expression, a mix of fear and bewilderment, but the prisoner made no protest, other than to drag his feet. As he stumbled, one guard cracked him hard across the shins with the baton. In a moment the trio had vanished.

The Ambassador turned to Matt, but the young staffer, who had seen only the man's back as he disappeared with his escorts, spread his hands helplessly. Strether tugged at Fred's arm. 'What was that about?'

'Dunno,' the fat man answered, his attention on the play. 'Often happens. Probably got behind with his alimony. Or taxes. Whatever it was, there's a good reason.'

'You sure?' Strether demanded.

'Oh, yeah. He'll have been spotted when he got here. Checked out. Probably made the mistake of using his swipe card – then they've got 'im. No rest for the wicked, no hiding-place. You've got to behave now. Best for everyone.'

For the rest of the afternoon Strether watched mostly in silence. In the basketball match the loping players, all astonishingly tall, were uniformly black, shaven-headed and aggressive. That had always been so, but now it made him think. The women soccer players were more varied, though four of the defenders had the same sturdy build and, from what he could tell at a distance, identical complexions and facial bone structure. And similar ferocious scowls.

By the end of the last contest he was glad to order up his winnings – Fred had been a competent tipster – and leave with Matt. The other staffers followed at a respectful distance. They joined the crowds on the walkolators towards the tube.

'Thanks, Matt.' He patted the young man's shoulder. 'A remarkable day. I'm thirty euros better off and I've learned a thing or two. Come up with a few conundrums as well. What is it with these people? They seem extraordinarily laid back, don't they?'

'Oh, they're content enough.' Matt frowned and sighed. 'I've been here a year, sir, and that's what you'll find everywhere. Makes you wonder.'

'Maybe there's something in the water.' Strether half

laughed, then regretted his levity and continued more soberly. 'Maybe folk have got so complacent they don't react to the strangest events. That man Fred didn't blink an eye when someone was arrested under his nose, quite violently too, and I didn't hear anybody reading out the guy's civil rights. They weren't even proper police.'

Matt walked quietly beside him. 'We can't assume anything. We ask, but we get nowhere. Unless it's an American citizen we're fobbed off.'

'But you have your suspicions?' Strether realised that he had spent the whole day taking in a host of impressions but had not been quite as dazzled as he had expected. Something was wrong, but he could not put his finger on it.

'Well, sir. It makes me twitch. These Europeans are so well fed, well housed, well paid and kept so well entertained that they've become indifferent. They simply give the benefit of the doubt to the authorities. They never complain – have nothing much to complain about. They question nothing.'

'Bread and circuses? Keep the populace quiet?'

'Sir. But if something was dodgy, who'd notice?' Matt swept an arm at the milling hordes, so orderly, so pleasantly disciplined. Most faces had a bland, almost vacant tinge, as if tired, though many were still discussing the esoteric points of play. 'And, if they noticed, would they care – or do anything about it? Complacency, inertia. This is modern Europe.'

'In which, if Fred is right, we are all expected to behave. No, dammit, to *conform*. But to what?'

Chapter Five

Outside the glazed window of the Maglev, the country-side flew past. Strether marvelled at the swift, noiseless motion; in the old days train travel had meant vibration, clatter, the smell of diesel and indecipherable announcements over a bad Tannoy. The French TGV had been the forerunner, electric-powered at 500 k.p.h. on arrow-straight tracks across Europe. But in heavily populated regions like southern England the Maglev soared silently on an elevated rail, elegant and triumphant.

As an ambassador he had permission to travel by car, but frequent use was bad manners in the Union. Petrol had been far more costly here than in the USA, but it was not a question of expense. Crowded Europe simply took its Rio responsibilities, as the international environmental policy had become known, far more seriously than Americans ever had. He could have used the chauffeured embassy electric motor; but 'when in Rome', Matt had said, tactfully, when he had suggested taking it to the mall. And, to be fair, with public transport as splendid as the Maglev to Porton Down, he was happy to comply.

Marius had been as good as his word. Indeed, the

Prince had volunteered to accompany Strether round the
laboratories and would meet him there. Strether had proposed travelling together, but the quick demurral had told
him that the Prince would probably arrive well ahead
and brief those who would be showing him around. Brief
them – or warn them, perhaps. His predecessor had
shown no such curiosity, Strether knew. Again, it was a
question of manners; however bold the population policies of the Union might be, the practical elements were
kept under wraps – solely to guarantee absolute cleanliness and avoid contamination, naturally. He'd be the first
overseas visitor for some time. An exception was being
made.

In return, almost as a courtesy, Strether had let it be
known that his interest arose not out of prurience or nosi-
ness but as a cattleman who wished to be better informed
about techniques with which he was wholly familiar.
That seemed to satisfy them.

The landscape undulated in the morning sun. On a far
hill the blades of wind turbines turned lazily. The maize
was already tall and would soon turn golden. It would be
cut before June and a second crop planted. Here in
England a double harvest had been possible for over half
a century, though in northern Scotland a second oats or
barley harvest was attainable only in the warmest years.
Rice-planting trials were under way near Portsmouth
with a new hardy strain. Those areas of the civilised
world that did not lack water had gained tremendously
from the increase in ambient temperatures. It was not
clear to Strether, as he gazed with a rancher's envious
eye over the greenly rippling fields, why anybody likely
to benefit from it, as northern Europe had, could ever
have objected to global warming.

That view, had he articulated it too often, would have raised eyebrows. It was another example among many of the quirky perspective he sensed he brought to his post. He was aware that the diplomatic community regarded him as an outsider.

Some of the reasons were obvious. He had not attended their universities nor engaged life-long in diplomacy. He was unfamiliar with the conventional wisdom. An alternative choice of ambassador, schooled at Georgetown or Princeton would have known the score and been acquainted with senior figures on the circuit. Many US Foreign Service professionals had attended European universities; Strether now suspected that they were alumni of ÉNA. The reflection put him on his mettle. A doctorate in farm management and animal husbandry might not rate as highly as a PhD in international relations from the Sorbonne with three languages. But he had earned his living in the real world. He held cussedly to what he regarded as real values. He was prepared to be convinced; but he was no pushover.

The train slowed; air brakes whispered, friction increased between the coach body and the magnetised rail. A well-modulated woman's voice announced that they were approaching Salisbury East and reminded him to take all his belongings with him. Nobody mentioned Porton Down. Officially there was nothing secret about it. He could have applied to see its annual accounts or the Director's last report to Parliament. But the phone number was not listed and it was not on the tourist maps. It existed, but everyone behaved as if it did not. The Europeans, and the English in particular, seemed to have no difficulties with such contradictions.

Strether rose, stretched and headed for the door. The

warm breeze on his face was a pleasure after the carriage's chill air-conditioning. On the platform he watched
as passengers alighted and boarded. The doors hissed
shut, the whole train seemed to breathe, a faint hum
could be heard. The hairs rose on the back of his neck in
response to the electric field. The linear induction motors
lifted the machine vertically a bare twenty centimetres
from the track and it slid away without a sound, slowly at
first then with increasing rapidity until it disappeared in
a flash of silver over the horizon.

'Good journey, I hope?'

'Oh, hi, Marius. Yes, fine. Wish we had those in New
York or Chicago.'

Marius grimaced. 'Horribly expensive, I'm afraid.
Capital costs are astronomic. We have to subsidise this
line. Still, it's pollution-free, so needs must.' He took
Strether by the arm and led him to the walkolator.

Marius was dressed less formally than at the Palace.
His cream tunic was undone a notch at the neck and was
cut from a linen fabric with a faintly crumpled look. That
must be deliberate, Strether decided at once, since
Marius's black slacks were perfectly pressed, his loafers
immaculate. He wondered fleetingly if his new friend
would regard it as rude if he requested help on a shopping expedition. His own clothes – the lapel suit, the
white shirt, the tie – marked him as an incomer a mile off.

'Here we are.' The moving walkway ended. Three
routes were signposted: to Salisbury Old Town, to
Stonehenge Visitors' Centre, and to cross-travel transfers.
Marius ignored them and turned smartly on his heel
down a nondescript passageway. The door at its end,

plain and unmarked, had no handle; it appeared sealed.
Marius stood upright in front of it. At such a distance he
could not be observed from the concourse. He waited.
Then the door opened and he ushered Strether through.

'Deters sightseers,' he grinned at Strether. 'New
system — works quite well, don't you think? All done by
mirrors.'

'I'd have thought you'd be using something more
advanced,' Strether commented. 'Testing DNA, for example.'

'Oh, sure, we've tried that. But too many of the official
visitors here have very similar DNA. Sends the machine
barmy. Frankly, it took too long checking. Can't keep a
Perm Sec waiting, you know.'

The procedure was repeated at a second set of doors.
Once inside, they were met by a trim male secretary in
narrow trousers who showed them to an anteroom. A
small black camera followed their every move. Scientific
journals were scrolling on the wall screen. A coat of arms,
intricately carved, hung opposite. To Strether, apart from
the tree of life and an array of scientific instruments, its
main motif resembled a hand holding a fried egg. The
motto on top was unmistakable: *Pro bono publico*. And
another, underneath: *Omnes unique sunt.*

'Every one an individual, of course,' Marius hissed, in
response to his request for a translation. 'Bit of a joke,
here.' Soon they entered a light, airy office.

A tall thin man, a middle-aged version of the
Permanent Secretary and others Strether had met,
stepped forward. The elongated, spare figure, the hands
with their bony fingers, the receding blond hair and pale
blue eyes were creepily similar, as was the slightly
reserved manner. Strether could not avoid feeling that

such men were searching him for clues, but would give no information he did not prise out of them.

'James Churchill, Director.' The men shook hands. 'Welcome. Forgive me, Ambassador, but you'll have to robe up before we can take you any further.'

Five minutes later Strether caught a glimpse of himself in a reflecting glass and laughed out loud. The all-enveloping white garment reached from his chin to his knees. Loose cotton trousers covered his own. His feet were encased in lint-free socks; the same material made up the gloves on his hands. A net of stretchy fabric covered his hair and dug into his forehead. A surgical mask hid his mouth and nose; above the mask were a cattleman's sunburned forehead and two slightly bulbous eyes, their veins pink in the glare. 'Not a pretty sight,' Strether muttered to himself. Marius and the Director, similarly attired, looked rather better.

The tour began. He was not sure what he had expected. Rows of bottles, maybe, as in *Brave New World*. Filled with foetuses, revolving slowly in their own fluid, monitored day and night by banks of computers. Eyes shut, thumbs in their mouths, dreaming of days in the light yet to come. They must exist somewhere, he reasoned. Instead the Director propelled him smoothly down corridor after corridor, pointing through glass windows at white-garbed workers in a neon-lit world, many with visors over the entire face. There would not be much opportunity here, Strether thought mischievously, for languorous glances across the lab bench. Some had pipettes in hand, others carried Petri dishes or reaction agents in conical bottles. Many were seated at terminals tapping information into keyboards, or at screens reading, pointing, analysing the data displayed. Everyone was busy and preoccupied. No one paid the newcomers the slightest attention.

There were fewer cameras here. Many rooms had none, other than an occasional white-painted one hung unobtrusively at the corner of a corridor, as if placing them were so much a habit that even the most central of government activities could not be excluded. Yet the sensation was strong that he was, for once, on the inside. These white-coated, masked operators, and whoever was behind the surveillance operations, were as one.

Or, maybe, in reality there was nothing to see. Strether felt a swell of disappointment. To add to his frustration, the Director's explanations were frequently beyond him. As nucleotides tumbled over ribosomes, adenine swirled about cystosine, amino acids melded into glutamic acids, his brain felt like an unravelling double helix itself. He began to lag behind.

Marius whispered to the Director, who coughed delicately.

'Right, Ambassador. The Prince and I have some parliamentary business to attend to, if you'll excuse us. Let me introduce you to my assistant director, Dr Pasteur. Prince Marius and I will return for you in forty minutes or so, if that will suit you? Yes. Through here.'

Strether's heart sank. They must assume that if they fobbed him off and bored him enough he would not trouble them again. He could report back to Washington that the genetic programme was remarkable, the laboratories magnificent, the outcomes nothing much to be concerned about. No one would complain if he did precisely that. The boat people seemed light years from this sterile, clinical nothingness. The solution to the queries they posed might well lie elsewhere anyway.

'Good morning, Ambassador. I'm Lisa Pasteur.'

Strether blinked.

The young woman before him was wearing neither mask nor hairnet. Her glossy dark hair was swept back and tied neatly; loose, it would have framed an extraordinarily sweet face, heart-shaped, a full mouth and handsome brown eyes. She wore no jewellery. She might have been in her early thirties.

'Good morning.' Suddenly, unaccustomedly, Strether was lost for words.

She was looking at him, an amused expression on her face. She motioned him into a tiny cubby-hole which passed as an office. The door shut, she pointed at his mask and hood. 'In here you're safe to remove those.' Then she sat at a small desk, spoke into a voicephone to order coffee and for her calls to be held, then indicated another chair.

Strether seated himself. In the narrow space there was no camera. He examined her more thoroughly. The white coat and trousers covered everything important, but she had small trim feet, tiny hands and a skin colour neither fair nor dark, as if she had Italian blood but from Lombardy rather than Sicily. Her eyes were brown flecked with honey. Strether found his voice. '*Dr* Pasteur, did I hear? Is that a medical doctor?'

The coffee arrived on a tray through a chute, neatly presented with a tray-cloth, digestive biscuits and linen napkins. 'I'm a stickler,' Dr Pasteur explained, with a wry smile. 'Bit old-fashioned, maybe. No point in taking infinite pains with our charges then poisoning ourselves with synthetic rubbish. To answer your question, yes, I do have a degree in human medicine, but no, I'm not that kind of doctor. I'm a medical microbiologist, and I'm responsible for the development part of our programme.'

'Your charges? What exactly are they? So far I haven't seen much here to thrill the folks back home.' He spread his hands inquiringly.

Lisa stirred her coffee. 'It's good to have a visitor, Ambassador. Mostly, you know, apart from other scientists, we're left to our own devices here.' She looked up, again with that cool, amused half smile. It was as if she were willing him to ask her questions, to take more than a humdrum approach. Strether found himself gazing rather too directly at her. She did not flinch. 'You expected to see babies in bottles, didn't you? Sorry, but that's not on display. Not to anybody. But first you need to understand exactly what we do, and why we think it is so valuable.'

The young woman was friendlier than anyone he had met on his tour so far. Perhaps her manner was intended to disarm. Maybe, with shrewd interrogation, he could begin to delve to his own satisfaction. With this charming informant it would be a pleasure. Strether settled down to listen.

'What we are doing is tidying up genes, usually to order. My personal work involves finding better and simpler means of carrying out the therapy, so we waste fewer embryos and make fewer errors.'

She began to sketch on a pad. 'You'll be familiar with some of this, so stop me if I go over old ground. The cell is fertilised and becomes an embryo – the eight-cell stage is ideal. That's a day or two after fertilisation, which usually we do *in vitro*. We take one cell, remove the nuclear material and examine it. Most genes will be normal – that'll have been determined when ovum and sperm were

selected. There should be no obvious defects. That's where
the first checks are so essential, and that's stage one.'

She ticked off on her fingers. 'Stage one is the elimination of known disorders. Anything inherited that the
parents don't want – the asthma gene, for example, or
diabetes or myopia. It can be a fiddly business if the condition is multifactorial. Of course, some of the choices are
trivial and we do try to educate parents: each alteration
costs money so the more simple discrepancies they can
accept the better. Adds to human diversity. And we don't
like to meddle too much if we can help it – you never
know what damage you may do.'

What an extraordinary woman. She's so matter-of-fact
about this, thought Strether. I could almost believe she is
talking about bovine breeding. But she's not.

Lisa had not paused in her narrative. 'Some defects
must be removed by law. Mental handicap is one – anything easily spotted such as Down syndrome. That's
trisomy 21, three copies of chromosome 21 instead of
two. Though to be frank, if we found a serious chromosomal deficiency like that – and there are still lots – we'd
probably discard the entire embryo, notify the authorities
and start again.'

'What else do you – discard?' Strether kept his voice
even.

'By law? Well, we're supposed to remove any predisposition to excessive aggression and violence; certain
mental illnesses – not depression; that's acceptable.
Manic depressives are often useful members of society,
sometimes geniuses. But obsessive personality disorders,
which produce rapists, psychopaths and the like, schizo-
phrenia, psychosis and such are eliminated. The
predisposing gene to alcoholism is still a matter of

parental choice, but that's highly controversial. They're hot on mental illness, the Health Commission, but they don't realise it's not so simple.'

'Yes, I can see that,' Strether agreed. He wondered what on earth had persuaded such a pretty woman to abandon attractive clothes, turn her back on any occupation that involved mixing with other young people, and adopt instead this drab white garb to spend her time peering down a microscope. Then he caught himself: that was not merely sexist, but unjust. She was patently a brilliant scientist or she wouldn't have risen to the rank of assistant director so early. Her looks were a bonus.

He must have shifted in his seat for unexpectedly Lisa did the same. They were very close in the tiny office. Last time he had sat as near to a stranger it had been with Marius and the King on those creaky old thrones. Dr Pasteur was a distinct improvement. She wore no perfume but his nostrils detected a clean freshness about her. A natural fragrance, perhaps; was that bred into them too?

His reflections were unworthy and he chided himself. It was fortunate that these Europeans had not yet discovered how to add telepathy to their genes. Not as far as he knew, anyhow.

Yet, as he gazed, she wriggled in her seat. He was aware that she was dividing her attention between her notepad, now covered in squiggles and arrows, and himself.

'We are learning the whole time. Years ago,' Lisa continued earnestly, 'it was policy to remove any genetic proneness to cancer. That was before tobacco was banned throughout the Union. But it was discovered we were creating new problems. Take breast cancer. The gene was isolated quite early, BRCA1 at location 17q12-21. In the old days nothing could be done and healthy women had mastectomies as a precaution: that must have been dreadful. So the moment we had the skills, out came the gene and the women of the civilised world cheered. Then we realised our mistake.'

'Go on.' Strether reached furtively for another biscuit. His hand brushed her knee, inadvertently. Or perhaps not. He was surprised at himself. She did not move away, but flashed him that tantalising half smile.

'Well . . .' Lisa hesitated then squared her shoulders. Whatever else, she was absolutely professional. 'We'd interfered with female hormone production. The babies born were physically unblemished, but when it came to their own pregnancies the daughters could not produce the right hormones. They were, in fact, infertile. We'd swapped one tragedy for another.'

Strether found part of his brain asking other questions, which he dared not put. Was this attractive woman – normal? Had her genes been checked? She did not lack breasts, though he could barely make out their shape beneath the voluminous protective garment. Did she have normal ovaries and eggs? How might she reproduce? *Was she married, or otherwise spoken for?* She wore no ring. He caught himself, startled. That was foolish thinking. He felt his face colour, though the furrow of concentration deepened on his brow.

'So that particular form of gene therapy was halted and another solution was sought. That's where stage two comes in.'

'Stage two?'

'That's right. Stage one is genetic cleansing – taking out anything undesirable. Stage two involves adding

something. We were barely in time with enhanced resistance to bacterial infection: the bugs mutate faster than
pharmaceutical companies can develop new antibiotics
to beat them. Anti-viral resistance is also now routine,
though as the second and third generation come through,
we don't need to enhance again: they've got it already.'

She paused as if mentally checking her facts. Strether
stayed silent. Then she continued, more slowly, 'With
breast cancer, it was decided to try adding an increased
generalised resistance to malignancy. The families
weren't keen on any more disasters, as you can imagine,
so there was opposition. Then came a widespread epidemic of breast cancer, linked with the mid-twenties
explosions. It was horrific – my great-aunt was a victim.
Fortunately, extra resistance works, and is now standard.
We don't even have to ask for permission; it's automatic.'

Strether grunted. 'Forgive me, but this is revolutionary
stuff to an American. We're not totally ignorant about
what you do here: CNN covers it occasionally, there are
calls for it at home from time to time, but it's not allowed.
Been banned from the start. I have to put it to you.
Doesn't anyone object?'

Lisa thought for several moments. 'They don't have to
ask for the treatment. They can have unexamined
embryos, if they want. Low-caste people mainly don't
bother.'

'Isn't that better?'

'As a scientist, I have to say no. That's so risky. Every
parent wants a perfect baby. Who'd want to bring into
the world a child who's deaf or deformed or prone to disease, if it could be avoided? Or with a chromosome
deficiency – my God, have you seen those kids with their
elephantine heads and tumours growing out of the chest?

Fused oesophagus and windpipe, transposed heart arteries? The cost, the pain, the misery . . . And that got harder, as you well know, Ambassador, after the mid-twenties explosions, with all the genetic mayhem the radiation caused. *Causes*,' she corrected herself. 'Still getting a lot of it. Awful – I see some of the poor patients when I lecture abroad.' She shuddered.

Strether tried once more. 'But at home it's argued that the problem isn't disability, it's our cruel attitudes to it. If we stopped seeing one way, one kinda body as perfect – if we saw them as people, first . . .' His voice trailed off; she gave him a withering look.

'That's all very well. But we don't have the right to inflict tangled limbs and defective organs on our children. Not when we have the power to change them. *That* would be wicked.'

Strether drank his coffee and munched his biscuit thoughtfully. This lady was remarkable, far more forthcoming than the Director had been, more comprehensible too. And quite lovely. Here was a chance not to be missed. The cosy quarters in which they were seated, the easy hospitality they were sharing, enabled two intelligent adults to speak to each other with maturity and compassion. What else might she say?

'Stage two,' he mused. 'I'd heard there was more to it than that. Not just resistance to disease?'

Lisa looked at him across the coffee cup. 'Does that interest you especially, Ambassador? I heard your wife died of malignant melanoma. Perhaps if her genes had been inoculated . . .'

'Call me Bill,' Strether answered. He sighed. 'Maybe, or maybe not. We have the treatments Stateside, but they are as unpleasant as ever. Beating cancer is not easy.

She'd simply had enough.' He hesitated. 'I miss her still, though it's a while now. Never had any children – they'd have made a difference, I guess.'

Lisa let her fingers touch his knee. 'So many people never know love,' she said softly. 'You must feel yourself lucky.'

'I do. But it leaves – a terrible gap.'

She nodded once. 'Yes. I was married. No kids either.' She seemed to shake herself, and resumed her narrative. 'Look; the justification over here for this programme is that, here, cancer is almost unknown. We don't only inoculate the embryos of cancer-prone families. We do it for every applicant now, unless they tick the box to say they don't want it.'

He could not stop himself: it came out in a rush. 'You could say that's what my wife did. She ticked the box. If she couldn't live healthily, doing the things she'd loved, riding and living out in the open – she was half Navajo – then she didn't want to live on a cocktail of drugs or vegetate in a wheelchair. I tried to dissuade her, but I respected her decision. In a way, that's why I'm here. After she died I needed another interest – another passion, you might say. Politics came along at exactly the right moment.'

Lisa smiled. 'I'm glad, Ambassador.'

'Call me Bill, please.' He ventured a lop-sided grin back. When she smiled, dimples appeared lightly at each side of her mouth. She was uncommonly stirring, no doubt about it. With a profound sense of shock, he realised that this was the first time since his wife's death that he had noticed another woman, as a woman. He took a deep breath. 'It'd give me great pleasure if you would use my name – a good-looking girl like you. If you don't mind my saying so.'

To his alarm, her expression hardened.

'I'll take that as a compliment, Ambassador, but you should be careful. Comments like that are deemed sexist under our code here in Europe, and are thus illegal. If you weren't a foreign citizen you could be arrested.'

'Lord, I'm sorry. I didn't mean to offend you.'

'You didn't.' She relaxed and tilted her head to one side. 'In fact, Mr Strether, you're not a bad-looking chap yourself.'

She was making fun of him. Strether's embarrassment was complete. 'I shall be more guarded in future. I apologise. But *Bill*. Please.'

'Are you sure? We would regard that as a bit . . . familiar. Bill. Then you must call me Lisa – that is my given name.'

'And Pasteur? You related? To Louis Pasteur, I mean?'

'Certainly.' Those dimples again. His naïvety seemed to amuse and reassure her. 'My grandparents chose very carefully. We are a medical family with direct inherited links with Marie Curie. She was Polish – that's why I have dark hair and eyes. They checked the range of selections open to medical families and surnamed my father after the main genetic introduction, Louis Pasteur. The cell material came from a lock of his hair preserved at the Institut Pasteur in Paris. My family are tremendously proud of the connection. And so am I. Bred to perform top-grade medical research, Bill, that's what I am. And fortunate to be so.'

There was not a trace of shyness about her statement, or arrogance. Strether gestured at the office, the printouts, the computer terminal. 'Doesn't it bother you, working on this – this manipulation? Don't you have any feelings of conscience about it?'

Lisa sat back, a pout on her lips. 'Not at all, not as a woman. Which would you prefer, Bill? Thousands of aborted handicapped foetuses sent to the shredder, or a little tidying up before re-implantation? Most Europeans – most educated women – feel there's no contest.' She bit her lip. 'Me, for instance. I'd love a child, but I'd be terrified if I wasn't sure it was absolutely normal. That implies using the best science on offer.'

Her manner had become challenging. He said, so quietly that she almost couldn't hear, 'All that means is that you've never been in love. Not properly.'

With a movement of his hand Strether tried to make peace. Lisa persisted. 'You do the same with your cattle, Bill. You want greater conversion between food intake and muscle weight, don't you? You need resistance to parasites, the capacity to withstand drought and poor conditions? Sure, I know you do. Heavens, the pioneer work with mammal embryos was done with cattle in Texas. In 1985 Steen Willadsen cloned hundreds of prize bull embryos. Unfortunately for him, farmers were not prepared to pay. Frozen semen and live cows were a lot cheaper.'

Strether nodded: he had heard the story. But Lisa was not to be deterred.

'It's the same with us. *Pro bono publico* – for the public good. And we mean it. We proceed with the utmost caution. The results are awesome – arguably, one reason why Europe is so far ahead of America. We've taken a major scientific advance and instead of wishing, or pretending, that it isn't possible, we made it work for us. What's wrong with that?'

Strether shook his head but could not answer her.

There might be no camera recording the exchange and

the body language, but there were other pressures. Time was nearly up; Marius and the Director would soon be back. Strether felt a sense of urgency, and suddenly realised that it was being communicated by her, to him. He leaned forward and looked hard at her.

Under his examination she wilted, then recovered herself. 'Look, Bill, we're civilised here in Europe. Or we try to be. That's not just propaganda.'

Lisa seemed upset, as if he had touched a raw nerve. Strether drew back; he had pressed her ferociously, and now half regretted it. She glanced down. 'It is so unusual to get an interested outsider. There are problems, inevitably. Scientists like to pretend that everything in the garden's rosy, but that isn't always so. Not at all,' she concluded, and looked away.

Footsteps and muted voices could be heard in the corridor. He rose abruptly and, with Lisa's assistance, began to tie on his mask. As she stood on tiptoe her face came close to his own. Those brown, honey-flecked eyes were fringed with long lashes. And he could smell her anew – that fresh, clean smell, as of a healthy creature, alive and alert. And quite lovely: his first impressions had been absolutely correct.

'Lisa, I'm so grateful to you. But I feel I've –'

'Barely scratched the surface?' She completed the sentence for him. Her face was wistful. 'You're more correct than you know.'

The remark left a powerful feeling of unfinished business between them. Strether took a chance. He mumbled, through the face-mask, 'If I wanted to see you again, could I? Would that be unethical? I can leave you my vidphone number . . .' He rummaged, found his power-book and printed out a gold-crested card for her.

'Thank you. Here.' She bent and scribbled rapidly on her notepad, tore off the page and handed it to him. 'This is mine. You should ring me and come out again for a drink. Or I can meet you in London – my family keeps an apartment there, so I'm not stuck in Porton Down the whole time.'

'Thank *you*.' Strether stuffed the piece of paper quickly into his pocket. The two of them emerged from the tiny office into the laboratory. As the door from the corridor opened he was once more fully robed and masked. He drew himself to his full height.

'Dr Pasteur. Thank you. You have made things much clearer for me, and set my mind at rest. Please accept the gratitude of the people of the United States of America.'

She laughed good-naturedly, as if she understood his need for cover. 'Mr Ambassador, it's been an honour. Have a nice day.'

Her eyes met his. Strether was certain she was trying to say more to him, but did not betray the confidence. He hoped she had not been humouring him or merely being polite. He wanted to see her again, very much.

In the Maglev returning to London Strether needed to talk. As if anticipating him, Marius sat in the facing seat.

'Impressed?' the Prince inquired. That slightly mocking expression again, but it was not unkind.

'Who couldn't be?' Strether answered. 'I've never seen anything like it. Mind-boggling.'

'I'll get you some material from the House of Lords library,' Marius offered. 'The debates are worth reading – the old fears, the refutations. The finance – the work is highly labour-intensive so it costs a packet. Estimates have to be agreed annually. Nothing goes through without the most intense scrutiny.'

Strether privately doubted that; few parliamentarians in any country had the skill to put sharp questions to scientists. He himself had floundered. Yet he was puzzled. Beneath her professional enthusiasm, Lisa's evident discomfort at his probing would not leave his mind. Her parting shot was almost an admission that the programme might have holes in it. He had found more than he had bargained for – but what?

'Dr Pasteur explained to me that there are two stages, one to take out defective material, and the second to insert . . . something better, I suppose. What I didn't understand is what happens before that. She mentioned parental choice several times. What does it mean? How is it exercised?'

'Ah, yes. That is not part of her duties, more the province of politicians.' Marius had resumed his most urbane manner. 'When a couple decides to have a child, they apply for a permit. What with the rapid increase in the numbers of elderly, this part of the world takes its population responsibilities to heart, though we can't prevent unplanned conception entirely. Poverty, however, has a powerful disincentive effect. Long ago we abolished those perverse payments that encouraged single parents or unsupported families to reproduce willy-nilly. It still happens but is rare. And unknown among educated and upper-caste families.'

'Go on. Who decides on the – permit? What are the criteria?'

'Slow down, Strether – Bill. It's similar to the old methods for adoption. Are they suitable? Is the partnership stable? The system prefers heterosexual married couples, but anti-discrimination codes mean nobody's ruled out. Can they offer a child a good home? If the answer's yes, they can proceed. Vanity usually dictates that they opt to use their own genetic material, egg and sperm, though we have spare banks of both.'

'And if no?'

'In law refusals do not have to be spelled out but I've handled cases like that through the Lords. Often there's an obvious explanation – cruelty or abuse of a previous child or of a spouse, financial incompetence, or serious genetic problems within the family that can't easily be corrected.'

'You're telling me you'd refuse a bankrupt?'

'Not necessarily, dear chap. But no sensible government would give the go-ahead to a baby about to become a burden on the state. We'd certainly refuse a family with, say, Huntington's disease unless they accepted genetic modification. It's not the tussle you imagine. Most would-be parents are desperate to have healthy offspring.'

'Yes, Lisa said the same,' Strether mused.

'Lisa? You're well in there, Bill!'

'No.' Strether wriggled in his seat. 'Don't change the subject. She mentioned the choices available to medical families. What did she mean?'

'That's stage two, when abilities can be added. Not only the obvious improvements, like disease resistance, say, or a facility with languages. Upper-caste families are offered enhancement of pre-existing tendencies, as long as there's a statistical need for them. Loads of options, but certain categories are preferred. Doctors, researchers – most of the lab workers you saw today will have had enhancement at conception. They're vital to the well-being of the state. So are mathematicians, or teachers, or creative writers. Up to quota, that is. So are politicians with a desire to serve the Union and not themselves, and a civil service which is sea-green incorruptible.'

'You are kidding, of course.' Strether gaped.

'I'm not. Most of the people you've met so far, Bill, have had stage two enhancement, particularly of their intelligence. We add up to five points as a matter of course.'

'God in heaven. What I'm getting at . . .' Strether was struggling. 'Who makes the rules? Lisa mentioned the Health Commission – is that part of the European Commission? Where do they fit in? Who decides that it's OK to add a bit of IQ, or make a man creative?'

'The would-be parents, of course.' Marius seemed a bit huffy. With an obvious effort he recovered his equanimity but his eyes were cold. 'Parliament. These matters are decided by the elected representatives of the people, no one else. The Commission are merely administrators, who respond in turn to the pressures exerted by those same parents. Millions of them. It's circular, I grant you. But another way of describing it is *consensus*. It so happens, Bill, that the consensus over here favours harnessing knowledge to meet human need. We simply do not have the terror of scientific advance that paralyses your anti-Darwinian fundamentalist Congress. We are not starry-eyed. We're not duped by quacks claiming to have the panacea to every ill. But where it works, we use it. Free of charge, if we can. *Because it is for the public good.*'

Strether lowered his voice. 'You don't think it's against nature? Or God?'

Marius laughed without restraint, to such an extent that other passengers twisted around. 'My *dear* Bill. The things you do come out with! It was God – or Mother Nature, if you prefer – who gave us these powers in the first place. You might as well declare that we should not use anaesthesia during surgery, or insecticides, or lasers, or fuel cells to fly planes, or rocket propulsion to go to the moon – or electromagnetic levitation to drive this train, for instance. We could still be living in wooden huts and using open hearths for cooking. How about it?'

Strether let his eyes rest coolly on his companion's face. 'And you, Marius. What was added to you? Do you know?'

Marius laughed again, more softly. 'Not in so many words, no. I know that my mother Princess Io, who is of Japanese stock, opted for the Asian slit eyelids to be eliminated. That was when she married my father, a Hungarian royal, so I'd have probably looked half Western anyway. After that, it's in my printout. I could find out more if I wished, but it becomes significant only when I want to marry and have children of my own.'

'Your printout?'

'I'll show it to you some time. Children get a printout of their genetic map on their eleventh birthday. It's quite an occasion. It means we know who we are. All part of growing up and becoming an adult.'

Strether gazed out of the window. His mind was in turmoil.

Everyone took it for granted that society's well-being was being served, even Fred, the ice-cream taster, and his wife. It was as if a better baby was regarded as a quality consumer product, an aspiration for those in the lower strata, an assumption for their rulers. Yet he had glimpsed enough, out in the street, at the games, in the tube, to think it possible that the system was being abused – or at least, deployed in ways that could not have official approval. Unless somebody was turning a blind eye.

Opposite him Marius waited. Once it was clear the discussion would not be resumed, the Prince calmly pulled out his powerbook and was soon engrossed in it.

Strether bit his lip. The doctrine was the creation of better human beings. Yet he had met at least one today: Lisa, with the honey-brown eyes and the fresh, healthy aura. He patted his pocket where her number was hidden. Then he dozed in a dreamy, uneasy reverie as the rich land outside slipped by.

He arrived back at the Residence late and weary. The housekeeper had long gone; he was alone. He poured himself a drink and sat lounging, his feet up. But it was no use telling himself to let a day or two lapse. It had to be done at once.

He dialled her home vidphone number and was relieved when her face appeared very quickly, as if she had been waiting for him. This time, however, she was in a blue sweater, and wearing small amber earrings which twinkled fuzzily on the screen. And lipstick. It made it harder for him to concentrate. But work came first.

'Lisa – so many new questions. I don't know where to start. Can I ask you anything?'

What emerged from the vidphone was almost a giggle. Perhaps she, too, had had a drink. 'You can ask. I'm not sure how secure this line is, though. *Ambassador.*' It was a warning. He readjusted his features, became immediately more serious.

'Well, for example, you talked about stage one, when

defects are tidied up. And stage two, when additions are made. Is there a stage three? I mean, when you've finished, you've got something unique, haven't you? Or can you make . . . copies?'

Lisa pondered. 'Under a microscope it would be straightforward. Remember I started with eight identical cells. I can repeat the modifications to the other seven, but that's tedious and prone to mistakes. It'd be quicker to introduce the improved genetic material into a denucleated host cell, grow it to embryo size, split the new cells up and then implant the eight identical nuclei into more empty shells. That's why they're called NTs – nuclear transplants.'

'How often could you do it – in theory, anyway?'

Lisa seemed uncomfortable with the query. 'In theory, any number of times you like. Even with some failures, if the process were repeated three times – eight to sixty-four to 512 – you could have hundreds of identical embryos. You grow the chosen embryo to blastocyte stage then it's implanted, in a surrogate, or the biological mother if that's what's been booked. Or in the laboratory, though that's so tricky and dear it's only done for top-caste families.'

'Such as?'

'The royals, obviously. Others – I'm not at liberty to say. People like me.'

'Wait, Lisa,' Strether said urgently. 'It's not the mode of pregnancy that I'm asking about. It's how often you duplicate the – the ideal embryo you've created.'

Lisa averted her gaze. 'We don't. It's not allowed. Can't you see? It wouldn't be in the public interest.'

'Why not? Everything else about that goddamned programme is. It's National Health Service money, isn't it? Paid for by the taxpayer, every last cent of it?'

'Mostly. The research certainly is,' Lisa admitted. 'I'm a grade six civil servant, that's true. But the state only pays for the therapy under certain conditions.'

'Oh? So who gets it free, and who doesn't?'

Lisa now looked distinctly ill at ease. 'If I had my way, everyone would, but that'd be astronomically expensive. So, all upper castes, of course. Any family with a history of defects. And anyone requesting preferred improvements.'

'Including modifying the fat gene so they can eat as much as they like?'

Lisa frowned. Strether noticed that even when her expression softened a moment later, the frown mark remained. 'No, not at present. They'd have to pay for that at a private clinic. The list is a matter of debate. It's not for me to decide.'

'But those who do decide are upper caste, I'll bet,' Strether thrust at her. 'So how about it? If they said to you to go ahead, make six of these beauts the same, would you? Must you?'

She paused, a look of great anguish on her face. 'Bill, don't. It isn't policy. That'd be cloning. Think about it – DNA's used for many forms of identification. In criminal cases, suppose there were two hundred people with identical DNA, how could you ever get anyone convicted? Answer, you couldn't. Access to cash machines, paying bills and the like: if lots of us were the same that'd be impossible. Everyday life as we know it wouldn't exist. Now do you see?'

'But is it forbidden?' Strether insisted. The football match was still vivid – the stocky quartet of women players, the strikers linked to stars from history – but he held his tongue. He had to absorb the official version cleanly to understand it.

Lisa sighed. 'No, not exactly. It isn't encouraged, but it isn't absolutely forbidden. At least, we don't do it at Porton Down, and it's stopped by the courts whenever examples emerge. Unless it's under licence.'

She twiddled with the knobs and her image went briefly out of focus, then returned, still speaking slowly. 'I know what troubles you, and it does me, too. When people look too alike, psychologically it's extremely disturbing. Everyone is an individual – that's Porton Down's other motto. But genetically it could be disastrous. If clone copies started breeding then damaged genes we might have missed, or which mutated spontaneously, could cause havoc. We could have a race of idiots, or madmen, or worse. That's why there's the age-old taboo against incest. Why go to the trouble of putting things right if we can avoid a mess to begin with?'

'Quite,' Strether agreed. He kept to himself Marius's casual remark about visitors to the centre having very similar DNA. He did not want to antagonise her further, yet her stubborn defence of her work, even under pressure, was confused and unsatisfying. 'I'm glad to hear you opt for individuality.'

'I do.' Lisa smiled once more and to Strether it was as if the sun had come out. 'Not that these matters are entirely under our control. The urge to replicate, to make uniform, is extremely powerful.'

'So that's why so many upper-caste people resemble each other, is it? Tall, blond, blue-eyed, long thin fingers – they look as alike as cattle bred from the same sperm.'

She shrugged. 'In western Europe Nordic looks have dominated for centuries. It's the fashion, Bill, but none the less powerful. Mankind is a conformist species.'

'So it does happen. Or, at least, it can.'

She seemed very downcast. 'I won't deny that. Anyway, that's not really the problem. Bill, is that all you wanted to ask me? Because I am busy here . . .'

'Oh, Lisa, I'm so sorry. No, that wasn't all.' He gazed at the screen. So what if somebody else's gimlet eyes were on them? It was a free world, wasn't it? 'Look, I'll accept it if you say no. But could we have coffee, maybe? Or that drink you mentioned? Or would you enjoy going out for a meal? I'd love to see you again. And maybe talk about — something else.'

The dimples broke out afresh; she raised her head and laughed sweetly. 'D'you know, Bill, I've got so bogged down in work here, my social life has all but disappeared. Yes, what a terrific idea. When? Have you your diary handy? How about Tuesday?'

Chapter Six

'Yes, but what is it? Is it supposed to represent anything in particular?'

Strether and Marius were standing beneath a geometric complexity of gleaming tubes and globes, which soared above them into the cloudless blue sky. Marius consulted his guidebook. 'It's the Atomium,' he offered helpfully. 'Heavens, Bill, one lives in Brussels half the year and yet one never sees the place properly. It says here it's a crystal molecule of iron expanded to 165 billion times life-size. It was built in 1958, so it's just had its hundred and fiftieth anniversary, like the Union itself. We can take the lift to the top for the panoramic view. Interested?'

Strether shook his head. His mind was elsewhere, with a pretty woman with dimples and amber earrings. But, for the moment, he had to concentrate on politics.

'Sure? Then how about Mini-Europe, with scaled-down versions of the principal monuments of every region in the Union?'

The answer was a grimace. Marius did not argue. 'Me neither. We're due for lunch at the Palais de la Nation in less than an hour. Do you know the etiquette? Belgium's effectively two regions. Both Flemish and French have equal status. Whichever you're spoken to in, you answer in the same one. Get it wrong and they're insulted.'

'I can't manage either. My German is coming along slowly, but I didn't have much use for Flemish where I came from.'

Marius grinned. 'As an American you're excused. Play dumb. Literally. Or use your auto-translator. You haven't left it at home, have you?'

Strether fumbled in a pocket and found the neat leather pouch, assembled the ear-piece, programmed it to 'E' for Europe, and slipped it over his left ear. As long as he stared directly at a companion, speech would be translated into English (of a sort) from any of thirty languages. The result was hardly great literature, and idioms would be badly mangled, but it served.

The two men strolled north along the Boulevard du Centenaire and headed into the Line 1A Métro. At Beekant they changed trains and rode six more stops to Park. Here trim lawns stretched smoothly away, carved fountains flowed sweetly. Date palms grew high over their heads, their green fronds moving slowly in the warm air. It would be hot today, over 30°C. Strether adjusted his straw Panama and hoped it sat well with the new suit in summer-weight fabric, modishly cut by Marius's tailor.

The Prince indicated their destination, a stolid twentieth-century building. At the park's far end stood a much more elaborate edifice from a more elegant era. As they spoke, a small group emerged from a side door and began to walk in their direction.

Marius peered then nudged Strether. 'I knew we would be presented to the Belgian Crown Prince before lunch, but it looks as if we'll meet him a little sooner. Prince Adolf Leopold. Bit of a stickler for protocol, I'm afraid – the less important they are, the more they insist on their status.'

'That never seems to trouble you, Marius?' Strether inquired.

'No, but then I don't have any proper status. The Hungarians decided thirty years ago to ditch their royal family so my parents, somewhat miffed at such treatment, left for London. They sensibly advised me to get a job and make myself useful.' The figures were coming closer, a bent old man in a peacock-blue cloak with several nimbler acolytes scurrying around. Marius pointed discreetly. 'That's him. I have a lot more fun than he has. As an elected peer in England I can get progress on issues. I don't have to keep up appearances too much. I have excellent contacts here in the Commission, and relatives in every European capital, so I never need stay in a hotel. Who could ask for more?'

The royal party was upon them. Marius bowed exaggeratedly low, deftly reminded the elderly Crown Prince of his own name and lineage then introduced his companion.

He must have been almost ninety, Strether reckoned; Crown Prince because the King his father was still alive, the oldest monarch in the world at 115, though bedridden in the Laeken Palace and reportedly senile. Adolf Leopold had a tetchy look.

'Your Excellency.' Adolf Leopold held out a limp hand and removed it almost before Strether could make contact. 'I have been to the United States,' he continued, in a querulous voice. 'New York World's Fair, 2065. The Belgian Village Exhibit. It felt as if *I* was the exhibit.'

'I'm sorry to hear that,' Strether murmured.

Adolf Leopold's slack lips worked as if more was to emerge, but with a despairing little cry he tugged his cloak about him and tottered on. Strether and Marius fell into step behind. The Crown Prince suddenly halted and addressed the American.

'Have you seen the Manneken-Pis yet?'

'Ye-yes, I have. Sir.'

'Good. Then you've seen the lot. That was put up about the time your Pilgrim Fathers were sailing for America. The only bit of authentic Brussels left, after the – the –' he waved a gnarled hand furiously in the direction of the Robin Schuman memorial where the Union blocks clustered '– after *they* took over.'

His courtiers shuffled their feet. One seized the Crown Prince's elbow and propelled him firmly on his way.

Marius sucked his teeth thoughtfully. 'You know, that happened ages before he was born,' he whispered. 'Shows you how persistent an opinion can be.'

Strether could not resist. 'Hasn't he been bred like that, though?' he teased. 'Isn't it in his genes? His country before the Union?'

'No, not him. He's not an NT. He'd be a sweeter personality if he were. He's just a miserable old curmudgeon, the true son of his father. That royal house is descended from Queen Victoria, and it's pretty obvious at times.'

Strether was silenced. When he glanced at his companion he saw that Marius was chuckling to himself, though whether at the Crown Prince's remarks or at his own remained a mystery.

The entrance to the Palais, as for every public building in Brussels and major cities during the year of the Grand

Celebration, was a forest of regional and Union flags. Strether wished he held shares in flag-makers – somebody was making a fortune. The arrivals were greeted by obscure folk-dancing troupes; a frequent game was to guess their origin. Strether's knowledge of mid-Continental ethnic styles was improving, especially since the embassy's library had yielded a diskette gold-mine of back issues of *National Geographic.* This time, as he examined the sheepskin leggings and hoop earrings he chose Uzbekhistan while Marius hazarded Azerbaijan. Both were wrong: this was an invited group from Welsh Patagonia.

'But they all drink Galactic Cola and wear Diana jeans at home,' Marius whispered as they followed Albert Leopold up the steps, 'and drive Ford-Mercedes family pick-ups, watch Yamaichi vidscreens and eat at California Raisin Hut. Doesn't everyone?'

The hall's parquet floor gleamed, the chandeliers sparkled. Strether, champagne glass in hand, moved towards the centre. He no longer felt quite such a beginner. His face and name were becoming better known; he had a modest repertoire of jokes and confidences in various languages, sufficient to converse for two or three minutes. Many guests wore an earpiece though a few, like Marius, seemed to manage easily without. On others, mainly young men with a superior air, a tiny titanium aerial behind one ear revealed an implant. Strether shivered at the idea: never to be able to turn it off – that would not suit him. Better, he felt, to *use* one's brain than to try and replace it.

After this weekend President Kennedy was expecting a report. His ambassador would be able to answer truthfully that the Union appeared to function splendidly; as

in a strong family, its members humoured each other's
foibles, but sensitivities were adroitly recognised. That
was no surprise. More than one speech he'd heard had
described a Union born out of conflict with millions
killed in savage wars. Bitter enemies now worked in harmony – France and Germany, the Irish and British, or
Turkey and Greece. He wished his historical knowledge
was less vague. Hadn't the Danes and Swedes once
slaughtered one another? And the Estonians had loathed
the Russians, the Romanians hated the Hungarians, the
Poles . . . At this juncture his mind began to wobble. It
was like trying to remember the myriad tribes of the
American Midwest, which he had tried to learn out of
respect for his wife's antecedents.

What he would convey to his chief was that this vast
empire served its citizens superbly. If the New White City
games or Portobello Road were any guide, the citizens
had blessings to spare. Though Fred the popcorn-eater
might not know it, the lifeblood was trade. Boundaries
and frontiers had disappeared. Crime was far less than in
the US; most adults seemed gainfully employed.
Wherever Strether went, an air of satisfaction seemed to
prevail. If he could put his finger on something he did not
admire, it was the smugness of the people he had met so
far, though even that was tempered by their affability.
With one exception, of course. Lisa was far from smug.

The Union, however, was an enigma. He could not
quite see how it was run. For a start, the Europeans
denied there was a centre; no federal government existed
as such. True, the Central Bank in Frankfurt decided on
interest rates and majestically controlled the stability of
the currency, but it had done so for a hundred years and
was irreproachably above politics. True, the President of

the Union was elected. Herr Lammas had defeated three women candidates (a Cretan, an Italian and a Dane) by picking up second preferences even though he had come third on the first ballot. Nobody in Europe thought that was unfair since the voting methods were modelled on Ireland's. It meant that nothing was quite as it seemed, and no outcome was predictable. At any rate, no electoral outcome. It was unmissable, though, that leading politicians all appeared to come from a handful of genetic families, so maybe it made precious little difference who won.

Government decisions at the centre – the 'Brussels' of which everyone complained – were a collective operation, as far as Strether could deduce. Collective, but not invariably consistent. Environment Ministers would scheme to remove chemicals from rivers and sewers while Health Ministers proposed the addition of new compounds to cornflakes, chapattis or pasta. Transport would extend regional subsidies to this port or that airline. Trade Ministers would thunder that no region should obtain an unfair advantage through taxpayers' money. Heated discussions would stir the night in a dozen dialects; but agreement was invariably cobbled together and hands shaken on a deal, even if in the final photographs some smiles were a mite forced. Then they would fly home, complain bitterly, and prepare for the next fight. It was a time-honoured tradition.

Thus Ministers, elected in their own regions, ruled collectively. The European Parliament had a part to play also. Debates there, Strether had been told, generated more heat than light: MEPs would become agitated about saving the world's few remaining whales, or the desirability of fishing permits for their particular patch – subsidised, naturally, by everyone else. Strether was familiar with such log-rolling in Washington. And Parliament, like Congress, had the constitutional right to interrogate the President of the Commission, Herr Lammas himself, on the exercise of his duties. But that had deteriorated into a 'State of the Union' event, a ceremonial used to put across whatever the leadership wanted publicised and no more. Too many platitudes and too little probing. So where did power really lie?

Strether was seated on table four. Through the smoked dolphin (Norwegian) and the moose tournedos (Icelandic) he had conducted a stilted conversation in German with a stout woman on his right who had turned in relief to the Austrian on her other side. To his left Marius was entangled in a lively discussion in what might have been Czech. It gave Strether an opportunity to take in his surroundings.

The Crown Prince was seated hunched over the top table, sawing away grumpily at his meat. Next to him was the Speaker of the Belgian Parliament, the hostess, a colossally fat woman rumoured to eat her fried potatoes with mayonnaise. Further on, he saw a thin ascetic figure he did not know but who from his figure and throat decoration, was probably one of that ÉNA-trained élite, a senior civil servant. The English Prime Minister and a bunch of MPs were somewhere about. At a further table he spotted Maxwell Packer, the media mogul whom he had met at Buckingham Palace. Packer caught his eye and raised a glass in greeting.

'Penny for them.' It was Marius's voice.

'So where does the power lie?' Strether asked aloud. In answer to Marius's raised eyebrow, he added, 'I'm looking at them. The MPs decide what they're allowed to decide.

The MEPs waste time on frivolities and fancy dinners. Ministers sign papers stuck in front of their noses, much of which they know nothing about, and mostly when they're dog-tired. The President's a figurehead. So who decides? Who writes those papers, props up the ministers, sets the parliamentary agenda, writes the President's speeches?'

'Who are the guardians, you mean?'

'Are they called that? Is there some sort of secret society?' Strether was astonished.

'No, no,' Marius murmured. 'I was thinking of the saying, *quis custodies custodiet?*' Strether looked blank. 'Who guards the guardians? The answer is, nobody does. We each do our best with the limited faculties at our disposal. I say that as an elected peer. It is an onerous responsibility and we are ever conscious of our imperfections.'

Strether peered at him suspiciously, but Marius's expression was studiously bland.

'Oh, great. There's no overall authority?'

'No. How could there be? Only God, I suppose, if you are a believer. Or your conscience.'

'Hum.' Strether paused. 'No, Marius, it won't do. Somebody puts in the homework, somebody writes a priority list, and sorts out what's affordable and what's shelved. Or, at least, makes the recommendations.'

The meat course was cleared. A shout went up as a Bombe Bruxelloise was brought in, its snowy meringue illuminated by lit sparklers. Strether handed the half-spent sparkler to the German matron who held it at arm's length with an expression of profound distaste. He quickly turned again to Marius and placed a hand on his arm.

'Who?'

Marius glanced about warily and lowered his voice. 'Who do you think? Who is in charge, has been for millennia? *Not* elected, *not* public figures, nameless and unknown. Protected from prying eyes. Invisible, immaculate, irreplaceable. Who do you think? Come on, Strether, you're far from stupid. If I say "faceless", does that help?'

'Bureaucrats?'

'Of course.'

Strether was deflated. He had expected something more – bizarre – to pass on to his President. Gently, with a half-crooked finger, Marius indicated the man next to the Belgian Speaker and slowly, one at a time, similarly dressed men and a couple of soberly suited plain-looking women, each with jewelled decorations, scattered at tables throughout the hall. 'Them. Chefs de cabinet, Commissioners, Perm Secs, advisers.'

'And every one of them went to ÉNA, I suppose.'

'Certainly.'

'Did everyone else here, too?'

Marius laughed again, but with an edge. 'Apart from yourself and the cooks and waiters? Probably. That's the cement which holds the lot together.'

'That's what Packer meant by the Énarchy, then. He mentioned it in London. The Perm Sec was not pleased with him.'

'Packer is a tease. But he's very much one of them.'

It was not till much later that Strether remembered that the Prince might have said, 'one of us', but hadn't. He brooded through the coffee. The Crown Prince was at last helped to his feet; the assembly stood and politely clapped him out.

'You are busy this evening, I suppose?' Marius stopped as if it were a sudden thought.

Strether calculated. 'Embassy reception at six then I'm free, if I wish to be.'

'Splendid. Then you'll dine at our club, the Forum – I believe I may have mentioned it. You will have to dress for dinner. *À vingt heures* – eight o'clock, then. Good.'

He would have preferred dinner with Lisa. Strictly speaking, *another* dinner with Lisa. The previous evening had indeed been spent in her company, tucked in a corner table at the Pont de la Tour restaurant, with the magnificence of Tower Bridge picked out in blue and pink light bulbs in the background.

She had arrived in a fluster, apologising for being late. The journey down-river to near Greenwich, the new location for the extended bridge, had involved two changes. Not for the first time Strether wondered why such an inaccessible spot had been chosen to celebrate the millennium in England. Matters had not improved in a century.

But she looked wonderful, and instantly it was he who was flustered. She wore a dress, the first time he had seen her in one; and she turned male heads, for most females in the dimly-lit restaurant wore trouser tunic suits that graced their slim figures. As she walked quickly towards him he could not help noticing once more the trim calves and neat ankles. She stopped, pointed a toe and swirled her skirt, showing off girlishly. Strether could not stop himself blushing.

'I have a cattleman's eye for a fine leg, Lisa,' he confessed, as he helped her to her chair. 'You're not going to start berating me again for paying you a compliment, are you?'

'No, not now I'm off-duty.' A waiter leaped forward and lit a waxless candle, which flickered, then settled and glowed softly. She smiled: the dimples caught the light.

For the next hour Strether was a happy man. Whatever he ordered, Lisa welcomed. Whatever he said, she found amusing or intriguing. When he swayed one way or the other with the enthusiasm of a subject, she seemed to sway in sympathy. He told her of his ranch, and of his love for his homeland, and the peculiar coincidences that had made him Ambassador to London. With a little encouragement he told her more about his marriage and the exquisite, mystical woman who had been his wife; and how, even as he held her hand in death, he had felt that he had never entirely understood her, nor could follow where she walked. And Lisa spoke, but simply, of the fellow student she had wed, and the sense that they had never touched souls at all.

It struck him that both were operating with the greatest delicacy, taking trouble to say nothing negative about themselves or those they had loved. Maybe he was absorbing a restrained, polite European style. Coming from a world in which carping was more commonplace Strether was fascinated, and began to relax.

'I'm so glad you could come. I hope this won't be the only time,' he said at last. Then it came out, too bluntly, and he wished he had not said it: 'A man can get lonely, you know.'

Her eyes widened. The candlelight made them golden, like a marvellous cat's. She bowed her head and pushed the remains of her food around on her plate with a fork.

'A woman, too. But I'm not into casual relationships, Bill. I'm not a female who has to experience her life through men. European women are different, at least, upper-caste ones are. The most important thing to me is, and always has been, my work.'

'Yes,' he mused. 'I can see that. Not a homemaker. Though you might enjoy having a home, and a family?'

'Oh, yes,' she answered, revealingly quickly. She recovered herself. 'But not yet, I don't think.'

A pause. Then he continued, 'Your work. When we last spoke, you mentioned problems. I thought you were referring to, well, copies.' His voice dropped as she darted a look around. The nearest camera was on the far side; that was why he had opted for this table. 'But you said that wasn't it.'

'You don't miss much, do you?' She had smiled at him, then placed a hand swiftly over his, as if her next statement was offered to cement a bond between them. 'The Porton Down experimental work. That's where the queries are arising. I'm right in the middle of it. You'll have to come and see.'

'What – back to your laboratory?' He was startled, and began mentally to juggle dates.

'No. To the records centre. Ask Prince Marius. Maybe he'll come too.'

'Can I trust him?'

'Who can say? Can you trust anybody, Bill?' Then she laughed. 'Except me, of course. Only be careful. I might just break your heart. Though not your pocket. You will let me pay my share, won't you?'

Strether bit his lip. He twisted his head helplessly from one host to the other, then sat down wanly on the nearest red plush bench. 'I can't.'

He, Maxwell Packer and Prince Marius Vronsky were deep in the basement of what had once been the medieval Hôtel de Ville in Grand Place. One should be thankful, Strether supposed, that the style of the Forum Club was not sixteenth-century slashed velvet breeches and be-ribboned codpieces. Given the attire into which he was now being bundled, that might have been preferable. At least then his naked knees and calves, the bits of his body of which he was least proud, would have stayed hidden.

'They won't let you in without it, dear chap,' Marius muttered crossly. 'If I'd thought you'd any objections to the formal dress the offer would never have crossed my lips.'

'But why do we have to wear togas?'

'Because this is the Forum Club. Here gather, for conversation and conviviality, the élite of the Union, the rule-book says. By invitation only,' Marius informed him, with a mere trace of mischief in his voice. 'Since the model for the Union is the Roman Empire, we adopt the garb of the Senate. And its eating habits.'

Maxwell Packer was ready. Strether noted grudgingly that the media man's full head of hair and tanned, muscular forearms and legs were splendidly set off by the cream cashmere cloak and metallised belt. Marius's heavy silk cloak was sapphire blue with an embroidered border, and he wore a white tunic. About his head was a narrow gold band, the mark of his royal rank. Had there been more notice Strether could have acquired something closer to his own taste, instead of renting a club spare. Had he known about this in advance, he would have refused point-blank to come.

'Come on, we'll be late.' Marius hauled Strether to his feet and set about pouching the striped toga over the belt and pinning the folds firmly to the left shoulder. 'There, you won't disgrace us. Or your country.'

Strether examined himself in the full-length mirror. Then he pulled back his shoulders and smoothed his ruffled hair. The middle-aged, rather paunchy man who stared back, he had to admit, could well have been a tribune on his way to declaim on an emperor's birthday. He looked more closely: the image was familiar. Then he recalled the statue, in Parliament Square in London, of George Washington as a Roman, complete with laurel leaves and a breastplate. Strether sniffed, half mollified.

The dining room was a further revelation, but this time Strether held his tongue. The long, low room was furnished with fringed couches and *chaise-longues* upholstered in sumptuous fabrics, with plump tasselled cushions in piles. Thick plum velvet curtains had been drawn. Great vases held displays of flowers, lilies, white lilac and tuberoses, whose perfume hung heavily in the warm air. Light came from classical-style lamps on pedestals; real wax candles stood like sentinels on brass stands. A trio with harpist, lute and a zither-like instrument played, their plaintive notes mingling with the buzz of conversation.

About half of the sofas were occupied by men in togas reclining gracefully on one elbow, sandalled feet tucked under their robes. Some had auto-translator implants. There was not a woman in sight, but most of the diners had that elongated, disciplined body, those bony hands and fingers and the pale blue eyes that Strether could now spot so readily. And this time he was sure it was not his paranoia.

Servants in short tunics glided between the diners. Strether saw guinea fowl carried past, a haunch of venison, an enormous poached shark-salmon, several mega-lobsters, and a boar's head with tusks intact, its mouth stuffed with a white-fleshed peach, its crisp skin studded with cloves like black diamonds. A polished carvery dish laden with dripping roast beef, crown of lamb and veal, steamed its way tantalisingly around the room. Its chef, a burly man in a floor-length apron, looked capable of wrestling a bullock to the ground single-handed. It dawned on Strether that much of the menu was banned elsewhere, but here, apparently, the usual rules and codes did not apply.

Strether, Marius and Maxwell Packer were shown to an arrangement of sofas. Cold starters (extremely rare North Sea herring, *foie gras*, quails' and ducks' eggs, oysters in champagne, baby octopus unobtainable in the markets, caviares absent from European catalogues) and breads appeared. Soups and hot entrées were offered, here dressed with walnut oil, there with balsamic vinegar or the finest emerald olive oil from Cyprus. A *kir royale* sparkled brilliantly, pink and inviting, before him. A voice in his ear murmured choices of other aperitifs and wines; Strether experienced the odd feeling that he wanted to refer to the staff as 'slaves' but checked himself quickly.

'So, do we get dancing girls and gladiators, too?' he inquired jocularly.

'Don't be silly.' Marius had reclined on a sofa as to the manner born with a goblet of purple wine. 'This is a gentlemen's club. Your main contribution tonight, Bill, will be the quality of your discourse. We've invited the Perm Sec and Sir Lyndon, the English Prime Minister, to join us. They're all members here. Sir Lyndon sometimes makes jokes about the club in private, but I warn you Sir Robin doesn't. Here they come.'

But it was three, not two, men who approached. In his dazzling white robe and tunic Sir Robin seemed even taller and skinnier than before; his age showed in the tiny lines about his face and in the pale hairs on his thin arms and legs, as if the vitality had begun to drain from the furthest parts of him. The Prime Minister wore a black tunic and a silvery toga, which created a flashy effect. On his forehead he sported a wreath of some kind; as the evening wore on it slipped askew and gave him a rakish air. The third man, however, was new: trimly elegant like Sir Robin, but in his young sixties, with a mass of blond hair and a piercing gaze. Packer and Marius leapt to their feet.

'Strether, this is Graf von Richthofen. How good to see you, Heinrich. Will you join us? Chef de cabinet to our President, Herr Lammas.'

'And a companion of the President since childhood. How do you do, Ambassador?' The Graf was courteously, effortlessly dominant. It was instantly obvious that he was the most important person present, despite the use of his first name.

Within the hour Strether was hooked and had begun to toy with ideas of starting such a club in Washington. He watched and imitated as other diners motioned for their food to be cut so that it could be eaten with a fork, one-handed, or with the fingertips. The waiters were ever-attentive, noiseless. The lilting music, some modern composition, seemed exactly right. Smells of meat *jus*, garlic, cardamom, fenugreek, balsam, cinnamon, roses and something else, more delicate – the personal perfumes of the guests, perhaps – filled Strether's nostrils. Candle flames leaped and guttered, casting shadows into the corners, making fruit glow richly in its golden bowls.

His head buzzed with something akin to longing, and with tantalised awe. These diners certainly knew how to look after themselves. The place seemed to operate under different rules from those imposed on the *hoi-polloi.* He wondered how one might be proposed for the club, and if there was a waiting list.

The Graf wiped his fingers on a napkin and nibbled at a grape. 'So, Ambassador, how do you find our club?'

Strether was more than a little drunk. 'It's brilliant. How come I've never heard of it?'

'It's private. No press, except Maxwell here, one or two other owners and editors, distinguished men in their own right. It does not advertise. No need.'

'Yeah,' Strether muttered. 'But d'you have to be an NT to get in? Or an Énarque? Or both? Why aren't there any women? Any . . .' he peered around '. . . any blacks? Why do so many of the guests look the same?'

'The club abides by the anti-discrimination codes, my dear Strether.' Sir Robin reached for a handful of nuts and dextrously wielded a silver-backed nutcracker. 'But you should have realised by now that those of us blessed with good genes and the finest education are proud of both.'

Strether shifted. He prodded his empty goblet, which was instantly refilled by a hovering waiter. 'Would you be upset if I asked you about all that?'

Four men glanced from one to another, laughed indulgently and shrugged. He heard the Permanent Secretary hiss behind his hand to the Graf, 'Tension on the Chinese border, a flu epidemic kills thousands in Russia, and that's what he's interested in. Typical American.' The Graf smiled but did not reply. Strether waited.

Marius sipped Madeira. 'You were impressed, weren't

you, Bill, with your visit to Porton Down?' It felt like an
opening sally.

'"*Pro bono publico*" – that's the motto in the waiting
room. But is it? All that . . . tidying up, the doctor called
it. It's not allowed in America.'

'So your women come here, to private clinics, and
they pay for the *in vitro* treatment.' The Prime Minister
fixed his eyes on Strether. 'Especially those who have a
history of congenital problems. Only the rich can afford
to do that. The poor give birth to deformed children who,
if not disposed of right away, suffer brutish short lives,
and their parents with them. Where is the public gain in
that?'

'And the USA does have such programmes, which perhaps even President Kennedy hasn't seen,' Sir Robin
joined in, 'for key members of the armed forces or the
space and nuclear projects, including civilian nuclear
power. Anyone who might be exposed to radiation in
their normal course of employment. Brought in by
Congress in great secrecy after the mid-twenties explosions.'

Strether stared at him in astonishment. 'Good Lord.'
He paused to let the information sink in. How did they
know that, if he didn't? Did James Kennedy really know?
Was he, Strether, the only person in the dark? Was this
some kind of conspiracy? With an effort he continued,
'That's the key, isn't it? So tell me about these nuclear
explosions. From your point of view.'

The Permanent Secretary took up the story. 'Well,
that's when these programmes became widespread here
in the Union. At least, in those regions – states, then –
able to finance and regulate them. It was felt wiser to
encourage their existence where standards could be set

than to drive them underground, to South America, or somewhere like that.' Sir Robin put his fingers together in an exact V-shape. 'I was a child but I can still remember the bitter arguments. Was it ethical to let nature take its course? The worst mutations would die out without intervention, it was said. Or should we use our God-given technologies to stem the avalanche of human misery, to clean up the damaged gene pool, and return quickly to something near normality?' He faced Strether squarely. 'For my part I'm convinced the right moral choices were made. Nothing could persuade me otherwise.'

Strether backtracked. He recalled his own President's comments. 'I suppose you were more badly affected by the explosions here than we were in the States.'

'And possibly we felt more guilty,' the Graf joined in. He had a slight lisp, which combined with his accent, forced Strether to pay close attention. The Ambassador suddenly had the clear conviction that his hosts had discussed his ignorance before his arrival and had cleared with each other what to say. It was no accident that he had been invited. Or that the Graf had turned up, apparently so unexpectedly. It had been planned, and for his benefit. This was not a conspiracy of *silence*. On the contrary.

The Graf was speaking. 'Europe should have acted after Chernobyl. Those old nuclear stations were of atrocious design and poorly maintained. Governments in the wealthy nations were aware, but nothing was done. Fission material was stolen, rods left unprotected, workers off moonlighting elsewhere. Then – *boum!*' His hands described an arc in the air, mushroom-shaped, then another. Diners nearby twisted to look. '*Boum! Boum!* A chain reaction through Siberia, Ukraine and western

Russia. Archangel'sk, Vologda, Cerepovec, Vitebsk. Zitomir was the worst, near Kiev. A dozen power stations, one after another. And a radioactive cloud drifting westward.'

'Which can still be detected in residues on the Rhine. Parts of Siberia are still uninhabitable,' Sir Robin continued smoothly. It was extraordinary, Strether saw. They all spoke with similar inflections. And thought along the same lines. They did not need to be telepathic: it was true, then, that great minds think alike. Closely related ones certainly did.

'But, Heinrich, if I may say so, we should not accept the blame,' Maxwell Packer intervened. He can do it too, thought Strether woozily. It's as if they're tennis players, all at about the same high ability, and I'm the spectator. Not even on the court. He absorbed as much as he could, as Packer hinted that money had been on the table but had ended up with the Russian Mafia, who didn't care much about ancient nuclear reactors. 'The new stations were never built. I know for a fact that Germany offered huge sums to the Russian Federation government to replace their most dangerous units, but the Kremlin was very sniffy about it. The implication, they claimed, was that the Germans thought the Russians incompetent.'

'We did, and they were.' The Graf smiled ruefully. 'Am I allowed to say that? It was a long time ago.'

'The lesser of two evils,' Strether mumbled. He felt seriously out of his depth. 'Well, I suppose if you must have genetic cleansing, it couldn't be done better. I grant you that.'

Sir Robin caught his eye. 'A great deal of thought has been given to it – a *great* deal. These technologies came through research on genetically engineered ruminoids, which you know more about than I do, Ambassador.'

'The early work in England was financed by the Milk Marketing Board,' Marius intervened wickedly. 'The hunt for bigger udders.'

'Don't trivialise, Marius,' Sir Robin chided. 'In the same era, the Human Genome Project was under way – the mapping of our genes, to establish which amino acid links had which role. The significance of that success could not be over-estimated. I liken it to the translation of the Bible into the vernacular; the precursor and genesis of spectacular social change. The techniques of, ah, *alteration*, were not far behind.'

'But the *need* wasn't there, not in sufficient numbers, not till after the explosions.' The Prime Minister pushed the leafy wreath, now somewhat battered, back from one eyebrow. 'You'd be surprised – some groups campaigned for these techniques to be banned on the grounds that we should value every human being, however damaged.'

'It is a viewpoint,' Strether sighed. He was feeling slightly sick. The others did not appear to have heard him.

'Legalised, regulated, inspected, standardised. Don't forget, in Europe we have the strictest controls. Some activities are not legal.' Sir Robin dipped his fingers in a lemon-scented finger bowl and reached for a towel.

'Like cloning?' Strether said automatically.

The atmosphere turned frosty. Four faces glared at him. The Prime Minister glanced at the ceiling and whistled softly. Marius prodded his arm sharply. 'Nobody here is a – what you said. It isn't done. I'd have thought your friend Dr Pasteur would have made that amply clear.'

Strether blinked rapidly at his neighbours, three of whom resembled each other so closely they could have been triplets, though of different ages. Maybe they *were* triplets, parts of a frozen embryo, defrosted from time to time so that another cell could grow to maturity. He bit his lip. 'I 'pologise. Didn't mean to offend. So you tell me. How d'you regulate? What's allowed? How do you decide?'

The Graf and the Permanent Secretary whispered briefly again to each other, their faces turned away. The evening's lesson, Strether judged, had not gone quite in the direction they had intended.

'My dear chap,' Sir Lyndon spoke distinctly. 'The procedures can be carried out only in a licensed facility. We are particularly hostile to certain – types of activity.'

'Such as?'

'Personal vanity. The individual who wishes to preserve himself for repetition after death. That's a misunderstanding, of course. The megalomaniac thinks it'll be *his* thoughts, *his* soul inside those baby heads. They won't. They are separate human beings. Different environments. The very fact that they're *not* him makes them different from Daddy.'

'That's not science fiction, you know. It's been done,' the Graf spoke quietly as if he did not wish them to be overheard by other guests, 'usually by religious or political fanatics. Remember when the North Koreans created ten identical embryos of Kim Il Sung? And a faction in China was putting together a new Chairman Mao till their government found out. The last Dalai Lama, the one who died in 2015, was preserved partly in a freezer, and partly as five growing foetuses, perfect in every respect. Europe was not able to stop that. Fortunately they each turned out good and honourable men, quite harmless, but there's no guarantee.'

'But most science fiction has been tripe, you must agree,' Maxwell Packer joined in. 'Creating a race of slave labourers, for example. Why ever, struggling as we are against over-population, would anyone want to do that? We have enough trouble finding space and food for the world's billions, let alone creating any more. Anyway, slaves are useless. Intelligent paid workers are best. The better you care for your operatives, the better they perform. Slavery was always bad economics. The north of your country, Strether, beat the south in the Civil War, did it not?'

'It did. That is correct,' Strether conceded. He could hear his own speech slurring. 'You're talking quality versus quantity. I *see*.'

Tea and coffee – fourteen flavoured infusions of the former, seven of the latter – were being served. Minute *petits fours*, shaped as moons and stars and flavoured with white chocolate, Drambuie and Amaretto tempted even Strether's sated palate. An elderly attendant in a black tunic wheeled in a hookah, which gave off a pungent odour that Strether identified in stupefied amazement as unmodified marijuana. Marius and Packer indulged; the others waved it away. The evening was drawing to its close.

The Prime Minister swung his legs over the sofa and sat up. 'Dear Strether. You have finally grasped the point. We need more brilliant brains, not dumb slaves. Another Beethoven would do nicely. Health specialists. Computer freaks. Writers – we never have enough creative people. If I had my way, we'd enhance appreciation of the arts, and put mathematical ability into every citizen at the same

time. The performing companies would be financially
smart enough to stay out of debt, and there'd never be an
empty seat. We'd never need to subsidise another theatre
or orchestra. Eureka!'

The joke was an old one, but was greeted with indulgent laughter. The men rose, stretched, tidied garments
into place, wished each other good night.

As Strether changed back reluctantly into daytime
clothes, his head ached and his feelings were as jumbled
as the discarded toga at his feet. He oscillated between
unfeigned approval of the club and dismay at the conversation. The wine, the food, the ambience were
dazzling. These remarkable men had overpowered him
with their knowledge, their style. He felt tossed and pum-
melled by their intellects, incapable of matching them
on any level.

They operated from inborn instincts: they were bred to
their jobs, to their lives, as he was not. His clumsy prodding had been parried with ease. They had patronised
him completely, but he deserved it. He envied them, and
the glamorous, erudite society through which they glided
with so little effort. *Over which they presided.* For if
Marius was correct, then these were the men in charge –
or some of them. And they had not gained their positions,
as he had, by writing cheques for election campaigns.

He could even picture himself, on his eventual return
home, explaining their genetic programme to his fellow
citizens. Stage one was no more sinister than corrective
surgery to a club foot. Stage two could be compared to
orthodontics or the fitting of crowns to eroded teeth. No
one, not even the most hellfire-breathing preacher, could
raise sustained objections. It was science at its most
triumphant: truly for the advancement of mankind.

And yet: what about intelligence enhancement? There
had been no opportunity to inquire. If the objective was
to help *all* mankind, wasn't that an exception? Mightn't it
create too big a gap between those who benefited and
their offspring, generation by generation, and those who
didn't? In time, upward mobility for the non-enhanced –
for ordinary people – would become impossible. Surely
that was on no one's agenda . . . but might it happen without anyone noticing?

His mind could not cope. Ambivalence mocked him at
every turn. He had been given sanitised responses, yet so
much was going on that he had not been told about. And
Marius seemed to blow every which way about the
issues: Strether could not fathom him.

Lisa, however. The lady with the honey-flecked eyes.
He would ask her. She at least, he sensed, might give
honest answers. As far as she could.

When he entered the embassy his vidphone was bleep-
ing. He turned on the message recorder and was startled
to hear a female voice and see a sweet face fill the small
screen.

*'Ambassador Strether – Bill? This is Lisa Pasteur.
Thank you so much for a pleasant evening. Could you
call me? I'd like to fix up a meeting. Speak to you soon.'*

The image vanished; suddenly the screen fizzed with
static. Over the jagged black and white lines came an
urgent voice:

*'Demonstration in Trafalgar Square. Protect the work-
ers! Support us! Tonight . . .'*

Strether stared at the machine, knocked its side, twiddled a knob. The screen had gone dead. When he tried

to run the digital recording back, only Lisa's face reappeared. The static message appeared to have wiped itself.

He rocked back on his heels, and resolved to call her early in the morning.

Chapter Seven

Lisa Pasteur pressed the icon for the orange squeezer, reached in the fridge and removed the fresh juice. Absent-mindedly, glass in hand, she opened and closed cupboards. Since most foods were irradiated, everything kept for at least half a year; nothing went soft or overripe, no fats went rancid. The refrigerator's main purpose was to keep her drinks chilled.

Her job was too demanding to allow browsing through the shopping mall. The vidphone link brought a repeat order monthly to her apartment, skinless bananas or oranges and long-life skimmed milk and oatmeal, ready-packs of fish and chicken, salads, breads. Plus a small box of her only vice, chocolate walnut whips, to be nibbled while wrestling with some intractable problem brought home. Once she had been caught eating one when she answered the vidphone to her office, and her staff had teased her. She did not cook; canteen fare at Porton Down was excellent – a perk – and she could eat out with friends when an evening came free, which had not been often, lately. An orderly life, but one driven by work, she reflected moodily. From which something was missing.

Lisa walked restlessly around the kitchen-diner. In the background the radio played a news magazine programme. Interviews with Ministers were getting more anodyne day by day. The newspapers, when scrolled down on to the wall screen, were no better: government statements delivered in a flat, toneless voice, trifling personal stories that were mere pap and gossip, with no serious inquiry or analysis. 'Today Prime Minister Sir Lyndon Everidge welcomed improved inflation figures . . .' 'Retired nurse Dolly Wilmut celebrates her four million euro lottery win . . .' 'Convicted murderer's father admits to love nest tangle . . .' 'Manchester United club chairman Maxwell Packer today signed Arsenal forward . . .' That man Packer seemed to pop up everywhere, but seldom with reports of substance. Frustrated, she told the radio to switch itself off.

Had she been working too hard? Was that the explanation? She passed a hand worriedly over her eyes. In a mirror she caught sight of her face and the beginnings of a frown-line between her brows. She touched the holograph symbol: within five seconds the image of the back of her head came into focus, moving about as she turned her head this way and that. The hair curled damply on the nape of her neck. The new earrings were charming and set off her small lobes. The jaw-line had not sagged, not yet. The eyes looked tired from every angle, the skin under the lids puffy. Overwork was certainly to blame for that. It would be some years before she would qualify for, or need, her first free bout of cosmetic surgery.

The Ambassador. It was as if he were in the room, with her. Him, and not the tiny ubiquitous camera in the kitchen, which she could ignore. She had often talked softly to herself when things troubled her; now, for all that their acquaintance had a duration of mere weeks, she had begun to talk to him in her imagination.

Why him, of all people? Was it to do with his stolid, shambling presence, so different from everyone she knew? Alien but oddly comforting, he was also gentle, honest and kind. He had been shy yet pleased when she had let slip that her singledom was no longer her preference. An admission, he seemed to suggest, of which she should not be ashamed, and which he appreciated without question, for it applied also to himself. That alone must draw them together. Alien and quirky, a puzzle. He was certainly a big contrast to the thin-lipped men who were the usual visitors to Porton Down. But that could be only part of the explanation.

Because he wasn't an NT? Surely not. That fact made it harder: he was instinctively hostile to the programme, or had been originally. But she'd vigorously done her duty to defend and justify it. She could be content with her performance. She'd persuaded him that the inherent dilemmas and potential ill uses were not forgotten by scientists. Yet it had been an unusual and disturbing experience to find herself hinting so strongly to Strether that the problems were real and no longer entirely theoretical.

Why him? Because he was an outsider? A foreigner? The frown-line deepened. That was dangerous. The rule-book at Porton Down was crystal clear. Outsiders were to be avoided. Anxieties should be discussed with a line manager. There was a disputes procedure. In a disagreement, the prestigious Chartered Institute of Human Genetics would back her up, or the First Division, the trade union for top civil servants. She had toyed with these possibilities. Or, risking dismissal, she could discuss the matter with an MP, a route guaranteed to cause a public fuss. Had that been her intention, Prince Marius would have been useful. But he had that knowing upper-caste cynicism entirely missing from Bill Strether. One could be trusted, the other could not.

The timepiece on the wall pinged. She would have to hurry. Strange, that time had begun to matter so much. Time, for herself, and her body – that was foolish, for at her age a wait of five or ten years before seeking a partner in marriage was insignificant, given that she'd reach her hundredth birthday with ease, barring accidents. But the mental image kept emerging, insistently, of the applica-tion for a child permit, the interviews and form-filling, and the delicious joint task of choosing the baby's eye colour, its personality traits, its future. Most of all, after peering down a microscope for so long at other people's embryos, she dared to dream of the wonder of creation. She had begun to face her own jumbled feelings squarely: she ached to hold her own child in her arms.

There was no rationality about it, but it was a fact. And how might Bill Strether cope with all that?

She drained the glass and placed it in the ultraviolet box along with the used cereal bowl and cutlery. They would be washed sterile. Banana in hand, she wandered towards the study. The time pressure came not merely from that biological clock and her own indecipherable psyche. It came, most definitely, from the increasingly confused mess at the laboratory itself.

She paused at the study door. These converted car show-rooms had their advantages: in antique buildings ceilings were high and space was cheap, but surfaces were not self-cleaning and attracted dust while the air-conditioning could be erratic. This one, the agent had assured her, had been a top-class garage. He had mentioned Jaguar,

Porsche, Alfa Romeo, names that meant nothing to her.
She had virtually no use for a car, and no curiosity about
their history.

At the desk she spoke crisply to the computer and
logged into her module at the laboratory. It was a convenient arrangement; she could hibernate at home,
uninterrupted, and cudgel her brain. Some top-secret
material was barred, as might be expected. As Assistant
Director she could request access, but needed a reason.
Anything she had developed herself, or with which her
section was involved, was open to her.

Just to be sure, she tapped in her password rather than
speak it. The camera in the kitchen could not see in here
but it could listen. Not that any electronic links were
secure – that much was obvious. She shook her head as if
to free it from a blindfold: never before had she found the
constant surveillance oppressive. It used to reassure her
that all was well, that her well-being was under control.
So why did it suddenly bother her so much?

She was in.

The year's files were listed. The computer asked, in its
throaty male voice (her choice, that), what she required.
She tapped in the date of the last batch of missing files.
The screen went blank. The voice sighed, 'No such files
found. Sorry.'

Same as before. The mystery of the missing data had
been shared with Professor Churchill and recorded. But
the Director had been blandly dismissive and had suggested that next time she learn to save them. It was after
a further, thoroughly unsatisfactory session with him that
it had dawned on her that he wasn't nearly as worried
about the loss as she was.

The Director had hinted that she was over-anxious.

Said she shouldn't concern herself. Why, in heaven's name, should he take that approach? And, if he persisted, what should she do?

Whistle-blowers were never popular. They under-mined the system, pointed fingers at colleagues, made the air ring with accusation. Such people were to be despised, excluded. Sneaks. It had never been her way. On the other hand, she had never before found herself in a spot where things were going badly awry, or when it had become so peculiarly difficult to use the usual chan-nels. Nor could she see why that might be. *Unless somebody was deliberately sabotaging her research.* Somebody quite idiotic. But capable of covering their tracks – and of avoiding detection.

Lisa peered closer. She put the machine to *Record* and repeated the attempt. Same result. Then she commanded it to replay the recording at its slowest speed. It seemed an age until she saw the evidence in front of her, a single screen that must have taken less than one-hundredth of a second, but which her sharp eyes had not missed.

Flickering before her nose was the simple phrase 'ACCESS DENIED.'

But why?

Pulling on her tunic she told the computer to close down and to erase her most recent instructions. Four times files had been lost, at irregular intervals; she sus-pected that were she to run the recording trick for each erasure, the outcome would be the same. The files hadn't been lost. They had been placed under lock and key.

After a moment's hesitation she slipped on her old ring, the one with the tiny insect set in Baltic amber. In all likelihood Strether would not know what to make of the mystery either, but the process of telling him might clear her mind, and her conscience. Her records clerk, Winston, at Milton Keynes, would have some ideas. He was so smart at the odd quirks of their joint work. It would be great to see him again, although they were in e-mail contact as tasks dictated. For the Bunker, as it was known, was where both she and the Ambassador, by arrangement, were heading.

It could be a very important day.

Winston Kerry gritted his teeth, then gave up. He picked up the control and aimed it at the camera. Only he knew that this would run a loop of film of him toiling away at his console. With a sigh, he opened a drawer in his desk, took out the black tape, dragged his chair over to the ceiling smoke detector and blanked out its apertures. Then he loped back to his desk and took out an illicit packet of South American cigarettes. There was time enough, just, before his visitors arrived. He was standing thus, cigarette and lighter in hand, when the door hatch began to hiss. Hurriedly he threw the packet back into the drawer and slammed it shut.

On the threshold stood his senior scientific officer, Lisa Pasteur, and a tall, shambling figure in a smartly cut tunic whom he did not know. Lisa herself was in a cerise tunic and skirt, which set off her dark features. Her hair, he noted, was not scraped back as usual but allowed to flow over her shoulders, a style of remarkable femininity for her. She was wearing jewellery. Winston glanced from the woman to her escort. She seemed more than usually conscious of the man's presence, turning to catch his eye frequently, touching his arm. Not the cool ice maiden. Interesting.

'Winston, this is Ambassador Strether, from the United States.' Since Winston was already on his feet, he ambled across the room and shook hands. He was taller than the Ambassador, who had to look up to him.

'My family were domiciled in the USA for a while,' Winston remarked, 'in what's now the state of the West Indies.'

'Really?' Strether was a little unsure how to proceed, Winston noted with private amusement.

'Oh, sure. But we were not willing immigrants. Not exactly.'

'Ah, yes.' Strether nodded, his eyes watchful.

'My name Kerry comes from a slaver. He was, by all accounts, a prolific Lothario. I'm a Macdonald of Clan Ranald. We're none of us as black as we're painted. Sir.'

Lisa pursed her lips. 'Stop talking politics, Winston. Put that family history away, please. We haven't time for tomfoolery.'

The Ambassador's face registered surprise that Winston did not seem to take offence: but then, he wasn't to know that this was his usual opening gambit, a provocative line offered to test a visitor's reaction. Winston knew himself to be impelled by a cool, laconic resentment towards most of the world, tempered by a respectful admiration for Lisa. He saw the American bite his lip.

Lisa walked Strether about, pointing out various pieces of equipment and outlining their uses. The Bunker was linked by fibre optic cable to Porton Down. Many decades before it had been decided that records and research should be separated to reduce the risk of contamination or catastrophic loss. Back-up files were maintained in Edinburgh with alternative passwords. It would be impossible either deliberately or by accident to destroy the lot.

'You should understand, Ambassador, that Mr Kerry is the crucial element of my entire operation,' Lisa was saying. 'He inputs my data daily. He checks, cleans and analyses it. That frees me up to concentrate on the laboratory, but he'll answer a query for me day or night, virtually, as if he were in the next room.'

'It helps that I'm not,' Winston said gloomily. 'What with you with your chocolate, and me with my . . . personal habits. You'd have thrown me out in five minutes.'

Lisa paused. 'Winston. You've been jumping about from one foot to the other ever since we got here. And,' she peered closer, 'you have guilt written all over you. What's up?'

'I'm desperate for a smoke, that's all. A ciggie. I was about to light one when you arrived.'

Lisa laughed. 'Addict. You are a dope, Winston. You know what those narcotics do to you? And they're illegal. You could be dismissed – purged, even, deprived of your right to employment.' She glanced up at the camera: it had not moved to register their arrival. She smothered a giggle.

'I know. But here in the Bunker underground people are allowed some indulgences. C'mon. I won't puff in your direction.' He waited, took their silence as acquiescence, then gratefully dived into the drawer, found the packet again and lit up at last, inhaling the smoke deep into his lungs.

'What they do for me,' he said, a moment later, 'is make me feel alive. Like a human being. A pinch of grass, unreformed, is even better, but you'd be strolling outta here with your eyes rolling and *then* the game'd be up. Now then, lady, gent, what can I do for you?'

'Why are underground workers allowed indulgences? What do you mean?' the Ambassador asked him quickly. 'D'you have to stay here the whole time? Aren't you allowed on top?'

'*I* am,' Winston replied with dignity. 'I'm a higher clerical officer, the highest rank you can get without being an NT. I live in a cottage near Stony Stratford.' As if to defy them, he blew a smoke ring in their direction. Lisa coughed discreetly.

The Ambassador took a chair at the side of Winston's desk. 'You seem to be, if I may say so, Mr Kerry, a rather unusual chap,' he said, cautiously.

'Oh, yeah, I am that,' Winston said, but there was bitterness in his voice. 'I'm black, I'm brainy, I'm as ugly as sin. And I know what goes on – what *really* goes on – in the NT programme. More than Dr Pasteur does.'

'Why do you say you're ugly? You look quite normal to me.' The Ambassador seemed genuinely nonplussed.

'Oh, come *on*. I'm type A-C 14, skin colour B3. Hair F-16 – and that's F for frizzy, mind. Almost as black as you can get. Thick lips, flaring nostrils, buck teeth. In a world where the upper echelons are Anglo-Saxon blonds with long thin hands and enhanced IQs? They don't think me cute. Not by a long chalk.'

'Does it matter?'

Winston got the impression that his physiognomy was not quite what the Ambassador had come to investigate. A softening-up exercise? Yet the American's manner exuded sincere concern. Maybe he meant it.

'Does it matter if we look different? Sure it does. If I wrote an essay and a blond white NT wrote an essay I could probably beat him hands down – not in breadth of knowledge, since people like me are denied the education *they* get, which I have to pay for with my taxes. If it's creative stuff you're after, I have the edge. I might even be preferred. But put us both in the interview room, and there's no contest.'

'But physical appearances are not important,' Lisa interposed gently. 'The codes make that much specific. Discrimination on any grounds is forbidden. On race, religion, age, gender, sexual orientation – especially on race.'

'That's balls, and you know it,' Winston responded. The cigarette had burned in his fingers down to a glowing butt. Without asking for permission he lit another from it. 'Whatever the codes say, it's easy to keep people like me down here. The same prejudices keep you in your place too. How many women are directors of laboratories? How many are professors? And the only black professors are in Afro-Caribbean Studies. Fat lot of use that is.'

'The majority of MPs are women,' Lisa responded stoutly.

'Right. And that proves my point. That's because it's an insignificant job. Glorified social workers, most of them. And when did we last have a woman Prime Minister, let alone a black one? Nineteen ninety, that's when.' Winston snorted and sucked at the cigarette.

'How would you respond,' the Ambassador seemed genuinely curious, 'if I suggested to you that you have a chip on your shoulder?'

'I'd say amen. Sure I have. So would you in my place. Hip, hideous and unhappy.'

'Stop that,' Lisa chided. 'I brought Bill here to understand the programme, and maybe to share one or two problems with him that I couldn't easily in Porton Down. The walls have ears there, I swear. Now are you going to be co-operative, or is that nicotine poisoning your soul as well as your lungs?'

By way of apology Winston stubbed out the cigarette and folded his hands across his chest. He had not missed Lisa's slide into first-name informality. 'I'm ready.'

For ten minutes he called up documents and explained the classification system, with comments from Lisa. The Ambassador was trying hard to follow, but became animated when Winston touched on the issue of parental choice.

'So let me get it,' he said. 'The couple have been granted their permit. They've decided to use their own egg and sperm, and in many cases you have their print-out. That must save you a lot of effort.'

'Yes – provided it's genuine. We gotta run a check to be sure.'

'It can't be faked, surely?'

Winston grinned. 'You'd be surprised. That printout is a *very* precious document – more important than birth, marriage and death certificates rolled together. There's a lively black market in high-quality forgeries. If I wanted, I could get one for myself that said I was a light-skinned Caucasian with pale blue eyes and an IQ of a hundred and sixty. Only the last bit'd be true. It'd cost, 'cause that's what everybody wants. We *always* check.'

Strether was shocked. 'What then? The parents present you with a list of preferences?'

'Correct. And we tidy them up, too.'

'You are being remarkably frank.'

Winston glanced at Lisa, who nodded imperceptibly. He shrugged. 'Yeah, why not? You're here for secrets. I got 'em.'

'In that case, please continue. You – what did you

say? – tidy up the requests? You mean, you interfere with parental choice?'

'Not officially, natch. Parental choice is inviolable, says the code. Well, those choices are so silly – even the professional families'. Most parents want their kids to be smarter and neater than they are, non-fade yellow hair, straighter white teeth, brighter blue eyes – though pale ones are heading the list recently. Some pop star they're taken with. If we didn't play around down here, we'd have the whole of northern Europe looking alike in one generation. They might not be identical NTs, but they'd look it.'

Strether took a breath. 'Clones?'

Winston shrugged. 'You been told it's not done? It is, but not in state-run laboratories. Me, I do my best to ensure that the common herd's yearning to ape the latest TV idol is tempered by good sense. I can't control what they call the kids – Alepha or Zedoko or God knows what – but I can improve on other temporary fads. Like, I fiddle it, with a bit of randomness. When I get stuck I take a pack of cards and play poker with myself. That does the trick.'

'Good Lord.' Strether pondered. 'Tell me, are there any official changes you have to make without telling anyone, where parents have made a request which is apparently OK, but you're required to change it? Or where they've named no preference, but you think there ought to be one?'

'He's a smart cookie,' Winston remarked to Lisa. He turned back to the Ambassador. 'Several. Skin colour, sir. If a black or Asian family demands a lightening of skin colour, that's fine. If they don't, I'm supposed to do it anyway.'

'What do you mean?'

'If Mr and Mrs Patel decide that little Nirmal's future genes are to be checked out, he will emerge a lighter colour than they are – several shades, typically from B5 to B7 or B8. And I can tell you, because we do the market research, that they're delighted. They think it's a side effect of cleansing. Nobody suspects – and, of course, their own consciences are absolved, since they didn't ask for it to happen. That's why the programme is so popular with a certain class of upwardly mobile non-white.'

'Doesn't it bother you?'

Winston shrugged again. 'They shouldn't ask for the cleansing in the first place. There's no need. The worst contamination died out decades ago. The gene bank is pretty clean. A century ago there were four thousand known human genetic disorders. After the explosions it went up to over ten thou. Now it's down to under five – more, I grant you, than before but not *that* many more, and the chances of most are less than one in ten million. They do it out of vanity.'

He paused a moment before continuing. 'D'you realise what's happening? Ever heard of regression to the mean?'

Lisa smiled, Strether frowned. 'A simple old theory of mathematics,' she said quickly. 'The more examples you take, the more the results will tend to hunker down to a mean – the average.'

'It works with people, too,' Winston added. 'The bigger the mass, the more they want the comfort of some broadly standard pattern. Odd bods like me are not wanted on voyage. Given the choice, most adults would iron out any miseries for their children they've experienced in their own lives. Big noses become moderate noses. Chinese eyes disappear. Acne's abolished. Asymmetric faces become perfectly heart-shaped. Big breasts smaller, small ones bigger.' He hooted suddenly. 'There's one exception to that.'

'Really?'

'Men always want larger pricks. For themselves, and for their sons. Serious tackle. Nobody wants a pinkie for a penis.'

He snickered. Lisa blushed and twiddled her ring. Strether smothered a smile and leaned forward, chin cradled on his hands. 'But, Mr Kerry, aren't you ever tempted to ignore your instructions? Especially when they clash with your own laudable principles.'

Winston's eyes bulged. He cackled with laughter and slapped his thigh. 'Oh, man. It's more than my job's worth. That's one thing they *do* check up on, from time to time. In fact I suspect that a couple of the Asian or Afro-Caribbean cases I deal with every month are test runs. To make sure I know my place.'

'Why don't you resign? Find some other post? It wouldn't be difficult with your talents,' Strether pressed.

'I've thought of that.' Winston's expression became brooding. He glanced at Lisa and his face softened. 'Because if I left, some other idiot'd take my place. The mistakes'd be mistakes, not the occasional undetectable twiddle. And I'd be cut off for ever from being able to do anything, even those little bits of sanity I do manage. Once you leave here, you never come back.'

'I think,' said Lisa quietly, 'that you have made your point, Winston. Thank you for that. Now, look; I have a dilemma.' Rapidly she sketched out the issue of the missing files and handed Winston a note with the approximate dates, culled by tracing accessible records and marking the gaps as far as she could.

'D'you want me to do this now? It could take a while, if access is denied.'

'No, when you have a moment. I'll spend an hour or

two showing Mr Strether round the Bunker. Maybe we
can see you again later. *After* you've switched the camera
back on, Winston. This is not a clandestine visit.'

'Yes, ma'am.' Winston grinned and reached once more
for the forbidden tobacco. 'Shut the door after you – and
hold tight to that dude. I like him.'

The underground complex was mind-boggling, Strether
was willing to admit. Marius had a point. Not that it was
unique: Strether had once visited the original
Disneyworld in Florida during a Democratic Party convention in Orlando nearby. They'd been proud of the
antique mini-Maglev there, which connected the airport
to the resort. The over-lifesize puppets and cartoon characters irritated him; Mickey Mouse should long since
have been retired. The artificial concoctions of land-
scapes and deserts had also failed to please, so far
removed were they from the open skies and clear air of
his home. He suspected that, had he ever visited the cas-
tles of the Loire or Rhine he would have held the same
low opinion of the fairytale vacuity that teetered over
Main Street, USA.

But he had been fascinated by the subterranean network that maintained the park in pristine cleanliness. A
piece of litter was placed in a bin; but the bin had no
base. It was a rubbish chute. Ten metres below it led into
a wheeled skip which, when full, was automatically
trundled away and replaced. Below ground were the
heating and air-conditioning which enabled buildings
on the surface to reproduce accurately the style of an
earlier era: no radiators, no bulging pipes. The only
chimneys were for Santa Claus. The kitchens remained

cool, the staff unflappable on warm days, the ice-cream solid, yet all without visible means. Both music and scent could be wafted out to customers. The sewage system naturally ran underground: at a discreet distance the output was churned, filtered, the water returned to the complex's reservoirs, and after sterilisation the separated solids became fertiliser. The whole place was a perfection of recycling, and all done for purely commercial reasons.

In later theme parks miniature nuclear reactors were buried deep, with the close-down processes required for their end-life decommissioning built in from the start. At DisneyCity – and at most new factories, such as Toyota's in China – enough space was set aside for three generations of nuclear-power units, sufficient to last a hundred and fifty years. And not a scrap of pollution, visible or otherwise, sullied the air.

All below the surface: that saved space and reduced exposure to sun, ultra-violet rays and other potentially damaging radiation. Since earth was a natural insulator, energy was saved. The combination of warmth from lighting and from human bodies was enough, with no need for extra heat. What had been experimental had become fact, and well accepted.

What struck Strether about the Milton Keynes 'Bunker', by comparison with Disney's imaginative creations, was its sheer scale. With little evidence of its presence overhead, an entire city hummed beneath the earth's surface.

Much pleased by his appreciative comments, Lisa trundled him about the under-earth town on an electric buggy. He was not surprised to see whole shopping malls; they had been widespread by the late twentieth century, and thereafter climate change had made them a necessity.

Indeed it was rare to find shops above ground these days, except in tourist areas (like Portobello Road) which attempted to re-create a lost ambience. Similarly he had expected stations, factories, colleges, dance-halls, places of entertainment, gymnasia, clinics, libraries, banks, accountants' offices, lawyers: there was nothing new in that as such, but the number and sprawl were remarkable. On top of such excess, however, the football stadium, skating rink, bowling alley and running track through a full-scale forest were awesome.

'Milton Keynes was always a go-ahead spot,' Lisa explained. 'I love it. If I had my way we'd shift the entire Porton Down operation here and return that site to sheep. It's too restricted to develop, with Stonehenge so near. Milton Keynes council was the first to license a full-scale operation. They'd been to see what happened below the halls at the old National Exhibition Centre in Birmingham, and they began to think big. I think it's terrific – and it's so much safer than on the surface. And more fun.'

Strether had put to the back of his mind the anxiety evident in her vidphone call. She would explain to him in her own good time. He wondered if she needed help, and whether he would be capable of providing it. But that was speculation, and must wait.

For the moment he was willing to be mightily impressed. The buggy attached itself to magnetic lines in the roadway and whizzed along a dedicated route. Having tapped in their destination, Lisa did not have to drive and could concentrate on their conversation. At intersections the buggy waited for some invisible signal, or sensed itself whether to proceed. Though the streets were crowded no buggies touched each other; a crash was virtually impossible.

All about him, Strether could see people both at their daily tasks and at leisure. He was struck by the physical similarity of many of those in dungarees, especially in the factories, the printing works, the sewage farm. Male and female, they were small, nimble, dark-skinned – with Cypriot blood, perhaps, or Arab. The majority wore eye-shades, except in dimly lit areas, of which there were many. There, they seemed to manage quite happily in the half-gloom where Strether could barely see his own feet.

'They are colour-blind,' Lisa explained. 'They have a genetic condition that reduces the number of cones on the retina so that they're ultra-sensitive to light. Obviously they're much happier in low illumination. And as that's cheaper, they're welcome. They're hard workers too, so they're prized employees.'

'Where does the colour blindness come from?'

'It's natural. It used to be found in isolated communities such as the Polynesian islands, but later it became widespread in Europe. Probably caused by the explosions. The mutation is linked to an increased flesh pigmentation – that's why they're so brown. Odd, that. They have increased protection against the sun as far as skin's concerned, but are distressed by excess light. Most live down here permanently.'

'Why wasn't the defect cleaned up? Aren't they entitled to gene therapy?' Strether was not sure he would like the answer.

Lisa cast him a glance. 'Because it's useful. The gene bank is not immutable, you know. They're well paid.'

They travelled on, Strether lost in his own thoughts. Then Lisa spoke again. 'I'll show you the hospital, then we can go for lunch. I've a particular reason for taking you to it. You should know why Porton Down still has to fight for its budgets. It has a lot to do with the demands posed by the numbers of elderly. Oh, I suppose I'll be old some day, and grateful for the services. But the founding fathers believed that as people got healthier, their need for hospital treatment would diminish. That turned out to be rot.'

The buggy entered the sweeping grandeur of the hospital forecourt. The main construction component was a kind of lilac concrete, functional, though hardly endearing. So busy was it that they had to wait several minutes for a parking space in the multi-storey park. Strether experienced a slight feeling of vertigo as they came back up ten floors in the lift.

Lisa ignored the main entrance and led him round to the back. Here, the light was bright, the equivalent to a mid-morning sun. A gentle breeze blew from hidden vents. A garden had been created, complete with living plants and shrubs; the illusion of a summer sky with scudding clouds floated high above. 'Hologram,' Lisa answered his question. 'Clever, isn't it? The plants are completely fooled. Here we are.'

She pressed her palm on the door and waited. It admitted her and she pulled Strether in quickly. 'I have access because sometimes I have to attend surgery on a newly discovered defect. They don't invariably show up at birth. That way I can recommend the simplest method to correct it *in vitro*, whether via the bone, the marrow, or whatever. And this entrance has no camera.' She halted suddenly. 'You're not squeamish, are you?'

'I don't think so. Seen many a disembowelled cow in my time. The main beneficiaries from those explosions in Colorado were the vultures – the modern variety are twice as big, twice as nasty.'

Lisa's nose wrinkled. 'Then I'll take you into theatre. Don't say a word, you might get us thrown out.'

In an anteroom she handed him a green gown, a hood, a surgical mask, and helped him cover his feet and dip his hands in sealing solution. As she did the same for herself she examined the surgery lists on the wall. Nobody was about, apart from a couple of orderlies; every theatre was busy, their exits and recovering patients unseen on the far side.

'Let's try number fourteen,' she said. Strether followed her meekly as she slipped through sets of swing doors. Then he stopped dead.

Under the arc-lights a green-sheeted body lay prone. A bevy of staff surrounded the raised operating table. One glanced up as they entered. Lisa whispered, 'Dr Pasteur,' and the nurse turned back to her task. Machines and equipment pinged in rhythm: pulse 100, blood-pressure 130 over 90, haemoglobin 12.6. A healthy body. The hands that peeped from under the sheet, plastic tubes in both wrists, were small and elegant though with wizened skin, the fingernails delicately manicured. A female. As Strether's eyes roamed up the covered torso, he swallowed hard. He wished Lisa had prepared him better.

The face had disappeared. A bloody mess had taken its place, composed of oozing flesh, skin and silvery bone, the teeth grinning like a skull's.

The surgeon was seated at the woman's head, facing the feet, cradling the chin in one hand though the cranium was held rigid in a frame. The scalp had been cut just above the hairline and hung back down between his knees, dripping slightly in a retainer hairnet. The surgeon was humming to himself behind his mask; he did not look up. With an instrument shaped like a flat spoon he was scraping away between the skin and the bone. He had deflapped the entire forehead and started on the cheeks. As Strether watched, his gut tightening, the surgeon pushed too hard and the instrument came through the skin. 'Darn it,' muttered the surgeon, and switched the instrument to the other cheek. 'Have to repair that later.'

It appeared that the eyes were to be avoided; Strether craned and saw that they must already have been attended to, for they were yellow with disinfectant and surrounded by crescent-shaped blood-encrusted scars. The surgeon was making his way down the jawbone, pushing hard as if he were skinning a bear. 'Bit tough, this one,' he muttered. 'How old did you say she is? Eighty-six? Should have more sense.'

Strether was rooted to the spot. He was aware that Lisa was glancing in his direction. Perhaps this was her idea of a bizarre initiation rite he had to survive to win her confidence. If so, then he could do it. He forced himself upright, cleared his mouth of the bile that had risen unbidden, and made himself watch intently.

'That'll do,' the surgeon announced. A nurse reached across and wiped the sweat from his brow. 'Two hours, sir,' she intoned. He wriggled his shoulders and set to again, this time using his hands to pull the flaps of skin hard away from the nose. Miraculously the face reappeared, its wrinkles gone. The lips were unpinned and pushed back over the teeth. Using clamps, he tried various shapes and tightnesses until some aesthetic standard was met. With a grunt, the doctor clicked the clamps shut and began to secure the ends under the ears with a gadget like a stapler. The edges were trimmed with bursts from a laser; spare triangles of skin dropped to the floor.

Lisa tugged at Strether's arm. With enormous relief he stumbled out after her.

'What the hell –?' he gasped, as he tore off the mask.

'Completely pointless surgery, I agree,' Lisa answered. 'A full facelift. We are each entitled to two under the Health Service: the first at fifty, the second at sixty or over. I've no quarrel with that, not when so many men are on their third marriage by then. Why should men have only young women to choose from? What makes me *mad* is that this patient is on her *fourth*. And we're paying for it. My attempts to eradicate muscular dystrophy for ever are frustrated by that lady, and people like her.'

'She gets it free?' Strether saw it would be useless to do other than follow Lisa's train of thought.

'*She* does, yes.'

'Why?'

'Because she's Princess Io, that's why. As upper caste as you can get. She could probably afford to pay for it, too.'

Strether cleared his throat. 'I don't think you should have told me that, Lisa. It's a name I know, though I've never met the lady. Till now. She's Prince Marius's mother, isn't she?'

Lisa was crestfallen. 'Yes. You're absolutely right. Forget what I said. But it's just that people like her can hog the money, and there are so *many* of them. Yet my section struggles at the end of each financial year. Politicians like Prince Marius boast there are no waiting lists, and it's true. But everything else takes a lower priority, and that's not fair.'

Back in everyday clothes they walked slowly through the garden. Still feeling tense and nauseous, Strether eased himself on to the nearest bench while Lisa strolled about quietly. Above his head a purple hibiscus gracefully dropped scrolled buds; nearby a yucca was in full bloom, its creamy cups raised to the make-believe sky. Roses fluttered their petals in the breeze, their fragrance softening the air. He drew in deep breaths and held them until his stomach had stopped churning.

'You wouldn't deprive the elderly of health care, would you?' he asked gently. 'It's been an agonised debate in America as long as anyone can remember. The rich pay, the poor get the basics. Everyone else insures or goes without. I had a sneaky feeling that European socialised medicine was a big improvement.'

'No. I wouldn't deprive them, but I'd ration them. If she pays to get her apartment redecorated she could pay to get her face rearranged.'

Lisa sat beside him and crossed her legs. She clasped her hands around her knees and stared into the middle distance. Again, Strether admired the shapely thighs and neat ankles.

'The cult of the third age has gone too far,' Lisa mused softly, a wary eye on a distant camera that had trained itself on them. 'Age discrimination is banned, so it's illegal to suggest someone's too old for treatment. And the distinction between what's cosmetic and what's health-related gets blurred. For old people most interventions are both. What's politically correct, as they used to say, is practically stupid.'

'But surely, people refuse of their own accord? My wife did. Not everybody wants a fourth face-lift, Lisa.'

'Well, the Princess does. Her doctor will have signed to the effect that without it, her psychological state would deteriorate or she'd lose her independence or some such. Not everything's worth doing – yet where's the doctor who'd stand up and say so?'

'At home the fundamentalists are in charge. They rail against science, but they took against euthanasia too. They think suffering's good for you. Europe seems ahead of us. Your codes outlaw excessive attempts to preserve life, don't they?'

'Sure. Euthanasia and living wills are perfectly legal. And cryogenics, though that's now obsolete. But the pendulum's swung too far the other way, Bill. Now whatever treatment a third-ager demands – provided he or she has connections – it'll be done, and no refusals.'

'Even if all that's wrong is a few wrinkles?'

Lisa's shoulders slumped. 'You saw it. What can I say?'

'Lisa.' Strether waited until she gazed up at him. 'I don't get it. So much effort to make things perfect. Your work, and what's going on inside that hospital. It's as if nobody can cope with . . . well, *normality*. Mess. Disorder. Ageing. Defects. Disability, dammit. You say that cosmetic surgery is hostile to your work. Winston says your work is cosmetic. And –' He stopped and pulled out a handkerchief to wipe his brow.

'Look about us,' he continued, exasperated. 'Nothing is as it seems. The whole darn thing is a fake. I'm hot right now, like I've been in the blazing sun. But the sun's kept at bay by fifty metres of rock over our heads. So much effort to create so much illusion. And I keep asking myself, what other illusions are there? What other guff am I being fed, where everything looks hunky-dory, and isn't?'

She was silent, though her face was perturbed and she was biting her lip.

'I heard a thing or two in Brussels that I didn't like,' he said heavily. 'Those smooth world-weary Énarques – they give me the creeps. We have civil servants in America, but not an army of 'em, like here. And ours don't all try to look alike, and don't act as if everyone else is inferior.'

'But they're right on that,' said Lisa, with sudden asperity. 'That's the trouble. The civil service and their friends have been bred to be ultra-smart for years. Throughout Europe. The programme is a success, Bill. I know – I make it so.'

He stared at her then, scrutinised the heart-shaped face, saw her distress and bewilderment.

'Lisa, why are you telling me this? You sounded so worried on the vidphone. And why me?'

'I don't know the answer to that last question. Maybe because you have kind eyes, Bill. Or I fancy your accent. Put it down to instinct.' She laughed shortly.

He took one of her hands in his. The skin was soft, the fingers slim. He touched the gold ring with the amber stone on her third finger, twiddled it gently round, once.

'So what's going on – at the lab, or here? What is it you're trying to tell me?'

'I don't know that either. It may be I'm inventing conundrums. If not, then it could be something alarming. Before I could take any action I'd have to be sure – or closer than I am now.'

'Those missing records are significant,' Strether hazarded.

'They could be. Combined with my Director's off-hand response.' Her voice became a whisper and she bowed her head, as if to ensure that the camera could not eavesdrop. 'You see, they covered some repeat experiments I tried, which hadn't worked first time either. The chromosome kept breaking. A weakness, somewhere – and at the crucial 21q11 location.'

'You've lost me. What does that imply?'

'Personality. It's where mongolism used to occur. I've never seen any examples, but Down syndrome children were supposed to have sweet, loving characters. If that bit's missing we get instead a predisposition to violence. If my suspicions are correct, that's seriously bad news. For everybody.'

The risks of talking in such an unguarded environment were too great. For her own sake, he had to stop her. 'Then let's hope you're wrong.' He rose, lifted her fingers to his lips and kissed them.

Strether never knew quite what made him say the next few words. He had linked her arm in his in an old-fashioned gesture. But now a surge of emotion touched his heart.

'It saddens me to see you upset. Lisa, d'you realise how fond I am becoming of you? I've never met anyone like you before.'

A hesitant smile lit up her face and the dimples re-appeared briefly.

'And I don't mean as a colleague. Or a daughter,' he added hastily.

'No, that much was obvious,' Lisa murmured. 'We're pretty direct here, Bill. Am I to take it you think of me as a friend – or even, as a lover?'

But he was too tongue-tied to answer that. Instead he led her away towards the buggy, arm in arm, a lightness in his step, and spoke once more.

'Now, did you mention lunch? I'm hungry. But do me a favour. Can we avoid red meat, just this once?'

Chapter Eight

He looked a new man. Staff at the embassy remarked to each other that their ambassador seemed to have a freshness, a spring in his step. Never unkempt, he was paying far more attention to his appearance. One attaché had seen him emerge from Harrods in Abbey Square accompanied by Prince Marius Vronsky, the two giggling like a pair of naughty schoolboys, laden with packages. Another had inquired at his behest about riding schools in Hampstead; he would, he said self-deprecatingly, enjoy the feel of a saddle again, and it would help combat a too-evident middle-aged spread.

It was the chauffeur, Peter, who confirmed it. One morning, as he polished the gleaming blue metalwork of the electric car in his basement lair, he was not surprised to be visited by Matt Brewer.

'I suppose we must keep those things, but it's an expense we could save,' was Matt's opening gambit, with a gesture towards the car. The chauffeur's scowl halted him. 'I didn't mean you, Peter. You have many talents. Aren't you a qualified engineer?'

The chauffeur kept his head down. Inside the garage it

was hot. Beads of sweat stood out on his lips and fore-head as he rubbed at an imaginary mark on the bonnet.

'It has been in use a lot more lately, though,' Matt continued hopefully.

The chauffeur paused in his rubbing. 'It has that. But then, you can't go canoodling on the tube. Not when you're a distinguished public figure, can you?'

'Canoodling? What do you mean? Who's canoodling?'

They both knew the answer. Peter grinned wickedly, fetched a can of chrome polish and started on the bumper, which was already spotless. The vehicle was a copy of a mid-twentieth century tail-finned Dodge, a previous incumbent's choice. What went on under the hood, however, was pure *fin-de-siècle*; the latest V20 300-horse-power reversed four-cam unit, powered by rechargeable lightweight NiCd batteries packed in circular formation around the Wankel engine itself to give maximum thrust. Range 300 kilometres, ideal for city driving. Exhaust, nil.

'Of course, we could change the car,' Peter agreed, reluctantly. 'If the boss doesn't like it. Or keep the body-work – it's beautiful, though I say so myself – and install a fuel cell instead. The trunk's big enough for the liquid hydrogen and oxygen tanks. The exhaust's only water-vapour – that goes mostly into the air-conditioning.'

'But water-vapour's a factor in global warming as you well know, Peter, so this electric one's more eco-friendly. You didn't answer my question.'

Peter chuckled. 'Him. That's who. Got a lady friend. Pretty thing – dark-haired and a smashing figure. Great legs.'

'You've been ogling them through the mirror, Peter. For shame,' said Matt sternly, but both men were pink with amusement.

'She's all right, I reckon,' Peter went on. 'He treats her real gentlemanly, not like some men I could mention. No hanky-panky; just out to a restaurant, and I'm asked to come back a couple of hours later. Then back to . . . I suppose it must be her apartment, though from the conversation she lives near Porton Down. She's a scientist.'

'She is,' Matt confirmed. 'We had her checked out – security. In case. No problems, from what we could establish. So, what happens at the apartment? Are you told to come back in a couple of hours then, too?'

'Indeed I am not,' the chauffeur replied firmly. 'Far be it from me to gossip, Mr Brewer. I've gone too far as it is.'

'Don't leave me in suspense!' Matt pleaded. 'We need to know, for his safety. And yours, come to that.'

Peter sniffed. 'Nah. He doesn't get up to nothing. He puts the glass divider up and I close my ears. But it all looks chaste to me – a quick kiss or two, and then she's away.'

'He's not said a word to anybody. I can't tell whether that makes it more serious, or less.'

'Oh, it's serious,' the chauffeur nodded knowingly. 'He looks so wistful when she's gone. I think he's a bit lonely. He sits and watches her door for several minutes before telling me to drive on. Then we come straight home.'

'We await developments.'

'We do. Mind, I think it'll have to be her that makes a move. Bit forward, young women today. Won't do him no harm. Now, was there anything else? 'Cause if you don't mind, I have to get on.'

The Europeans celebrated anniversaries at the drop of a hat, and there were plenty of them. Strether had been warned not to miss the Bastille Day bash on 14 July at the French embassy. The St Patrick's Day event at Dublin House was legendary. Every single one among the forty-two former European countries (a couple of which had split, including Scotland from the UK, to make forty-six regions) had its national day, usually commemorating some bloody event whose outcome of self-government had vanished long since in membership of the Union, or some half-mythical saint of scant interest to the largely secular population. In addition each commemorated Union Day, 9 May, which this year had produced the extended Grand Celebration in Brussels. If he'd heard Schiller's 'Ode to Joy' sung to Beethoven's tune once he'd heard it a thousand times.

In response, the 4 July Independence Day party at the United States embassy was to be a far bigger affair than in previous summers. The acceptance list totalled almost two thousand. Strether had arranged for beef from his own herds to be shipped over for the hamburgers and T-bone steaks, and wines in quantity from northern vineyards. A container full of temptations not on sale in Europe – root beer, Hershey bars, peanut butter cups and the most lurid sugar and gum confectionery he could lay hands on – had docked that morning. Stars of Barnum and Bailey's Circus (humans, not animals) would perform. It was a pity that numbers were too great to use the Residence and its garden; there, it would have been possible with a squeeze to have laid on a mini-rodeo with his cowhands from Colorado. Maybe he'd hold that in reserve for another year.

On the morning of the party Strether strolled around the embassy halls. To his regret, the US ambassador of half a century before (when the building had been moved from Grosvenor Square) had tastes both dull and mean. Precious little had been spent since. The building, though spacious, did not have voice controls; swipe cards, an unreliable technology, were still required for staff. The atmospheric monitoring was ramshackle – in high season it could be as searingly hot inside the offices as outside. The vidphones were ancient and creaking. Facilities for DNA testing for passports were rudimentary and meant long queues. It was like living in a third-world country at times and irked Strether. The gibes he had wilted under at Buckingham Palace were all too true.

It came down to money. In world terms, America played third fiddle to the European Union and China; its days as lynchpin of the United Nations were history. So its Foreign Service was kept on short rations by Congress. The 4 July celebrations, however, were his to order, especially as he was subsidising them himself.

'Morning, sir.' The young staffer twisted precariously on his ladder. Matt Brewer was hammering a vast American flag to the wall as high as he could get it. At the far end, hot-dog, hamburger, spare-ribs, popcorn and ice-cream stalls were being set up: Union food-hygiene laws, Strether had dictated, did not apply since this was foreign soil. A ten-metre screen would relay parades from around the States via CNN. The lobby was to be a Manhattan-style club bar serving a bewildering array of powerful cocktails. In an adjoining room Dixie jazz was in rehearsal; discordant snatches of music could be heard, along with the panted shouts of New York's finest, the women police baton twirlers' formation team in practice. The Air Force marching band had been banished to the backyard since nobody could hear himself speak within fifty metres of them. If nothing else, it would be a raucous night.

'How are you getting on, Matt?' Strether asked. Of all his staff, Matt Brewer was the one he liked best. The crew-cut young man gave the nail one last wallop then shinned down the ladder.

'That's the last, sir. In here, anyway. Looks grand, don't it?'

'I guess so. Should be quite a party.'

'Yessir. And, sir, on behalf of the staff may I say how much we appreciate it? We haven't celebrated July Fourth on this scale in years. We think it's great.'

Strether did not conceal his delight. 'Thank you for that. We like to indulge in a real hoe-down out west.' He helped Matt fold the ladder.

'Sir, your way is fine by us. In fact . . .' The young man hesitated. 'Forgive me if I speak out of turn, sir, but it's about time you knew. You're a big improvement on recent holders of your post, and that's the general view in the embassy. You're more . . . normal. Less stuffy. You listen, and you take notice of what we say. You don't waste our time. You make it a pleasure to work for you – and an honour.'

'Just doing my best, Matt.' Strether clasped his hands behind his back in what he hoped was a dignified stance. He had seen Prince Marius do it several times. He wondered what Matt was getting at.

The staffer dropped his voice. 'You see, most of our bosses are content to go along with whatever the smart guys in the Union tell them. They report back to Washington and the reports are all the same; I could write them in my sleep. "*Our great ally is doing fine, their technical edge over us is slight but nothing to worry about, their social attitudes are a bit strange, but all's well*" – that sort of stuff. Nobody ever delves, as you do. I can't recall anyone at your level properly checking out the genetic programme, let alone going underground at Milton Keynes. They visit the games, sure, or go racing or watch polo, but they sit in the diplomatic box. Not you. You were quizzing that fat guy next to you and his wife. It's admirable, sir.'

'Now I'm embarrassed.' Strether put up a hand. 'But let me into a secret, then, Matt. How did my predecessors spend their days, if not like that?'

'Going to other embassies. Eating, drinking. Recycling chatter as fact and innuendo as truth. Putting themselves absolutely in the clutches of those pale-eyed clones, the perm secs and chefs de cabinet. Since you ask. Sir.' The staffer's eyes were bright, but his mouth was set.

'We don't use *that* word here, Matt. Not even in asides. But I take your point.' A thought occurred to Strether. 'You courting at all, Matt?'

The young man grinned. 'No, sir, not yet. Playing the field. The girls here are gorgeous. The only minor problem is they tend to look alike. California girls are the rage at the moment, so I'm suited. Can't tell whether it's fashion or – you know what.'

'I tell you why I asked,' Strether said. 'I have an invitation to the nightclub called the Toy Shop; Prince Marius says I must go. I thought there might be safety in numbers. Would you and a couple of the other staffers care to accompany me? I won't cramp your style, but it might be better if we go as a crowd.'

Matt looked at him curiously. The Ambassador's physical side must have been thoroughly awoken – or reawoken? – for such a suggestion to have been considered, let alone accepted. The Toy Shop was not a place to take a respectable woman; like a Japanese geisha house, on which it was modelled, it was designed exclusively for the entertainment of men. That said, it was reputedly not to be missed.

'Certainly, sir. I've heard a lot about it. That'd be great. Now, please excuse me; I've been asked to taste the Tex-Mex chilli. Duty calls.'

It was acknowledged as the best party London had seen for ages. Strether had revelled in the power his engraved cards briefly conferred. The senior echelons of the business world attended, including billionaire friends who had flown over from the States, the entire diplomatic corps, department heads and students from seven universities which had offered Strether honorary degrees, doubtless in hope of largesse; sports personalities, including the teams he had seen at White City, his favourite film, theatre and TV stars. The press corps turned out in force, with Maxwell Packer in the vanguard. A crowd of MPs, MEPs and peers milled about with partners both licit and illicit, alongside the management of the Milton Keynes hospital, who had been bewildered at the missive since they had been blissfully unaware of his visit. Plus anyone who'd ever fed him since his arrival four months before in the early spring, what seemed a millennium ago, on board *King William V*.

Prince Marius, resplendent in a purple velvet tunic with blouson sleeves, raised a glass of frothy green liquid topped with spangles and a tiny umbrella. 'Congratulations, Ambassador. So this is how you like to enjoy yourself.'

Strether, flushed and happy, half bowed. He had chosen an ivory linen jacket and sported a silk stars and stripes tied jauntily at the neck. 'Good to see you.'

'I hear you're a horseman again?'

Strether patted his middle. 'After Brussels. I couldn't go on like that, Marius. I'm not genetically cleansed like you to avoid heart disease. I seriously missed my riding, so I started up again. I go hacking on the Heath trail first thing every morning. Got a bay gelding called Jefferson: big brute, but it's doing me good.'

'Pity we don't allow fox-hunting any more. You'd have loved it. The French were the last to bow to public opinion – the Commission's, not theirs. These days, the nearest you'll get is bear-shooting in the Urals; and if you don't pay your beaters well they're as likely to shoot *you*.' Marius put his head on one side. 'So, Bill, you like it here.'

'I could become very used to it.' The two men had gravitated towards the french windows and emerged on to a balcony. Behind them came vivid snatches of 'Jeepers Creepers' and 'Maple Leaf Rag'; it sounded as if the various bands were competing with each other. A fragment of Sousa music – the circus, probably, on the floor below – came floating up as an echo from a nearby building. Below, street lamps gave a muted light as dusk began to close in. Electric cars whizzed around corners several storeys down. The air was warm and limpid.

Strether checked they were not overheard; the embassy was free of cameras and clean of bugs, in the public rooms at any rate. 'Maybe you can help me with one small matter, Marius. It can't be all sweetness and light here, and I don't care to be treated like a fool. I keep getting messages on my vidphone about demonstrations. From an unlicensed operator, at a guess – the quality's terrible. Bit garbled and frantic, about protecting someone. Yet there's never a whisper in the news. Is something happening I should know about?'

'There's been some restlessness, yes,' Marius answered slowly. 'I've had one or two on mine. I think they put a blanket call to – well, anyone they think'll be interested.'

The two men's eyes met. 'But are there demos? Are people taking to the streets? And why? What's wrong?'

'Things don't have to be wrong for protests, you know that. Often it's the most privileged who squeal loudest. The lower castes can't be bothered.'

'From what I've seen of the lower castes, as you call them – the ordinary people who work their twenty-five-hour week, love the wetties and support their local team – they're remarkably well taken care of. They don't have much to bother about, that's so. But *somebody* is up in arms. You haven't denied it. Who, and why?'

'Fools. Idiots. Over-educated people with too many principles and too little sense. Purged, most of them. Usually for breaking basic codes, deliberately.'

'That means they're denied employment, doesn't it? Their insurance cards are taken from them, so they have no pension or health rights, unless they provide for themselves. Bit drastic, isn't it?'

Marius shrugged. 'Better than putting them in prison, as we used to. Or fining them – pointless exercise that was. Anyway, "protecting the workers" is what they claim to be about, and *workers* is precisely what they're not.'

That accurate quote proved to Strether that the Prince had also been a recipient of the messages. His replies had been odd, elliptical. At times an aura of obfuscation hung over Marius like an illusionist's mantle. Dissidents making contact with a foreign power? That was standard practice. But Marius, with his noble background and elected peerage, quintessentially Establishment, was hardly an appropriate outsider.

Strether spoke more slowly. 'You're not levelling with me, Marius. I've been repeatedly told that here, in this earthly paradise, all is for the best in the best of all possible worlds. I've read sufficient to know it was a sick joke when Voltaire wrote it, and it can't be true now. I've seen hints enough in four months to have my doubts.'

'Like what?' Marius leaned back against the wall and perched a neatly shod foot on the balcony rail. His chin was up and he appeared to be contemplating the flight of a starling on its way to its nest. Strether thought quickly. Probably he had little option but to trust Marius. In the absence of those bloody cameras, perhaps the Prince was here with a dual purpose. So be it. The authorities might as well hear Strether's views from a reliable source. But not everything.

'Like – if I were being blunt – the whole Union appears to be in the grip of a self-perpetuating élite. Identical or not, they operate to the exclusion of everyone else. The enhancement of IQ I find particularly sinister. That'd make upward mobility for anyone else virtually impossible.'

Marius dropped his eyes and twirled the toy umbrella around his drink. 'There's nothing new in that. The civil service always was a form of secret society. It functions well; they know and understand each other. Saves a lot of wasted time in conference, I do assure you. And the enhancements are not sinister. Don't let your distaste for the programme interfere with your judgement. If more public servants were as dedicated, by genetic planning, by birth, by upbringing – call it what you will – then the world would be a more efficient place. There have been no corruption scandals involving an NT, not ever, not even at Commission level.'

The Prince had spoken, as if he were repeating a given line, one which he could not fault but which he personally found less than absolutely convincing. It intensified the Ambassador's growing unease that the *whole thing* was corrupt, or at least in danger of turning that way.

'Okay, then. What about the way the codes are ignored? They're not worth the paper they're written on. Ethnic diversity's being discouraged, women don't get on. It's a man's world, but a particular group of men appear to have put themselves squarely in charge. Led by some geriatrics who give me heartburn. They crow about the diverse culture of Europe but it's tinsel – folk-art and dancing troupes. Like in the old Soviet Union. At least,' he jerked his thumb backwards towards the sound of the Sousa march, 'I know the difference. Why doesn't anybody object?'

Marius eyed him. 'Who have you been talking to, I wonder? That's subversive stuff, my dear Bill.'

The Ambassador grunted. 'Marius, you're a friend. I hope. You're smart, a great guy, and sophisticated in ways beyond me. Surely you must be anxious about this? Élites are fine, if they operate to everyone's satisfaction: as long as they're open, and the ladder's in place for others to climb.'

The Prince sighed. 'Don't knock Voltaire. His Dr Pangloss had a point. When it's done well, the result is good governance – not good, *excellent*. It suits a lot of citizens, you know, to leave decision-making to those in charge. No one starves, nobody suffers. Their wants and needs are anticipated by opinion polls and in-depth surveys, then attended to, even before most are aware of it. It's the kind of regime Utopians have dreamed of over the ages. And we have it here in Europe.'

Strether leaned over the balcony. He could feel
Marius's eyes on him, part curious, part veiled. 'Yes, I
can see that. But don't some people get fed up being kept
out of decision-making? Isn't that part of the quality of
life? Sometimes the citizenry want what's bad for them –
and that's also a kind of freedom. Like overeating, I
guess.' He laughed ruefully. 'But nobody wants to be shut
out when it matters. And Parliament goes along with it –
parliaments, indeed: from what I've heard, assemblies in
other regions are also mostly indifferent. Flummery and
ceremony but little substance. I'm puzzled, to tell the
truth. It doesn't feel like democracy as I know it.'

'Nonsense. Registered voters have more chance to take
decisions now than at any time in recent history,' Marius
countered robustly. 'The English have more referendums,
on average ten questions a year, than any region but
Denmark. Blame *that,* if you like, for the decline of
Parliament. Once every big issue is settled by plebiscite,
the Commons is bound to feel like a rubber stamp. Which
is why I prefer the Lords, where we don't take ourselves
too seriously.'

'The turnout's so low. What – twenty-five per cent on
the last ballot? It doesn't increase my confidence.'
Strether modified his tone. He would have to go back
inside.

'That does worry me,' Marius conceded quietly. 'If so
few participate, far more issues will be decided by executive action. Possibly not even published. Like the
current proposal to limit all grade five and above posts to
certain types of NT. It hasn't been possible before – the
numbers available were too small. But now there are sufficient, the idea's resurfaced. And will probably go
through on the nod.'

Strether had been about to rejoin the party. He turned quickly. 'What types of NT?'

'Oh, it's no big deal,' Marius muttered vaguely. 'You didn't hear it from me. But what type? Like our colleagues Graf von Richthofen, Sir Robin, Sir Lyndon. Their close relatives, you might say. Pure blood. Perhaps you should interrogate them rather than me, Ambassador. I'm off to get myself another of your excellent cocktails.'

The dialogue had been abruptly ended. Strether followed Marius back through the french windows towards the brass band. Frustrated, he resumed what he hoped was a majestic progression through the rooms and lobbies. He had gained the impression that the Prince, once he was certain of the Ambassador's train of thought, had been trying to give him information. To confirm, perhaps, that his fears had some substance?

With an effort Strether reset his expression into a wreath of jolly smiles. The celebration was in full swing, with energetic boogying and jiving, the latest dance revivals, filling the larger rooms. Streamers and balloons impeded his path and he had to dodge brightly coloured paper balls shot from pea-shooters thoughtfully provided at the entrance. A juggler in a fluorescent leotard, barged past, tossing Indian clubs, with open bottles of cola balanced on both forehead and chin. A fire-eater was attracting an appreciative audience in a corner. At the bar a team of perspiring barmen were trying to keep pace with demand. The Dixie musicians, their faces streaked with sweat, waistcoats unfastened, paraded round the edge of the hall with an inebriated conga line in tow. The smell of grilled hamburger mingled with popcorn and the acrid, burning odour of the fire-eater's petrol. The whole event was hot, steamy and a huge success.

Strether dabbed his brow with a handerkerchief and felt a surge of pride. He had striven for the finest way to celebrate his country's nationhood and had triumphed. Nobody Stateside could have done better. He did not feel especially homesick: there was nobody at home to feel homesick for. Only for the open air and the feel of the dawn sun on a broad-brimmed hat. He put his more sombre worries firmly on to a mental *Hold*, to be re-examined with more care later. Life in Europe, meanwhile, had its compensations.

Such as Lisa Pasteur. She was here, somewhere. At last he found her with a group of companions in a cluster surrounding Porton Down Director Professor Churchill at the Manhattan bar, cream-frothed concoctions in hand.

He took a moment to examine her frankly before she could notice him. Her dress was full length and slinky, made of a shimmery black silk cut on the bias so that it clung as she moved. A slit up to thigh level made Strether look twice and gulp. Her glossy hair had been piled on her head but tendrils escaped, framing her face. Suddenly Strether knew for certain that he yearned for her – needed her, to be more than his consort for private dinners, in a way he had not wanted a woman for a long time.

The Professor rose and stretched out his hand. 'Ambassador, what a tremendous evening. Allow me to present my wife.' An angular, narrow-chested woman came forward; armed with his new knowledge, Strether's glance strayed involuntarily to her chin line. Aged sixty or so, she must have had a lift. Or maybe two. No surplus folds, no jowls, no wrinkles marred the smoothness. He caught Lisa's eye: she had noted his surreptitious examination of Mrs Churchill and was greatly amused by it. Cross with himself, he realised that never again would he be able to look older people in the face without checking. Women, or men.

'I was grateful for the time you gave me during my visit, Director. Dr Pasteur, too.'

The exchange continued blandly until Strether could manoeuvre himself away. As he turned a corner Lisa deftly caught up with him.

'Well done,' he grinned. 'They can't be easy to slip away from.'

'I told them I was going to find the loo then explore. It'd be boring to spend the entire evening with colleagues from Porton Down – I see quite enough of them.'

'You look stunning, Lisa. That dress! I'm glad you don't wear it when we go out. You'd have had me in the rumour magazines in no time.'

Their liaison, such as it was, had been kept low key by mutual (and unspoken) agreement. It could not be completely private – but nor was it trumpeted abroad. Strether guessed now that nobody at Porton Down was in the know: their body language had displayed no prurient curiosity.

Both knew that nothing might come of it, or that the results, should they get together, might turn out unsatisfactory. Both, as they had discovered in cautious conversations, were wary of casual relationships – Strether had agreed wholeheartedly with that. They had found each other's company delightful, stimulating. Yet each was wary of using the other; and, paradoxically, that had turned them into comrades, co-conspirators, almost.

But the springing awareness of her physical presence, of her femaleness and attractiveness, which had struck him the first moment he had seen her despite the white lab coat, had stayed with Strether and grown vigorously within him. Lisa had entered his dreams, increasingly in images he would have described to no one. Now she stood below him, her face tilted upwards. The black folds of the neckline set off the curve of her shoulders. A simple gold chain lay about her throat. The little earrings she had worn in Milton Keynes twisted delicately and caught the light. He could see a tiny blue vein on her temple; the fine skin was almost translucent there, and in the vulnerable hollows of her collarbones.

'I want to kiss you,' he whispered to her.

'Mm, I know,' she replied mischievously. 'It must be the heat. Excites the hormones. I'm glad your air-conditioning doesn't work too well.' She put a hand on his arm and stood quite still as if making a decision. 'Maybe it's time,' she said, almost to herself. Then she half-smiled, and glanced around. 'D'you have somewhere quiet?'

It was the act of a moment to guide her to the back elevator. His office was in the west wing and fairly well equipped, with a bathroom and a small bedroom. He wished he had prepared it better, with flowers or a gift for her. It was sparsely furnished, suitable for a catnap between engagements when it was not worth the trek to the Residence: but it did guarantee privacy. And, away from the crowd, it was blessedly cooler.

As he unlocked the corridor door, Strether was laughing softly. He had not drunk much that evening; he had been too busy. Yet he felt hotly intoxicated and madly out of kilter. And totally thrilled that she had seized the initiative.

'You make me feel like a big kid, Lisa. Here am I, the host. Oh, I won't be missed for twenty minutes – but I should be offering something a deal more romantic for you.'

In the elevator they had been so close, touching knuckles, not holding. As she walked into the office and gathered her bearings, Lisa spoke. 'I'm not a very formal person, Bill. We aren't, in Europe. The days of elaborate courtship disappeared with Queen Elizabeth.' She smiled over her shoulder at him. 'If we see what we really want, we go for it.'

Someone had left a window ajar and the night air came in, heady with the perfume of late blossom from a clutch of trees below. A few petals had landed on the window-sill. Nearby a cricket sang sleepily. She lifted her arms and rubbed her skin, enjoying the soft breeze.

Without switching on the light he locked the door and put the key prominently on the desk. She could leave at any time, if she chose.

Then he took her fingers in his hands and, as he had done on the garden bench, lifted them to his lips and kissed each one. She slid her own hands to the side of his head, smoothing his hair as if to get his measure, and pulled his face down to her level. Then she kissed him, lightly first then harder, till he gave in to the ache buried deep inside and caressed her shoulders then her breasts, cupping them in his big hands. Her body under the silk was taut and warm. He pointed to the bedroom. 'In there. Come on.'

The dress had no zip or fastening. The fabric was yielding and fluid; with a wriggle, Lisa slipped her arms out of the top and let it fall away, then kicked off her shoes. She wore only a scrap of black lace as panties; the breasts were firm, the aureoles rosy. Her waist was narrow, the hips rounded and feminine. In the dim room her eyes darkened to blackness, their honey flecks elusive and secret.

Then as Strether watched, hardly daring to breathe, she stepped out of the garment and placed it casually over a chair. 'If we're a crumpled mess when we leave here, it'll be obvious what we've been up to.' She took a step back. 'The new jacket's terrific, Bill, but you'd better get it off. Here, let me help.'

As she leaned close to him, Strether held saw how the shape of her breasts caught the moonlight, how sturdy she was on those handsome thighs. He did not mind that she readily took the lead – it felt right, as if the imbalance of his age and status was reset. 'Lisa. Oh, Lisa. I haven't – for ages. It's been such a long time. Forgive me.'

She slipped open the velcro of his shirt and slacks and laid them also, not too neatly, on the back of the chair. The silk stars and stripes scarf slipped to the floor. He tugged off his shoes and socks, his shorts. In a moment he stood before her, the hairs on his torso stirring in the air.

'Me neither,' she whispered. 'I don't sleep around. Here, love, hold me; I want to feel your arms around me –'

He swallowed hard. 'Should I – I mean, are you –?'

She smiled, and smoothed her hand over his shoulder so that the touch of her fingertips made his skin sing; her palm floated lightly over his abdomen, so close he could sense its warmth, then came to rest on his thigh. 'You don't have to worry about that. I have an implant. I suspected you were getting interested. Some day I want a baby, but not this way, and not tonight.'

And she led him to the bed, and bade him lie on it, and propped him up with pillows; and she perched agilely before him, her knees each side of his, she with her lithe body and natural grace. She guided his hands, and murmured her pleasure, till he gathered confidence and tried old movements which his wife had loved, long ago when they had first been married. Perhaps something in Lisa's dark looks reminded him, or her spirited independence. He reached up and rubbed his thumbs over her nipples and watched them harden, laughing softly with her. He bent his face and took the precious nibs of flesh between his teeth, first one then the other, and sucked like an infant till she gasped and arched her neck. Then he pushed her on to her back and did the same between her legs, relishing the taste and moistness of her. At last he took her firmly, turned her over and entered her from behind, his mouth buried in her tangled hair and his breathing in short gasps, quicker, quicker – until it came, for them both, with a deep drawn-out moan from him –

– then a collapse on the strewn pillows, in a gurgle of spent excitement and shared joy.

Lisa rolled over and stroked his sweaty face. 'Dear, sweet Bill. D'you know you're good at this?'

He lay on his back, his arm relaxed around her shoulders. 'Had a bit of practice, but years ago.' He lifted himself up on his elbow and gazed happily down at her. 'Haven't got much time, so I'll say this now. You are a fabulous lady. So smart, so womanly. I want to see you, I'd love to do this, over and over again. More romantically, if we can manage it. Not just a one-night stand. How does that sound?'

'Sounds great.' She was smiling at him, her honeyed eyes bright.

'Better warn you, I'm not a one-night-stand sort of a fellow.'

'Fine by me.'

He felt drunk, wild. 'I mean, Lisa, that if you're not

careful I could fall in love with you. I'm an old-fashioned
kinda man.'

She gave him a gentle push. 'Got it. But if we don't
move now, sweetie, your Secret Service guys'll be sending out a search party. Then you'll be in hot water. That'd
do wonders for your reputation and authority.'

In a few minutes the two had showered, sharing a
towel, and dressed. Lisa switched on the light and
attempted to restore her hairstyle. By the time she gave it
up as a bad job, rather more curls framed her face than
when she had arrived but, combined with her flushed
cheeks, the effect was sensual and alluring. Strether told
her so as he combed his own hair and checked himself
back and front in the hologram mirror. As he refastened
jacket buttons and fumbled with velcro his hands trembled. Lisa, with a conspiratorial chuckle, had to help him.

'Wait.' He went to the main door and unlocked it
slowly, checked up and down the corridor then ushered
her out. In the elevator they stood side by side and
demure, but her expression none the less kept breaking
out in grins and dimples.

'You look like a dame who's been enjoying herself,' he
murmured. 'Have to get you another drink so you have an
excuse.'

As the elevator hummed Strether struggled to bring
himself back under control; he felt light-headed, and
wanted to sing with joy, rather than embroil himself once
more in affairs of state. He wanted to dwell on his adventure and how lucky he believed himself to be, and how it
would be even better next time, more relaxed. They
would get to know each other's bodies, and he would
plan a future for them –

He pulled himself up short. He barely knew the young

woman beside him. He must not take for granted that his
interest was reciprocated. Despite her assurances, to Lisa
he might be merely a passing fancy. He had no idea what
she was truly like, nor any other European women. Other
than her passion for her strange profession, her belief in
its efficacy, her fears about some lost files, she was as yet
an unread book. She had taken the lead with him tonight;
for that, there could be another motive. Surrounded as he
was by puzzles, perhaps she was just one more piece in
the jigsaw. He had little notion what motivated her, what
inspired her.

Then it would be fun to find out, he resolved. He
shook his head to clear the fuzziness; he still tasted her
lips on his. He was deeply reluctant to re-enter the hard
world of duty. But she had made it plain that a repeat
episode would be welcome. He would cling to that.

As they emerged from the private corridor Matt Brewer
was waiting. 'Sorry to bother you, sir, ma'am, but we've
received . . .' He pulled his chief to one side and dropped
his voice. 'We've had a call from the police. There's some
trouble three blocks away, near Parliament Square. We've
been asked to keep the guests here for a while, till we get
the all-clear. And not to alarm them.'

'Still got plenty of booze?'

Brewer nodded.

'Then that bit's straightforward. Put a couple of guards
by the exits – choose big ones, but ultra-polite. Do people
know?'

'No, sir. It's not on the news networks. I've seen one or
two guests using mobile vidphones. Mr Packer has gone.
And Sir Lyndon has had to slip away – he presents his
apologies, sir.'

'What sort of trouble? Criminals, a shoot-out? Or

what?' Strether began to stride beside him towards the
crowded rooms. Behind, Lisa made to rejoin her group.
He halted and spoke to her direct. 'You're not to leave
until it's safe. Any of your party.' His face softened. For
the second time that evening the Ambassador strove to
put his jumbled feelings in order. This time he did not
entirely succeed. 'And thank you for – for the discussion,
Dr Pasteur. You're a very special lady.'

Matt Brewer allowed himself a fleeting smile. 'The bar
is that way, ma'am.' The two Americans waited while
Lisa glided away, her hair bobbing insecurely on the top
of her head. At the far door Prince Marius hovered, and
spoke a few words to her. She nodded vaguely and disappeared in the direction of the Manhattan bar.

Then the staffer continued, his voice urgent. 'We don't
know who's behind it, sir. The unit involved down on the
street is a crack team against organised crime. But our
guess is it could be political.'

No one seemed to have noticed his absence, though
Strether suspected Matt Brewer had missed little. The
officer would be far too discreet, and loyal, to mention it.
In a moment their tour took them to the balcony where he
and Marius had spoken earlier. The french windows were
still open. He stepped outside.

Down below cars had been halted in a double stationary line, headlights ablaze. Several drivers had got out
and were leaning on their cars or standing in a gaggle, all
eyes in one direction. There appeared to be a police
blockade of some kind. Blue lights winked, a siren
wailed. Strether leaned over the balcony, craned his neck
and peered into the night. Behind him Marius reappeared, his face studiously set, as if he had expected
the Ambassador to return to this spot.

Strether could hear shouting, but too far away and faint to identify any phrases. Then somewhere in the distance came a sharp crack. A high-velocity rifle? Instinctively he pulled back, then cautiously leaned out again. The rifle was answered by the distinctive buzz of max-power laser weapons, familiar from his National Guard days. Car drivers dived and scattered with yelps of terror. Red beams zinged from behind police vehicles and were directed at windows two or three blocks further down. A block of masonry at third-floor level slowly detached itself and crashed to the ground, scattering singed chunks into the road. The rifle fired back angrily and a police officer slid sideways. A woman in a car screamed.

'Get inside, sir.' Matt Brewer grabbed at his jacket and closed the windows. 'Not safe.'

Strether's gaze switched rapidly from Brewer to the silent Prince and back again. He erupted, his face working in fury and fear. 'So what the hell's going on? The police are shooting the hell outta somebody down there. Not for the first time, is it? I bet it's linked with those pirate broadcasts. So what's happening? Some kinda revolution, or what?'

Marius shook his head. 'Don't get involved, Ambassador. That's the best advice.'

But Matt's expression was grim. He answered the question directly. 'Dunno, sir. But someone sure is lying to us. Probably somebody in this building.' He glared at Marius. 'Or maybe, every man jack of them. What do you think?'

Chapter Nine

There can be few more desolate places, Colonel Mike Thompson considered, than an airport at the end of a line: ramshackle buildings, a passenger hall that smelled like a toilet, toilets that smelled unspeakable, cash machines long since wrenched from the wall, automatic doors defunct and propped open with wedges. Tattered posters hung from a tourist shop barely larger than a cabin, whose window display of stained vodka bottles and Russian dolls was barred and forbidding. The surveillance cameras looked as if they had not been functional for years. He pitied the civilians huddled around a creaking luggage conveyor. With luck, their bags would come tumbling out eventually, zips half open and clothing strewn about, greasy fingermarks on the handles. The more luxurious luggage would not reappear at all.

A blast of noise hit the cavernous hall from a loud-speaker: tinny martial music, somebody's anthem, or, perhaps, a national march. A sallow man nearby stood to attention, pebble glasses misty. He at least had come home.

Thompson shouldered his kitbag and began to walk towards the exit, avoiding the stinking puddles. Aided by a tail-wind, the fastjet had been ahead of schedule. He would wait for his transport away from the intrusive noise and odours of this batch of humanity.

It was not his first tour of duty on the Euro-Chinese border. If tempers flared, it might not be his last. In a way, however, his current posting suggested the area was fairly quiet; for he had trained as a traditional soldier, normally a commander of fast-moving mobile troops in Eurocorps, not of specialised units involved in nuclear warfare or chemical or biological protection. His forces relied on intelligence and speed; their usual task in a conflict was to move in once an area had been declared clean and take possession of bridges, secure utilities and crossing points. After that it would be the turn of the infantry to dig in. And after *that*, the politicians would arrive by the plane-load, and would make better or worse the gains their military had secured.

It had to be admitted that the politicians had had some success. The nuclear arsenals were sheathed, for the time being. Chemical and biological weapons had proved notoriously difficult to eradicate, but had not been used between the great powers for nearly a century. Between them the European Union, the United States and the Chinese Republic colluded, openly or otherwise, on what should appertain in many other parts of the world, where local firefights broke out with much the same depressing frequency as ever. It was not clear to Thompson, brought up on Union codes that guaranteed and celebrated diversity, why it was still the case that ethnic Malays hated their ethnic Chinese neighbours with such ferocity or why Sudan and Eritrea insisted – even now – on fighting over arid desert while their people starved. Peace had replaced ancient strife in the Balkans and Ireland, in

Cyprus and, more or less, in Afghanistan. If his efforts could help establish calm in other strife-torn areas, then he would die content.

It suited him far better than Buckingham Palace. He could now admit to himself the truth, that despite a sneaking liking for the empty-headed young King, he had been bored rigid. He was a soldier, not a courtier. Attendance at dinners, listening to arcane or shallow discourse, trying to stay smartly upright for hours of public duty, had tested his powers of endurance to the limit. It had not however been entirely useless, which is why he suspected his superiors had arranged it. He had met the highest in the land and begun to form opinions on them. And he was not impressed by what he had seen.

He sniffed the breeze: it hinted at dry heat devoid of moisture. Beyond the terminal building were palm trees whose dusty fronds waved limply. The deserts were still advancing. Although climate change had been so beneficial in the West where water was plentiful – indeed, London was plagued with too much as sea levels had risen – in the great inland areas of Africa and central Asia vast tracts had become virtually uninhabitable. Populations had trudged across borders, become refugees, sat down as homeless and survived on UN rations. They never went back for there was nothing to return to but bare scrub and hopelessness; they never settled and became prosperous, for they knew nothing but poverty and bitter displacement.

Thompson sighed. A hand tugged his trouser leg and he looked down. At his feet a legless beggar crouched, an adult but no bigger than a dog. The face was twisted and deformed, the hand had a single blackened thumb and no fingers. The whole thing stank and was filthy. The product of genetic damage, no doubt – a lot of that in this region. Trying not to recoil, Thompson searched his pockets for a local coin and gave it to the creature, who scuttled away.

A lean young soldier, swarthy and moustached, came running towards him, then skidded to a halt and saluted.

'Colonel Thompson sir! I'm so sorry. We heard you were going to be late.'

'No, it was a good journey. Surprisingly so, for Russian Commercial Airlines.' The Colonel handed over his bag and shook hands. 'Captain Neimat Vesirov? Where are you from?'

'I'm Azerbaijani, sir,' the officer answered proudly. 'The first commissioned in your regiment.' The two men fell into step and walked out into the blazing heat.

'I thought Captain Mahwala was going to look after me again,' Thompson commented as he climbed into the hover-jeep and strapped himself in. 'Has he been posted?'

The adjutant shook his head. 'He had an accident, sir. To be honest, there was some trouble.'

'Really? I never thought of Ranjit as a hothead. Is he hurt?'

'He had to be sent home on medical leave, yes. But he had been most unhappy beforehand. He did not enjoy service at the prison camps. That was well known.'

Thompson shrugged. 'Lord, have they put us in charge there again? Then his reaction was quite understandable. Pity, he was a fine man to work with. I'm sure you'll be excellent too, Captain. Let's go, shall we?'

It was hard to concentrate. Lisa pulled her lab coat round her as if to remind herself that she was seated at her console in Porton Down, not on the tousled bed in Lambert

Strether's embassy. The events of a few days before had been profoundly stirring. To focus instead on microbiological specimens was proving almost impossible.

Would it always be like this? Was her reaction normal? It annoyed her to think that a single episode like that should knock her sideways for days. If this was the way the biological clock affected her, then it was more than a little irritating. She had read that pregnancy made women cow-like, as their hormones adjusted to the demands of the growing foetus. Nature ensured that the baby came first and the adult second. That, among other reasons, was a powerful argument against natural pregnancy even with an approved and enhanced embryo. Far better to let science take over in the most pristine conditions, and thereby ensure both that the baby would be born immaculate, and that its parents could continue to fulfil their economic potential as long as they wished.

So why this buzz in her head, this ache under her ribcage? She was not ill, not dehydrated, not suffering from any low-level infection – every physical possibility had been checked and eliminated. But she felt disoriented and light-headed, as if strange compounds were circulating in her brain, making her less incisive, less acute. More feminine. *Dammit*, as Strether would say. That was not in the game-plan.

So what did it mean – was this love? Was she love-sick, was that it?

Lisa leaned back and folded her arms. An observer would have noted the frown-line between her eyes, the loosely tied brown hair, the slight smudge to the lipstick she had taken regularly to wearing. The tired look and worried expression were present only when she stared hardest at the computer screen. More often, when she was gazing into space, her face was dreamy rather than anxious.

She did not feel love-sick. She did not feel *in love*, if truth be told. Her body had thrilled to the touch of a man after such a period of abstinence; if she listened to her innermost soul carefully, which she had tended to do rarely, she could detect a delight that certain parts of herself, blanked out and forgotten till Strether had kissed her, had returned boisterously to full use. It bewildered her, this loss of control, this *pleasure*.

With the greatest caution, for she did not want to come to any unbending conclusions, she explored her emotions. She liked Bill. A lot. Of that she could be certain. He was a big, shambling man whose character, what she knew of it, would commend him to anybody. The fact that he was so different from almost everyone she knew added spice and excitement, and a frisson of – what? – maybe fear, too: fear of the unknown.

She adored the way he treated her with such courtesy. And the way he talked, especially about his own life. It had taken a while before he had been at all forthcoming about himself; he was insignificant, he had told her, it was purely fortuitous that he was in England, and his main worry was that he was not up to the job set for him by his President. But when she had asked him what his President wanted he had clammed up instantly. From which she had deduced, and joshed him lightly, that he had no cause for concern. He was, rather, an excellent diplomat.

He had spoken of his wife, with such sweet adoration that Lisa had found herself admiring him and seeing him through her eyes. On reflection it told a great deal about him, that he had married a Native American; in his circles, surely an unusual choice. Lisa had a vague picture

in her head of a typical Texas oilman's moll, a brassy
piece in high-heeled cowboy boots with a Stetson
perched on bottle-blonde curls. But Strether's wife had
not been like that. Perhaps Colorado was more tolerant.

She had gained the impression that, while he might
not be immune to more garish attractions, the qualities he
was most drawn to were thoughtfulness and a warm
heart. That was deeply flattering, but it also gave Lisa
pause.

She sucked her teeth and breathed slowly. The views
he had let slip about the role of a wife in marriage were
almost old-fashioned. It was best, he had ventured, if it
were clear from the start, and agreed, who was the dominant partner, at least in public: what went on behind
closed doors was entirely between the couple. He had
been especially blessed, he admitted, because his wife
had always insisted it should be him.

'I don't think that's me,' Lisa whispered to herself.
'Somehow.'

The screen before her had been left undisturbed so
long it had gone into standby mode. She tapped it to
bring it back to life. The computer programme flipped to
the main menu and asked what she wanted to do next.
She was unsure of the answer.

Darling that he was, Bill Strether could be no more
than a friend. She would have to be careful that he did
not fall in love with her. Kid-glove treatment, and the
greatest consideration for his feelings, would be necessary. But it was delicious, nevertheless, to have restarted
sexual activity. The sheer pleasure that gave – the lingering sensations, days afterwards – suggested that celibacy
had been wrong for her, and should have been abandoned
much sooner. Bill wanted to carry on an affair, and she

was not about to refuse. But she would behave responsibly, and try to ensure that whatever happened he was not hurt.

So if Strether was not to be the love of her life, who might be? Wicked thoughts began to flit unbidden through her brain. With an oath she tried to discipline them, but not before the following had registered: that he should be younger than Bill, and in better shape. And preferably European, and an NT. Call that prejudice, perhaps, but at least, she told herself bluntly, she had had the clarity to recognise it.

He would have to be at her own level. Not necessarily a scientist – of course not. But someone who could understand her life's work, her passion for it and, in guarded moments, out of sight of automatic eyes and voice-monitors, her deepest fears about it. Not an innocent, not a strident advocate of the system, yet wise enough to be a guide and mentor, and to push her in the directions that scientific probity urged her to take.

A face floated into her mind. With a quick laugh, she dismissed it. The idea was preposterous. But where had it come from? Ah, yes, she had seen him fleetingly just as she and Strether had parted at the embassy, when that aide had drawn Bill aside and she had been warned not to leave. The face was quite familiar: she had seen him on television with that mocking smile and those shrewd eyes, dark like her own. It came back: he had asked her then if she was enjoying herself, taken in the tousled hair and the flushed cheeks, and smiled at her. She had reckoned that he had guessed what she and their host had been up to, and was most amused. He had glanced back at Strether, then realised that something grimmer was under way, and had moved away from her to follow the Ambassador.

The guest knew her from official trips to the laboratory, such as the day he brought Strether. But he had seen her only in the clothes she wore now, the white coat and trousers, devoid of makeup or jewellery. She had been putting out no sexual signals then, and the visitor, who had a reputation for escorting society women, must barely have noticed her. Until that night at the embassy, when she had been so aroused, and he had come to her like a bee to a honeypot, and had leaned so close.

How strange, that such a momentary encounter should come back in such detail. Probably because it had occurred when her own awareness had been so heightened. Or because in some recess of her subconscious the younger man, so smart in his velvet tunic, his dark eyes sharp and teasing, had come closer to her ideal. If so, that insight was not to be dismissed lightly, but savoured and considered with the greatest care.

For the man was Prince Marius. And the opportunity might arise – or be made to arise – to meet him again.

Strictly speaking the Queen Anne public house was named after an eighteenth-century monarch, but it had received a new lease of life with her formidable namesake, the grandmother of the present King. The swinging sign outside, a sop to heritage laws, showed a haughty woman with the prominent nose and receding chin of her clan, characteristics that had been corrected in subsequent generations. Indoors, tradition was maintained, with wood panelling, sawdust floors and the odour of ale, tobacco and sweat. Nor did the royal connections do the pub any harm, for it was the favourite watering place of officers of the Metropolitan Police from the nearby station. Even after retirement they would drift in for companionship and solace.

Captain Wilt Finkelstein's expression was bitter. He chewed his lip ferociously. The old uniform was stretched to bursting across his now ample middle and the belt was on its last notch; his wife had had to sew the brass buttons more securely on to his tunic. He strode into the pub ahead of a small contingent of sombre figures, ignored the fat man seated precariously on a stool and slammed a hand down on the counter.

'Four litres – not halves – and be quick about it,' he demanded.

The fat man shifted on the uncomfortable stool. 'You look like you had a hard morning, Officer,' he ventured.

'Too bloody right,' Finkelstein grunted. 'Been to a funeral. One of my old partners. Shot dead.'

'I'm sorry about that,' the fat man said sincerely. 'Nobody realises what you guys have to put up with.' He pushed the four full glasses towards the police officer and placed a large paw on his fist. 'No. I'm getting these. Mark of gratitude.'

'Thanks, pal,' Finkelstein muttered. He gave his name. 'What do I call you?'

'Fred Hoyle. Fred to you.' The two men shook hands.

Finkelstein settled himself on the next stool and took a long draw on the beer. 'You're spot on,' he growled. 'Nobody appreciates. That guy was not yet forty. Promoted to an élite corps in February. Got a family – two kiddies. Then there's a shoot-out three nights ago and – pow! Blown to smithereens.'

Fred made suitable noises and took a swallow of his own drink.

'I'd string 'em up, that's what I'd do,' Finkelstein continued. 'We haven't had capital punishment anywhere in
the Union for a hundred years, but that's a big mistake.
The bastards think they can take pot-shots at police officers and get away with it. And they can. All the bugger
will get is a few years in clink. That's if we catch 'im. And
what's my mate got? Nothing. Cut off in his prime. Them
poor kids.'

'What happened?' Fred had sensed that the officer
needed to talk.

'Terrorists, that's what.' Finkelstein dropped his voice.
'Not supposed to know that, are we? It's listed as a street-
crime shoot-out, but it was political. A group got into the
Channel 5 TV annex and tried to start broadcasting. But Mr
Maxwell Packer, the owner, wasn't having any. He called
his buddy, the Metropolitan Police Commissioner. Some of
the group were armed. And my mate got blown away.'

'That's odd,' Fred mused. 'Didn't see nothing about it
in the papers.'

'No, well, you wouldn't. Nobody likes to admit there
are problems. All's well, all the time. Except it ain't.'

A frown had appeared on Fred's podgy face, threatening to distort his genial demeanour. 'I don't know of no
problems,' he said cagily. 'Seems to me that if some
lunatics invade a TV station the owner is within his
rights to have them thrown out.'

'Yeah. Only it wasn't as simple as that.' Finkelstein
buried his face in his beer mug then wiped the foam from
his mouth with the back of his hand. 'What gets me is
they keep us in the dark. I never made detective, so I
can't suss it out. But that bunch were armed, and the
police unit sent after them was ready for trouble – the
latest high-powered lasers, the lot. Yet nobody's been

arrested or charged. An' nothing in the press, nothing at all, like you said. It's as if it didn't happen.'

He leaned forward and poked Fred viciously in the chest, his finger disappearing repeatedly into the folds of flesh. "Cept it did, and my mate's dead. An' something's going on, and more men will get killed. And for what? That's what I'd like to know. For what?'

He lapsed into silence. The two men drank in mutual sympathy till the glasses were drained. In the far corner the other police officers were seated, talking glumly to each other. Finkelstein put his glass down on the bar. 'Another? My shout.'

'Yeah, why not? It's Friday, short shift, only three hours. If I go home the missus complains I get under her feet.'

'When I think of it,' Finkelstein continued over his refilled glass, his voice more mellow, 'my life these days, on civvy street, is a big improvement over police work, any day. I used to do thirty or forty hours a week, half the night, running from one bun-fight to another. We thought nothing of it. Mind you, I was younger then.'

'You not in the force now?' Fred eyed the uniform and noticed the worn cuffs and shiny elbows: the marks of hours spent seated at a desk. His manner became slightly less respectful.

'Nah. Got invalided out. Still got a bit of bullet inside me. I work for RSS – Rottweiler Security Services.'

Fred nodded. The company was well known.

'Big operation,' Finkelstein began to boast. He talked animatedly for several minutes about his job, much of it in the language of the recruitment brochure which he had just helped to write. Then he glanced about and spoke in a conspiratorial whisper.

'You buy shares ever?'

Fred shrugged. 'Yeah, got a few. Virgin, Yamaichi. I tried for the BBC issue but was too late. Any tips?'

The former police officer leaned close. 'Our firm. RSS. Being taken over, so I hear. Foreign interests. Could be big money. Shares are at ten euros – could be three or four times that in a few weeks.'

Fred's eyes shone. 'Thanks, that's worth knowing.' He paused to drink. 'And who are the interested parties?'

'Dunno.' Finkelstein shook his head. 'Far East, rumour has it. Keen to buy into the security sector. God knows why. An' who cares, anyway, provided they pay our wages?'

Marius was restless. His usual weekly visit to his mother, arranged for the days when Parliament wasn't sitting, had been postponed again. She was indisposed, she declared, and would be for a while, as if she could conceal her surgery from her son, her next of kin. But she would still be quite bruised, her flesh purple and green in patches, with the scars visible. It was kinder to respect her vanity, and let her be.

He walked down the street aimlessly until it became too hot, then sat at a sidewalk café in the shade and ordered an iced coffee. The liquid was cold, but not strong enough, not the way he preferred it; the lacuna made him unreasonably fractious. Opposite was a pub, the Queen Anne. He could see men inside with big hands wrapped lazily around lager steins. As he watched idly, one overweight figure ambled out and headed purposefully down the road. A workman going home, probably, or to a match. Only the unfortunate had to work after Friday lunchtime.

It came to Marius out of the blue that he had no home. His mother's apartment was very much hers; her children had given it to her as a seventieth birthday gift. The house he had grown up in was the rococo palace in Budapest, overlooking the Danube, but he had been a small boy when they left and had revisited only as a famous stranger. For years the family had trudged about Europe as lodgers in other palaces and embassies; he had become accustomed to elaborate ceilings and dusty, over-filled bedrooms. The nearest he had come to a home of any sort was the apartment he had acquired after entering the House of Lords. But that was no more than a convenient *pied-à-terre* at a smart address, with few redeeming features.

The apartment was comfortable enough. The block, not far from Parliament, had originally been constructed with MPs and senior civil servants in mind. While their personal security was paramount, their privacy must also be protected. Thus the property came with full mechanical portering and cameras only in the common areas, a somewhat unusual arrangement. It meant, however, that Marius could entertain without surveillance. Not infrequently that had included the wives and daughters of colleagues. He smiled at the memories, then felt obscurely ashamed.

The iced coffee grew warm in the soft air as condensation ran wetly down the tall glass. Marius brooded. His mother's chiding came insistently to him. In her words, maybe it was time he began to grow up.

Had he seen his mother she would inevitably have raised the question she had aired since he had reached his thirties. When was he going to settle down? She would pluck his sleeve and murmur about how happy it would make her, and how he had a duty to ensure that his heritage was passed on, her voice like the caress of a silk scarf over his face, suffocating and unavoidable. He would joke that the passage of his genes could be done at any moment, and that instead it was an outcome he took great care to avoid. *Planned* conception, he would tease, was what he assumed his mother had in mind. In turn the old lady would pout that an official wedding and a proper wife were what she meant, as if he needed to be told. The exchange was familiar and increasingly frequent. Until recently Marius had dismissed it as the natural preoccupation of a loving parent. But lately he had hesitated in his standard responses, sufficient to have his mother eye him closely; and the discussion had embarrassed him, in ways he could not quite fathom.

His mother was ambitious for him, though it was not clear what gains a suitable spouse could bring. Marius sensed that, in career terms, he had gone as far as he wished to go. Had he yearned for high office, he could simply have made those views known and would probably have been invited on to the front bench with alacrity; hints had been dropped more than once that he would be welcome. But that would have meant abandoning the freedom and independence of his chosen lifestyle in favour of endless days and nights in committee rooms, cabinet and the Lords chamber, explaining, defending, parrying policies for which he might have only the most tenuous affection. The appeal of such office was limited, the pay terrible. Nor could a determined wife push him, he was sure, into something he did not want to do.

If she were wealthy . . . Marius caught himself sharply. He was far from poor. The glossy jetset, many of whom were long-standing acquaintances, were casually generous

with their homes, with holidays and cruises on yachts;
provided he made himself excellent company, he lacked
nothing but their responsibilities. It was a cadger's life,
perhaps, but its lack of ties suited him admirably. To be
honest he did not ache to own anything, only to enjoy his
time on earth, to avoid pitfalls, to fill his days with pleasant and absorbing activity. He would say he was a happy
man.

Or, rather, he used to say it, under his breath, swinging
along a sidewalk, squiring beautiful women to theatre
first nights or to private showings at galleries. Taking his
place on the second row of their Lordships' House when
the King came for the state opening, representing his kin,
the crowned heads of Europe, at sessions with the
European President Herr Lammas whenever money or
precedent were on the agenda. Making new friends such
as the American Ambassador, whose solid nature and
inquisitiveness had impressed Marius from the first.
Escorting such distinguished visitors to places like Porton
Down, where his more laconic approach was challenged
by their concern. Indeed, some of his current malaise
could be put at Strether's door: the man was a sea-green
innocent, and yet the questions the American asked and
his worries about the genetic programme had intrigued
Marius and stayed with him long after the conversation
had ended.

He let his mind dwell on Strether. *Bill*, as he liked to
be called. Marius chuckled to himself – it was that example of easy familiarity, the willingness to expose his
cultural quirks to scrutiny, to risk ridicule, even, which
separated Bill so effectively from self-regarding
Europeans, and rendered him so satisfactory as a friend.
One felt instinctively that Bill would listen to any worries

and have words of simple shrewdness to offer. Yet perhaps he would also benefit from a little extra European
sophistication. He was a degree too solemn, too earnest. It
might be time to resurrect an idea that had been briefly
alluded to that afternoon months ago at the Palace. It was
time to take Strether to the Toy Shop, and give him a rollicking good men's night out.

That was mischievous, and Marius knew it. Strether
abashed, out of his depth, would be amusing and the
source of endless dinner-party stories. The Prince examined his motives and found them slightly impure, but no
matter. There was no active cruelty in it. Strether would
find the Toy Shop an amazing experience, and would
dine out himself on tales of what went on – his own
behaviour excluded, of course – when he went home. As
family men would whisper in all-male company the
secrets of a geisha house after a sojourn in Japan, so
would Strether the cattleman regale his closest pals back
in Colorado. If he could be persuaded to come.

The prospect of the fun ahead detained Marius a little
longer, then the restlessness returned. The afternoon was
wearing on; shadows remained short, but the sun was
losing its intensity. Soon the streets would be filled with
strolling young men and women out for the cooler hours
of the evening, eyeing each other in a swish of skirts, a
hint of scent, a twist of the head. Maybe he should pick
up a girl tonight, and take her back to his apartment; not
least to prove to himself that he could still do it, a master
at seduction as ever. Or he could call up one of a dozen
ladies who would be delighted to share an evening with
him, stylish females with perfumed hair and perfect
limbs, who would rebuke him for his neglect of them and
beg him to stay.

He took out his powerbook and began to scroll down names, then with a soft curse switched it off. This was not what he sought: he wanted to go home, to have a home, and to have waiting there a lovely woman who was wedded to him and him alone. Who was committed to him and had made promises she would always keep. And for whom promises of lifelong devotion on his part would seem to be mere statements of fact, an assertion of obvious truth. But where might such a woman be found?

He leaned back and squinted at the cloudless sky through the lush leaves of a fragrant beech tree. Images flickered through his mind as the diffused light came and went. His retinas were dazzled and for a moment he was blinded.

His mother wanted somebody royal and preferably rich; he didn't care about either. Physical beauty these days could be virtually guaranteed – as his mother could testify, once her scars had vanished. Brains and intelligence were more important (a view which might surprise the Princess), plus wisdom and good humour. A person with some of Bill Strether's better qualities, then. How unusual that a stranger should have had such an impact, and have altered, however imperceptibly, Marius's ordering of what made people worthwhile.

What kind of woman might Strether like? The Prince found himself chuckling. The two had shared days out shopping but the Ambassador had not been especially forthcoming on the subject of female company – except about his wife, whom he had described with a loving awe. But Strether had recently found himself a replacement, if the gossip was correct. That lady he had been with at the Independence Day party, the woman in the slinky dress, her hair falling down about a pretty heart-shaped face full of character, her cheeks flushed as if they had been making love only a few moments before.

She was a doctor at the government laboratory; of that much Marius was sure, for he had been introduced to her more than once. Each time they would smile at each other and say, 'We've met,' though he had never exchanged more than a few words with her. She was quite senior: Assistant Director, he recalled, so she must be astonishingly bright. Yet she gave an impression of sweet vulnerability, especially in such feminine garb. The curve of her bare arms, no longer hidden under her day clothes, made her distinctly desirable. Strether, poor fool, probably didn't even notice these finer points.

What was her name? Marius closed his eyes. Suddenly her head and those creamy shoulders, the dusky hollow of her neck, came clearly into focus. He was startled. *Lisa Pasteur*. Lisa Pasteur – it ran over the tongue like moist grapes, like a superb wine, and left a lingering taste of freshness and depth. Lisa Pasteur.

But she was Strether's girlfriend. He might be quite smitten. As an older man Strether's emotions might be a minefield. He, too, might be searching for someone special. And it would be a shame to hurt Strether for the sake of a bit of fun. Though Lisa, he sensed immediately, would be a serious proposition from the start, and would not play games.

A saying from his younger days came back to Marius. *All's fair in love, war and politics.* It made him laugh out loud, and drain the rest of his tepid coffee.

She was Strether's. Or was she? And if so – *so what*? Only the lady herself could decide. Perhaps it was right to consider offering her a choice.

Chapter Ten

'Ambassador, we are so delighted to welcome you.'

The Mistress of Dulwich College was a solid, muscular individual with steely hair cut in a bob about her square jaw. Her tweedy brown tunic and skirt, her flat, laced shoes seemed entirely in character. Her calves, Strether noticed, bore witness to continued prowess at hockey, a game that had mostly fallen out of fashion. That was probably the reason she still played; she gave an impression of considerable force both physical and intellectual, yet of disdain for passing style.

The Mistress crushed his hand in her own. 'The boys and girls will be so pleased to see you.' At his side, Dr Lisa Pasteur, former pupil, cleared her throat, as if to stifle a giggle.

An invitation to present prizes to the school's leavers at the end of the summer semester — or, indeed, an appearance at any school, since he did not have children — was not one he would normally have accepted. With a diplomatic diary crammed with engagements from morning till night he should have demurred without further ado. But Lisa had persuaded him, choosing her

moment one evening as he had been melting into those
honeyed eyes. It would have taken a man of stone to
refuse her.

The Mistress strode ahead. Her muscular bottom
bulged through the skirt which see-sawed rhythmically to
accommodate it. Both Strether and Lisa gaped helplessly
and exchanged glances.

'Of course Miss Molotov wasn't the Mistress when I
was here,' Lisa whispered. 'But it's invariably somebody
fearsome. And usually plain as a pikestaff.'

'Is she a – you know, an NT?' Strether hissed back.

'Oh, absolutely. Doubly enhanced, at a guess. She's
unchallengeable. IQ of one hundred and sixty at least.'

'She doesn't look it. I don't mean to be rude, but . . .'

'Not all families make appearance choices. A surname
like that probably derives from Russian or Slav stock. If
her parents didn't request visual refinements, they won't
have got them.'

'Not even with Winston on the job?' Strether grinned.
Lisa dug him in the ribs and did not reply. From her
sudden frown, however, he knew that Winston's efforts to
find the missing files were still on her mind. She had
mentioned that no more had vanished, but neither had
the original material surfaced.

The school buildings were as forbidding as the
Mistress, mainly brick-built at the turn of the nineteenth
century. It had once been exclusively for boys, with a
Master; the bleak masculinity of the place was redolent of
cold showers and brisk runs. Lofty narrow windows had
high sills to deter any schoolchild's wandering eye.
Sallow paint predominated, wall upon wall of it up to
beamed ceilings. In corridors narrow bookshelves were
lined with untranslated classics. Footfalls echoed on

stone floors or were muted on parquet polished to a hard shine by thousands of shoes.

They turned a corner and were met by two pupils, the head boy and head girl, officially their hosts. Whether the Mistress's family had requested visual refinements or not, it was obvious that the parents of both these children had. The pale blue eyes and blond hair, the well-bred high cheekbones and the elongated, spare figures were startlingly similar to those of Sir Robin Butler-Armstrong, the Lord Chamberlain, Graf von Richthofen and others Strether had met. He could spot the template a mile off.

The boy stepped forward. 'My name's Fenton, sir. Welcome.' He had a calm, adult manner, assured and in control. Inherited, probably, Strether briefly reflected. The girl introduced herself as Bridget. She had the same small pretty earlobes as Lisa, but no earrings. The youngsters were nearly Strether's height; their gaze was direct and unforced. The Ambassador felt himself under polite scrutiny.

No doubt he must be an object of curiosity to them: he, a foreigner, and quite evidently not an NT, but in a position of some authority. They must wonder how he approached problems, whether he could think logically, if he ever found his natural abilities to be inadequate. Given what they were told so early about themselves in the printout, they must wonder how someone like himself came upon self-knowledge. How would a non-NT find out what his tastes and talents were? How discover what made him happy, what frustrated? The randomness of real life must resemble a casual drawing of lots to them. Except that for these children, and their families, *real life* meant knowing everything about oneself, right from the start. There could be few secret desires harboured in such

a breast. Unless they had been put there without anyone
saying.

He tried to concentrate on his duties. First, lunch; parents and friends of award-winners would arrive as their
coffee was served. The great hall would be full as the
platform party entered. Then a speech and the handing
over of prizes; that would just give him time to return to
the Residence to change before the night's adventure at
the Toy Shop nightclub. The thought of that outing to
come made his pulse race.

Marius had suggested that he did not tell Lisa of the
escapade. Women did not approve of such places, he
warned, though mostly their activities were utterly innocent – or as innocent as guests might wish. The inference
was left for Strether to draw that should he want a more
vigorous evening, that too would be possible.

The arrangements had been made. In itself that had
been an astonishing experience, one which he had felt
obliged to note in his private diary.

*27 July 2099 . . . Marius helped me. We had to book
about two weeks in advance, but even then some of
the popular names had gone. Some guests make
block bookings for years ahead with their
favourites. Fresh stock is ordered as necessary, we
were advised, but it can take decades to come on
stream. If a particular type has a surge of exposure,
for example when an old movie is played on main-
stream TV, big problems can arise. That happened
recently with the retrospective cinema season of
late twentieth-century wetties. Demand for the Kate*

Winslet and Leonardo DiCaprio models was so high
they collapsed from exhaustion: no more bookings
are being accepted for either of them till October.

It's done by vidphone conferencing. Marius came
to the Residence and clocked on – you need to be a
club member with a password and he, inevitably, is.
I was puzzled at some details required – date of birth,
nickname, that sort of thing. The operator was a
swarthy man with gap teeth, a pencil moustache and
slicked down hair. Like a 1920s Chicago gangster.
His mouth was lop-sided and his eyes darted about,
as if he thought we couldn't see him. Choosing was
one of the hardest things I've ever done.

It'd have been great to ask for Lisa herself, but
the real Lisa – and, probably, a cloned one – would
have threatened me with death and destruction, I'm
certain. You'd think a person would be flattered.
Marius soon picked Lucrezia Borgia. He said that
contrary to legend, she was a beautiful and intelli-
gent Italian countess much loved by the citizenry;
she didn't poison anybody – that was her father,
the Borgia Pope, her husbands and their cronies.
He was assured she'd been modified to be sweet-
natured, though he commented to me that he'd
prefer a fiery witch any time. In any case, given the
time lapse since her death in 1517, he doubted if
much of today's version was original. He reckoned
he was quite safe.

Various suggestions were made for me, mostly
from the entertainment world of the recent past.
Among those who'd died sufficiently long ago for
authentic copies to be available were Emma Mirren
(her mother Helen was also in their brochure),

Sophia Loren, Jeanne Moreau and Liz Hurley. The latter looked most fetching, I must say, though her dress was held together by safety-pins – she didn't make the best of herself. In truth I'd never heard of some of them: the Atlantic's a big pond, even today. They were probably free, Marius whispered, because their popularity was somewhat overblown – he urged me not to compromise, but to take only what I wanted. I declined them. The operator sighed and flicked back a few decades. Then we struck pay-dirt.

How about Mae West? he asked, and which age: when she was first famous and wrote dirty plays, or in later years as a wise-cracking old madam? He played a clip from Myra Breckinridge *as a taster. Or Marlene Dietrich, blue angel in fishnet tights and topper, or mature in spangled gown? Elizabeth Taylor, who smouldered adorably, violet-eyed and svelte (Cat on a Hot Tin Roof) or black-browed and busty (Cleopatra)? Or if I preferred an intellectual beauty, the Jodie Fosters are perennially successful. I began to feel spoiled for choice.*

Special permission was required for certain models, the operator said, and moreover we'd left it a bit late. The Margaret Thatchers were a bit prim and unfortunately, since they were exact copies, would never stop talking, but were much admired by grey-haired gents in their fifties. At this I swore under my breath; the operator must have heard me, for his hopeful expression turned sour. They go back further in history, he continued, but was beginning to sound desperate. Queen Marie Antoinette is a terrible flirt and specialises in feeding her clients cake. Alexander's Persian queen, Roxanne – widow

*of the defeated Emperor Darius – is a coquettish
little minx, but then she married in turn the two
greatest men in the ancient world, which can't have
been easy. And the Empress Josephine, wife of
Napoleon, is both regal and rampant. A certificate
of good health is required for a night in her company. They didn't want any heart-attacks on the
premises, though doctors were in attendance.*

*I asked Marius in a whisper what would happen
if I wasn't hetero. He chuckled and said he had
another vidphone number and I could choose any
number of desirable partners – Oscar Wilde (though
he was a bit sensitive, poor soul), Rudolph
Valentino, Rock Hudson and Quentin Crisp among
others. It was particularly helpful when, as in Crisp's
case, the body had been left to medical science so
the NT was a precise copy, right down to the witty
one-liners. Some stars, hetero in life, had been
genetically altered to accept the attentions of gay or
bisexual men. The Arnold Schwarzeneggers, David
Nivens and Clint Eastwoods in particular went
down well. In fact it got confusing as other versions
of the same men were also the biggest earners at the
women-only club in Knightsbridge, the Hen Party.*

*It's a pity no current names are on the list.
Copyright is held on all living stars by the individuals themselves, who naturally insist on their
uniqueness. No clones for them, and under
European directives their estates have exclusive
rights for seventy years after their deaths. So I'm
stuck with an effort of memory; but then, this is a
fantasy world made flesh, so the images of my adolescence seem entirely appropriate.*

The operator was becoming impatient. I asked
for a few more old names. I settled on American
nostalgia: I chose Marilyn Monroe. God knows what
I'll find when I meet her, but apparently she's been
made from the original Marilyn's gall-bladder so
she's absolutely authentic. If nothing else –

Strether became aware that the young student, Fenton,
had made a remark which required a response. They
were seated at high table in the refectory. The wood-
panelled walls displayed a dozen honours boards dating
back centuries, with letters picked out in black and gold.
Two had carved laurel wreaths – the dead of world wars.
In the body of the hall hundreds of pupils bustled,
dressed in regulation brown tunics with the school badge
on the shoulder, and simply-cut skirts or trousers.

The dominance of graceful blondes of both sexes was
overwhelming. The largest minority after that resembled
Marius or Maxwell Packer – trim, dark-haired. Lisa was
similar – a mid-European style, striking by contrast with
the generally Nordic preponderence. A few were of Asian
origin, neat-featured and black-haired. Strether looked
closer. Not one was as dark as he or she might have been.
Given that Winston, the records clerk, had been at work
only ten years, it was unlikely that their light skin colour
was his doing. It must be a policy of long duration.

'I beg your pardon,' Strether mumbled. 'Would you
repeat that?'

Fenton did not blink. 'I asked, sir, if you have children.'

'No, I don't. My wife and I were never blessed.'

'May I ask why not? I apologise if this is personal, sir,
but I have an essay to write on the contrast between
European social attitudes and those of other cultures.

Here, among the upper castes, it is regarded as important to procreate. Either one should ensure that one's genes are passed on, cleansed or enhanced as necessary, or an improved embryo can be used. Provided a stable environment pre-exists, naturally.'

Strether put down his fork. 'May I ask how old you are, Fenton?'

'Eighteen, sir.'

'Then perhaps *you*'ll tell *me*. Why, in a world where global resources are under such pressure from excess population, should anyone bother with offspring – apart from untrammelled biological urges, that is? Why isn't childlessness admired?'

The young man stared at him coolly. In three years' time after university he would be a candidate for the civil service exams, Strether realised, and almost certainly would qualify as one of the favoured breed ready for the highest ranks. A couple of decades or so from now, he could be running the country.

'Quality, sir. If there are to be restrictions – or discouragements – they should apply to the lower castes. You are right, Ambassador. We don't need *more* people. We do need *better* people.'

That was unarguable. Strether tried a different tack, his tone jocular. 'So what did you do with your eleventh birthday printout?' he asked. 'Pin it on the wall alongside the biker posters?'

'Certainly. Though it's mainly a collection of numbers – hair colour and such. And my posters are of politicians and statesmen. My surname's Gladstone-Bismarck.'

'Heavens. I might have known. What was your IQ?'

The boy smiled. 'Enough,' he answered.

Strether reached for a stoneless peach and peeled it with a small knife. On his other side the Mistress was engaged in a lively discussion with Lisa whom she was trying to persuade to become a school governor.

'Tell me,' Strether pursued, 'how do they make sure your potential is fulfilled? I mean, in the USA that's left to chance. Yet we still have some of the world's greatest writers, musicians, artists and so on. On the whole we muddle through. We call it freedom. But here in the Union you go to such trouble to improve on nature. How do you make sure it's not wasted?'

Fenton allowed himself a superior smirk and indicated the children scurrying below them with full trays, each searching for an empty seat. 'You are in the right place. Here you will find the key, and in higher education, Ambassador. Our leaders try not to leave anything to chance, at least for the upper castes.'

'How do you mean?' Strether filled his mouth with yellow-fleshed peach and chewed appreciatively. Whatever criticism might be directed at the human outcomes, genetically modified fruit was delicious.

Fenton put his knife and fork down on his empty plate, neatly parallel. 'A great deal of trouble went into my conception, sir,' he replied seriously. 'My parents come from political stock. They required a permit – that took several years, since the political clan is often over-subscribed. They had to show they were a loving and stable couple. It is particularly important in fields such as mine, since statesmen with traumatic or unhappy child-hoods tend to cause havoc. I, however, was blessed, as you put it, with remarkable parents. And because I was an agreed conception and within quota, I qualify for free health care, recreation and education, right up to the

point when I can earn my own living. Most children here
are the same – allowances, grants, additional payments,
are quite generous. The taxpayer ensures that my breeding is not wasted. The taxpayer is the ultimate gainer.'

'Quota?' Strether was mystified.

'There is a quota – a limit – for the most popular pro-
fessions. Or for those where we simply don't need
many – ballerinas, for example. As you have in the USA
for immigrants. You are familiar with such selection
processes, Ambassador, though you may not be aware of
it.' The boy's pale eyes had a gleam of triumph.

'I see. Supposing, then, that you had been born out of
quota. And yet you wanted to be a politician. What
then?'

'That doesn't happen among upper-caste families. It
did in our grandparents' day, but not now. People struggled, sir. They had no help. That system still applies for
people born into the lower caste who, shall we say, wish
to rise above their station. Unless they aim for a shortage
activity.'

'It doesn't seem to bother you, Fenton.'

'What should bother me, sir?' The boy was icily polite.

'This lack of choice. This darned shoe-horn they use
on you. Supposing you wanted to be a musician? What
then?'

'But I'm *bred* to be in public service. That is my
nature. To serve the Union with pride, devotion and
incorruptibility. I have only the most rudimentary musical appreciation – sufficient to give me pleasure at the
opera, where I am likely to meet others in the same occupation, but not to earn a living. And you should
remember, sir, that the child whose nature and nurture
coincide will be both a high achiever and very happy,

contented and fulfilled. I'd feel "shoehorned" if I were forced to function against my genes. Our system's designed to ensure that can't happen.'

'You approve, then?' Strether was grave. 'No more hit and miss?'

'Certainly. We are building here the greatest society the world has ever seen. And some day, without undue modesty, I hope to play my part.'

'What's happened to the rebelliousness of youth?' Strether finished the peach and wiped his fingers.

'What rebelliousness – sir?'

The boy had such unshakeable confidence that Strether felt quelled. For the next few moments he answered questions about life in Denver and the attitudes of his countrymen and women to leisure drugs, selective abortion and financial crime. The tone of the questioning depressed him further. The boy seemed to think that it was not enough to enunciate a problem; action must follow to obtain the desired outcome. More than once the Ambassador found himself protesting, 'It's not as easy as that,' only to be met with that baleful glint, as if he were confirming the young European's moral superiority; and that such was the boy's intention.

The coffee appeared. The boy offered cream and sugar. 'Let me put it like this, sir,' he said emolliently. 'My great-great-grandfather served under Margaret Thatcher. She was remarkably decisive and would not tolerate discursive interventions – fools, in other words. She approved of those who brought her solutions, not problems. We have taken that several stages further. If we have a shortage occupation, we allow lower castes to fill it at least temporarily – and the pay and allowances will rise – but we also increase the permits available and request suitable parents to select enhancements in that direction. It's quite straightforward.'

'And what happens to the lower castes when the new NTs come on stream?'

The boy did not flinch. 'But that can take twenty years or more. By then the inserts may be ready for retirement. Long before that, frequently, they're keen supporters. Having shown a natural aptitude, and enjoyed high rewards and security, they want their children to be sure of the same. They'd like their offspring to be upper caste too. That means assisted conception. So they join the queue and are often fast-tracked.'

The boy spoke with the same earnest enthusiasm as Lisa had that first day at Porton Down, but with none of her anxieties. Strether wanted to prod harder, to ask the youth why anybody was permitted to manipulate the system for unworthier objectives; the fact that ice-cream taster Fred's younger child was an NT, and paid for, gave the lie to such ideals of seamless perfection. *Because they wanted to* would not be an adequate answer in a world so devoted to the common interest. It was, however, an expression of personal liberty, which Strether could easily understand.

But there was no time. The meal was over; the Mistress rose, clapped her hands for silence and crisply thanked the Lord for his bounty. Then she led the guests towards the door and the main hall where the parents were seated.

An hour later Strether and Lisa were making their farewells to their hosts and to each other. She would go back to the laboratory by Maglev. As he climbed into the electric car and gave Peter his instructions, Strether reflected that he had heard more truth from the mouths of babes that day than ever from Marius, Sir Robin or their friends.

And what he had heard had chilled his very soul.

The club was housed in a magnificent old circular edifice named after the consort of Queen Victoria. With its whitened pediments, upturned U-shaped windows, pink stone entrance and painted frieze supporting a flattened dome, the Royal Albert Hall in Kensington was one of the few locations large enough (after the Millennium Structure had blown down) to house the circus, orchestra, restaurants and hundreds of private boxes that made up the Toy Shop.

In the foyer Marius waited, resplendent in a milk-white multifibre tunic. Strether had decided on dignity and chosen navy blue with a fine pinstripe; now he felt under-dressed. The more so, for next to Marius was a fabulously caparisoned doorman dressed as Mr Punch, complete with a hook nose, hunchback and gross belly, in crushed red velvet and black knee-breeches. At his side sashayed an enormous Judy – loftier than a basket-ball player and three times as hefty, a man, surely – in striped pantaloons with an exaggerated ginger wig. The 'baby' she carried, wrapped tightly in grubby waddings, was used to batter arrivals over the head. 'Roll up! R-r-roll up! This way for the greatest entertainment in the wor-r-rld!' The entrance was lit by the flickering light of torches carried by strapping young men in leather loincloths and not much else. As Strether watched, agog, one put the torch into his mouth, licked the flames lovingly then blew a stream of orange fire safely over his shoulder.

'My God,' he muttered to the chuckling Marius as they entered, 'you didn't tell me it was like this.'

'It's a house of fantasy. Whatever you dream, you may have – that's the slogan. The design's based on the Cirque du Soleil who were such a hit here a century ago, with a pinch of virtual reality and the odd hologram thrown in – but mostly it's genuine, I promise.'

Within a few moments they were joined by Strether's young staffers, Matt Brewer and his companion, a red-haired Virginian, Dircon ('Dirk') P. Cameron III. Four adjacent cubicles had been booked, each with a private entrance; the four and their hostesses could, however, sit together at a balcony in the red-velvet-lined boxes to watch the show.

Marius opened his door and bowed low to the unseen personage inside. A rustle of silk and a low purr, or so it sounded, greeted him. The door was then firmly shut. The staffers had vanished further down the curved corridor, pulling and punching each other like little boys. As he opened the door of 31C Strether lifted his head and sniffed in thrilled anticipation. The perfume was old, almost forgotten and no longer on the market, but deliciously unmistakable. When asked what she wore in bed, Marilyn Monroe had answered, 'Chanel No. 5.'

'Hi! I'm Marilyn.'

She was, too.

Strether took a step back and gaped in utter amazement. Marilyn in a slinky black sequined dress, halter-neck and backless, which she had worn at the Golden Globe awards in Hollywood in 1962 when she was the world's most popular star. Marilyn slim and enchanting, not the blowsy overweight moll of later times shortly before her death at thirty-six, but at her finest.

Marilyn with swept-back tresses, off the face, the purest
platinum blonde, the skin alabaster, her blue-grey eyes
emphasised by thin black eyeliner and lashes like paren-
theses, the beauty spot on her left cheek highlighted like
a breathtaking full stop. Marilyn with not a single piece of
jewellery except tiny drop sapphire and diamond earrings nestling at the angle of her heart-shaped jaw.
Marilyn. Marilyn Monroe.

'And I'm all yours for the evening,' she breathed, as if
reading his thoughts.

'My God,' Strether muttered again, and reached for a
chair.

In an instant she was at his side, all solicitude. 'Oh!
You poor man. It's such a shock. Didn't you see me on the
video?'

Strether shook his head. He had spent too long trying to
decide between *Destry Rides Again* and *Cleopatra*. But as
he accepted the glass of champagne and rapidly drained it,
he took in those extraordinary wide eyes, filled his lungs
with her presence, and knew he had chosen – magic.

'You – you look just like her,' he said weakly. 'You
sound like her. You move the same, exactly. It's uncanny.'

For answer Marilyn turned and wiggled her remark-
able curves. 'I *am* her. You gotta understand. Do I call you
Bill? And I adore your accent! I'm not a copy. I'm *her*. Me!
Oh, it's so complicated. Don't worry about it. Just enjoy.'

The gown was so restricting she could barely walk.
She wiggled closer and refilled his glass. In the spangled
high-heeled sandals her toes were healthily pink, the
nails painted scarlet. Strether felt his throat contract with
panic and adoration. Behind them the lights dimmed. A
squat, muscle-bound man, his body shiny with oil, mallet
in hand, strode out on to the circular stage below and hit

a huge brass gong. He was followed by the fire-eaters, whirling blazing batons. Marilyn jumped theatrically. 'See, the show's about to start. Shall I order some supper?'

Strether still could not stir. He stared. 'You look as if you would glow in the dark,' he said at last. She answered with a hectic squeal. 'Yes! That's right! That's what they said about me in *Gentlemen Prefer Blondes*. Luminous, they said. I was in love – with Joe. I guess it showed.'

For the next half-hour Strether, shaking inwardly and forcing himself to breathe, sat with Marilyn's thigh pressed up against his own. He could feel the warm firmness of her flesh as she leaned across him to the plates, could smell not only the perfume but the fainter, more enticing pheromone of the woman herself. Her red-tipped fingers offered him goujons of fish, sushi prawns, a sauce-coated spare rib, which he refused; she did not seem to mind but wiped his chin with a napkin, all the while chatting inconsequentially in that breathy, earthy voice. She kept his glass well-filled, but his heady intoxication was not due to alcohol.

Below them the strong man and the fire-eaters completed their act and retired to loud applause. Tumblers ran forward and criss-crossed in the air, bouncing off hidden trampolines so high that they could peep expressionless into the boxes above. Skimpy costumes of gold and silver lamé with an overlay of macramé gave them the appearance of agile lizards. The next act was a pair of young female contortionists. Tiny lithe girls with olive skins, sheathed in blush silk from the top of their smooth heads down their pre-puberty torsoes to their nubs of infant heels. They writhed together like snakes, limbs slithering in and out and reappearing sinuously at impossible angles. Their joints seemed capable of smooth rotation through 360 degrees. Under any other circumstances Strether would have been glued to the performance. Indeed, when one particularly inexplicable manoeuvre resulted in a neat mountain of buttocks, face, buttocks, face, he sat back with an exclamation.

'Amazing, aren't they?' Marilyn agreed. 'Nomin and Chimed. Such adorable children. I don't know how they do it either, bending their spines over backwards like that. But they're Mongolian, double-jointed. They say it's natural, genetic.'

She snuggled closer to him and he could feel her full breasts pressing on his arm. 'You,' he choked, 'are not wearing any underwear.'

'Sure,' she giggled, and shook her shoulders so that he could see her breasts move. 'Never have done. I don't like to feel wrinkles.'

Gently she took the glass out of his hand. 'Let's draw the curtains,' she urged. 'A little privacy. And if I press this button here . . .'

Before Strether's startled eyes plush curtains swished silently across the balcony. The interior lights, rose-coloured, cast a delicate glow over Marilyn's arms and shoulders. The diamond earrings twinkled tantalisingly as she unclasped first one then the other and dropped them on the table. At that moment, behind her, a quiet hum came from the wall and a luxury *chaise-longue* slid out, smothered in cushions and a velvet throw.

Marilyn stood up. 'Here,' she murmured. 'Can you help me undo the zip on this dress?'

This could not be happening. Strether's mind jarred and struggled. Fantasy made flesh: it appeared only in dreams, never in reality. He would wake up in a moment, his face wreathed in wicked smiles, reaching out for a

caress that had vanished with the morning light. Stars
like Marilyn Monroe were fantasies: that was their purpose, the reason they flitted past, two-dimensionally, on
an oversize cinema screen. She was correct – the likeness
was uncanny simply because it was no likeness, no copy,
but absolutely the real thing. It was not her, but the manufacture of this – thing that was so creepy. And yet, as he
gazed mistily at that swaying back, that superb backside
and the shimmering black sequins over the haunches
touched into flame by the shaded red lamps, his heart
melted. No mechanical doll, this. A live human being,
with every scrap of the vulnerability, no doubt, of the
original whose psyche had been so fragile. With feelings,
emotions. Hopes, even.

Strether's arm trembled as he reached up. The metal
was warm to the touch and he could feel the smooth,
dewy flesh behind it. Then he dropped his hand.

'No, I can't.'

'Oh, it's not stuck again, has it? It's always doing that.
What a nuisance.'

'No. It's me – I can't. Not tonight, anyway. Too much,
too much. I'm sorry.'

Marilyn dropped to her knees beside him. 'No, it's me
that should be sorry. I overdid it, didn't I?' Her breasts
this time were against his legs, her lovely arms and
creamy shoulders spread over his lap. Clumsily he tried
to get her to stand. Then he knew what stopped him.

'No, it's not that. You are truly wonderful. But – I have
a lady friend, and I guess I'm half in love with her. This' –
he gestured about him, at the empty bottle upside down
in its ice bucket, another ready to open, the scattered
food remains, the inviting bed – 'this would take far too
much explaining.'

'But you don't have to tell her,' Marilyn pouted. One strap had slipped sideways and Strether found himself gazing down a spectacular cleavage. The desire to put his hand down it and lift out a gorgeous breast was over-whelming.

'I'd have to explain it to myself. My conscience. My dear,' he added, as if mild affection would reduce the heady intimacy.

'Well,' Marilyn continued dubiously, perching on the *chaise-longue*, 'we can just talk, if you'd prefer.'

'Thank you.' Strether found a handkerchief and mopped his brow. He hoped she would not notice or comment on the substantial erection her closeness had caused.

'What would you like to talk about? I could tell you about my film career, and how I was voted Best Young Box Office Personality of 1953. That was my best time, I reckon. Or how I met Khrushchev – he stared and stared! I could sing you "Happy Birthday", though I'm not in the proper dress for that – we checked your birthday and it's not today, is it?'

The open, solicitous expression on her face touched Strether, who answered her with difficulty.

'I can't get over it. You're right – you *are* Monroe. Except, come on, *you* never met Khrushchev. Not you personally. That's just a line.'

Again that naughty giggle. 'Yeah. I don't even know who he was. Seen pictures of him – glad I didn't have to kiss *him*.'

'But I don't get it. Wouldn't you rather be yourself?'

'But I *am* me. I'm not a person dressed up as me. This is me – this flesh, these legs, these bosoms. Pretty well, anyway.'

'What do you mean?'

Marilyn tilted her head and frowned exquisitely. It made Strether's heart turn over.

'The body, that's me. But my life's been much easier than – hers. Nature versus nurture, in my case.'

Strether had heard that before, earlier in the day. 'So, how are you different?'

'Oh, for example. Marilyn was abandoned by her mother when she was eight and had a miserable time in foster homes. And she was – abused. And not believed. So her approach to men wasn't simply inherited – it was learned. I had to learn it too. The behaviour, at least. Though it must have been genetic, up to a point: her own mother had mental breakdowns. I get badly depressed some days just as she did.'

'You do? About being a clone?' It slipped out. Strether could have bitten off his tongue. Marilyn went white.

'I'm not a clone . . .' The glowing head twisted and turned, then a tear slowly formed and tilted over the lid and down one cheek. 'Oh, why pretend? We all are. Not the circus – the Toys. That's what we are. Clones.'

She flapped her hand at the curtain. 'They're out-landish, those human rubber creatures, yet they're normal – born in a bed to a mother, not in a test-tube. We're the freaks. You think so, don't you? I can see it in your face. You don't need to lie to me.'

Strether felt helpless. Her distress was quite genuine. Then she tossed that ravishing head with a loud snuffle and turned on her heel.

'So: what if I am? Does that make me worthless?'

He offered his handkerchief but it was declined. She sniffed and wiped her eyes on the back of her hand, leav-ing a tragic smudge of mascara on the pearly cheekbone.

'How many of you are there – I mean, how many Marilyns?'

'Ten – no, nine at the moment. I'm Marilyn Six. One just retired. I'm next.'

He goggled. 'I don't get it. How old are you? Do you have to retire when you reach the age of her – death?'

'No, no. In that case I'd have disappeared years ago. That'd be too expensive – they'd get only twenty years' work out of us. I'm forty-six. We retire at fifty. That's the rule for this model.'

'What happens then?'

Marilyn's face crumpled and the tears really began to flow. Mutely Strether offered the handkerchief once more; this time it was accepted. 'I d-don't know,' Marilyn sobbed. 'That's what makes me so de-depressed. They vanish. Betty – that's what we called the Marilyn who's just gone – Betty promised she'd be in contact, and she hasn't been. We've not seen hide nor hair of her.'

'Do you have a nickname too?' Strether was eaten with curiosity.

Marilyn nodded dumbly. 'Y-yes. I'm Marty.'

'Hi, Marty, pleased to meet you.' Strether felt idiotic, but was relieved when Marilyn – *Marty* – bent forward and shook his hand. Her fingers were wet with her tears. It seemed safe at last to leave his chair and sit beside her. He put his arm round the heaving shoulders and hugged her. Like a brother.

'You know, in a crazy sort of way, that makes it easier for me,' he remarked quietly. She looked up from blowing her nose, uncertain whether that meant she had to resume the Marilyn pout. 'I mean, I'm in my fifties, so you're nearer my age than Marilyn was. I must say, you look superb. Wearing well, Marty.'

'Thanks.' She gulped, but the sobs were finished. 'Fraying a bit at the edges. D'you know, I reckon Marilyn was jinxed by some of her doctors. I'm cloned from her gall bladder, yet there's nothing wrong with mine. I reckon there wasn't much wrong with hers, either, but some knife-merchant cut it out anyway for the publicity.'

'Here, let me pour you a fresh glass.' He lifted the champagne bottle. 'Come on, let's talk like mature people. My head's bursting with questions. Would you answer a few for me?'

She sniffed again, hiccuped like an infant, then sipped the frothy wine. 'Sure. You're a gentleman. And an American, like she was. I love her, y'know? It feels like she was my mother. She never had children – she wanted them so much. Me neither – not allowed in this job.'

'Do you have any choice about the job, Marty?'

'You kidding?' Her voice had resumed its sensual breathiness. That, at least, came naturally to her. 'I'm bred for it. I only exist because the Toy Shop exists. It's very successful, you know. We make terrific money. Live in top-rated furnished apartments. Hairdressers, clothes, holidays, all found. At least, as long as we're fit for work.'

'A high-class brothel? That's what it is. Splendid, mind-bending. But no more. How do you feel about that?'

She shrugged. 'I'm a very high-class tart. Look, Bill, it's how we're raised. From childhood, in the Toy Shop nursery. I'm *proud* to be who I am. I make Marilyn Monroe available to paying guests – most of whom aren't half as darling as you – but it's my role in life to make them happy in a *unique* and *positive* way. What's wrong with that?'

Her justification was painfully close to that of the upper-caste NT, Fenton. Strether groaned inwardly.

Marty had regained the initiative and knew it. She gestured at his crotch, now detumescent. 'You weren't immune. And if you come another night, maybe I'll persuade you.'

'Will you get into trouble because I wouldn't?' he asked anxiously.

'Silly boy,' she laughed throatily. 'Who's to know? This box isn't wired, I checked before you arrived. You can boast afterwards as much as you like. And no, I get paid the same, as long as I have customers.'

She rose and pushed the button to draw back the curtain. Musical snatches filtered into the box along with a brilliant green light. Above their heads in the recesses of the dome, six trapeze artists in white leather thongs clung upside down to their swings, flew in arcs and wheels, hands reaching out to clasp, hold and release. The breathtaking display of power and absolute trust, the sinewy limbs, the beauty of their strong bodies glistening with sweat, moved Strether more than he could say.

Marty's voice was wistful. 'Marilyn used to say she wanted to be an artist, not a freak. So that's what I try to do – be an artist.'

He took her hand in his. 'Marty, you're an amazing woman,' he said quietly. 'I don't mean Marilyn, I mean you. But how do you cope – really? How does it feel to be exactly the same as another person? Even if you rationalise, by thinking of her as your mother?'

Marty sounded far away. 'I'm not exactly the same. Nobody ever is. Like, I'm taller than Marilyn because we eat better. And the newest Marilyn, Debbie, our baby who was born last year, has those pale eyes which people prefer now. That's a deliberate change, but it's only fashion. And our upbringing ain't the same, as I explained.

Nobody beat me as a child, poor thing. My heart goes out to her, y'know?'

Strether nodded wordlessly. Marty continued, 'And then, if you consider, no human being's ever a replica of another. The fact that Debbie and I have virtually the same genes doesn't stop us being two people. We both know about the existence of the other, see? So you work secretly on having a little bit of yourself inside that's just – *you*. You differentiate, in private anyhow. Otherwise you could go nuts. In fact it's harder for those models who are unique – they've nobody to talk it over with. Betty and I used to discuss it a lot. Oh, I do miss her.'

The trapeze artists had been replaced by a thundering band of clowns and acrobats in striped vests and over-sized dungarees. Strether glanced past her and was reminded of the Bacchanale in Venice of which he had seen a video. He pointed at the spectacle.

'We're all performers, Marty, all seeking our identity. You seem to have a clearer idea than most people of who you are. I've never met a – a proper clone before. Not one who'd talk about it, anyhow. I keep being told it doesn't happen.'

At this Marty's eyes opened wide and the beautiful mouth broke into an unladylike hoot of laughter. 'They're having you on, Bill. It's done all the time. Not for the upper castes – they take care to ensure they're differenti-ated in the test-tube, in one or two cute details. Then they can breed again with impunity. But there are thou-sands of cloned toys in clubs like this throughout the world. Didn't you realise?'

Strether was dumbstruck. Marty, her expression grim and upset now, pressed on. 'Toys, human toys. Like

Crufts with dogs. They can be a lot weirder than here.
And – scary – you know what happens with interbreeding. Things can get nasty.'

The two held hands tightly as Strether shuddered.
Below them the clowns were tumbling cartwheels,
squawking grotesquely, in a mad parody of the acrobats.

Marty tipped her glass back and emptied it down her
throat. 'Clones are everywhere, Bill. Open your eyes.
Security guards, identical, down to being brain-dead.
Footballers, jockeys, pop-stars. Find an outstanding type
and you can be sure there'll be a dozen in a decade or
two. The joke is, it takes years to bring them to maturity
to start earning their keep. Whoever can speed up that
process'll make a fortune. So the money-men are forced
to second-guess tastes far ahead, and often they get it
wrong.'

'Not in your case, though,' Strether commented. At
that she grinned and planted a chaste kiss on his cheek.

A pair of wild-eyed heads peered round the curtain:
Matt Brewer and Dirk Cameron. Matt appeared to have a
lady's silver shoe jammed on his crew-cut. They winked
at the Ambassador and Dirk made a crude remark. Both
were then dragged from behind and vanished. Of Marius
there was no sign.

He rose and stretched, reluctant and fascinated. 'I
think I should leave you in peace, Marty. But if I come
back again, may I see you?'

'Sure. And it'd be a pleasure, Bill.' She treated him to
a dazzling, incandescent smile and he took her in his
arms, for a melting, precious moment. When he stepped
back her eyes were brimming. 'But don't leave it too
long.'

Chapter Eleven

'And that, Ambassador, is China.'

Colonel Mike Thompson swept his baton towards the shimmering distance. The sky was a steely white, as if it had never known night, or rain. The earth had an exhausted, drained appearance, testament to endless beating by a brutal sun. Marius and Strether squinted and shaded their eyes. On their shoulders and the crowns of their wide-brimmed hats, the heat was an oppressive blanket that threatened suffocation. The thin air made Strether pant.

'Used to be a sea, this,' the Colonel remarked. He and his guests walked slowly back to the hoverjeeps. Their soldier escorts, squatting in oblong patches of shade, jumped to their feet and adjusted their Eurocorps blue berets. 'Hard to credit. Same sand as on a beach. We often pick up sea-shells or fossils which are obviously aquatic. We've quite a collection back at base.'

Strether mopped his brow. His skin was sticky and itched; his mouth knew how a dry-roasted peanut felt. The temperature must be 50°C. 'Shows you what climate change can do,' he murmured.

The Colonel seemed to conserve energy by instinct. Strether envied the loping, rangy man in his forties whose body sat easily in his khaki shirt, whose skin was tanned like leather, the eyes behind their reflecting shades narrow and observant. 'Meteorites caused this lot,' the Colonel answered. 'Not our fault, this time. D'you know, there's enough carbon dioxide in the atmosphere to put global temperatures up another two degrees next century? One of the most durable compounds known. Shove it up there and it'll last almost for ever.'

They were somewhere not easily identifiable, in the no man's land between what had been the Russian Federation and the high steppes of the Chinese Republic. Strether and the Prince had landed by fastjet at Alma Ata. A sardonic poster in the airport foyer announced, 'The end of civilisation is here. Get your shots at Dr Krapov's clinic. American nurses.' A short hop in a battered Mitsubishi 838 had brought them to the frontier town of Kashi. From the position of the sun, they had then headed east. The distant mountains were massive and had snow on their peaks. Beyond that, however, he was lost.

'How long,' Strether asked weakly as he climbed into the Colonel's hoverjeep, 'would a man last out here?'

The Colonel shoved the gearstick and pressed buttons. Mini-jet engines hummed and the vehicle rose a metre into the air, hovered in a whirling cloud then took off, skimming the dunes. Behind them the four escorts arranged themselves in formation, Marius perched in the foremost, which happened to have a female driver. 'Sorry about the dust-storm,' the Colonel said. 'Latest model has a negative pressure filter, which keeps it at bay. Due for delivery next year. Now, your question? About four hours without water and shade, six with shade, though he could get hypothermic at night without shelter. With water and shelter, a fair while provided he doesn't go mad.'

'Christ managed forty days and forty nights.'

'Not here, he didn't. The Judean desert's a lot more hospitable. You a believer?'

'Of course. Most Americans are.'

The Colonel chuckled and glanced over his shoulder. Above the roar they could not be overheard. 'I am, too, in my own way. When you've seen as many dead bodies as I have, you do look for a meaning to life. But one doesn't bleat about it.'

'But the Union is officially God-fearing, isn't it?' Strether had learned to glean information wherever he could. 'At a school I went to not long ago the head teacher said grace both before and after the meal.'

'Yes. Absolutely. But what they actually believe is that the supreme being is mankind. They don't have much time for a deity, nor much need of one.' The tendons in the Colonel's forearms knotted as he strained to keep the clumsy vehicle steady. 'My theory is, people used to turn to priests to explain what they couldn't understand or couldn't control. Once mysteries are solved, and science brought reassurance – for example, ill-health's virtually abolished through the genetic programme – then God is redundant. A lot of religious belief wasn't much more than superstition, anyhow. Nothing more sophisticated has turned up in its place.'

Strether clung tightly to the side bars. 'People still have spiritual needs. If that wasn't so, why the queues at the Diana shrine and those miracles attributed to her? It's more than a hundred years since she died. And churches like Westminster Abbey are full.'

'Yeah, but it's hardly a traditional outlet these days. New Age, Buddhist, Tao, Dianist, Bahai'i, they're doing well. Love-ins, eat-ins, happy-clappy stuff. Everything but the guy you mentioned, Christ. Nobody's keen on suffering now. Putting up with it's not a virtue but a vice, or at least foolishness.' The Colonel swept his baton out at the waves of dunes. The hoverjeep, driven one-handed, veered and rocked. 'Out here, you see how insignificant we are. We don't control anything. Somebody does, though, I'm sure of that. Anyway, I'm not an atheist – that'd be tempting fate, given what I do for a living. Here we are.'

Strether was glad to be out of England for a while, though he would not normally have chosen August to visit the troops at the front. But his relationship with Lisa had taken a sharp downturn, which had left him ashamed and bewildered.

He had not meant to tell her. Marius had joked that the visit to the Toy Shop would not have met with her approval. But by temperament Strether was an honest individual. He had wanted a wholesome, open liaison with her, not least to show her respect. To himself he could confess that such respect had been dented by his eagerness to visit the infamous nightclub. But the ferocity of her response had startled and confused him.

He had seen no reason to lie. One evening after supper in Lisa's apartment near Porton Down she had asked, casually, whether he had yet managed to see any of London's night-life. So the admission had slipped out, quite without intent. In that instant he knew he had made a big mistake.

'You went *where*?' she rounded on him.

'The Toy Shop. It was Prince Marius's idea.'

She had jumped to her feet and paced furiously up and down the living room, her image appearing and reappearing in the hologram mirror with the frown line ever deeper between her brows.

'And you do everything that aristocratic idiot tells you? Have you no sense?'

'He's not an idiot, Lisa. He's a highly intelligent and thoughtful man, and he's a friend. And it wasn't what you think.'

'Oh? In what way? Which toy did you choose to play with, may I ask?'

He sat on the sofa, his drink untouched, aching with misery. 'Marilyn Monroe, if you must know. And she was lovely.'

'I'll bet, Bill. And how old was she? Sixteen? Twenty?'

It dawned on him that Lisa was jealous. That emotion he could deal with. 'No. She was older than you, Lisa. In fact she was worried about retirement – it's compulsory at fifty. That's what we talked about, mostly.'

'You *talked*? And, forgive me asking, was that all you did?' Lisa sat down suddenly. 'Oh, Bill. I shouldn't have said that. You're a free agent. You can do what you like. It's just that I thought – that is, you and I –'

He took her hand in his. The instinctive gesture reminded him of the last occasion he had sat like that, in the red plush-lined box at the Albert Hall. He squeezed Lisa's fingers and stroked the soft skin of the inside of her forearm, as she liked him to.

'We talked, Lisa. Nothing else. I promise. And that was because of you.'

Her hunched form relaxed a little. 'But what was it like? Wasn't it – spooky?'

He laughed shortly. 'Lord, yes. Weird, wild. Yet she was Marilyn exactly, right down to the voice and moods. And that quality of innocence and basic decency. She had that, too. She was an amazing person.'

'Of course she was Marilyn. She's probably an exact copy. D'you think it's only physical traits that are determined by our genes?' Lisa's brown eyes were blazing.

'Lisa,' Strether asked gently, 'now that you know I didn't *do* anything, what precisely do you object to? If I went there again, would you be angry with me? I wouldn't want it to hurt our friendship. I've become – well, more than fond of you.'

'I object – as a scientist – and as a woman, I suppose.' Her voice grated. 'Look, Bill, the genetic programme's set up for the public good. The Toy Shop is not. It's an aberration. It's what you'd call – oh, damn. *Cloning*. Endless repetition for nothing more than the most degrading form of entertainment. It's a prostitution of science, disgusting to people like me. Coarsening to those like yourself who patronise such establishments. You shouldn't go there. You shouldn't exploit those poor women.'

'They clone men for it, too, Lisa,' Strether responded bluntly. He paused. 'She mentioned Cruft's – what we've done to dogs for over a century. I saw a three-eared dog the other day. Two-headed ones will be next. We humans have a trivial side as well as a yearning for improvement, you know. That doesn't make it wrong. She said it happens all over. You told me it didn't, that it wasn't allowed.'

'Professionals like myself have always opposed it. No one of any distinction would work in those – factories.' Her face was raised to his, her expression anxious. 'D'you see how it cheapens my work? If those skills are spread about, unregulated, the whole business could get out of hand. No licenses like that were issued till twenty years ago. I was still at school, but others fought tooth and nail to stop it.'

'She's forty-six, Lisa,' Strether replied gravely. 'And she wasn't the first. It's been going on most of this century.'

'It is *wrong*,' Lisa insisted. 'Just because there's a demand, and the sensitivities of people like yourself get blunted enough to think it's okay, doesn't make it so. We shouldn't play games with science. It has a nasty habit of jumping up and biting us.'

Strether had never seen himself as a philosopher. He did not want to lose Lisa; nor, it came to him silently, did he want to lose the right to see Marty again.

'I dunno about that,' he mused. 'But I do know that in human advance you can never say, *This far and no further*. You scientists recognise no limits. If you see a horizon you go bounding towards it, even if the naysayers are calling "*Don't*." It isn't knowledge itself that's dangerous. It's what's done with it; and who's to decide what's good and bad about that? The Toy Shop seemed harmless enough to me. They're members of the human race too. Not robots.'

'They have no say in the matter,' said Lisa brusquely. 'They're brought up to it.'

'And you're not?'

'Christ.' Lisa rose and walked woodenly away from him.

Helplessly Strether reflected that one new skill he had acquired in Europe was that of reducing attractive women to tears. 'Darn it, Lisa. We're all programmed, I guess. Me too. I was brought up to be a cattleman, not an ambassador. I love what I do now, but some day I'll go back to my wide-open skies and my horses. And perhaps –' He stopped.

She stood still, her back to him. He could see her wiping her nose with a tissue. He had not intended to make a declaration, but the turn of events seemed to demand it.

'Oh, Lisa. Don't break my heart. I'm so very fond of you. I haven't felt this way about any woman since my wife died. Maybe this is premature, but – would you consider it, in three or four years' time, when I've finished my tour of duty here, – would you think of coming home with me?'

Lisa turned, her face set. 'I'm sorry, Bill. This isn't the moment. Not when those problems have resurfaced at work. I'm worried sick, I tell you. And I'm still horrified – I keep seeing you in that sleazy hole. If it didn't have any customers, it wouldn't exist.'

Strether opened his mouth to retort, 'Then neither would Marty,' but thought better of it. There was no answer to an argument like that. Most of life – of his life – was a market-place of willing buyers and suppliers. If nobody ate meat, his herds would not exist. They wanted it cheap so it was ranched in huge herds tended by a handful of microlight-riding cowboys. If dim fashion-followers like the woman on the tube filled their hours with novels instead of pets, then three-eared poodles and floppy kittens would never be born, or loved. If no one needed security then Rottweiler's guards and ten thousand camera operatives would be unemployed. But Marty was as much a real human being as Lisa – of that much she had convinced him – and, however vulgar and low-life, had been produced in much the same way. And, he suspected, was somewhat easier to deal with.

They had parted with a degree of coolness. Strether cursed himself that he had handled it so badly. Yet he also sensed that he had got away with something. Lisa had not asked him for a promise not to frequent the place again. Nor had she rejected him out of hand as the loving friend he ached to become. That blurted proposal lay on the table and could be resurrected by either party when the time was right. It had seemed wise, none the less, to take up the invitation to visit the frontier, and he had fled with a distinctly guilty sense of relief.

Both women, and the dilemmas they posed, would keep till his return.

The war rooms were situated in an ancient palace of red-brown stone. Around it had grown a plethora of prefabricated huts and concrete hangars and silos some ten storeys high, plastered with cryptic symbols and labelled with the Union flag in blue with gold stars. 'EU' in square white script was plastered over tracked vehicles, missile launchers and hoverjeeps, as if that might deter their loss or theft. The detritus of previous occupants was still detectable: on the doors were signs for Exit in French and Russian, and on the entrance portals were chipped carvings of Hindu gods, their chubby arms straining forlornly south towards India.

The Colonel, cheroot in hand, was highlighting locations on the screen map on the wall. A swarthy young adjutant kept notes. 'Where you stood today, Ambassador, used to be China. Cold War maps call the area Chinese Turkestan. Base camp here is in one of those former USSR republics, Kazakhstan. End of the world — or roof of the world, depending on how you look at it.'

'But it's not theirs now, is it?' Strether felt he ought to know. He could feel sweat running down from his armpits. At his side Marius was also smoking, cool in a navy suede tabard and silk shirt, almost oriental in style. No smoke detectors bothered them here. Not for the first time Strether envied his friend the chameleon reflex that enabled him to fit in with any company.

Colonel Thompson spread his rugged hand, palm downwards, and wiggled his fingers. '*Comme ci, comme ça*,' he answered. 'The Chinese consolidated their hold on Tibet ages ago and disposed of the last bits of Tibetan culture. Only remnants survive in Scotland and Canada. They saw off a Russian invasion in 2015, independent Russia's last gasp. After that the People's Army dug in, but in effect they conceded areas west of longitude eighty degrees. By that I mean it doesn't cause an international row if we carry out patrols, and there's little activity. But it can be tense – incidents flare up occasionally.'

'I suppose the fact that it's so inhospitable may have something to do with it,' Strether suggested.

The Colonel shrugged. 'That, plus the lack of any strategic or economic value. Geological surveys indicate oil deposits, but they're of no great value now. The uranium mines are worked out. And, despite the latest modern weaponry, the mountain ranges are an effective barrier. The air here is too thin for sustained air strikes and human activity is fairly restricted, too.'

Strether had found it disorienting to be in a high-temperature desert with snowy mountains within sight and yet feel breathless. It was not a pleasant mixture.

The Prince had been listening carefully. 'It can be useful, Colonel, to have a stretch of land between the great empires, no? In effect a sanitised zone?'

'Yes, that's right. But not demilitarised. And we still have to fit in with the regional autonomous government. Frontier life has its advantages, though. Some Union laws simply don't apply.' He grinned and flicked ash into an antique brass spitoon.

'So what do the locals do round here?' Strether asked. 'Farmers, or what? Nomads? Is there a modern economy, of sorts?'

'Certainly. Us, for a start – the bases bring in millions of euros, and our Russian hosts are only too desperate to help us spend them. This is R&R territory. D'you fancy a visit to one or two of the nightclubs?'

Strether swallowed and shook his head. 'No, thanks. It'd be misconstrued back home.' He was happy to let his host infer that that meant the USA.

The Colonel smiled and prodded the glowing multi-coloured map. He scrolled it down a thousand kilometres. 'Here,' he pointed again, 'where the climate allows it, is the Golden Triangle, source of most of our recreational drugs. Natural cocaine, heroin and marijuana, crudely grown and manufactured but still big business. Some goes west, a lot east. Do you indulge, Ambassador?'

For once Strether refrained from asking his companion to call him Bill. This dialogue, he felt, had an edge. Too much familiarity might not be desirable. 'No, I don't,' he said. 'And if I did, I'd prefer the genetically modified variety. Much safer.' A thought occurred to him. 'Are the growing areas affected to any extent by lingering radiation from the mid-twenties explosions? I heard there were some accidents near here.'

The Colonel scrolled back. Afghanistan and its neighbours slid away to be replaced by Outer Mongolia. 'The nearest were at Semipalatinsk and Novokuznetsk. And

Irkutsk further east. Doesn't affect the drugs merchants –
or if it does, they aren't saying. But pockets can be nasty.
I don't send young married troops out *there*.' He tapped
the screen to the right.

'But they weren't accidents, Ambassador. Not in this
region.' The young adjutant spoke for the first time.
Strether tried to place him. The name badge, Vezirov,
indicated Azerbaijan, one of the later Caucasian nations
to have joined the Union.

'Oh?' Strether was puzzled, but instantly alert.

Captain Vezirov checked with the Colonel. A silent
nod gave permission. 'In the west, and in Siberia, the
explosions may well have been accidental,' the adjutant
went on, his voice solemn. 'Given the ramshackle state of
the nuclear reactors, it's hardly surprising they went
hypercritical. At this distance in time we see those incidents as having occurred all at once, but in fact that
wasn't so. They took place over about five years or more,
until shut-down could be achieved. So the records say.
But in this region half a dozen units went up in the space
of *three weeks*.'

'How do you know?'

'It's local legend, and – for accuracy's sake, you understand, it was a while ago – our unit head checked. The
dates when electricity generation ceased at each location
are listed.'

'I think I'm missing something.' Strether was conscious of Marius's cool eyes on him. 'What went on? Did
one trigger off some kind of chain reaction in the others?'

'No-o. Then it'd have happened in a few hours.' The
adjutant paused, as if doubting the wisdom of enlighten-
ing their American visitor. Then he continued, slowly.
'Sabotage, we reckon.'

Marius and the Colonel exchanged looks. Strether struggled. 'But why? And who?'

'It suited somebody to paralyse the Russians at that juncture. You could argue that they never really recovered.' The Azerbaijani spoke impassively.

'One of the poorest regions in the Union now, that I do know.' The Ambassador found himself wishing he had absorbed better the reams of Union history downloaded on to his powerbook. 'The disasters had a big effect on Russian ambitions. Stopped 'em in their tracks. Who gained from that? There'd been fears that they were preparing to challenge the European Union, but those turned out groundless. And China must have been nervous of Russia's posturing. So was it the Chinese?'

'You're not a career diplomat, are you, Ambassador?' the Colonel remarked. Strether flushed and did not respond. 'Reflect for a moment on what you said. Who had most to gain, seventy-odd years ago, from the weakening of the economic and physical strength of the Russian Federation?'

'Well . . .' Strether cudgelled his brain. He looked up at the two soldiers and the Prince. It came to him, but was hard to believe. 'You did, I suppose. The Europeans. But surely the Chinese . . .'

'The Chinese don't care.' Marius was too obviously familiar with the arguments.

'And they don't need to,' the Colonel added crisply. 'Look. Two billion Chinese. They control nearly ten million square kilometres of territory, and though it's only half the area of the Russian Fed, most of China's land is useable. Much of Russia is permafrost or desert and fit only for prison camps. Take another chunk out through contamination, plus two generations weakened by

genetic defects – the figures are still secret, even today. It
mattered a lot, further west.'

The penny dropped. Strether half rose from his seat.

'You mean – the Union ordered the sabotage? The
European Union destabilised Russia by blowing up its
nuclear power stations?' He felt his mouth drop open.
The cynical, rehearsed discourse at the Forum Club in
Brussels, so obviously staged for his benefit, returned in
a rush. No wonder the 'accidents' had been so significant. 'But how could that be? Weren't you supposed to be
allies, of a sort?'

'We were. Like after the Second World War. Allies,
and rivals. And potentially, murderous enemies.'

'But – but it was bloody stupid. The contamination
fouled up most of Europe at the time, and since.'

'All war is stupid,' the Colonel responded swiftly.
'There's always some fall-out. Collateral damage, it's
called. Civilians who get in the way. The European
President of the time could be accused of over-
enthusiasm. He was Latvian, hated Russia. His loyalty to
the Union, however, was beyond question. That's why
Europe is the supreme free state today. Far more powerful
than the USA, if you don't mind me reminding you,
Ambassador.'

Marius intervened: 'And because of the way it was
done, there was no war. Just a barrel-load of – well,
regrets, you might say, plus offers to help.'

Strether did not feel able to reply.

'Anyway, that's why we are *here*.' The Colonel tapped
the screen; the picture jumped and buzzed like angry bees,
then settled back to Technicolor tranquillity. 'The enemy
is China, and always was. The Russians gave in eventually
and joined us. By then – 2060, wasn't it? – they were

reduced to a rump. Never again a threat to anyone. One minor advantage was that we were able to take over their prison camps. Turned out to be an unexpected bonus. You'll see one of those tomorrow, I believe.'

The Ambassador rose. His head ached. Frontier life might suit toughened individuals like the Colonel but the lack of creature comforts was not to his own taste. His crotch itched with heat and sand. His mouth was parched and his skin felt like singed paper left too long in the sun. He was probably badly dehydrated. So the Colonel's next words were like ambrosia.

'Enough lessons for today, Ambassador. You look done in. This is a punishing station for those new to it. The bar is open – can I offer you gentlemen a drink?'

It was after twenty-two hours. In the quiet of her laboratory, Lisa worked on patiently. In Strether's absence, the extra time available to catch up was a godsend. It took her mind off him a little, and what felt suspiciously like her lover's betrayal.

And the aristocratic Prince Marius was no better, though he could be excused as a European, brought up to accept genetic science's possibilities. His reputation as a man who appreciated beautiful women fitted also. The Toy Shop was famous for them. The Prince was almost certainly a member, and probably the instigator of the escapade. Like Strether he would probably defend the place as harmless and deride her view of it as sinister.

After Strether's expressed distaste for the programme, to find that he had so readily forgotten his principles as to patronise the Toy Shop had been a shock. Perhaps the American's sensitivities had begun to be blunted; that would be a tragedy, even if that came from her own insistence on the virtues of gene manipulation. Yet he didn't seem to see it like that. Rather, he had defended the production of 'toys' with some asperity. He appeared, indeed, to regard them as ordinary mortals – perhaps not *ordinary*, quite. But she had been brutally insulted at the suggestion that she, a top-range NT, might be in the same mould. Plus everyone else she helped to create.

Yet maybe Strether had a point. She pushed back her chair. If he were right – in part – the whole genetic programme could be judged as one. Her scruples would be worthless.

She bent her head once more. Her life's work. *Omnes unique sunt*. The eradication of disease. The enhancement of mankind's finest qualities. It *was* useful. It was essential. Bill Strether and Winston could be as critical as they liked – even four thousand genetic defects would have made the programme necessary, let alone more.

But if it went wrong – in however minor a fashion? She pushed buttons and gritted her teeth. Damn. That month two more files had vanished into thin air. Where were those results? Why did they each turn on chromosome 21? Did someone want them suppressed?

You are getting paranoid, she told herself crossly. It's the influence of that bumbling overweight foreigner. He was not good for her. He had disturbed her serenity. He had addled her head.

He had questioned her very existence.

The trip to the frontier had become an ordeal. Strether was accustomed to dry heat and a searing dust-laden wind in Colorado. Here the lack of oxygen was debilitating, while crude atmospheric conditioning inside official buildings added dampness and, he suspected, irritating spores to the air. Or perhaps despite bland denials there was a sub-atomic level of radiation present, to which he was sensitive.

The briefing had left him deeply unhappy. Brought up with the optimistic and ethical values of the United States in the twenty-first century, he was not prepared for the Europeans' worldly cynicism whenever affairs of state surfaced. In such matters he knew himself to be an innocent abroad. The loss of that innocence upset him profoundly.

The tale he had been told was not news to its other hearers. It should not have been news to him; that was probably his own fault. Yet, as he brooded, he was increasingly sure that the act of sabotage committed by Europeans on their Russian neighbours was not widely known. It was not, of course, the type of act any government would want publicised. Especially not once the Russians had accepted the inevitable and joined the Union; and, emasculated, had been welcomed, probably with that same snooty grace towards a tamed barbarian that Sir Robin, Prince Marius, the Graf and other NTs showed towards himself.

His own President, in all probability, was aware of the skulduggery the Colonel had described. James Kennedy, a keen student of international relations, would have been amused by – possibly, even admired – the decisive method by which the European Union had destroyed its most dangerous foe. But Strether was not amused. The fact that it had occurred in his father's lifetime and not his did not help him rationalise it.

The European Union had been modelled on his own

country's success. Its constitution had come increasingly to resemble America's, right down to the federal arrangements and elected president. Yet it had proved itself, if this story were true, far more ruthless than the USA had ever been. What had its founding fathers created? What kind of monster had it turned out to be?

Strether caught sight of his gloomy face in the mirror – no holograms out here. History, he remembered, is written by the winners. The Union had emerged the victor, and with credit. That alone would be held to justify what had been done.

A trip to a prison camp was hardly calculated to improve his spirits. But since this was the sole chance he might have, it would have been both churlish and a dereliction of duty to have declined.

Besides, the mystery of the boat people, which he had kept in the back of his mind since his appointment, remained unresolved. Some clues might be found here. Dispatches from Washington had mentioned them once more. Further boats had arrived, but again the occupants could offer only the vaguest recollections of their identity and provenance, and had died one by one. One batch had been tattooed with numbers and letters on the thumb, which immediately summoned up the historical comparisons of Nazis and gulags. Whatever inhumanity the Union could commit on its own citizens, Strether reasoned glumly, it was not beyond question that it could be done out here, in this forgotten land.

The Colonel volunteered to accompany him. Marius had made his excuses and stayed at the base; he said that as a parliamentarian he wanted to meet the troops.

Strether suspected he had a date with the woman driver, but said nothing.

'Godforsaken dump,' the Colonel commented, as his hoverjeep hissed to a stop before the gaol gates. After inspection of their passes they were waved through and parked in the shade before an administration building of bleached concrete.

The camp Commandant bustled out to them and shook hands vigorously. Beads of sweat stood out on his podgy face and on the flesh which bulged over his braided tunic collar. His accent announced he was a Scot. 'Good morning, Colonel, Ambassador. Please come this way. Tea? Tisane? Virgin Cola? We have everything here. We look after the prisoners very well, you will see.'

They followed him past watch-towers and thick-set RSS security guards with laser weapons at the ready. Strether pondered whether these guards were clones but could not decide: some black, some swarthy, they seemed drawn from several races. They would tackle an escapee without demur: that was beyond doubt. Despite the heat he shivered.

'We treat them with kid gloves,' the Commandant was saying. 'Single rooms, air-conditioning, satellite television in twelve languages. The Irish complain we can't get Gaelic programmes, but then they do have a choice about being here, I always say.'

They arrived at a workshop in a cavernous hall. Inside, its main activity appeared to be carpentry. The prisoners – all male – were listlessly planing wood, or drilling holes with old-fashioned hand tools. Two were assembling chairs, working lethargically. Dust hung in the air. Nobody reacted as the visitors entered.

'Remember that it isn't the policy of the European courts

to send people to custody,' the Commandant was explaining. He did not lower his voice or make any concessions to
the dozen listeners in the room. 'Normally conviction leads
to fines or to community service. No point in filling up
prisons. Our guests here tend to be rather special.'

Strether stared hard at the nearest convict. The man
was a thin individual of above average height with hair
that flopped into his eyes. A grubby leather apron protected his body; blue dungarees, a striped shirt and heavy
boots made up his uniform. As Strether watched, the man
became aware of his scrutiny. After several moments, as if
giving in, he paused to look up.

He had pale blue eyes, and under the greasy dirt his
hair was blond. The face had the same conformation as
many Strether had seen back in London and Brussels.
The bodily shape, as the man straightened briefly, was
also similar: spare and rangy but with strength and discipline. He was an NT, and of the highest caste. Of that
Strether was absolutely convinced.

The Commandant loudly invited their questions.
Strether pointed, but found it impossible to articulate the
notions forming in his mind. 'I was wondering,' he said,
'is the diet satisfactory? I mean, they all appear so – well,
limp.'

The blond NT bent his head to his task but Strether
could see a slight smile on his lips.

The Commandant grunted. 'The diet is excellent,
Ambassador. Better than many people eat back home.
And we keep 'em fit. You won't see any obesity *here*.'

The Colonel glanced sideways at the plump
Commandant, caught Strether's eye but said nothing.

'They learn not to waste energy,' the Commandant
added. 'Most of them are lifers, so there's no point.'

Strether turned and headed for the corridor. It was at best discourteous and at worst counter-productive to talk in such a way in front of the prisoners. Some instinct in him still wished to regard them as people. The Commandant followed with some reluctance, but stood holding the glass-windowed door ajar.

'You must understand, Ambassador. These men are the Union's most troublesome offenders. They have all served sentences in home prisons and on release have reoffended or ignored their parole restrictions.'

'Are they dangerous? Mentally ill? Murderers and the like?'

The Commandant pouted. 'This isn't a hospital. We're not dealing with psychopaths. No sex offenders, no. But some are murderers. Most of those you've seen are politicals.'

The Colonel strolled away down the corridor a few steps, baton in hand, as if to indicate to the Commandant that the military presence could be ignored. Strether seized the opportunity.

'Politicals? You mean you have political prisoners here? What – Chinese? Arabs?'

'No. Non-Union citizens get deported, if they have a state that will take them.'

'Dissidents?'

'That's more like it. Certainly. The best way to render them harmless is to cut them off from all contact. That's why they're sent to frontier prisons – we can minimise access. They serve their sentence where they can do no further harm. So, Ambassador, they're mostly Europeans. Some quite distinguished. Hence the kid-glove approach.'

Strether blinked through the glass. Nothing was ever quite what it seemed. The NT was watching him. He had been joined by another of similar appearance. The two were whispering. The roles of observed and observer had been reversed.

'But do they behave? Doesn't the concentration of so many "politicals" make it difficult to manage the prison? They must be a smart bunch.'

The Commandant's manner became confidential. 'Right. That's why the military are in charge, not us civilians alone. And the European Prison Service learned a lot from the troubles in the Maze, in Belfast. The diet contains everything they need. Including PKU. And they know it.'

'PKU?'

The Commandant looked taken aback. 'I'm sorry, Ambassador. I thought you were fully briefed.'

'Apparently not.' Strether allowed himself to sound annoyed.

The man's sweaty face went studiedly blank. 'It's a form of restraint. A non-artificial hormone. Chemical handcuffs, you might say.'

'You put something in the water? But that's horrendous.' Strether wished desperately that he could make notes. What on earth was PKU?

The Colonel was returning. The Commandant protested, 'Not at all. It's perfectly humane, Ambassador. These men – and women, in the female block – have been condemned, not to death, since we don't have capital punishment in the Union, but to life imprisonment. And life must mean life for the crimes they have committed. Effectively they've been banished. Our job is to ensure they don't escape.'

'Supposing they're innocent?'

The Commandant drew himself up to his full height,

which still left him an undignified few centimetres shorter than Strether. 'In your country, Ambassador, they'd have gone to the electric chair. Where's the compassion in that?'

Suddenly Strether wanted to get out as quickly as possible. He felt sick to his stomach. He twisted his head for one more look into the workshop. The two convicts had slipped from view. He took a step and peered around the door.

The NT was on the other side of the room as if waiting for him. Strether awkwardly raised a hand in farewell. With a half-smile the NT raised his hand also, but gave the Ambassador an old greeting, the thumbs-up.

And on his thumb were printed numbers and letters, clear as day.

Lisa Pasteur was wondering if she wasn't going mad. It was bad enough to be denied access to her own research findings. To be told they did not exist was ridiculous.

She had seen the genetic material, with her own eyes, under the laser microscope. She had emptied the unfertilised egg, sucked the fertilised nucleus with a fine pipette out of the embryo cell, tucked it tidily into the empty unfertilised shell and sealed the cut with a microsecond blast of electricity. She had coated the creation in a thin layer of agar to protect it from rejection in the host oviduct. It had been alive, then, with every chance of growing to maturity and birth.

But one chromosome kept disintegrating, for no reason she could fathom. The resulting foetus should have died naturally, quickly. It hadn't. It had survived, as had most of its identical copies, so painstakingly manufactured by hand by Lisa herself. Their details had been entered on the computer records, scrupulously, as always. Then they and their coded trail had disappeared.

She rose and rubbed her eyes. It was after midnight, the fourth night in succession she had worked late. She walked to the window and stared out at the yard. Behind her the lights in her workspace adjusted to her absence. The room became shady and quiet.

She did not know how long she stood there in the darkness, leaning her face miserably against the window-pane, nor what ragged conflicts were in her mind. But as a noise came up from the depot area four floors down, her attention was sluggishly reawakened.

This was a bit late for an out-delivery. Somebody else was working late. And what a strange lorry – huge, lumbering, old-fashioned. It emerged from below, out of her line of sight, then headed towards the back gates, which swung open without any checking of papers or swipe cards. That in itself was most unusual.

The back of the lorry was covered in a tarpaulin. Its contents appeared to be lumpy and shapeless. She watched idly, then with increasing horror, unable to tear her gaze away: for part of the lorry's hidden load, at its tail-gate end, was moving.

What she saw struggle free from under the tarpaulin was unmistakable. It was small, a child's arm, with five fingers and two thumbs. Prettily formed. And very much alive.

Chapter Twelve

Report of Ambassador Lambert W Strether to the Commander-in-Chief, 16 September 2099, encoded at 0930 GMT

Mr President, I apologise for the delay in sending this dispatch, but I wanted to ensure it could be put directly into your hand. It may be an excessive precaution not to trust any electronic media. But I do know that some subversive group has gained access to my private vidphone number – how, I can't tell – and if they can, so can the authorities. And though more open channels are suitable for factual reports, I felt a more personal overview might be timely.

As I indicated to you before, it would be easy to take everything here at face value. I confess that in many respects I am bowled over. One might think this vast agglomeration of disparate national states, the European Union, which so dwarfs the United States, could not possibly function with coherence and efficiency. Yet it does, and in fact – this is incontrovertible – it guarantees its citizens prosperity, peace and self-fulfilment on an unprecedented scale. From what I have seen, indeed, it may be said fairly to meet the admonishment of that great European, Voltaire, to provide for the greatest possible happiness of the greatest number.

That said, we Americans are steeped in what's missing. A nation composed originally of Europe's misfits, we pioneered a constitution that not only embodies the will of the majority in democracy, but protects the rights of everyone else, the minorities. We took that further by including the right to life in the thirty-fourth amendment. We fought a war over the rights of men – slaves – who were then barely seen as human. So any system that fails to ask about losers is bound to leave me unconvinced.

It's not a simple matter to figure out who the losers might be – certainly not here in the western regions, where I travel most. Poverty is not seen, or only rarely. The state chooses thoughtfully where it intervenes, and does so for the public good. Family life is the norm and is encouraged. The sick are cared for through public funds. And cured: life expectancy is an astonishing ninety-two for males, ninety-eight for females – far higher than ours. The work ethic is strong and widely adhered to, yet I've found no puritanical dislike of enjoyment; on the contrary, people do seem to be happy. Arts and sport flourish, professional and amateur. Crime is rare, Death Row unknown. Even mentally ill offenders are offered genetic therapy, and it succeeds better than one dare expect. States like Texas and Mississippi could do worse than copy.

But I am worried that notions of duty are so deeply instilled – especially among children – that free will is vanishing, and that can't be a good omen. The breeding programme – for that is how I see it, being a cattleman – produces remarkably able upper castes whose combined efforts are sure to continue the progress to which the Union is committed. But humility is not included in the qualities on offer, nor a willingness to admit to the risks of what they're doing. Instead the system imbues pride, at every juncture. Nor are they inquisitive about alternatives; nobody sees the USA as a desirable model any more. My own queries about the programme are met with disdainful denial, except from the odd isolated scientist whose own doubts are tinged by confusion and guilt. It's as if the programme itself is the new deity, whose existence and loving-kindness it is mortal sin to deny. They would put it otherwise – that the skills come from God, so why not use them?

Or maybe that's the effect on me of one particular group of NTs, in the civil and foreign service. Mandarins, they used to be dubbed, because they're inscrutable, self-perpetuating, effortlessly superior. They share more than an exclusive education. They run everything; wherever I turn whether in London or Brussels, smooth-faced men with pale blue eyes greet me. I am not being paranoid, Mr President. It is not just a matter of Nordic looks predominating as a form of adornment; it is genetic, and deliberate. Once I spotted it, I started seeing NTs of the type everywhere. And it's recently been quietly decided that only this brand of NT can proceed in future to the highest posts throughout the Union – the modern version, perhaps, of Margaret Thatcher's famous query, 'Is he one of us?' I was alerted to this by an NT of a different breed who was clearly unhappy about it, but it's excited no comment here in the press, not a word.

The door was flung open and Matt Brewer's crew-cut head appeared.

'Sir? I beg your pardon. I did knock.'

Strether slipped a piece of blank paper over the communiqué. 'Morning, Matt.' He did not invite the young man to enter.

The message was received. 'I can see you're writing, sir. Ballpoint and paper – must be important. I just wanted to welcome you back, and hope it was a good trip.'

'Thank you, Matt,' Strether responded courteously. 'If you invite the staffers to drinks in the reception room tonight – say, around eighteen hundred hours – I'll give them a debriefing. Did anything much happen while I was away?'

'It's been quiet, sir. Very hot and humid – the weather's getting worse. Three deaths from heatstroke in Islington.'

'Anything in the press about trouble? Like the incident outside here in July?'

Matt pulled a face. 'Exactly what you'd expect, sir – not a scrap.' He closed the door behind him.

Strether sat quietly and chewed the end of the unfamiliar pen. He read back a few lines then bent his head.

The press is not free, not as we know it. It must be censored, or controlled, in some way. I don't rule

*out self-imposed censorship. I shouldn't be sur-
prised (that paranoia again) if the media owners
aren't themselves NTs of the appropriate strand, or
their children are, so that promises of preferment,
or an alignment of interests, keep them on side. At
least one I have met, Mr Packer, fits this description.
But journalists ought to be suspicious outsiders, or
they are reduced to a mere propaganda machine.*

*No censorship office exists, and none would be
required if I am right. Freedom of speech is
enshrined in every code of the founding treaties,
but I'm not sure anybody here grasps what it should
mean. On several occasions I have become aware of
incidents of civil unrest, including the shooting of a
police officer by laser weapons which I myself witnessed. In New York it would have made the front
pages. Here, nothing. Why not? Who decided it
should be suppressed? And there's no underground
press to speak of – pop music papers and superfi-
cially anti-authoritarian youth culture magazines,
yes, but they come from the same stables. Hence no
independent media exist from what I can ascertain,
though the discovery that this must be true has
shocked me to the core.*

*Parliament ought to be the bastion of liberty. I
have brought forward plans to attend the
Commons. Of course I have met with the Prime
Minister and have been given open access to his
office and advisers – those darned blond NTs again.
He is not exactly the same model – less grand, more
swaggering in manner, but has considerable
shrewdness. I see no evidence of conflict between
the executive and the civil service – no falling out*

behind the scenes: they're in close cahoots, even though (unlike at home) the officials outlast each regime, and are supposed to be non-partisan.

But as for Parliament: its Members make headlines from time to time, a brief flurry, mostly on insignificant matters. Their main targets appear to be the love-lives or financial dealings of their opponents rather than any sober consideration of issues. News management is perpetual and effective there, too. I gather that the principles behind the genetic programme have not been seriously debated for over thirty years, while its annual estimates are passed on the nod. I shouldn't be surprised if the topic disappears from the parliamentary agenda entirely.

So we have an inbred élite riding on the acquiescence and contentment of their people, docile media, and a genetic programme the outstanding success of which has dulled the senses of all concerned as to the choices being made.

An example of the latter will illustrate my alarm. In at least one case, that of the underground workers, mutations are accepted (colour-blindness) which are regarded as useful but which tie the individuals to a narrow pattern of life for ever. They don't complain, that is true. A black clerical officer I met was deeply critical, hinting that certain racial characteristics (his own) were eliminated from the programme, with tacit official concurrence. He may have been exaggerating, since he had an axe to grind; but, perhaps not.

And then there are the political prisoners I saw in Asia; a separate report is appended for your eyes *only. I infer that somebody must object to the current regime, though on what grounds or by what means I have no further information, as yet.*

I confess that I am no nearer solving the puzzle of the boat people than when I arrived, though one or two clues have emerged which I am pursuing. You might ask the medics to check out something called 'PKU'. It could be helpful.

What I should emphasise, however, is that I have seen no signs whatever of this extraordinary society weakening or crumbling in any way. Our greatest ally is strong and indeed willing to be ruthless with its enemies. You have my report on the briefings at the frontier; I cannot vouch for the truth of what was alleged, and it is history now. That implies, and I believe it to be true, that in any conflict with the Chinese the Europeans would stand firm, which is excellent news for us in the USA. But I do not doubt that, given this secrecy and penchant for swift action, enemies within would also meet with short shrift. You will understand why I consider it wise to be careful.

Rereading this paper I realise that it sounds as if I am full of nameless and insupportable forebodings. That is not so; most of the time my staff and I feel at ease and totally safe. It is a pleasure to live without fear of crime, to breathe pollution-free air, to know that free, quality health-care is available even in an emergency. I can well understand your warning that some of my predecessors could not bring themselves to go home. But I am equally certain that this admirable exterior hides some rottenness of which its happy citizens are kept

*largely ignorant. I will endeavour to discover more
and will relay what I can find.
    Signing off at 11.31 GMT. Strether.*

Marius knocked on the door, waited for his mother's
high-pitched 'Come', adjusted his tunic as if he were still
a small boy, and entered her boudoir.

Princess Io was seated in a brilliant gown of irides-
cent blue at a dressing-table laden with a cornucopia of
cosmetics, potions, creams and pills. Before her was a
complex arrangement of hologram mirrors. She was peering into the front one and twiddling the focus. As her
son waited respectfully, she ran fingers with red-painted
nails over her cheeks, pausing at one faint hollow.

'I think he messed up, the surgeon,' she grumbled.
'There's a dark patch that wasn't there before. They get so
careless. Just because I'm a senior they think it doesn't
matter. But it does.'

Marius came forward, rested one hand on the silk-
covered shoulder and kissed his tiny mother on the other
cheek. He scrutinised the image in the hologram; it would
have been bad manners to have examined the old lady's
flesh too closely.

'I think they did a fine job. You look splendid. It helps
that the basic bone structure and conformation were
superb to begin with. Most women could never be as
beautiful as you, whatever their age.'

The Princess simpered. She reached for a perfume
bottle. 'Go on with you. Such flattery. It sounds as if you
want something from me, Marius.'

Her son pulled up a footstool and sat, so that his head
was roughly on a level with hers. He unfastened the top
flap of his tunic; the boudoir was warm. His mother's

muguet-des-bois scent filled the air, flowery and expensive. 'No, not really. I have come with an invitation. I should like you to meet a friend. He and I will be attending the debate next week on the budget. Might you like to come?'

The Princess picked up a powder puff and dabbed it delicately on her nose, the sole part of her anatomy entrusted to the knife but once, when she was a girl. That little upturn had made her slightly less Japanese, sufficient to satisfy her for the rest of her life.

'Darling, I don't think sitting for hours in the parliamentary gallery is quite my style. Unless you're speaking?'

'I thought you might say that. No, I haven't put in a request. And I want to take him into the Commons, not the Lords. But would you join us on the terrace for lunch, perhaps? Tuesday?'

'Now that is a much more entertaining idea. I haven't done that since you were last elected. Such a delightful spot with St Paul's opposite, and it will make my friends *so* envious. Shall I come about twelve?'

The Prince raised her fingers to his lips and kissed them.

'And who is this friend, might I inquire? You said "he". A younger royal, perhaps? Not a deadly dull politician, anyway.'

'Not this time. He's Lambert Strether, the American Ambassador appointed earlier this year. A delightful man. I am sure you will like him.'

'Darling, an American? That sounds too frightful. Will I have to work hard to make conversation?'

Marius considered. 'I don't think so. He's a bit unsophisticated, that's true, though I regard that as part of his

charm, frankly. He's a western rancher whom I have
rather taken under my wing. In more ways than one. But
he's upset by certain aspects of life in Europe; he won't
need much encouragement to talk. I suppose a foreigner
would be bound to stumble over some of the Union's
activities, but I find his comments quite intriguing. I'd
like your assessment of him. And he may bring his girlfriend. She's definitely special – a scientist, and beautiful
too.'

The Prince made no effort to leave. His mother glanced
at him, then scrabbled about until she found a bottle of
nail varnish from the vast collection before her and began
delicately to paint her nails, though it was not obvious
that they needed another coat.

'So, my dear son, you still enjoy being in Parliament?
It has not gone sour on you?'

'Not at all. Life is treating me extraordinarily well. I am
enjoying myself hugely.'

The Princess's laugh tinkled. 'You always did. You
have an infinite capacity for making the most of whatever
opportunities are at hand. And for ending up with everyone's approval, whatever scrapes you found yourself in. I
don't know where this ability comes from. Certainly not
me – I am far too conventional.'

'Maybe my father?' Marius relaxed, pushing one leg
out lazily under his mother's seat. He wished she were
marginally less conventional about smoking, but the
detectors were on and blinking at him.

'Your father, possibly. He was a bit of an adventurer in
his way. He would have loved what you get up to. We were
a strange couple, him with his penchant for a bit of swash-
buckling and me with my passion for the proper. It was a
love match, you know, Marius. We were very fortunate.'

The Prince smiled. 'So I'm an unusual mixture of genes, Mother. Maybe that's why I don't feel that I fit in, often.'

The Princess paused for a second in her painting, but did not lift her eyes to her son. 'What do you mean?'

'It's hard to explain. I've sensed it since my childhood. My schoolfriends and fellow Énarques would slip easily into whatever pattern was set for us. I, on the other hand, was mildly rebellious – not enough to make a fuss, and perhaps innately I did not want to draw attention to myself; your caution, maybe, Mother. But they had an unshakeable conviction that everything was tremendous, that progress was inevitable, and that nothing could ever go wrong in the world. At least, not as long as we were in charge. I didn't share that confidence. I felt . . . more irreverent and disloyal than I should have been. More like an outsider.'

'How strange,' his mother murmured. 'I can't imagine where you inherited that from. Does it show in your chart?'

'My genetic chart? I can't tell, it's too subtle for me. Anyway, on which chromosome is personality formed?'

'All of them, I expect.' The Princess laughed indulgently. She tapped Marius's knee. 'Which brings me to the obvious question, my dear child. Have you yet found anyone to marry? You should not leave it too late, if you want to use your own genetic material for reproduction. Even healthy men's sperm deteriorate, they say.'

'Heavens, Mother, you make it sound so clinical. No, I haven't yet found a partner. But you're right, the search has begun, just about. I need a woman who is intelligent and attractive, who is imaginative and supportive, but who is not *too* formidable.'

'Will you consider a royal?'

Marius snorted. 'No. With one or two honourable exceptions, such as yourself, Mother, they're too dim for words. We would really have to fiddle with the embryo if I were to have any sort of close relationship with my children. I'm fond of our cousin the King, but that's as far as it goes. An NT copy would not be my idea of a wonderful son.'

The Princess giggled and covered her mouth.

Marius rose. 'I have to go. I'm pleased to see you recovering so well, Mother. And don't worry, my marital status, or lack of it, is now in the forefront of my mind. You have given me food for thought, as ever. Take care.'

Winston Kerry, the records clerk, had no similar problems with smoke detectors. The advantage, he had discovered, of living in a small cottage on the surface in Stony Stratford was that the renovations could be made entirely to his specifications. When the builder had pointed out that a certificate of fitness for human habitation could be issued only if the gadgets were prominently installed on each ceiling, he had invited the man back the following week. Sure enough, white steel boxes had been placed where bureaucracy required and red spots blinked. That there was nothing inside was known only to Winston and his partner, who now offered him a Chinese cigarette.

Martin Kerry (for such was the surname he had adopted) was a rangy, thin man with a shock of ginger hair cut in a spiky crew-cut, a style made popular by punk designers of the previous century. He was a copy-editor for a publishing house and worked from home.

They had met five years before in a gay bar in Hampstead and had stood, beer bottles in hand, hips thrust forward, each transfixed by the other, until at last Winston had found his voice, made the ritualised inquiry about an AIDS test – the usual euphemism for sex, the disease itself having long been conquered – and had broken into a broad smile at the affirmative nod. They had left together immediately and had been lovers ever since.

Winston drew on the cigarette several times and blew a smoke ring. Then he ambled into the kitchen, collected a tray of Kentish mangoes, skinless bananas, mixed nuts, goat cheese and focaccia bread, with two cans of lager. One of the cans was handed to Martin, who had already eaten and was lounging on a leather sofa, his eyes half turned to the wall television, though the sound was low.

Winston sat at his side and they kissed for a moment, till Winston slumped back and began to eat a banana. 'I'm buggered at work,' he announced.

Martin switched off the television, helped himself to some nuts and curled his legs under him. He did not need to do more than listen. Winston, the extrovert, the wild boy, could then unburden himself in comfort, while Martin could offer calm and uxorious sympathy.

'What do you do, Marr, if you believe your employer's whole operation is deeply flawed? But you're stuck in the middle, and you know you're the best there is? Every day I do what I'm paid for. I keep their records, I adjust the parents' selections in line with the guidelines – not the published ones, but those that come through every six months or so. All I gotta do is reboot the computer so it throws up any genetic constructions that haven't been authorised or are no longer deemed desirable. Mine's not to reason why, and since I don't give a fuck about any of it, mostly I don't bother my head to find out what they think they're up to.' He halted, brooding, and gulped down half a bottle of the beer.

Martin stroked his arm wordlessly. His thin face puckered in concern.

Winston prodded the food. 'At times like this I wish I wasn't a veggie. I could eat red meat. I could *murder* somebody. Today I decided to test the instructions. I was watching for any anomalies – Dr Pasteur has been struggling and I'd like to sort it out for her. But what came up on the screen made even me yelp. What a shower they are.'

Martin cracked a green pistachio nut in his teeth, took out the kernel and fed it to Winston. He continued to do this until he sensed his partner relent a little.

Winston sighed. 'I knew that the IQ enhancement was to be restricted to specified A1 types. That's been the rule for some time, though by law it's available to everyone. The explanation, see, is that after three generations we've taken it as far as it'll go. Start creating too many geniuses and the result could be a lot of unhappiness. But the impact of the latest circular is that we are to take IQ *down* a little from here onwards. Two or three points. Undetectable to most recipients. Except for certain groups, who will be specially labelled – and they're to carry on going upwards. Somebody's trying to accomplish what nature itself can't do.'

His shoulders sagged, and he let himself slide gently down until his head was in Martin's lap, his long legs in their scruffy jeans hanging over the arm of the sofa. Meanwhile Martin broke off pieces of bread and cut slivers of cheese which he fed one at a time into Winston's mouth.

'The world's gone crazy,' Winston mused. 'First I'm asked to remove defects – but not all of them. I'm told to spice the genes up a bit, make the kids smarter – I don't have much argument with that. I'm obliged to lighten the skin of every Asian or Afro-Caribbean citizen's child, whether they like it or not. They like it and come clamouring for more. They'd all be blond and blue-eyed, given half a chance – shows you how hopeless the anti-discrimination codes are, don't it? In half a century true blacks will have disappeared, at least from the upper castes. They'll all be shades of grey. But now I have to make a big space between one bunch of triply enhanced NTs and the rest of the nation. Given my devious mind, I can just guess why. It makes my blood run cold, Marr, I tell you.'

He reached up and caressed Martin's face. His voice, when he spoke again, was soft and full of love.

'A right pair, we are. Lucky we don't fancy breeding. Nobody would have either of us. Our DNA'd be dumped straight into the bin. Gay means unsuitable. Me, black, nine-tenths, anyway. And belligerent, uncouth and ungovernable, I guess. And you, born dumb and never spoken. Genetic rejects, the pair of us. But who's to decide we're worthless? What gave them the right?'

Several thousand miles away, another public servant was frowning in annoyance at the orders that had just been handed to him. Colonel Mike Thompson read each line again and snorted. The flash had appeared on the screens earlier in the day, but had been confirmed by the white crested envelope and letter brought by fastjet courier. The signature of Morrison, the Permanent

Secretary at the Ministry of Defence meant there could
be no mistake.

'But I am a soldier,' he murmured, not caring that
Captain Neimat Vezirov, the Azerbaijani adjutant, was in
earshot.

'Sir?'

'I am to return. To relinquish this post. I am promoted,
and will take up ceremonial duties in London.'

'Congratulations, sir.' His master's glowering expression
meant that the remark was made without enthusiasm.

'I bet,' the Colonel continued slowly, 'I'll bet there's
more to it than ceremonial. I'm too bloody useful here.
Must be some reason for it. Half the regiment's recalled,
too. Not you – you'll see out your term here, Neimat.'

'You'll be missed, sir. The men think highly of you, if
you don't mind my saying so. Sir.'

'Thank you. Appreciated.' The Colonel half saluted
then turned on his heel. As he marched away, papers in
hand, the Captain could hear him muttering to himself.

'Why on earth would the MoD want seasoned troops
in the middle of London this winter? What will we be
expected to do, other than get bored out of our boots on
guard duty? There has to be another story. What, though?
That's what I'd like to know.'

Lisa stood stock-still in the corridor, the sound of the
door being shut firmly behind her still ringing in her ears.
Furiously her hand rubbed her cheek as if she had been
slapped. That was how it felt.

The label on the door was unchanged: Professor James
Churchill, Director. Yet her relationship with her supervisor, the man most immediately responsible for her

research, for her promotion prospects and her place in society, had altered for ever. And very much for the worse.

He had listened with obvious impatience to what, to be fair, was a barely credible tale of an unusual cargo leaving the premises late one night. He had questioned her closely as to what she had been doing there and whether she made a habit of, as he put it rudely, 'creeping round Porton Down looking for trouble'. He had tutted when she had explained her presence by the extra effort to locate the missing files, which, he remonstrated, was a problem resolved some time before, at least to everyone else's satisfaction. To his inquiry about corroboration of her sighting – her *apparent* sighting – she had had to admit that no one else had been nearby, and that neither photographs nor video had been taken. Nor, it transpired, was any material available from the gate security cameras, which happened to have been pointed elsewhere just at the moment Dr Pasteur claimed to have been observing such marvels.

At first Lisa was mystified, then increasingly tart. She had retorted that, since the event had been so unexpected, there'd been no time to prepare – one did not anticipate strange movements in or out of the building at that time of night.

'And we do not normally have our top scientists prowling about at that time of night either, Dr Pasteur,' Churchill had growled. He had glared at her until she dropped her gaze. 'Especially an assistant director. It sets a bad example. It offends against the health and safety code, if nothing else. It will have to stop.' And he had made her promise to cease her nocturnal activities, and to take some vacation.

Lisa realised she was shaking. This man, whom she had so respected as a professional colleague and her boss, had shown no respect to her whatever. Disrespect, more like. Contempt.

She began to walk away, head down, hands thrust deep into her lab coat pockets. It was so – unscientific. Trained men and women did not dismiss bits of evidence, however odd or unexpected, with a wave of the hand. Neither did they ignore information on offer and twist the conversation to trivialities. Instead they noted details, asked probing questions. What sort of hand? What made you think it was a child's? What was it attached to? Are you sure it was moving and not a trick of the light? They soothed, certainly, and might hint that a simple explanation was in order. They would announce some kind of investigation. They did not invite the informant to leave and to shut the door behind them.

She headed back slowly towards her own domain, her brain jangling. At a corner a notice peered down at her, the logo of the staff of life and the human egg prominent. With the motto. *Pro bono publico.* For the public good.

All science was inherently dangerous. Once a technique had been developed past the pioneering stage, it offered options that had previously been impossible. To blow a town to smithereens: nuclear weapons made it easy. To make travel between continents barely a matter of drawing breath: with Mach 3 fastjets, that was old hat. To ensure that a child saw its hundredth birthday: a combination of genetic therapy and medicine made that virtually inevitable. To grant parents the right to choose whatever virtues they wanted in their children – to provide them, if vanity dictated, with almost a carbon copy of themselves: those processes were in her own sure hands.

Every advance had been greeted first by dismay and pseudo-moral horror: what had been an Act of God had been downgraded to an act of man. The sermons were challenged by those who stood to gain direct benefit, who demanded angrily to know by what right bishops or fundamentalist politicians could hold up progress. In between were the mass of the populace, curious and fearful, and above them government, charged with turning each new revelation into practical policy.

Lisa had always felt more secure than the average person, knowing that the genetic programme was run in government laboratories by civil servants like herself. That decision had been made half a century before, in rebuttal of the previous trend, which had allocated most activity to private corporations. Like health, embryology was regarded in Europe *prima facie* as a public service. Access should be as wide as possible, and not denied because of inadequate wealth. The state gained if cleansing and enhancement, and the concomitant educational incentives, were open to all.

Private business would be too commercial, it had been successfully argued. There would inevitably be a 'dumbing-down', in the jargon of those decades. The finest enhancements would be on offer to the highest bidder. Look what had happened to broadcasting, to publishing. If the public good were to be paramount – and how, with such a powerful weapon to alter future generations, could it be anything else? – then the government had not only to regulate but to operate it as well.

Lisa raised a hand and tentatively touched the writhing tendrils of the tree of life. To play with it was such a – a privilege; such an extraordinary responsibility. She had always felt overawed, honoured, to have been able to take on this work. It mattered so much for itself. Above all, it mattered that it was done well, and honestly.

That was the reasoning behind that detailed legislation which gave government such overweening controls. The European preference was for state action; the European Commission had led the way. Discussions and consultations had been swift and thorough, though long before she was born. Action had had to be taken speedily before the technology got into the wrong hands – the analogy had been drawn with nuclear weaponry back in the days of the Cold War. The early years of embryo science offered another helpful model: if access were easy, it had been shrewdly argued, there would be no need for families to resort to underground or unlicensed facilities. Risk could be contained. And scientists' wilder imaginings could be channelled and monitored, it was believed, by comprehensive, even fierce, directives, not by waiting until a disaster occurred and then trying to pick up the pieces.

The disaster had happened, with the mid-twenties explosions. After that, the bishops went silent. The programme had advanced and become a proud part of European life. The relative decline of the USA could, at least partly, be put down to their unwillingness to embrace the latest technology; it was as if, in a previous age, they had refused on religious grounds to make use of computers.

But the powers? Lisa dug her hands deep into her pockets. Down the corridor a camera was trained on her; it would learn nothing from her body language. What had gone wrong?

She sighed. One element was obvious; and all the

efforts to foresee it, and to counteract it, were bound to
fail. People would get round the system. The human
ingenuity that had toiled over the new science was not
averse to hijacking it for quirky or private tastes. Silly
things to which she had turned a blind eye, as if they
were harmless, were commonplace. Genetic manipulation could be employed to avoid the consequences of
over-indulgence – heart disease or obesity. Toy breeds of
dog led to toy breeds of *homo sapiens*. The idea was
hideous to her, but undeniably attractive to a large part of
the population. And, of course, it was done. Under
licence. By men and women she had trained herself, and
who had been lured away from the public service by fat
salaries and facilities in palm-fringed locations.

Something else dug at her. It wasn't simply the fickle-
ness of human aspirations. The controls were there; the
licences could have been denied. Except that politicians,
elected by those same voters, would have forced the
issue.

And what if . . .? She found herself holding her breath
and let it out with almost a sob. What if the guardians
became just as irresponsible? If the controls were in the
hands of those who had different motives? Or whose
motives remained impeccable, who still saw themselves
as charged with maintaining the public good – but who
began to see it differently?

If that were the case, then where could she turn?

In her pocket her fingers closed on a piece of paper.
For distraction she took it out. It was Strether's vidphone
number given to her on his first visit, long ago committed to memory. What she had learned since, about the
programme and the man – and herself – made that original contact seem as though it had occurred in another

millennium. Common sense warned that her vidphone
might be monitored. In any case she would see him
shortly if she took up the invitation to join him for lunch
with Prince Marius in Parliament. And the Prince himself – if he could be persuaded to take an interest . . .

She started to walk away. The wall-mounted camera
picked up her motion and swivelled to follow, its black
eye incurious and efficient. Perhaps all her actions were
now under surveillance. Perhaps everyone's were. In
which case the fact that the gate cameras had been off
suggested human intervention, not an accident. Or that
the film had been erased. Somebody knew about that –
that *shipment*. Somebody who did not want it made
public.

Lisa stared up at the camera, a new malevolence
welling in her heart. She raised her right hand and
formed the index and middle finger into a V shape, much
as she had seen done in old films, and gestured at the
lens. Then she strode on.

Chapter Thirteen

Bill Strether shaded his eyes and squinted back, forth and up at the pale yellow masonry that soared vertically above his head, its gilded towers and gargoyled turrets yellow in the morning sun. To his left Big Ben pounded out ten o'clock. He whistled softly. 'Well,' he mused, 'it sure beats the J. C. Penney building in New York.'

To their left brooded the black statue of Cromwell, 'our chief of men', who had once led Parliament to victory over a recalcitrant king. Some had protested that, in these days of monarchy, the statue should be discarded but in the end the dying embers of republicanism had been appeased. To the right pranced the oversized equestrian portrayal of King Richard Lionheart, who had lived in France, mostly, and had spoken no English. Other than to glorify royalty *per se*, it had never been clear why this commemoration, of dubious artistic value, was given prominence. But it was popular with tourists, though many asked where to find the matching tribute to Robin Hood.

'The Palace is breathtaking,' Marius agreed. 'Wordsworth wrote, "*Earth has not anything to show*

*more fair;/Dull would he be of soul who could pass by/A
sight so touching in its majesty.*" Actually, that was two
palaces ago, and for balance I should mention that
Dickens called it "the Great Dust Heap".'

Strether took his bearings. Opposite was the Bank of
England, resplendent in fluted columns and architraves.
Westminster Abbey had been moved several blocks
nearer the shopping quarter; St Margaret's in its shadow
was now bijou boutiques. Parliament Square, an oasis of
palm trees, fountains and frangipani, was entirely a
pedestrian precinct. The copper dome of the New British
Library, built to replace an earlier version that had developed brick cancer and collapsed in a heap of dust, peeked
around the far corner.

'There was no choice about moving once the Thames
barrier failed,' Marius explained. 'Guy Fawkes's cellars
were awash with dirty water, the Commons rifle club and
the crèche in the basement had been abandoned and the
stink in summer was horrendous. Or so I've been told.'

He walked with Strether up the broad white steps from
St Stephen's entrance, handed over his swipe card,
planted his palm on the DNA tester, waited for the all-
clear and paused while the Ambassador also cleared
security. 'With that experience you'd have thought the
MPs would have preferred dry land, but no. The bulk of
the Union grant wasn't spent on relocating the Palace of
Westminster itself, block by block, but on creating the
artificial lake on the far side so that the Members' Terrace
would overlook water. Mad, I call it.'

Strether chuckled. He wiped his palm on his trousers.
The DNA machinery was so heavily used that the surface
was sticky. 'But it'd have been a tragedy to let this place
sink beneath the waves,' he remarked.

'Sure. And it could be improved on. Barry's master-piece had no electricity, no elevators or escalators, and only the most rudimentary air-conditioning. This build-ing's four storeys taller, though you can't tell. Everyone's on the same site, with staff and library in six floors under-ground and the MPs on the top floors. They love it – wonderful views. Of course, the cut in the numbers of Honourable Members down to three hundred made for a lot more room – and they were better paid as a result – though the total's crept up again since. And mostly women.'

'Can't have too much of a good thing,' Strether responded judiciously.

'Oh, you can. We in the Lords take the view that two hundred and fifty's ample for a legislative assembly. Any more is sheer pomposity, and then they're scrabbling around for something to do. The MPs can't see that the *fewer* of them, the greater the prestige. They think it's the other way round. Just about sums them up.'

The two were walking down the reconstituted St Stephen's passage, past white marble statues of Walpole, Burke, Pitt, Thatcher, Mandelson and Hague in charac-teristic pose. Most of them wore or carried hats, though the reason behind Hague's sporting headgear had been lost in history. A few more steps and they stood in the great octagonal cathedral of Central Lobby.

Marius straightened his midnight-blue tunic and pointed at vaulted arches lined with gilded Venetian mosaic. 'Quaint, isn't it? The old British constitution in stone. This way to the Lords, the other to the Commons. Up there St Andrew, St George, St David, St Patrick. It didn't matter that by the date the building moved here, neither Scotland, Ireland nor Wales were under this

Parliament's jurisdiction. The sole concession to modernity is that each has a tiny symbol of the European Union added somewhere. See it? St Patrick's got it under his shamrock, and St David has a blue leek. St Andrew was originally shown as a fisherman, but is now carrying a golf bag with gold stars on it. For St George, it's the dragon at his feet breathing starry blue fire. An ultra-nationalist, the restorer, or so it's alleged.'

Strether admired the view. 'I shall get a crick in my neck if I gaze at it too long.'

Blue and pink-cloaked figures hurried past, papers and powerbooks under their arms. A mobile vidphone rang shrilly. Two police officers in navy tunics and Victorian-style helmets, boots and buttons polished, guarded a desk at which constituents sent in small green cards in the hope of enticing their MP from his office or the Chamber. Marius explained with a cheery cynicism that without an appointment most would ask in vain. 'Legend has it that one wild-haired petitioner with an ancient grievance attended daily for twenty years. He used to sit, groaning to himself, on the same green leather bench over there.'

'Poor man! Did he get what he wanted?'

'Nobody knows. Late one night, when it seemed he had fallen asleep, he was shaken by a Serjeant. The body slumped slowly on to the tiled floor. The old man had died waiting.' He pointed. A tiny brass plaque marked the spot.

The Prince consulted his watch. 'The Commons debate has already started. It was opened by the opposition, so if we pop in now, we should hear the Prime Minister.' The route took them out of the lobby to the north, towards the Commons chamber. He eyed his friend. 'Did you say Dr Pasteur is joining us for lunch? If so, I'm delighted to hear it. I invited my mother. A grand old lady. I think you'll get on very well.'

Strether remembered the previous time he had seen Princess Io, on the operating table, and wondered with a suppressed shiver how the grand old lady's face would now look. 'Lisa couldn't manage time for the debate. She's never been inside the chamber, though she's been a professional witness upstairs to select committees.'

'Well! She's probably had more influence than most.' It was the Prince's turn to be diplomatic. A tall fair man in a braided cloak swung past and Marius bowed briefly. 'You're quite fond of her, aren't you, Bill?'

'I am, but I can't figure her out exactly.' Strether followed the Prince to the right, by a war-damaged archway and past more forgotten heroes – Lloyd George, Churchill, Gladstone. Another statue, this time of the first British European President Anthony Blair in old age, bald and hook-nosed, smiled blankly back. Not an NT, that one. The toe had been rubbed shiny by the touch of superstitious visitors hoping that his outstanding qualities – and his talent at comebacks – might be contagious.

The two men stood before a small lift. Strether carried on: 'She's totally engrossed in the Porton Down genetic programme – it's her *raison d'être* – but there've been some hitches with it lately, and it's made her a bit short with me. Maybe she thinks I'm too stupid to understand. If so, she'd be right.'

'Nonsense!' The Prince smiled. The lift arrived and both stepped in. 'Nobody's smarter than you, my dear chap. But its employees are covered by the Official Secrets Acts so maybe she's simply not allowed to talk. Especially about any – anxieties. It can be highly sensitive stuff, Strether. But I must say, you have taste.'

The Ambassador pursed his lips. Perhaps Lisa had told him too much already.

The two men found themselves on a narrow upper corridor, with the sound of a declamatory voice nearby. In a moment they emerged into the green-benched gallery above the opposition and were shown to seats.

Far below them Members lounged or listened attentively, on the government side in blue woollen or acrylic robes over their tunic suits, their opponents in pink or orange or green according to party. More senior Members, whom Strether took to be Ministers, bore two-toned stripes down the robe front with gold braid on the sleeves. The man to whom the Prince had bowed was apparently the Deputy Speaker. The gowns were a reversion to the sixteenth century when Sir Thomas More was Speaker, and had been introduced almost on a whim; the idea had been proposed after the interregnum, almost as a joke, to counteract attempts to abolish the wigs and court dress of the Speaker, Serjeant-at-Arms, Lord Chancellor and others. Instead the new garb had been an instant success. It gave Members, especially the ladies, an undoubted if unmerited dignity.

At the brass-bound dispatch box, the Mace displayed before him, a stocky figure was in full oratorical flow. He wore an embroidered black robe and chain of office but on him they sat sloppily and were flung about as he lunged across the table. Strether peered down and identified the Prime Minister, Sir Lyndon Everidge.

The Ambassador scrutinised him, as had become a habit. The solid, bullock-like body was not in the same physical mould as other important NTs; maybe seventy years before a variety of styles had been in vogue. Strether took in the rest of the echoing chamber. Sir

Robin Butler-Armstrong, the head of the civil service was also present, discreet and robeless in the officials' row behind the Speaker's Chair, almost hidden. Seated, and still, and watchful, with a half-smile playing on those thin, clever lips.

'This year, for the third year running, armed forces estimates have been held at the same level in real terms!' the Prime Minister was saying, apparently in answer to some taunt in the preceding speech. 'It is nonsense to suggest that we are warmongering. Indeed, I may point out, since the Right Honourable the Leader of the Opposition doesn't seem aware of it, we are spending a smaller proportion of the national income on defence than in any year under the previous administration . . .'

Beside Strether, Marius snorted. 'But that was nineteen years ago. Bretherton, the opposition leader, was still at school. There'll come a day when such comparisons won't wash any longer.'

The man to whom he had referred threw down his papers in a theatrical gesture, a disdainful expression on his refined features. A rangy, fair man, wrapped in his magenta robe, he seemed excessively youthful in comparison with the bald and sleek grey heads close by. To Strether young Bretherton had 'NT' – and 'Énarque' – written all over him; it was not worth inquiring.

'Right Honourable – they still stick to the traditions?' he asked.

'Absolutely. The more decision-making shifted elsewhere, the more members became sticklers for tradition. In fact extra ceremonial was invented to bamboozle the reformers – so now they have stately processions in and out every day, and the Speaker enters to trumpets on the first Monday of each month. I don't think His Majesty relishes the State Opening of Parliament each year, golden coach and all – his predecessors tried so hard to get rid of the palaver. But that's what MPs want. Rather what you'd expect, if you think about it. Those who preferred to exercise power moved as it moved – they're beavering away in Brussels and Frankfurt. The ones who stayed put are enslaved by pomp and circumstance.'

A hissed 'Hush!' came from behind. Marius continued his commentary in whispers. 'Bretherton's being groomed. Parliaments are an essential part of the set-up and, however incompetent the bulk of ordinary Members, the front benches have to be capable. He chose to be elected, though he comes from civil service stock – an ancestor was the official Board of Trade observer at the original Messina talks in 1955. D'you know the story?'

Strether shook his head. He loved Marius's anecdotes and the stylish courtesy with which they were offered.

'He was pulled out by the Eden government. Britain still clung to nostalgic dreams of empire; equality with a clutch of other nations did not appeal. He wrote to a French colleague, "*I leave Messina happy because even if you continue talking, you will not agree. Even if you agree, nothing will result. And even if anything results, it will be a disaster.*" Two years later the six signed the Treaty of Rome. The Union was born.'

Strether snickered. 'Another world,' he remarked. Marius nodded agreement.

Sir Lyndon had reached his peroration. His berobed arms flailed like black sails in an uncertain wind, his face grew puce, spittle sprayed into the ether. 'I am *proud* of this government, proud to be at its head! We have *doubled* average incomes in the last ten years, kept inflation below a *fraction* of one per cent a year, seen interest rates

fall to their lowest levels for two decades. The average
age of our population has at last stabilised at sixty, an
achievement which has eluded all previous administra-
tions. When the election comes we will face the voters
with confidence! That is my challenge to the Right
Honourable gentleman, and my answer to his empty,
mindless gibes. No party could go to the country with
more certainty of success, based on sound principles and
sound finance. I rest my case.'

He sat down, breathing heavily, to cheers and the
waving of order papers by supporters behind him. Marius
spoke directly into Strether's ear.

'The opposition has exactly the same policies, of
course. We Europeans gave up experimentation ages
ago – the Commission's directives don't leave much
scope, anyhow. The election will be fought, when it's
due, on personalities, whatever the contestants claim –
whether Sir Lyndon is past it or not, whether it's time for
a change, whether Bretherton's convincingly ready. The
Perm Sec will hover in the background to guarantee no
backsliding, whoever wins. Their brains all function in
precisely the same way, so there will be no surprises.'

Something acerbic in Marius's tone made Strether pull
away and look sharply at his friend, but the mocking air
had swiftly descended and the Ambassador could not
judge whether the Prince was serious or not.

Strether frowned. He may have hinted to Marius that
he found Lisa at times hard to make out, but the Prince
was often unfathomable. He was a cynic and an enthusi-
ast at the same time. He pretended to be a lightweight, yet
his remarks usually turned out to be accurate and were
unsettling. Marius himself did not seem sure which side
of the fence he was on, nor whether indeed he was sitting

perched uneasily in the middle. And yet this handsome, dark-eyed man was quintessentially part of the Establishment he so coolly criticised. Maybe Marius was so secure, in both birth and upbringing, that he could play the licensed jester, who had no wish to damage the system that sustained him. Or maybe, more disturbingly, Marius had the same fears as Strether. Maybe the Prince was trying to alert him, to point his attention in a particular direction. But why? *And where?*

Other would-be debaters were on their feet clamouring to be noticed. The Speaker called another NT, leader of the third party. Strether felt restless and disappointed. Whatever answers he might need, they were not here.

'Marius,' he murmured, 'I'm lost. In the USA, Congress holds independent powers. It can stop a President in his tracks. It can throw out his budget, tack extras on to his favoured legislation, impeach him. We expect rows between the oval office and the elected body – open warfare, sometimes. Those conflicts are the heart of American liberty. But here . . .'

The Prince shrugged. 'Here? Maybe you hope for too much, my dear Bill.'

'Nobody seems to have noticed. The form is maintained. It reminds me of an old tree in my yard at home, still upright and flourishing, dominating the landscape, but the trunk's hollow and inside it's dead. Down there,' he pointed sadly, 'your politicians make speeches as they've done for a thousand years. Oodles of fire and fury. Only what does it signify now? Almost nothing.'

On a sudden impulse Strether excused himself and went out to find a toilet. Inside a locked cubicle he took out his vidphone and punched in a number from his private directory.

'Yeah?' a sleepy voice answered.

'Marty? Is that you?'

'Yeah. Gawd, I'm not awake yet. What time is it? Who's that?'

'Bill Strether. Your American friend. Sorry I woke you.'

'Oh, gee. Bill. Great! Howarya?'

'I haven't got much time now, Marty. You free tonight?'

'Lemme see. Hang on. Yeah, my last appointment's early. I'll be clear twenty-three hundred hours. Eleven o'clock to you.'

'Can I come? I don't want to be a nuisance. To talk.'

'Oh, you and your talking.' The voice dissolved into a breathy gurgle. Strether felt his heart skip a beat. 'Sure, sweetheart. It'll be a pleasure. See yah.'

The Prince may have been scathing about the artificial lake, but to Strether the terrace was instantly a marvel. Its broad paving stretched over two hundred metres with a waist-high balustrade in Portland stone. In the near distance fountains played, lit by coloured lights in party colours, in a sequence said to symbolise harmony between the factions. Swans flapped and honked below while a herd of flame-pink flamingoes on the far shore stepped delicately, like an outing of fastidious old ladies. On the terrace itself striped awnings provided shade; a pleasant breeze came off the waters. Orange and lemon trees in white-painted tubs separated the tables, their fruit pendulous and inviting. Along the parapet spilled hibiscus and perfumed orchids, the latter a special genus, *parliamentaria*, with blooms in the hues of each main party on the same stem. A Member's pet monkey pestered for titbits and was shooed away, while piebald seagulls fought over scraps.

At the Prince's request the two women guests had been met and escorted. Lisa and the Princess were already installed at a trim wooden table, fruit-filled drinks to hand. Strether bent and kissed Lisa's cheek. She had picked two orchid blossoms and tucked them into her hair. Her close-fitting trouser suit was of amber shantung; with a start Strether realised she must have been spending some money on her clothes. Not that she needed to, but the effect was delicious. Her manner to him was warm, too, which augured well, though otherwise she seemed on edge.

The Princess rose and held out a beringed hand. She was barely the height of a young child and was dressed in a full-length brocade *cheong-sam*, fastened at the neck. Strether hesitated. He touched the fingers and bowed low, in what he hoped was an old European gesture. This woman could not possibly be – what had the surgeon said? – eighty-six. Her features were tiny and fine-boned, her jet-black hair swept back from a face that could not be more than forty years old.

'So pleased to meet you, Ambassador,' Princess Io cooed, as she rearranged herself in a chair stuffed with tasselled cushions. Strether could not stop himself checking whether the stitches had left any traces, but there was no sign. He mumbled inanities in reply and felt slightly foolish.

'What did you think of our wonderful English Parliament, Ambassador?' the Princess continued. With deft grace she forked slivers of asparagus and baby octopus into her lipsticked mouth and played with the Danish champagne.

'I don't think he was too impressed,' her son suggested. 'Reckons they do it better in the States.'

'But that's normal, surely. He's a patriot,' the Princess responded. Her voice was high, tinkly, yet her entire presence had gravitas. The regard between mother and son was evident as Marius quietly removed dishes and arranged for glasses to be refilled.

'I was a bit bothered,' Strether ventured at last, 'to hear that the main parties have identical policies underneath the rhetoric. They're surely supposed to go at each other, not merely replicate line for line. And, though I can see the point, I'm alarmed that the Perm Secs will ensure that nobody does anything untoward — whatever the results of an election.'

'Goodness! There's nothing new in that,' the Princess tinkled prettily. 'Better than chaos each time a changeover occurs. But they're all wonderful people. We are lucky to have them. I, of course, being royal, am above politics.'

Marius exchanged a flicker of private amusement with his mother. It made Strether cross, as if once more he was being excluded from some important secret. He nudged the Prince. 'Do they realise that inside?' he asked. 'And do they care?'

The Prince shrugged. 'Yes, and no. Most of them know it, if not when they arrive as energetic new MPs full of ambition then soon after. The best are spirited upwards, particularly the awkward squad. When they're offered a junior Minister's job and don the striped gown, that straightens them out. Or they're shunted off on delegations. Some remain dazzled for their entire career. Others

find a niche and settle happily for some minor achievement. One could do worse with one's life and gifts. It's
public service, and that's drummed into us here.'

'Do they have to be NTs to get on?' Strether felt the
Princess shift. Lisa was watching him as she sipped her
drink.

'No, not absolutely.' Marius did not seem embarrassed
at the inquiry. 'For the highest appointed jobs, yes, obviously. But some upward mobility is still possible in the
political world – new blood can be assimilated. This' – he
jerked a thumb at the edifice behind them – 'is one of the
few institutions where anyone can rise, still. Less and
less so, though. Breeding will out.'

A green-tunicked waiter cleared trays. Effervescent
ice-cream arrived in fluted glasses and caused lively comment. The Princess asked Lisa to describe her work and
smiled vacantly as Lisa struggled to make sense of it to
her. A second bottle of wine was opened. Strether felt
the company waiting for him to proceed.

'I'll tell you what bothers me, if I may. Here on the
terrace,' Strether waved a hand about, at the glorious
flowers with their heady fragrance, at the figures dotted
at other tables, at the tourist boats near the fountain,
'it's hard to credit that this great Union might have a
single problem. But we sat and listened most of the
morning to a debate which was a parody of free expression. As if there were a deliberate conspiracy to avoid
the issues of the day. I can't accept that everybody goes
along with this charade. You are too intelligent. All
three of you.'

The Princess threw back her doll-like head and
laughed. For a second Strether thought he spied a mark
under her ear, then it had gone. Marius was grinning, as if

pleased that the Ambassador had grasped an obscure but vital argument. Nobody replied.

Strether drained his glass, emboldened. 'Doesn't anybody object to this suffocating perfection? Is there no movement to question its underlying propositions? You, Lisa. You told me what you wanted to be the truth – that nobody misused the genetic programme. But they do, and it's widespread. And you knew that, even if you refused to face it. You, Marius, you're a prince and a man of the highest quality. And integrity, I hope. You're a Member here. Dammit, you're a member everywhere. Yet you tell me the MPs are playing convoluted games with each other and I'm sure that's so. You, Princess, say that's not new, as if the fact that something *slipped* generations ago is somehow satisfactory. Why doesn't anyone stand up and shout about it?'

For several moments, as the others sat in silence and toyed with their meals, he wished he had kept his mouth shut. The breeze stirred Lisa's hair but she kept her eyes fixed on her plate, her movements fidgety. Then Marius answered.

'They do. You saw that for yourself, the night of the embassy party.'

Strether sat back, startled. Lisa had turned away; he could not see her face. She had spoken little and had barely touched her food.

'Who are *they*?' he demanded. The Princess began to examine her painted fingernails.

'Various groups.' Marius dropped his voice. 'Here and in some cities on the continent. The most prominent is called "Solidarity". Another is "1848", though it could be a separate branch of the first.'

'How do you know about them?'

'I make it my business, my dear Strether.' The Prince's face clammed shut.

Strether grunted in irritation. Maybe the Prince could not talk with the women present. Strether remembered another tack.

'Lisa, what's PKU?'

'PKU?' She swivelled about and focused on him. 'It stands for phenylketonuria. Used to be called Fölling's disease, after a Norwegian doctor who identified it. Why?'

'What is it?'

'Oh, golly. That's a question from a twentieth-century medical exam. You don't see it now. It's a metabolic condition. Resulting, if I remember rightly, in a deficiency of phenylalanine hydroxylase. PAH. That's usually found in the liver.'

'Would you put it in somebody's water? PKU, I mean?'

'No, not at all. That's the name of the condition. The stuff that's missing is PAH.'

'But somebody ignorant might talk about adding PKU to the diet?'

'They *might*. But how weird. What for?'

Strether thought hard. The other three observed him, puzzled. He tried again. 'What causes it, Lisa?'

'Heavens, Bill. I got my doctorate years ago and I did *not* major in the history of medicine. It's genetic, an auto-somal recessive disorder on chromosome 12, I think. Relatively common – about one in twelve thousand before the mid-twenties explosions. It could be detected at birth with a heel-prick blood test, one of the earliest employed. Later it could be corrected by gene-transfer technology – again, one of the earliest tried successfully. A chunk of liver would be excised, transduced and rein-serted. Worked a treat.'

'But what happened if people weren't treated?'

'Oh, they went mad. The gut without PAH is unable to tolerate normal protein. Without treatment or special diets children, though normal at birth, became severely retarded. If it developed in adults they had psychological problems, tremors, spasticity and neurological damage. Something like that.'

'Would it kill them?'

'No-o, I don't think so. The main effects were developmental. But there used to be hospitals full of mentally retarded patients with PKU, until the tests and treatment. Those were so effective it vanished.'

'Could it be reintroduced?'

Strether became conscious that Marius was leaning forward, though his expression remained inscrutable. His mother was gazing out over the lake, her exquisite nostrils flared, her eyes half closed.

Lisa frowned. 'In principle, yes. What has been removed or repaired could be undone. Maybe in a slightly altered form. But why on earth would anybody want to?'

'Perhaps as a form of chemical handcuffs,' said Strether slowly. 'For prisoners. So if they tried to escape and were deprived of – PAH, did you say? – they would go mad.'

'You're crazy, Bill. No doctor would do that. It'd be deeply unethical,' Lisa retorted. 'Anyway, hardly anyone in the Union is sent to prison. It isn't policy.'

Strether and Marius met each other's eyes.

'OK, Lisa. I'll buy that,' Strether said easily. Her face had become flushed: Lisa, usually so much in control of herself and her surroundings, was obviously unsettled. Out of the corner of his eye he noticed that the pet

monkey, a jewelled red collar about its neck, was creeping timidly towards their table, attracted by the diners'
quiet demeanour. 'But tell me, Doctor. Everything isn't
sweetness and light in your neck of the woods, is it?'

'My results are excellent,' she answered bluntly.

Strether might have accepted that public denial a
week, even a few hours, before. But the empty shell of
Parliament had left him exasperated and impatient. Lisa,
he was sure, knew more than she was letting on. The
sting of their spat before his trip had faded, but still he
felt she owed him. 'Really? But you've been working late,
then suddenly you can take whole days off like today.' He
waited, then seized the moment. 'Did you find those
missing files?'

Her body sagged. Strether realised the power of cruelty. He held his breath.

'No. I didn't. And when I tried to repeat the experiment it failed again. Or rather it succeeded. And that data
disappeared too.'

'Failed? Succeeded?' the Princess trilled. 'How could
it do both? What did you lose – and what are you two
talking about?'

'Princess, you know I work at Porton Down. Among
other projects, I've been investigating chromosome 21.
Damage to it introduces – or possibly reinforces – a
vicious streak. That alone should render the embryos
non-viable. It always has before. We bred it out long ago.
Reasons of policy, sensible policy. But this batch thrived.
And if mine did, maybe somebody else has come across
the same phenomenon. As for those files, not only did the
data vanish into thin air, but the living material did too.'

'So somebody may have a few dozen healthy little
foetuses whose main characteristic is a penchant for

violence?' Marius asked, slowly. 'I take it you are not joking or exaggerating, Doctor? You are sure of this?'

Lisa did not reply but her anguished look was testament enough. 'And who,' Marius continued in the same measured tone, 'might be interested? Who knows about this?'

'My Director. He says I'm imagining things. He implied I was imagining what I saw the other night . . .' Lisa's hand flew to her mouth and her eyes widened in misery.

'Go on, Doctor,' Strether said gravely. 'What did you see?'

The title, the reminder of her status, seemed to reinforce in Lisa a deeply ingrained duty. As she heard it for the third time, she nodded to herself. Loyalty to science, to mankind must come before loyalty to an employer. She shook her head and for a few moments could not talk. The pet monkey pulled at Strether's trouser leg. He gave it a piece of bread which it snatched and carried away, squeaking. Nobody spoke.

Then, after gentle urging from both men, Lisa described as accurately as she could the shadowy tarpaulined lorry and its strange, moving cargo.

Her listeners digested what she had said. 'I asked you once about rejects, and you did not understand what I meant,' Strether reminded her gently. 'But that sounds to me like a barrel-load of rejects. Maybe they were supposed to have been disposed of – gassed, or whatever – but it was botched. Someone's doing a bit of breeding on the side, Lisa. Perhaps the experiment went wrong. You weren't supposed to see. None of it.'

'You are a very brave woman.' The Prince nudged his chair next to hers and held her trembling hand in both of his. Her face, full of misery, was turned to him, but she did not cry; that would have drawn attention. Her shoulders shuddered with the effort.

The Prince looked closer. 'You've never been asked to experiment on anything like that, have you, Lisa?'

'No. Never.'

'That's because you are a principled woman,' Strether intervened robustly. He put himself firmly on her side. 'If anyone had, you'd have told them firmly where to stuff such a proposition.'

Lisa found strength from somewhere. 'I'd have reported them. To the Chartered Institute. To anybody. It's dreadful. The whole ethos is being ignored, mocked – everything I care about most. And I don't know what to do. By contrast, Bill, your – your toys are quite benign.'

'Well, now. Enough,' came Marius's voice. He had resumed a patrician, insouciant air. 'So, we have more than a supine Parliament to flagellate ourselves over. How very intriguing. Let me ponder on this, Bill. Meanwhile, this poor girl's had sufficient interrogation and my dear mother's nodding off. Can we please change the subject?'

The monkey had leaped chattering on to the parapet a few metres away. It tore at the bread, ate, and scratched itself. Strether caught himself wondering whether it had been subjected to gene therapy or enhanced in some outlandish fashion. Maybe it could perform tricks such as screeching 'Rule Britannia' with perfect pitch. Given what he had just heard, he was beginning to believe that anything was possible.

Marty greeted him in a dressing-gown of white satin edged with fur, identical to the one Marilyn had worn on leaving hospital after her first miscarriage. It had marked,

Marty told him, her maturation from her empty-headed starlet period. Or, looking at it another way, had been the first step from hope to despair. Underneath it was obvious that she wore nothing at all.

Strether mopped his brow. He had caught the sun that afternoon, probably through its reflection off the MPs' folly, their darned poxy lake. Marty was a little tired, she told him; her previous job had been a mite over-enthusiastic. She lounged on the *chaise-longue*, the lovely limbs stretched like a cat's, and rubbed her knees.

'He had a Clinton tendency, that one,' she observed. 'Gawd, makes you wonder why they pay real money for it when gadgets can do it just as well.'

Strether removed his tunic and hung it over a chair. In Marty's company, for the first time in weeks, he felt comfortable, though not entirely relaxed – that would have been impossible. Yet her perfume filled the air, and the hint of a sexual smell was stronger than on his earlier visit. 'You have a remarkable attitude to your clients, Marty. I though it might upset me to hear you discuss them that way, but it doesn't. It's as if the body who – performs those acts, is someone else.'

'Yeah, I feel the same. Most are cute, y'know? Especially the young boys sent here by their fathers. I always feel I'm doing some nice girl a favour; when she meets the right guy, he'll know exactly how to please her. Makes for a far better marriage.'

'Doing your public duty, maybe,' Strether commented, but the import of the remark was lost on Marty. She passed him a platter of fruit. He took a handful of fat ripe strawberries and bit one, his teeth sinking into the sweet flesh.

'Your two staffers were here earlier this evening,' she said, by way of conversation. 'Did you see them on your way in? Matt and Dirk, the ginger-haired guy. You should warn them, though. Their toys are a bit peculiar.'

Strether accepted the obligatory champagne but waved away dishes of gravadlax and caviare. 'How do you mean – peculiar?'

Her manner became vague. 'Unreliable, then. They shouldn't attempt to meet them outside.' She sat back and crossed her ankles, a gesture that quickened Strether's pulse alarmingly. The rosy light made her skin luminous, the same magical glow that had enchanted him before. He started to eat another strawberry, but the taste on his lips made him aware of the great scarlet bow of Marty's mouth.

'That's all. Now, darling Bill, what can I do for you?'

Strether held his breath. His skin had begun to tingle. He forced himself to pause and reflect. What was he about to do? What duplicity was he capable of? He was so very fond of Lisa. That was a friendship founded on respect as much as anything else. Plus the fact that the doctor had been the first attractive woman he had come across, the first who had reawakened his dormant interest. It was a romance, but had a formal element. She would not have taken kindly to the idea of any repeat visit to the Toy Shop. He should have been utterly incapable of deceiving her, yet without hesitation he had come again, and hidden the arrangement from her.

But Marty was another world entirely: a kind, open personality, without pretensions, but wrapped up in the most luscious frame ever endowed on womankind. And her generous nature would extend to welcoming whatever advances he might make, without expecting anything in return. Nor need Lisa ever find out.

He would let the idea ferment for a little. Meanwhile he wanted information.

'Marty, I just need some wise company for a bit. Let me ramble on, will you? Then tell me what you think.' He sat nibbling fruit and talking for more than ten minutes, outlining his dismay at his visit to the Commons and his stupefaction that nobody seemed bothered by its weakness. He omitted mention of Lisa's work, since she could be compromised by gossip; and her name would feel like an intrusion. It seemed instinctively best, too, not to venture into the murky world of the prison camps or his sojourn in the desert. But when he reached Marius's hints that protest groups might well exist, Marty kicked up her heels and hooted with laughter.

'1848? Solidarity? What kinda names are those? Sounds like a slimming club to me!'

'You never heard of them?'

'Naw. We do get to hear all sorts of rumours here, when clients are in their cups, but I never heard tell of no protest groups. You're having me on.'

Strether sucked his teeth in frustration. 'I was hoping you might be able to add something, Marty.'

Her alabaster brow puckered, the lips pushed in a round pout. Her shoulders came forward artlessly and the nipples showed clearly beneath the white silk. 'Oh, gee, I'd love to help. I'd love to know more about it myself. Do they spirit people away? Do they have escape routes – tunnel under walls, secret messages 'n' that sort of thing?'

'I've no idea.' *The boat people.* 'My God. Maybe they do. Tell, me, Marty. If you wanted to escape, where would you head for?'

'Escape? West, of course. Where you come from. It's the closest, and big enough to disappear in. Isn't it?'

'America?'

'Sure. That'd be where I'd escape to, Bill.' Her face

became wistful. She slid closer to him. The silk slipped from her thigh. 'Maybe that's not so fanciful. P'raps if you get to know more about these Solidarity people, and they're short of candidates, I could volunteer. I still haven't heard a word from my best pal, Betty. I'm not sure I wanna stay around to find out what happens to fifty-year-old Marilyns, y'know?'

Strether caved in: the tensions of the day had been too great not to. He took the warm, sweet face in both hands and let himself melt into the candid blue eyes. He could no longer tell himself that this person, Marty, was an artificial creation. This was flesh and blood, and wholesome, living woman. He kissed her full on the scarlet lips and rested her dazzling platinum head on his shoulder.

Then he pulled awkwardly at the dressing-gown cord and let the slippery fabric slide away, revealing what he had never seen, but now realised he had dreamed about. Marilyn's breasts, full, creamy, firm, their nipples bold and aroused. Marilyn's hips, broad and almost heavy, the belly a slight curve, not flat, the high navel, the curly pubic triangle revealing that she had not always been blonde. Marty sighed and lay back, her arms up, hands crossed over her shimmering head as if she were a child. She ran her moist tongue over her parted lips, then laughed throatily. Her lovely legs bent up at the knees, slightly splayed, were an invitation to part them.

Strether stood up and unfastened his trousers. 'Yeah, Marty. I'll find out more, if I can. And don't worry. I'll make sure you're OK. Don't know how, but that's an absolute promise.'

*

It was more than two hours before he returned to the Residence, his head and whole being suffused with Chanel No. 5 and Marty's own musky odour, which had so entranced him. He felt weak, dazed, almost delirious. And quite extraordinarily happy.

The vidphone was blinking. Strether switched it on, half expecting another garbled message from some subversive group. The callers' numbers were never traceable; he wondered in annoyance quite what the urban terrorists, if that's what they were, expected him to do with such fragments of information.

But it was Marius.

'Hello, old chap. Hope you enjoyed the Toy Shop again – yes, my spies saw you. Are you genuinely interested in finding out more about what we discussed on the terrace? If so, I'm afraid it's back to Milton Keynes. Call me.'

Chapter Fourteen

The delivery boy stood on the footpath and whistled lazily. With his free hand he unwrapped a piece of testosterone chewing-gum and stuffed it into his mouth. He did not believe the claims made about it on TV but you never knew. It certainly made him feel perkier.

His was an unusual job, which his friends envied; these days, most household goods arrived overnight in anonymous packs from automated vehicles and were left ready for breakfast in the cooled acceptance cupboards built into most homes. He'd heard that communications such as post and newspapers used to be sent the same way, though letter-boxes, as they were called, did not require refrigeration. Electronic mail had put paid to that, plus the vidphone and wall screen. Nobody sent reams of paper any more.

He pushed the maroon cap to the back of his head and hefted his load from one arm to another. The electric van purred softly at the kerbside; he had taken care to park it in the shade, but if this dolly didn't hurry up the sun would have moved and made the metal too hot to touch. He pressed the doorbell again and shouted into the entryphone. The sound of crockery being dropped and a muttered curse greeted him. He grinned and switched the gum from one cheek to the other.

The door opened. A brown-haired woman stood on the doorstep, looking completely bewildered. Her tunic was half fastened and she had on only one earring. 'What on earth . . .?' she asked.

'Flowers, miss. Somebody loves ya. Thumbprint on the powerbook 'ere,' said the boy. This would be a tale to tell his pals.

'Flowers? Good Lord, I've never had flowers. What kind are they?'

'Dunno, I'm no expert. But, from the fuss made at the shop, summat special. Roses, maybe?' The boy grew a trifle restless. 'Will that be all, miss?'

'Er, yes, indeed. Thank you.' The woman had missed his hint entirely. Clutching the bouquet in her arms, she shut the door. With a disconsolate sigh, for tips were a substantial part of his income, he slouched back to the van.

They were indeed roses – rather a lot of them, the velvety scarlet buds several centimetres deep, wet with dew, wrapped in crinkly cellophane with scarlet ribbons. The thornless stems must have been half a metre long.

Lisa tried to remember what one was supposed to do with cut flowers. Shorten and crush the stems. Put a few sugar crystals in the water. Find a vase – a plastic jug would have to do. In the warmth of the apartment the blooms had begun to open slightly; a fabulous perfume filled the air.

Then she found the card. It was small and white, embossed with a red portcullis and a coronet.

'A great delight to meet you, Dr Pasteur. Forgive an archaic token, but I hope these will give you enjoyment.' The name followed. Lisa's eyebrows lifted.

She arranged the roses as best she could and ran her fingers over the glossy russet leaves. Flowers in homes had gone out of fashion before she was born, when pollen allergy had reached epidemic proportions; as with peanuts, some children in particular could become comatose at the mere sight of them. A vigorous campaign of genetic cleansing had removed most of the tendency in humans, and flowering plants were popular features in gardens and public displays, but by then the gift had become associated with thoughtless bad manners. Not from this individual, though. From him it was a charming if eccentric gesture.

Why on earth would Prince Marius be sending her flowers?

Later she shared the problem, still quite puzzled, with her records clerk Winston Kerry. A visit to the Bunker had become an urgent necessity. While there was no clear evidence that her e-mail and vidphone calls were being monitored she had started to act with circumspection. If she were in the Director's shoes, it would be prudent to check what Dr Pasteur, that prickly rebel, was up to. On the issues she had asked Winston to pursue, face-to-face discussions would be safest.

Winston had put his feet up cheekily on the computer console. Above him the camera was motionless and unblinking: put to sleep temporarily, Lisa suspected. He offered her a chocolate from a little box, as if sharing secret vices with her. 'Man, that's not a problem,' he chuckled. 'A guy sends you a prezzie like that, you say thank you kindly and wait to see what he sends you next.'

'But I've hardly met Prince Marius,' Lisa protested. She unwrapped the sweet and popped it into her mouth. The next words emerged indistinctly. 'I caught a glimpse of him when he brought Bill Strether to the lab – just a moment in the corridor. He was in cahoots with the Director then. They went off and left me and Bill together. And he was at the embassy party – we had a few words, nothing dramatic. Last week was the first time he's ever had a conversation with me.'

'Bill? Pretty familiar, huh? You got a whole harem there, ma'am.' Winston pronounced it *hareem*, lolling his tongue against the thick lips and rolling his eyes.

'Oh, don't, Winston. I'm in a muddle. Cracks like that are not helpful.'

'I'm not the best person to come to for agony aunt advice, dear Doctor,' Winston relented. 'But what's going on? You like this geezer the American?'

'I do. He's a darling. An absolute gentleman.' As she spoke she remembered his dalliance at the Toy Shop, but forced it firmly out of her mind.

'You trust him?'

'Yes. Increasingly so. When he criticised my research I was mortally offended, but he was right. He's a man of limited education and background compared with a typical European diplomat, but has sound judgement, I'd say.'

'Big romance?'

Lisa shrugged but her face was downcast. 'I sleep with him, if that's what you mean. And I'm immensely fond of him. I think he's a bit old for me; or maybe it's the fact that he's not from here, and finds much of our world not to his taste. At times it's like chatting to somebody from another century.'

'Bit of a hick, then.'

She laughed at that, and relaxed a little. 'He asked if I'd like to go back to the States, but it doesn't appeal, to be frank. So much of our lives here we take for granted. I like the way our government and the Commission are expected to take care of us — that's very European. I don't think I'd be comfortable in that fundamentalist paradise. And how would I earn a living?'

'That I can see. But you didn't quite answer me. When I asked if you trusted this Bill feller, you talked about his wonderful judgement. But would you trust him to keep his mouth shut?'

Lisa considered. 'I suppose he must report back. But I doubt if he would put anyone at risk. Why do you ask?'

'Because he's coming to Milton Keynes later today. I wondered if that was why you were here too.'

She was silent. After her ringing endorsement of his trustworthiness this was a surprise. Then: 'I was not aware of that. Coming to see you?'

Winston recrossed his legs. 'Not exactly. But there aren't many secrets underground. If you hang about, maybe you could tag along.'

She was dubious. 'I probably wouldn't be welcome. I'm beginning to feel something of a liability wherever I go.'

Winston pursed his lips in a kiss and made smacking noises. 'They all adore you. Prince Marius is coming too. A double reason. Go have yourself a soya milk-shake and I'll gather a few printouts. I'll see you at the caff in twenty minutes.'

*

Strether and Marius had chosen to drive by electric car to Milton Keynes. It was not far; the journey up Watling Street was hardly arduous, as, though the motorway had long since been ploughed up for vineyards, by historical standards there was little traffic during daylight hours. The speedy Maglev was too public for the confidential conversation, and Strether, being an American, was an accomplished driver.

'I tried an antique motorbike once,' Marius confessed, as he fastened his seat-belt. 'A Norton 732 with twin carbs from the Midlands museum. It completely petrified me. And the stink of unburnt hydrocarbons! Nothing whatever would induce me to learn to drive after that. Too bloody murderous, even if the road was empty. Anyway, in my profession it's best to use public transport. The voters prefer it.'

Strether eased the car into sixth gear. He had learned not to wrestle with the controls of the small but powerful English-made Toyota, chosen in preference to the Dodge. The night before, he had made the effort to sit down in the garage with a doubtful Peter, the chauffeur, and the manual. It had taken over an hour to master the systems and on-board computer with its instructions in an addled version of Microsoft English. He would return from the trip content to let Peter take over in future.

The car moved out north beyond the city towards Harpenden and Dunstable. Above their heads, and in an almost straight line into the distance, tall cypresses reached to a cloudless blue sky. Strether switched on the shader and adjusted the air-conditioning. It might be autumn, with the older deciduous trees losing their leaves – more modern species did not – but noon temperatures were still forecast to reach over 30°C. Fortunately

Bedfordshire was not humid. In the semi-tropical jungles of Sicily, today would be stifling.

'What exactly am I going to see, Marius? You've been nothing if not mysterious. "Wear stout shoes and clothes which you don't mind getting dirty." These are my sole instructions.'

The Prince pretended to look out of the window. 'I can't tell you much. Or, rather, it's not for me to tell. I'm not a fount of knowledge on this. It may be a learning opportunity for me too.'

Strether grunted. 'Damn you.' They drove in silence for several kilometres. Leighton Buzzard with its conservation areas of 1960s 'little boxes' housing slipped away to the west. Then he tried again. 'I can't figure you out, Marius. Am I wrong? You seem to know everybody, and you move in the most elevated circles. You're an NT, and an Énarque. Presumably you could, if you wanted, be a front-bencher. Or a top official – leastways, a person with considerable influence. Yet you play the dilettante. I don't get it.'

'Go on, I'm enjoying this.' A half smile curled on Marius's face. 'A little bit of character assassination does a man good. I've never had a proper job, that's true. Never felt any need of one. Maybe when they put my genes together, they forgot the most important ingredient.'

'What's that?'

'Taking oneself seriously.'

The two men laughed quietly. Marius continued, 'You sound like my mother. Except she wants me to get married and start producing embryos of my own.'

'And why don't you?'

'Oh, something lacking in my personality, I suppose. Put it down to prolonged immaturity – mine. And I've

never found the right woman. But I will admit, I have
started looking. I have begun to take steps – definitely.'

A road sign indicated access to the Woburn Abbey
theme park, which stretched from Luton to the edge of
their destination. In the distance elephant-giraffe crosses
could be glimpsed, and a pride of tame white leopards
asleep on the roof of the Moat House Hotel. Strether
slowed slightly. 'I did want to ask you. You're familiar
with the ethics of the genetic programme, aren't you?
What Lisa was saying at the Commons has been addling
my brain ever since. What actually happens to rejects?'

Marius folded his arms. 'I knew you'd ask me that,
sooner or later. It was discussed ferociously in the beginning, but, my dear Bill, that was over seventy years ago.
And when something's successful, and as widely
accepted as the programme is, then it ceases to be the
subject of debate. Criticism seems like carping. Some
questions are no longer asked. Who wants to know what
happens to sewage?'

'I worked that out for myself,' the Ambassador
responded grimly. 'I'm listening.'

'What was supposed to happen with failed experiments – rejects, damaged material and the like – was
covered by two separate considerations. First, its human
origin required respect. That meant, if it were viable, and
the parents wished it, it could be blessed or given the
last rites or whatever, and disposed of like a stillborn. It
couldn't be used for further research without express permission. The second element was really a contradiction
of the first. It stemmed from the need to understand
errors. Details had to be recorded, biopsies stored, medical audit would establish what went wrong and why. In
either case, a test-tube full of defective live cells would be

handled with the utmost care. Unfortunately, my meagre inquiries have shown that both systems have fallen into disuse.'

'But what you've just described are excellent proto-cols – if there has to be a programme, that is.'

'Sure. And that's how it was written – in 2032, anyway. But in practical terms it must have been a night-mare. Getting signatures on all those documents – what if the ova and sperm are donated? Who has paramount rights? Who were the "parents"? That sort of thing. With manipulated chromosomes a baby could have fifty "par-ents" or more. So other legislation came to predominate. Family law, for a start. For the last fifty-odd years, the official parents of an assisted-conception child have been whoever applies for the licence and accepts responsibil-ity for the outcome. They expect success: they're not interested in disasters. In other words, there had better not be any failures.'

'So the mistakes are not admitted. That must mean they go down the pan.'

'In all likelihood. Ask your friend Lisa. Legislation covering medico-ethics is biased towards her side, as a scientist. The positive assumption in law these days is that the needs of research override other considerations. The material becomes useful if a researcher wants it; if not, then it's quicker and easier to discard it. And a lot cheaper.'

'Money counts that much?'

'As ever. Start loading administrative and clerical costs on to the programme and the estimates would soar.'

'But it's not "material". It's human. Never mind the parents, does *it* have any rights?'

Marius laughed unpleasantly. 'Rights? Eggs and

sperm? Embryos, foetuses, mashed up bits of RNA and DNA? That really would be impracticable. You must be joking.'

To their left the great lakes of Little Brickhill lay flat and hot in the sun. Flocks of white herons wheeled and cried. To lighten the atmosphere, Marius remarked how wise it had been of the environmentalists to insist, once the clay quarries had been exhausted, that they should be left untouched to fill with water naturally. In his view they made a splendid contrast to the tinny artificiality of Woburn.

Strether would not be distracted. 'Our answer to those conundrums in the USA was simple. We banned it. The whole caboodle.'

Marius spread his hands. 'An impolite European would say, "More fool you." The ends justify the means here, Bill. Anyway, the means themselves aren't seen as posing any tricky moral dilemmas. Honestly. Instead, depending on the person's standpoint, they're regarded as ranging from the miraculous to the humdrum. You might as well question the mechanisms by which the electricity is generated that drives this car. Nobody's the least interested, as long as it moves when the buttons are pushed.'

'You're saying they don't give a damn. I see. Doesn't that strike you as morally shallow? Shouldn't somebody care?'

Marius paused. 'Most people don't care. They don't care about anything, much, provided life treats them well. But if anyone attempted to close or scale down the programme, Bill, there'd be an outcry. It's a source of immense pride to the Union authorities and its citizens. Who doesn't want to be healthy? Who doesn't want a healthy child? You start voicing doubts out there, and you'll get laughed out of court.'

'The "authorities" are all beneficiaries, I suppose. And had the hypocrisy bred out of them.' Strether was aware that he sounded caustic.

Marius murmured an amused, 'Well, not quite.' Then he frowned, and spoke more slowly, accompanying his words with emphatic hand movements.

'Bill, understand. History is against you. Even oppressed people seldom rise up, and our citizens are among the most contented on the globe, every opinion poll says so. Change only comes when a leader decides. The Roman empire, which two thousand years ago built the die-straight road we are travelling on, would have carried on worshipping Jupiter if Constantine hadn't declared for Jesus. England might never have had the Reformation if Henry VIII hadn't lusted after Anne Boleyn. And the old USSR could have been a super-power for another century if Gorbachev had never uttered the word *perestroika*. Change requires leadership. Forget that stuff about power coming from the people. It's crap. Forgive me.'

They must be nearly there: that last junction had been for Buckingham. The vidphone on the dashboard beeped. Strether glanced at Marius, who turned politely away.

'Hello?'

The screen buzzed into focus. It was Lisa.

'Oh, Bill, is that you? Can you talk? I heard you were on your way to Milton Keynes. I'm here anyway. Can I join you?'

Her voice floated round the car interior. Strether was about to answer when Marius touched his sleeve. The Prince was mouthing, '*No*.' The Ambassador looked quickly to his companion, who hissed, 'It might be dangerous.'

'Well, I'm not sure,' was the best Strether could manage, aware that Lisa could see his expression. They were on the outskirts. Signs pointed to the main tunnels, over which 'Welcome to Milton Keynes' billboards had been erected, complete with oversized holograms of John Milton and John Maynard Keynes. As they travelled downwards the vidphone flickered and cut off; the vehicle must be between transmission points.

By the time the car had reached a level again, however, the transponder was blinking. She must be using her instrument to track them. They could not evade her, if she were quick enough.

After Lisa had left, Winston sat another few minutes at the café table. He brooded on the sheets of hieroglyphics before him and brushed drops of carob milk-shake off the thin paper. A powerbook would have performed as well, but just as he felt at home in an antique stone-built farm cottage, there were times when paper and pencil (though those had to be hoarded when they could be found) were the best.

He had not managed to discover much that was new. Though Lisa's loss had been reconfirmed – and that could itself be counted as progress – the trail of exactly what had happened to the material on which she had been working was as cold as before. They had encouraged each other, however, with a recognition that they were no longer hunting missing documentation. The jigsaw-puzzle exercise on the terrace of the Commons, in which scraps of information had been tentatively merged from a variety of sources, had established firmly that some devious activity was under way, and not a mere paperchase.

Winston had spooned cottage cheese and salsa into his mouth as he had spoken; Lisa had seemed too worried to eat, but with some prodding had fetched bread and cereal bars for herself. She had lost weight and looked drawn and tired.

'It seems to me,' Winston had suggested eventually, 'that at least two different private projects are in hand. Number one: the senior NTs are hoping, in a couple of decades, to be able to put distance between themselves and the rest of us. That's long-term planning on a grand scale, but they're experts at it. Nobody would complain about further enhancement – it's the cut in IQ which is so objectionable. I'd like to bet that in a year or two the instruction will come to increase the degree of affability among the lower orders by a percent or two. That'd make them more amenable and easy-going. Now wouldn't that suit a governing race? Wouldn't it just!'

'Where do you get all this from, Winston?' Lisa slowly chewed the bread.

'That's easy. I'm the poor bloody infantry that gets told to do it,' he replied. 'I can't be the only one; and if I made a fuss they'd shift me or sack me, and get someone else. I'm not sure they realise I've cracked the codes. I certainly haven't let on to anybody in authority – except you.'

Her face did not register any pleasure. 'You said at least two separate projects. What's the second?'

'Oh, that's obvious. With your material. That's why it's so damned important to find it and destroy it. A gang of teenage thugs with a propensity to violence would suit some purchasers down to the ground. It's a crazy idea: defective genetics like that would be so unpredictable. I sure as hell wouldn't want them working for me. Or anywhere in my vicinity.'

'And the – the lorry?'

'Umm . . . That's a poser. Maybe nothing to do with the projects. Maybe simply a one-off mess somebody had to get rid of. Or p'raps it occurs quite often. Give somebody a lab, Doctor, and they're going to start playing sci-fi games. Not all of which have an innocent outcome.' He had pondered. 'At least time is on our side. Whatever they're playing at, it'll take a generation to come to fruition. Existing adults can't be altered, and that's a blessing.'

'True, but then nobody would destroy healthy infants either, even if they carried undesirable characteristics,' Lisa pointed out. 'So once this material gets out and starts to breed, the die is cast. We can't be complacent, or tardy. We daren't be.'

Then Lisa had risen with a determined air. 'You have not cheered me up, Winston, but at least I feel I have an ally. You and the Ambassador. Thanks.'

Winston had grinned slyly. 'And the Prince?'

'The Prince? I'm not too happy about him. Such a strange character – all things to all men. And women. But, my God, if he decided to help, what might he achieve?'

'You can't come, that's all there is to it.' Marius had now issued the injunction in various forms three times. 'It isn't safe. At least, I don't know what we will find down there, and I don't know exactly who we will meet. I do not have their permission to bring you along, Dr Pasteur. And they are incommunicado.'

The three stood in the seventh-level car park near the hospital. Its gloomy lighting and echoing halls made it seem far more removed from the airy light above than the mere metres between themselves and the surface. However much thought had gone into the attractive shopping and working environment nearby, those few vehicle parks not demolished or converted to other uses were dingy and neglected.

In any fight between Lisa and Marius, Strether would have put his money on the female. He stood back and watched the body language between the two with increasing curiosity. Lisa was the smaller, but she was a coiled, intense and angry person, all her energies directed into the confrontation with the Prince. He, sombrely dressed with a casual jacket over his arm as if expecting to encounter cold, was on the defensive and leaned away from her. And yet when it was his turn to speak, he bent close to her and seemed to want to conceal his remarks from Strether. It was as if the Prince sought intimacy with the young woman: as if he wanted to test her scent, or subconsciously to touch her.

'Whatever you're up to, I think I have to be in on it, Prince,' Lisa was saying, with studied ferocity. 'Those missing files, those damaged embryos, that ghastly heap in the back of the lorry: I cannot walk away. I cannot.'

'Then I should keep your voice down, Lisa,' Strether warned. 'Your sense of responsibility is commendable. A sense of self-preservation would also be smart.'

She gazed around anxiously; a security camera was looking the other way. Marius caught her arm. 'Okay, since you insist. If you carry on arguing you could put us all in peril by drawing attention to us. But, for God's sake –' He brought himself up short and snorted. 'I was going to say idiotic things like keep your eyes skinned and don't make a sound. This stink of conspiracy is getting at me. I feel like a character in one of those banned children's books – Enid Blyton, wasn't it? The Famous Five. All we need is a girl called George and a dog.'

His semi-facetious comments went over his hearers' heads. Marius pointed. 'Down there. Door 7-14.' He glanced about; they were alone. The camera was still aimed at the entrance; perhaps its ancient brackets were stuck. 'Have you got your vidphones with you? Can you be tracked with them? Switch that feature off, but they might be useful. Come on.'

The three moved off, avoiding the puddles on the floor. The water table had risen throughout England; although Milton Keynes' advisers had carefully checked forecast data for two hundred years, the climate change that had melted nearly half the polar ice packs had occurred faster than any prediction. So while the town's residents enjoyed an enviable lifestyle underground with Christmas lunch on the lawn in the shade of their own vines, pumps to keep level seven dry were on the council agenda.

Door 7-14 was in a recess behind pillars. At first it appeared blocked by fire-fighting equipment: rusty reels of hosepipe, fire blankets, cylinders of foam. With some straining the two men managed to move enough obstacles to clear a path. Marius stood waiting quietly, as if under scrutiny. For what seemed an age nothing happened. Strether began to shuffle his feet. It was chilly. Then a tiny red light, hardly bigger than a pinhead, flashed on above their heads, once.

Marius placed both palms on the door and pushed. It opened slowly. He stood aside to let Lisa and Strether slip through, then followed. Behind him, the door slid to without a sound.

They were in a narrow, dank corridor, lit by small wire-caged lamps in the low ceiling above their heads. There seemed nothing to do but start walking. Ahead was pitch darkness, though as they walked sensors switched on the lights above them and turned off those behind. That made it impossible to judge how far they had to go or had come. The gloom was disorienting. Lisa saw Strether check his watch and begin to count paces, his lips moving silently.

She touched the walls. They were cold and felt wet. The lining was cheap concrete; in places chunks had fallen off to reveal older brick underneath, which efflo-resced in furry bulges with the damp. Above them pipes were slung, painted anti-corrosion red, with faint mark-ings and tags. In places leaks ran down from encrusted welds, with ferns and sodden lichens in a greenish trail. Condensation dripped on to their heads.

The tunnel was too narrow for three to walk abreast but wide enough for the two slim ones, herself and Marius. She slipped back and let Strether go ahead.

'Thank you for the flowers,' she hissed. 'I wasn't sure what you meant by them.'

Marius chuckled. He coughed once; his breath hung in a misty fog about his face. It was getting colder. He pulled on his jacket, then looked at Lisa. 'You warm enough? Would you like this?'

She shook her head. They were walking quite fast and she was panting slightly. 'Fine for the moment. The exercise is sufficient. Prince, what the hell is this, please? Where are we going? Who – or what – are we hoping to meet?'

'I can't entirely answer your last question. But if I'm not mistaken we should make contact with the group the Ambassador was inquiring about on the terrace.'

'Oh, those odd names. Solidarity? What does it mean?'

'You are not a historian. Neither is our dear friend Bill. I had to spell it out for him as well. It was the name of a Polish protest organisation in the mid-twentieth century, as the Soviet Union was beginning to disintegrate. It had the backing of organised labour and the Roman Catholic Church – believe it or not, Poland was once profoundly religious. It was at the forefront of the fight for Polish independence, symbolising a struggle for freedom against tyranny throughout the world, and was totally successful. Until it became the governing party in its own right when everything turned sour.'

'Is this Solidarity a religious group? If so, I'm not sure I'd have much in common.'

'Can't say. It has links with continental groups, but I don't think the numbers are large. I pretend to my dear friend Strether that I'm a fount of wisdom, but you should realise, Dr Pasteur, that I'm somewhat of a fraud.'

She stopped dead, then saw the smile on his lips. 'God, don't tease.' She shivered, and carried on rapidly. 'If you'd seen what I saw in that horrible lorry – the way those little fingers reached out, as if pleading for help. I keep wondering what kind of body it might have had. It was a living creature, and it was human. Or it had started off human.'

'A world away from roses,' Marius said softly. 'Or d'you think those were genetically engineered too?' The quip had its desired effect; Lisa smiled back at him. 'I can assure you nevertheless, Doctor, that they were sent to you with genuine and unadulterated affection. And respectful awe.'

'You're aware that I – we –?' Lisa indicated Strether with her thumb. Was this being disloyal? With the longest stride he was now ahead of them by some twenty metres. Yet what did she owe him, other than the consideration of friendship?

'Yes. But there used to be a saying that all's fair in love and war. Have you not heard it? The fact that a man I admire is in love with you immediately puts you into a favoured category with me. And your self-discipline and your profound sense of duty, let alone your remarkable intelligence, have heightened my . . . interest, dear lady.'

'Lord. What it is to be wanted. You'd better call me Lisa.' Winston's earlier advice came back to her. She squeezed Marius's arm. Inside, something shrugged: she would let fate take a hand from here on.

Ahead Strether checked his watch. They had been marching briskly for some fifteen minutes – that meant at least a kilometre. He had lost count of the paces some while back. The path had begun to meander slightly uphill. Then the lights ahead showed that another tunnel was about to cross theirs.

They were at a crossroads.

The trio stood uncertainly, their breath heavy in the chill air. Strether could see nothing but was absolutely sure they were being observed; he could imagine the heated discussion that was going on, as it became clear to those who were scrutinising them that they were three, not two, and one was a woman. If Lisa was identifiable – say, from her vidphone signal – they would have ascertained that she was a high-ranking official from Porton Down, and was not on the guest list.

Down the tunnel to their left, a red light winked, once. They took that as a signal and turned towards it.

'Whoever these maniacs are, they are well protected,' Strether muttered. 'If they were attacked by this route they could pick off assailants one by one.'

'And I've not the least doubt we are under surveillance the whole way,' Marius agreed. 'Easy to do in tunnels like this. I've seen no escape hatches, have you?'

His companions shook their heads. Lisa moved closer to the Prince, her fear genuine. 'It is a bit claustrophobic,' she whispered. Her voice echoed down the chambers. 'I hope we get to where we're going soon.'

In the most fraternal of gestures, the Prince took her hand. Finding her fingers cold he tucked her hand with his into the pocket of his jacket, and kept it there.

Ten minutes later the tunnel began to narrow until eventually it was no longer possible to walk abreast. Strether found he had to bend his head to get under pipes slung from the ceiling. In single file they trudged on until another crossroads loomed.

'Bloody hell,' muttered Strether, blowing on his hands. 'How much further is it? What are these tunnels for anyway? They're not sewers. There's no smell.'

'Communications of some kind. Or they could have been purpose-built. Or the builders simply found old tunnels and decided to re-use them.' Marius's lack of his usual certainty revealed that he was guessing. In the half-light his face was drained and pinched. 'Our instructions are to keep going: they'll let us in when they're ready.'

'For Chrissake, I don't like this at all,' was Strether's blunt reply. 'Not what I was expecting when I accepted

the President's commission. I thought my toughest challenge was going to be the weight I put on at official
dinners.'

Lisa froze. 'What's that? Shut up, Bill, for a minute.'

The Prince closed up to her and put an arm around her
shoulders. She motioned angrily at both men to be quiet.
The roof seemed to press down on them as if it were
alive. The three moved together like animals seeking
comfort. Then Lisa grabbed the Prince's coat. Her eyes
widened in alarm.

'Listen. Behind us. My God. There's somebody else in
the tunnel. Oh, Christ, we're being followed.'

At first Strether could hear nothing. Then he held his
breath to still his thumping heart. A faint footfall could
just be heard from the blackness behind them. Not
boots, not a crisp or military crunch, but a sound more
sinister, in soft-soled shoes, someone who did not
expect to be detected, or did not care, some distance
behind them.

'Keep going,' Marius hissed. 'Let's get a move on.'
They began to run, covering ground almost faster than the
light switches could keep up with them so that they had
to stumble forward into the murk. The Prince led now,
with Lisa on his heels and the Ambassador heavily bringing up the rear, his breath rasping, mouth wide open.
Into Strether's mind came the remnants of unarmed
combat he had learned in his youth. He wished crazily
that he had thought to carry a weapon.

'Marius – did you bring – anything?' he panted. Lisa
tripped and let out a little scream. Behind them the feet
had also broken into a trot and seemed to be gaining on
them. Marius picked up Lisa without a word and did not
reply.

The tunnel suddenly twisted to the left and ended. The three cannoned into a blank wall.

'Holy Moses,' Strether gasped. He scrabbled for a handkerchief and wiped his forehead and flecked lips. 'What happened? Did we take a wrong turn? Where the fuck are we supposed to be?'

'I've no idea,' Marius muttered. 'I am heartily sorry I got you into this. Get behind me.'

They cowered grim-faced, their backs to the wall, and turned to confront whatever was loping steadily towards them. Strether could feel Lisa shaking with terror. He took in the Prince's profile, its aristocratic jawline set, the brown hair lank, the forehead beaded with perspiration, the eyes wide and impenetrable. Then he glanced down, and realised that Marius had had more information than he had ever admitted.

In the Prince's hand, half hidden in his garments, was the metallic glint of a gun.

Chapter Fifteen

The air-conditioning had broken down again. An elderly fan clattered in a corner, its head moving this way and that like a questing dog. On his desk the folders had to be held down by a paperweight, a piece of granite containing a fossilised tooth. The sweat ran down the groove of his back in a steady trickle. Colonel Thompson picked up the fossil and examined it dully for a moment. Perhaps one day, millennia from now, some genetically refined creature would do the same. Only the tooth in question might be one of *homo sapiens* – might be one of his own.

The fan turned malevolently towards him and the papers fluttered. Cursing, he jammed the rock on top, then clasped his hands together in a resolute refusal to set to work.

A return to London was not what he had anticipated or wanted. He could not deny that, in both geographic and career terms, the frontier posting was a dead end. The barracks were diabolical. The intricacies of commanding a mixed bag of Caucasians, Sicilians, Germans and Balts – even if their officers were the pick of the bunch – tried his patience and drove the autotranslator into a frenzy.

But it was soldiering. The enemy was in sight – if not to the naked eye (though occasionally a plane or helicopter hove into view, or puffs of smoke on the distant horizon confirmed a firing exercise) then definitely in the vicinity. Every screen in his control room proved their existence. Their movements were tracked by satellite; their emissions were analysed by gas spectrometer, their state of readiness pinpointed by infra-red sensors from a hundred kilometres away. He knew at what temperature their engines ran at idle and at peak performance. He knew the mixture of fuels, and that they relied on the cheapest form of diesel – proof of their backwardness. He knew they ate without fail at eighteen hundred hours. That regimentation had surprised him, till he realised that alarm bells should ring only if the pattern altered.

And it was the right enemy. The Chinese were not merely a different civilisation: they were the challengers. Given what he knew of their character, as demonstrated daily on his monitors, Mike Thompson had no doubt they were the main danger to the peace and security of the Union, a real and menacing threat to the way of life he and his fellow citizens enjoyed. Given half a chance, their brooding presence could switch to belligerence; were the Union to abandon these dismal steppes in Central Asia, the enemy would not hesitate to step in within a few days.

This was no idle fancy. It had happened where defences had been weak. In Japan, for example. The pacific nature of those people, the unwillingness of their flabby parliament to stand up to the aggressor, and the preoccupation of its government with the appeasement insisted on by commercial interests, had made the wealthiest islands in the world a sitting target. The military action had taken six

days; resistance had been brutally suppressed. Now, the
Japanese lived in uneasy co-operation with their overlord
occupier, and hoped they might be allowed to go on
making money without interference or penal taxation. It
was not freedom as he understood it. Neither had there
been objections in China itself. From what any outside
observer could judge, the celebrations over their country's
'victory' had been genuine. Human nature didn't change
much. If his job on the frontier, therefore, was to warn the
Chinese not to contemplate similar moves westward, then
he was willing to do it.

He wished the Union would take a firmer stance in
other parts of the world. It was a mistake, in his opinion,
to ignore Africa. True, much of the equatorial region had
become uninhabitable as daily temperatures soared. The
Sahara desert was twenty times its size of a century
before and now stretched from Ghana to Kenya, coast to
coast. But the Magreb, the Mediterranean coastal strip,
was an important manufacturing region, where German
and Dutch business exploited cheap local labour forces
and the lack of Union regulations on fire, health, safety,
working hours and the like. The south had become an
empire in its own right, an important market for Union
exports, though its standard of living was still well below
that of its richer allies. Yet whenever he visited either of
these regions – or South America – the airport lounges
were full of sober-suited Chinese with attaché cases and
raincoats over their arms. Hotel lobbies had signs in
Chinese, and many of the staff were conversant with the
language – enough anyway to say, 'Have a nice day,' in
Cantonese, Mandarin or whatever they guessed to be
appropriate. The invasion could come by blazing guns
from those tanks lined up ten minutes away. Or it could

come insidiously, through shareholdings and soft loans and debt-management, through smiling handshakes in the smoky air of closed boardrooms. There was more than one way to win a war.

Here, at least, he was in the front line and performing daily a task he justified with no qualms. He could kill the enemy if he had to; he could give the order to open fire, and would not hesitate. Naturally he would do his utmost to avoid any spat, for it would cause an incident with international repercussions. Thompson's maturity and tact were useful assets in this eternally tense theatre. He was aware of sniggering gossip about his faith, but among the military a rudimentary pattern of belief was not uncommon and not a handicap. Here, he was trusted.

London was another matter entirely. His instructions had been skimpy, which meant that something was afoot. The Colonel might have been bred as a simple soldier but he was nobody's fool. He sighed and scratched his arm where a bug had bitten.

Civil unrest. The phrase had leaped out of the terse communiqué. He and his unit, crack troops, were required to return to the regional capital and to prepare themselves for potential conflict. That could mean shooting people, and not Chinese. Yet he was in no position to refuse.

With an oath of savage impotence he banged his fist down on the papers. Several loose sheets fell away. The Colonel put his forearm on the table and deliberately swept the lot off the desk. The fossil fell to the stone floor and rolled away.

Thompson rose and contemplated the mess as the fan blew the documents about. That had been a pointless gesture which would irritate his adjutant. It did not make

him feel much better either. He rummaged about for the
fossil. The stone had cracked open: the mammoth tooth,
forty million years old, which had survived intact long
after the annihilation of its species, now lay broken in
pieces in his hand.

'We been took over,' Finkelstein announced. 'Again. I
thought so.' He pointed to the small paragraph in the
bottom corner of the wall screen. 'There. Never tell us
anyfink, do they?'

In the Rottweiler Security Services office behind
Westminster Abbey Captain Wilt Finkelstein and
Sergeant Dave Kowalsky were munching a mid-morning
breakfast, toast with real butter and marmalade, sugared
tea in mugs. The police world – even the private sector –
clung to its traditions with unrivalled tenacity.

His partner grunted through another slice of toast,
butter gleaming on his chin. 'Who is it this time?'

'Dunno. New World Securities, it says. Lemme scroll it
up. Company registered in the Malaccas. Far Eastern
interests. Could be anybody.'

'Well, as long as they pay us proper. I'll do anything
I'm told, if the readies are in the bank.' Kowalsky put his
booted feet up on the desk. The navy serge of his combat
trousers creased comfortably. He tilted his chair. 'You
worry about things too much, Wilt. Whatever it is, you
worry 'bout it. You got shaken up about that guy shot
near the American embassy, remember? An' when we
was in the force together, you worried then. Didn't wanna
hurt nobody. You put yourself in the firing line rather
than shoot a killer. You've forgotten why you got
invalided out, and that's the truth.'

Finkelstein brooded. 'We don't get appreciated. Police never do.' Then he sighed. 'You're right, this is a cushy number. An' I got a few of them shares – good price. May be able to take the wife to Deep Ocean Disney this year. All we gotta do is keep the bosses happy. Carry out the contract, whatever it is. Ask no questions.'

'Get told no lies,' Kowalsky put in easily. He drained his mug.

'Get told nuffink at all,' Finkelstein responded. 'I mean, who're we working for? Really? An' what do they want?'

'Who cares?' Kowalsky stretched. 'Oh, Gawd, I gotta helluva day ahead of me. New recruits. C2s, the lot of them. Thick as planks, but tough with it. Wish they didn't all look alike – still, it doesn't seem to bother them if I can't tell one from another.'

'They *are* all alike,' Finkelstein reminded him. 'Have been for the last ten years. Find a type that suits then repeat the recipe endlessly. Everyone recognises a Rottweiler Guard, like the slogan says. Brand image, it is. Secret of our success.'

'The new lot are coming in stupider, I swear.' Kowalsky rose and pulled on his leather jacket with its slavering beast's head, lettering in gold on the back and the four stars studded into the shoulder flaps. He fished his name-tag out of a drawer and pinned it on. 'Maybe they're giving new orders at the factory. Exact reproductions. Give us dimwits who'll do as they're told.'

Finkelstein helped himself to the last piece of toast. 'Don't joke about it, Dave. I reckon the fact they're so similar ain't no accident. Gives me the creeps.'

'It's fine by me,' Kowalsky shrugged. 'Provided nobody starts interbreeding like they did with the dogs. 'Orrible brutes they ended up, them rottweilers. Don't see 'em much now. I wouldn't fancy being around if some of our raw recruits decided we was the opposition.'

Finkelstein patted his holster. 'Elementary exam question: *"In a tight situation, what do you do with your weapon? Turn it on the attacker, or on yourself? Discuss."* Yeah, I know what you mean. Go on now, they'll be waiting. Don't wanna be late on their first day, do you?'

The safest place to talk. That was normal. But whether it was because the hiss and opacity of the steam made visual surveillance virtually impossible, or because a fellow could hardly carry a concealed recording device when he was mother-naked, Sir Lyndon Everidge had never quite worked out. He was, however, certain that the sauna at the London Forum Club was not his idea of a pleasant spot. Especially not when his companion was the Permanent Secretary, whose desiccated frame seemed to relish the richly-enveloping heat. For Sir Lyndon it was a crude form of torture.

'This had better be good, Robin,' he muttered. He could feel his blood pressure rising, the arteries pulsing in his temples.

'It is. We are close to our goal.' Sir Robin Butler-Armstrong folded his thin arms with an air of satisfaction.

'And that is –?'

'Oh, prosperity and contentment throughout the realm, of course. Permanently.'

'You're not telling me anything I don't already know.'

'My dear fellow. Don't get so aerated. The three-point plan. We are making great strides.'

'I'm listening.' Sir Lyndon slumped soggily into his towels.

'First, the economy. We are now in a position where four per cent growth per year can be confidently predicted for the foreseeable future. With productivity gains, that should mean five to ten per cent wage increases are easily affordable. You can announce it whenever you like, my dear chap. A substantial hike in the standard of living. Just in time for the election, too.'

The silvery hairs glistened on Sir Robin's chest. Nothing sagged on the trim torso; Everidge suspected the man had had a body tuck to remove excess abdomen skin, a common problem in older men. The way the scrotum hung, so tidily, suggested some delicate cosmetic surgery in that area also.

'Second, enhancement. My dream – so dear to my heart! – of a sustainable gap between the upper castes and the rest is now under way. The first children are at advanced foetus stage.'

The Prime Minister brightened. 'That I do know about. My younger daughter married that bloke Dainty from the Home Office and they've put in for one. Due next spring.'

'The Director of Porton Down is doing an admirable job. He assures me everything is going splendidly. No hold-ups whatsoever.'

'I'll believe that when I see it.' The Prime Minister reached for a hand-towel and wiped his pounding brow. 'He's not as interested in the acceleration project as I'd like. He can't see its importance. And his expenses are something chronic. I don't trust that bugger further than I could throw him. He'd swear everything in the scientific garden was rosy even when it was throwing up man-eating monsters.'

'You have no cause to say that,' was the frosty response. 'Of all the advances benefiting the Union, the enhancement programme is by far the most effective. And the best controlled.'

'I suppose that's so,' Sir Lyndon conceded. 'The fact that it's in our hands makes me more comfortable. But the day can't be far off when Mr Murdoch Junior acquires the technology and sets up his own facilities. Or our pal Maxwell Packer. He's been demanding legal amendments to make cross-patents possible. Then he could sell the output round the world. More profitable than news-making and sports, any day.'

'He won't. He can't. The computer programmes have a self-destruct built in. We've dealt with that.'

The Prime Minister, more aware of the machinations of commercial minds than the civil servant – whom he privately regarded as living in a world too esoteric for his own good – wanted to say, 'Balls!' but decided against it. He was already at an acute disadvantage and preferred the conversation to end as soon as possible. Instead he shifted his blotchy thighs and said gloomily, 'Go on. How's the third bit of the great plan going, then?'

'Third? Your allusion to our news media brings me to the elimination of dissent. It is so rare, but it does happen – cranks and idealists who assume they can per-form better than you, the elected representatives, and us, the selected élite. As you are aware, violence has flared up again in London and other regional capitals, though the news has been satisfactorily – ah – filtered. Our friends are proving their worth.'

The Prime Minister wanted to riposte that he didn't trust them either, but thought better of it.

'Behind the scenes,' Sir Robin continued, 'we have

key dissidents under constant observation. There appears
to be some foreign influence – to our alarm, from so-
called friendly nations. You should be wary.'

'You're kidding. Who is it? The pesky French, I'll bet.
Can't leave them alone a minute. Or the Germans? Or are
the Russians at it again?' The Prime Minister's love of
intrigue shone on his streaming face.

'No. Good Lord, Lyndon, those are not *foreigners*.
They're our partners in the Union. It may be fashionable
still to refer to them in xenophobic language, but it isn't
practicality. No, it's further afield. I'm afraid the
Americans appear to be encouraging the subversives. The
Ambassador in particular – a most naïve and foolish
man.'

'Why should the Americans want to do that?' Sir
Lyndon asked. 'Wait – I suppose their President thinks
that if the Union falters a wee bit, they'll be able to take
over. Idiots, if that's the case. Anyway, what are we going
to do about it?'

'My main anxiety is over the sporadic, but increasing,
outbreaks of trouble. "Terrorism" is more apt. We have to
nip it in the bud or it may become harder to maintain
news black-outs. Several divisions of front-line troops
are on their way home. Their loyalty is unquestioned.
And we have negotiated more civilian back-up from the
private security firms. They will play a far bigger part in
future.'

'I hope Rottweiler are included,' the Prime Minister
said. 'I made a killing on those RSS shares. Fifty euros
each this week! When I got involved in the business
twenty years ago they were ten cents apiece.'

Sir Robin pursed his lips. It was not illegal for politicians to have substantial shareholdings, nor did they

have to be declared. Parliament had long since abandoned the archaic practice of registering personal financial interests. There were too many, for a start. Provided the tax authorities were happy – and, in Sir Lyndon's case, that could be guaranteed, or arranged – it was nobody's concern but their own.

'I'm not entirely happy about that, I must admit.' Sir Robin's aristocratic brow puckered. 'I have no reason to doubt that the new owners will fulfil all contracts to the letter. My difficulty is that we can't find out exactly who they are. The trail of interrelated companies is highly complex – the convolutions have defeated the Stock Exchange. We couldn't have interfered: competition laws forbid it. But good Lord, Lyndon, for all I know it could be somebody hostile.'

'Like who?' Sir Lyndon sat up straight. 'I dealt with Branson. The cleanest credentials you could find. What are you accusing me of exactly?'

'No, no. My *dear* chap. You will give yourself a heart-attack, and that would never do. You acted with total propriety. And, in the end, Rottweiler is only one of many private security firms, even if it is now the biggest in Europe. But – Far Eastern certification – that makes me uneasy.'

'Could be Indonesians, or Singapore. Or our own chaps trying to avoid tax.'

'Quite reasonable, in the circumstances. You will be able to announce cuts in taxes, too, in your next budget. But suppose it's somebody else?'

Matt Brewer and Dirk Cameron stood together in the washroom, brushing their hair and tweaking their tunics.

Dirk's red hair stood up in a startling crew-cut. He spat on his hands and smoothed down the sides, but the hairs immediately sprang back upright.

'Yeah, but that's what we want tonight, ain't it?' he pointed. 'Up and at 'em! No surrender!'

'Those girls. Insatiable. I've taken tomorrow morning off. I could hardly walk after the last episode,' Matt agreed, with a giggle.

'They're wild. Never met anything like it. You know, I came six times, and still she begged for more? They'll never believe us back home.'

'Almost inhuman. Forget New Viagra, just gimme a Toy Shop girl. But then, they're bred for it.' His voice fell to a conspiratorial whisper. 'Mine has a taste for the wild stuff. Suggested I spanked her. Or she'd do it to me. Offered to tie me up in chains.'

Dirk's eyes bulged. 'An' did you? That's kinda spooky. Mine's got whips and handcuffs and that in her cupboard too, but I told her I like it straight, hot an' strong. I don't need no restraining!'

'We ought to be careful, though. They aren't quite normal. Mine's on something – some drug. Or maybe there's a sado streak. So what's it about us they find so irresistible?'

'Maybe our boyish innocence, Matt. Or our fresh-faced charm. Who can say? Come on – you ready yet?'

The lights in the tunnel went out. Cowering together, their backs to the dead end, Marius, Lisa and Strether could feel the heat of each other's bodies, could hear the rattle of breath in the throat and sense the pounding of each other's hearts. Strether, the tallest, his mouth clamped tight shut for fear of screaming, could also sense something faint but dank hovering about both himself and the other two. It was the smell of terror.

He reached for Lisa's hand. She scrabbled about in the pitch black and clasped him so tightly her nails dug into his flesh. With a wrench he realised that this could be the last time he touched her, if death was round the corner. He wanted to blurt out how much he had valued her, some babble about the joy of knowing her. Forced behind her as she resolutely turned outward he slid his arms around her waist and pulled her to him, so that he could bury his face in her hair. She trembled but every tendon was rigid. He whispered something to her, some endearment, he could not afterwards remember what. Behind them the walls were cold and clammy. It was a terrible place to die.

He struggled to concentrate but already his mind was fragmenting. Is this what it meant, that one's whole life began to flash before one's eyes? He could see the endless Colorado plains, could hear the wind in the eaves of his ranch house, the thunder of hooves in the distance. A night fox called out, that eerie squeal that had transfixed him as a child out camping with his father. The odour of sweaty leather enveloped him afresh as he cantered across a gully, the horse straining and muscular beneath him. He had never faced his own death, but had struggled against its lingering cruelties with his wife: he would be spared that, and would spare others the need to care for him in a dribbling dotage. That was a blessing at least.

But what overwhelmed him was a powerful ache of regret: so much not done, so many useful years ahead lost. Most poignantly he grieved that he had not had time to say goodbye to Marty, and would not now be able to keep his promise to help her. He would never again be able to make love to her, to stroke those fabulous breasts and hear her breathy laughter. Hers was the most jarring of all the unfinished business snatched from him. And she would never know that she had featured among his fleeting reflections in this chilly tunnel which was to be his tomb.

He heard a click as Marius pushed in the gun's laser cartridge. A vicious little weapon, it could drop a victim at half a kilometre. Suitable for an assassin who wished to make one hit where it would be most brutal. At close quarters it could blind. Strether prepared to shade his eyes the instant firing began, though a hole punched through his hand would be equally dreadful.

'*Don't shoot.*'

The voice hung in the darkness, around the corner from which they had come. It was male and had a vaguely familiar resonance, but was edged with authority and caution.

'*Don't shoot. Put up your weapon. You have nothing to fear.*'

Marius cleared his throat. 'Who the hell are you? Identify yourself.'

'I'm here to identify you, Prince. Or, rather, your uninvited guest.'

As the pursuer rounded the corner the motion switched on the lights once more. The trio stood rigid, eyes staring, fright now mingled with curiosity.

It was Lisa who recovered her wits first.

'*Winston!* What on earth —?'

Before them loomed the lanky figure of the records clerk in his unmistakable sweater, jeans and sneakers, a woolly hat on his head, his neck swathed in a knitted scarf and leather gloves on his hands. His eyes were wide and wary but he carried no weapon.

Winston pointed at the gun. 'Disarm it and put it away, please, or you're not going any further.' Marius, shaky and confused, did as he was ordered. 'Now stand a few steps away from the door.'

Strether began to ask, 'What door?' then he grasped from the direction of Winston's look that he meant the wall behind them. Obediently the three shuffled back several paces and Winston walked forward, his long neck inclined as if he were peering through a spy-hole, though the wall was smooth and featureless.

Then the dead-end wall swung back as if on hinges, and Winston ushered them through. The corridor ahead was not much broader than the tunnel from which they had come, but it was well lit and the floor had rush matting. The air was immediately sweeter. Behind them the enclosure shut silently. A camera slung from a bracket in the ceiling surveyed them with a low buzz.

'Say your names – they like to use voice recognition,' Winston instructed, and they did so, one by one. The camera seemed particularly interested in Lisa. As it concentrated on her, Winston nodded firmly at it. The anonymous eye moved on. She bit her lip. The subsiding panic had left her drained and exhausted.

'You decided to tag along, Dr Pasteur,' Winston explained in a formal tone. He began to move along the corridor and the others followed. 'They freaked out when they saw three people heading their way, not two. Especially when your ID came up – a government employee, high-ranking – so I got an emergency call. I blame myself. I should have maintained total secrecy, and I let it slip. I should not have mentioned that the

Prince and the Ambassador were coming. You were bound to jump on that. Anyway, I've vouched for you. Hope that's okay.'

Lisa stopped dead, a look of utter amazement on her face. Winston turned and began to chuckle.

'I think *you* have some explaining to do, Winston,' Lisa chided. 'What is going on? How are Prince Marius and Mr Strether involved? And where the hell are we?'

'That's simple. Under the Milton Keynes public library, at a rough guess. There are tunnels everywhere beneath the complex. Some old, some new. It was designed as a government bunker in the last century's Cold War, in case of nuclear holocaust. Never needed so the system was forgotten. But it's ideal for our use.'

'Who's *we*, Winston?' Strether inquired. 'Is it Solidarity? Are you a member?'

'Of course I'm a member,' Winston grinned. 'My God, it's the sole thing that keeps me sane as I punch out those goddamned codes – knowing I can record the nastier bits to show somebody else who'll take it seriously. And who isn't forever spouting on about how fantastic the genetic programme is, and how lucky we are to have it.'

Lisa averted her eyes. They were at another barrier which opened to admit them into some kind of great hall, a treble-storeyed room like a hangar, big enough to house a small aircraft or helicopter. Around its walls were storage racks with anonymous boxes and pallets neatly stacked. A shadowy figure in overalls slipped out as they entered. The light was dim, power-saving but adequate.

'This way.' Winston strode across the hall towards a glazed supervisor's office at the far corner. It was empty. In a moment they found themselves standing, somewhat cramped, in front of an untidy desk. The windows of the office gave out on to the darkened hangar. Above an empty armchair another camera watched and paced, as before, from one visitor to the other. All the cameras looked new and hastily installed; no attempt had been made to merge them into the background. As if satisfied, this one suddenly looked down and stopped moving.

The welcome, if such it was, was grudging, though they no longer felt in immediate peril. Marius ostentatiously placed the gun on the table before him, close to his hand.

Out of the corner of his eye Strether saw that the Prince had taken Lisa's fingers in his other hand, and was holding them tightly. It dawned on him that the two had walked together, behind him and out of his sight, in the time – it seemed like an age – they had been in the tunnel. And had whispered to each other, and not shared their remarks with him. Marius and Lisa were the same generation, he noted, and similar in colouring and stance. Part of Strether's mind flickered. She had Polish blood; the Prince was Hungarian as well as part-Japanese. They were closer genetically, and culturally, than he was to either of them. It was not impossible that they should be attracted to each other. A strange, sonorous alarm bell began to ring somewhere deep in his soul.

Then his attention snapped back. Fear flooded through him once more.

A dark-haired, thickset man entered. He seemed to have a slight limp, but he carried himself with an air of authority. He wore a khaki uniform with badges of rank. His eyes were black, his greying beard was neatly enclosed in a small hairnet that disappeared up beyond his brown skin and ears, and ended in a startling blue turban.

Chapter Sixteen

The three dishevelled adventurers stood stock-still in the crowded office and stared openly. Lisa pushed a lock of damp hair back from her eyes then covered her mouth with her fingers as if uncertain how to react. At her side Marius relaxed visibly and squeezed her hand once again. She did not remove it. Strether noticed the slight movement; embarrassed, he found a handkerchief in his pocket and blew his nose.

'I'm Ranjit Singh Mahwala,' the turbaned man introduced himself. 'My code name is Spartacus, and I'd prefer that you use that. Sit down, please.'

'Good Lord. I'd expected –' In truth Strether did not know what he had expected, except that a trim, muscular Sikh officer with a mobile, intelligent face had not been anywhere near the frame. He sat down heavily.

'You expected a tall, blond NT, no doubt. Everybody does: it is the unassailable icon of leadership. Racism is endemic in the Union, Ambassador, as it is everywhere else, whatever the law may say. People such as myself and Winston are relegated to the lower ranks of society not merely because we are not NTs, but because we don't conform in any way to the image of NTs.'

'You're all so accustomed to the ruling class and its style that it's assumed the likes of us can't possibly perform in command roles,' Winston added, with a twist of a smile.

'So Solidarity is just blacks, is it?' Strether was nonplussed. He had been challenged once before on these supposed supremacist tendencies by Winston and resented it.

'No. Absolutely not.' Spartacus's voice was sharp. 'We have many NTs in the group. Responsible individuals who are alarmed at the trends. Who have reason to believe that something sinister may be going on. Who want it stopped, and normality restored.'

'Why are you called Spartacus?' Lisa's brain felt weary. It may be silly, but unless she could settle trivial details she could not focus on larger questions.

'He was the leader of a great uprising against the Romans,' Marius answered her. Up to that point he had been very quiet. He no longer attempted to hide that his hand was entwined with Lisa's.

'An uprising of the slaves, so perhaps it is not the best analogy,' Winston continued.

Strether grappled with the reference. There'd been a movie in the distant past. The name had another defect, he recognised. Spartacus had lost.

'Perhaps I should explain,' the Sikh continued. 'I was a soldier, an officer. Still am; officially I am on leave recovering from injuries sustained when my vehicle blew up. A frontier posting I was not sorry to quit. Anyway, I am not a fugitive. But for the last few months I have worked full time for this organisation. It is my intention to hand over the task as soon as I can find a suitable replacement. Then I can return to my regiment, and there carry on whatever good work I can do.'

'You will note, Dr Pasteur, that we do not have a slave mentality,' Winston murmured mischievously. 'We welcome anyone in a senior position who can support us. Passive personalities are no use whatever.'

Lisa had caught up. 'I'll buy that. If you know about my work, Spartacus, then you'll have heard from Winston that I'm very unhappy. The purposes of the programme, the public-service element especially, are being eroded and replaced by some other, more sinister objectives. It's complicated, and murky. I can't find out who's responsible but it must be reversed. That doesn't mean I want to join any underground movement.'

'You don't have to join us, though naturally we'd hope you would. For the most obvious reasons we don't keep any central membership register. This is not the kind of club to which you pay your subscription by direct debit, Dr Pasteur.'

A silence fell as the five people in the little office warily assessed each other. Strether had a distinct feeling that everyone present knew a piece of an important story, like part of an old-fashioned jigsaw, but nobody had the entire picture. With the right encouragement each might offer their contribution, but the atmosphere was edgy and distrustful. They might break up without having made any progress, with lingering enmity, frustration and fear, or a dramatic fusion might occur. He wondered how much of it was up to him, and groaned inwardly at the state of his own ignorance. But his courage was returning.

He broke the silence. 'Is Prince Marius a member?' he inquired softly. It was easier to put the query to the Sikh rather than directly to the Prince. 'I suppose he must be, to be so well informed about it.'

Spartacus gazed for a moment at Marius who was pre-occupied with a bit of fluff on his sleeve. Then, 'We should like him to be more than a member, Ambassador. We think he would make a fine leader.'

Every eye turned to the Prince. His handsome face darkened. 'We have had this conversation before,' he said grimly. 'It is a compliment of the highest order, though I'm really not sure why I should have been singled out. And not at all happy about it.'

'Because you're on the inside. You move in the highest circles. You are widely respected and liked. If anyone can initiate effective action against the forces of evil, you could – and you could bring in many more, who'd be horrified to know what's been going on. Up to now all we've managed is sporadic action, a few strikes here and there. The same with our contacts on the continent. It isn't enough. You, Prince, you could lead us all forward.' Spartacus's voice had taken on an earnest, almost plead-ing quality.

'And you don't have freckles,' Winston added drily. Lisa glanced sharply at him.

'Freckles? What does that mean? What difference . . . ?' Strether was irritated at the superficiality and intrusive-ness of the remark.

Winston slouched forward and spoke as if confiden-tially to the Ambassador, though in the cramped office his words were audible to everyone.

'It means he ain't what he seems. His parents requested freckles, but for reasons known only to himself, or them, he hasn't got 'em.'

'What makes you think his parents requested freckles?'

On his friend's behalf, Strether felt annoyed. Family material of this kind was not for public display.

Winston grinned again but did not reply. Lisa answered for him, speaking carefully. 'It means Winston has located and checked the Prince's printout – the one given on a child's eleventh birthday – but unlike most readers who learn nothing from the tables, Winston can analyse their content. The Prince differs in distinctive respects from his own chromosomal makeup. Freckles are linked to particular NT lines. Either the clerk made a mistake forty years ago, or someone else did. The computer doesn't lie.'

'The freckles could be on a recessive colour gene which was subsumed by something stronger, such as Japanese pigmentation,' Marius spoke up in his own defence. 'You're wrong to assume I was unaware of the discrepancy. But I do not consider it significant. And it has no bearing whatsoever on my decision not to lead this group of worthies – to what can only be their destruction.'

'But that's precisely why we need a remarkable individual like you,' the Sikh urged. He gazed at Marius till the Prince returned his stare, then held it steadily. They resembled nothing so much as two gladiators testing each other in mortal combat. Strether found himself listening in fascinated perplexity as the two men verbally parried and side-stepped, unsure which protagonist he wanted to win: but the advantage lay with the Sikh who was circling, net in hand, to catch his unwilling prey.

'You have a duty to lead. You have all the qualities necessary. You could help us.'

'I cannot. You flatter me. It is dangerous. You are heading for defeat.'

'We cannot stop. The Énarques are tightening their stranglehold on society. Soon it will be impossible for anyone else to enter the élites. And with increased passivity and reduced ambition at lower levels, nobody else would want to.'

'I do not have it in me. I may be independent, but I'm a loner. I could never lead a full-scale rebellion. I wouldn't know where to start.'

'You would leave that to us. Plenty among our ranks have military or police experience – in fact, they've been among the quickest to join. They've seen what's happening and how it flatly contradicts their training and the Union's laws. The true subversives are those upper castes who have their own game-plan. Men at the very top. They are the conspirators, not us. We need you.'

'I am not a leader. I could not make decisions. I've never made decisions. In fact I've spent my whole life avoiding them. Conflict is not my line. I respect what you're trying to do, it's utterly admirable. If I could, of course I'd help. But I am not your man.'

'But that's precisely why you were picked out – your arrogance is a front, a pretence. In reality you're a vastly more civilised and thoughtful person than you let on, Prince. We've been observing you for months. That should come as no surprise. You have the perfect balance of history, birth and integrity to make this mission a success.'

The Sikh's language had drifted into the messianic. His eyes bulged in his head, his lips were tensely pursed. In the background Winston, still upright, hovered like a vengeful sprite. The pressure on Marius was enormous. Strether watched in mute, shared anguish as the Prince wrung his hands, as if they were being entwined by ever-tightening invisible bonds. A biblical allusion came hazily to him, of Jacob wrestling all night with the angel. Only when his will was broken was he granted the strength to overcome his enemies. And to lead his people.

What was needed was an act of free will, a choice. The Prince was right when he said that he had always shunned commitment. If he held to that view, their journey underground was wasted. Yet Marius had arranged the episode in the first place; he must have been aware that the stakes would be swiftly raised. And in front of both Lisa and Strether, newcomers to the group. Had he perhaps – unwittingly or otherwise – put himself into a corner where to refuse would be to lose face, friends, everything?

The Prince and the Sikh. Each clearly grasped the stance of the other. On whatever occasions they had met before, Strether realised, the identical arguments must have been rolled out. Yet here, now, a palpable sense of destiny hovered about them. Not least because of his own presence, and Lisa's. There could be no going back, not now.

'I am not a leader. Don't ask me to do this,' the Prince said, sadly.

Spartacus scented victory. 'You have some persuading to do, Prince, but not of us. Or of yourself. Your task would be to persuade others – to use your prestige and your contacts to spread the word, then to identify and brief those men and women who would replace the Énarchy at the right moment.'

'But *I'm* an Énarque,' the Prince answered, with asperity. 'I went to school with these monsters you so roundly condemn. You're asking me to betray my relatives, my parliamentary colleagues – a whole class. And for what?'

'Because it must be done. Because the codes are being betrayed as we speak. Because the world we've grown up in, sworn loyalty to, is being destroyed before our eyes – and you will be one of the culprits if you don't call a halt to it. You can't wait on the sidelines. Soon enough there won't *be* any sidelines.'

They backed off for a moment. Strether pondered. Then he spoke. 'Marius, what have you got to lose? If you accept that the Union's in trouble, it'd be immoral not to try. It's not a job for someone like myself – it needs an insider, Spartacus is spot on there. Nor, I suspect, would anyone accept strictures from Winston or even Lisa – sorry, but this is *realpolitik*. It has to be somebody exactly like you. One of *them*. Absolutely, one of them.'

'And, with respect, Marius, this is urgent. You have to decide.' Lisa touched his arm, her expression pleading.

'On the other hand,' Marius responded, a sarcastic edge to his voice, 'what have I got to gain? I'm a privileged mover in every élite. I have a fabulous life – power without responsibility or, at least, influence without accountability. It has suited me so far. I'm at a decision point, that is so: hardly a mid-life crisis, but more a feeling that my playboy days are behind me. That's personal, not public. My best years are to come and I wish to share them, to find a partner. Somebody like Lisa here – who knows?'

Everyone present saw him tighten his grip on her hand, and the uncharacteristic shyness with which she bent her head, only to raise it to gaze fully at him. The Prince did not pause. 'That's hardly a recipe for becoming a full-blooded revolutionary against the NTs, my blood and bone, and it does not appeal to me, not one jot.'

'But you're not an NT,' Winston said softly.

The whole room froze. Strether felt his heart skip a beat. He glanced at Lisa, but she was sitting bolt upright, clutching the edge of the desk for support with her other hand, staring at Marius intently as if the computer print-out were etched on his cheeks and brow for all to see.

'What did you say?' Marius demanded, half rising in his seat. His fingers reached for the silvery gun.

'Calm down. You can find out for yourself easily enough.' Winston spoke clearly so that everyone could hear. 'It's not just the freckles. A whole host of things don't add up. Not least your personality and IQ. You're supposed to be barely beyond average intelligence, Prince, like most royals. That ain't so, as you demonstrate every time you open your mouth. And your classification is F-645, which is bland, lightweight. You're neither – that's what makes you such a find. You are learned, and passionate, and wilful. The combination is unusual – so much so, that it must have come through natural selection. That's why I'd lay a big bet that you're not an NT.'

'That's a terrible thing to say, Winston,' Lisa upbraided him crossly. 'How dare you? You commit a criminal act by poking around in somebody's private records and then you accuse him of being a fraud. And a non-NT. How could you? D'you think that's going to convince him, if nothing else will?'

'The trouble with you, Doctor, is that you've swallowed the whole lie hook, line and sinker,' Winston retorted angrily. 'You think the world revolves around being an NT. What's wrong with the rest of us? What makes you so superior? I'm not one. Neither is the Ambassador, nor Ranjit. Nor, I am spot-on certain, is your bloody boyfriend here. The Prince. If he's a Prince. If he's anything.'

Lisa's mouth opened as if to reply, but suddenly she pulled her hand away from Marius and lifted it to her face. Her eyes glazed over and she seemed turned to stone.

Marius stood up jerkily and straightened his tunic. His face was working furiously, his expression a mixture of the genuinely outraged and a high-caste NT at his most haughty. He reached for the gun, checked the safety and put it carefully in his pocket.

'I think this is the point at which I leave.' His voice grated. 'Whatever is going on in here, I cannot be part of it.'

He turned to Lisa. 'Will you come with me? I fear I got you into this. My apologies. Perhaps these good people will be kind enough to let us return unmolested. Strether?'

But Lisa did not move, and Strether seized his friend's arm. 'Sit down, Marius. If what they've said is correct, then you are an extraordinary individual. They have not insulted you. But it alters the picture out of all recognition.'

'Indeed? How, would you say, my dear Bill?' Marius's dark eyes were cold fire.

'Because if these guys have figured out you're not what you claim, then others can't be far behind. That means you're in serious danger. You would find yourself pushed to the fringes – subtly, somehow. You could become not simply a – culprit, as Spartacus said earlier, but a victim. What you hold most precious could vanish tomorrow.'

'Nonsense. This is entirely speculative. An outrage. I won't hear any more.'

He took two strides and was outside the door, but then stood uncertainly a few paces off, glancing unhappily in the direction of the dank tunnel from which they had emerged. His back was to them, but they could see his shoulders shaking with tension. He was no longer wrestling with the angel, but with himself.

Then the Prince turned back to Lisa, one hand held out, his expression full of pain.

Lisa gave a little cry, as if she had been touched by electricity. It was impossible for Strether to guess what raced through her mind in that split second, but he did not attempt to stop her as she jumped up and went to join the Prince, without a backward glance.

The door slammed behind her. She ran after Marius and halted him several metres away. Through the glass window the couple could be clearly seen, though their voices were reduced to muffled murmurs. The observers left behind made no pretence but watched them intently: nobody in the stuffy little office dared utter a word.

As in the car park, Strether was riveted by the vivid and tempestuous body language on display. Lisa seemed vociferous and intense, trying hard to convince Marius – of what? Before, she had begged to be allowed to come – insisted, indeed. Strether strained to hear but caught only snatches. Her hands gesticulated, pointed, jabbed; the Prince's hung limply at his side, or were held up half-heartedly in protest. Marius was twisting backwards as if to avoid her ferocity, yet he coiled about her as if their bodies independently ached to entwine. Some force beyond their consciousness was drawing them irrevocably into each other's orbit. Some magic was afoot.

The Ambassador was sure Lisa was determined to get action over the Porton Down disasters. She could be the technical, professional heart of the dissent, its convincing solidity. The Sikh's objections were broader, drawn more from the nature of society as a whole. She could not lead any revolt herself, as a woman, and an insufficiently important NT, but with Winston's back-up she could provide the necessary forensic evidence to make any objections stick. In fact she was vital to the future success of Solidarity. She was also young, so beautiful, and healthy. Moreover, as Strether had unwillingly begun to recognise, she was deeply attracted to the good-looking Prince, with whom she seemed to be bargaining fiercely.

And, he realised, with a dreadful sadness, *Lisa was aware of the attraction.* Neither was it one-sided. It had been there the whole time; the Prince had held her close even back in the tunnel. She was conscious of it and recognised it, and was now turning it selflessly from herself alone to a far greater purpose.

She was trying to persuade Marius. She held his sleeve and tugged it in emphasis. She tapped her breast with both hands and then placed her palms on his shoulders. I am yours, the gesture said, but on one condition. He could have her, and she would support him unquestioningly in the role of leader. But he could not have her alone.

Both. Or neither. It was for the Prince to decide. She would brook no compromise.

And Marius had his palms up, in protestation, half in surrender, as if waving away an undeserved gift; but he was gazing at her as if he wanted to melt into those brilliant honey-flecked eyes. Strether, too, had gazed, often, and found her impossible to deny. The Prince's mocking manner had vanished completely. Instead his face was suffused with anguish, and something so akin to love that it made Strether's heart turn over.

Strether did not want, at this extraordinary instant, to

believe that the woman he had loved could have
deceived him. It was the other way round: he had been
the guilty party. She had been so angry about Marty, but
then contrite, and had reminded him that he, Strether,
was a free agent. Her response to his offer to take her
home to America had been lukewarm; no obligation survived. And, knowing Marius – or, it had to be said, the
old Marius – Strether would not have put it past him to
pursue Lisa behind his back. The Prince would have
regarded her as fair game. Maybe something had happened between them before today, though what exactly it
might have been was irrelevant. Far more important were
the biblical trials of strength in the hangar, nakedly visible to the silent watchers: Marius with Spartacus, Marius
with himself, now, finally, Marius with Lisa. It was a
struggle towards an irrevocable decision. It could end in
triumph and freedom: or in disaster for every one of
them.

Strether forced himself to breathe in and out, very
slowly. The sight of the two people who had become
more dear to him than any other Europeans arguing
intensely with each other brought one fact home to him
forcefully: he was not included in their considerations.
Nobody had said, '*but what about Bill?*'

Strether could understand the Prince's quandary. Even
if he were not what he had seemed – if he had no entitle-
ment to the printout with freckles, if his conception
somehow involved a conundrum, or a lie – Marius was
wily enough to cope. The facts would probably never be
revealed. And if they were known to a handful of key
personnel, what would be the outcome? Again, in all likelihood, nothing. Parliament, including the Prince's
beloved second chamber, was a place of pomp without

power. The controls had shifted into other hands many
ages since.

What about Bill?

Lisa and Marius had moved from the window. Their
voices could no longer be distinctly heard. Then Marius
strode away and was hidden as Lisa stood, still speaking
rapidly, face flushed, her lips mouthing words Strether
could not grasp.

Then Marius reappeared, seized the girl in his arms
and held her tightly, rocking backwards and forwards.
Strether shut his eyes.

He had lost her.

They were a pair. Their bodies were as close as if they
had been made for each other, and had always expected
this moment to come.

Bill Strether's spirit wept. But his generous nature saw
that his sorrow was solely for himself. For he had witnessed the best outcome. Both Marius and Lisa had once
defended the genetic programme. Their acceptance of its
ethical vacuity had saddened him even as it showed
unarguably why the Union was so far ahead of his own
country. If sophisticates like the Prince and honest minds
like the young doctor's could go along with it, he had felt
the more a hick for his fumbling criticisms. Now they
were all on the same side, lined up with objectors such as
himself, and committed to exposing its failings. It was
some kind of consolation, and made him feel almost
serene.

There they were, the two of them, together in the shadowy light of the underground hall as if they had never
been apart, radiating courage and hope, facing a future
that could be filled with dreadful dangers. His breast
stirred. They needed each other, but they did not need

him, neither Lisa nor Marius. He had seen their unification. They would be a formidable partnership. And he, a stranger, relegated once more to mere acquaintance, would pledge to do everything he could to help.

The door reopened. On the threshold stood the Prince, his face haggard and wet with tears, his arm round Lisa whom he hugged protectively to him.

'God in heaven, I must be mad,' he muttered. 'But you can count me in, from right now. What exactly do you want me to do?'

Chapter Seventeen

Lisa had returned to Porton Down. It had been agreed that she should take care not to draw further attention to herself; she should ask James Churchill for lighter duties, avoid any more reference to her missing files, and keep her eyes peeled. Meanwhile Strether was invited to tour the Bunker, and tactfully left the new leader and his mentor together. He would rejoin them later.

For Spartacus it was an essential opportunity to introduce the Prince to the principles and strategy of the organisation. Marius frowned as their secretive structure was explained to him. Nobody knew the names of more than a small band, no meetings were ever held with more than four present. Despite the paucity of their numbers and the constant risk of betrayal, secrecy had been maintained so far.

'We don't like it, but it works,' Spartacus commented. 'You will only ever meet your own cell, even as overall leader. You could find yourself in a roomful of distinguished men and women and be quite unaware that several are our operatives. They would not be able to identify each other either, though one or two might. If you remain under cover, most would be ignorant of your status also.'

'But what about our methods?' Marius asked quietly. The afternoon was drawing on. He and his guide were relaxed in an inner sitting room where battered sofas and a low table provided a modicum of comfort. A bottle of J&B rare whisky had appeared; the Prince found it soothed his edgy nerves while heightening his sensitivities.

'We have debated such tactics as blowing up Parliament or putting bombs under the vehicles of MPs, if that's what you mean, and so far have decided against,' Spartacus replied carefully. 'The argument goes both ways. History suggests that that might be counterproductive. It could set the nation against us, gives us the label terrorists – which we are not. We have genuine grievances which we want addressed. Yet direct action is gaining adherents, especially when so little else makes an impact.'

Marius swilled the whisky round and took a gulp. 'You should know that I will not be associated with any unit, covert or otherwise, that starts killing innocent people. I witnessed the shoot-out involving the police on July the fourth. Was that us?'

Spartacus played moodily with his glass. 'Nobody was supposed to get shot. They were cornered. It was an attempt to liberate the news media, for an hour or two at least. To highlight the appalling censorship we suffer. I might try to justify it, Prince, by telling you that the dead police officer was a brutal man who had been involved in treachery and murder. If he was picked out as a target I can't say I'm sorry.'

Marius felt himself being tested, like a barefoot man

instructed to walk on broken glass, as if to prove his mettle. He forced Spartacus to meet his eyes, then, only half mollified, grunted in reply. The Sikh adopted a softer tone. 'A campaign of civil disobedience is more effective, in my view, though some of our activists strongly disagree. It draws attention without hurting anyone. It irritates the government and provokes overreaction. That, skilfully handled, can help the cause.'

The model was not the Marxist-inspired liberation armies of the previous century, therefore, but closer to early Gandhi, Marius suggested. The Sikh, delighted that the Indian reference had been recognised, nodded enthusiastically.

'But Gandhi was a master of publicity,' the Prince pointed out. 'He made sure, right from the beginning, that whenever the British Raj beat up unarmed civilians – especially women – a top press reporter was present.'

A cloud crossed Spartacus's face. 'I think,' he answered slowly, 'that this will have to be one of your priorities as leader. At present the European media are too tightly controlled. The Énarchy have it down to a fine art. Key media owners seem to have their own reasons for misreporting, or not reporting the truth at all: the relationship is almost incestuous. We may have to seek help from beyond these shores. Much of Gandhi's most vigorous support came from Americans, remember. Our friend Mr Strether, perhaps?'

'But he's a diplomat. And inexperienced – he hasn't served a year yet. He may not be able to make a fuss.'

'He could on his return. Or via his own press. His President might not be averse to taking a stance.'

They left it at that, aware that Strether was about to join them.

Marius brooded. It was not settled whether, or how, he should announce his conversion or his new position. Those decisions were up to him. Spartacus himself was completely under cover: his family believed he was on a secret posting outside western Europe and largely incommunicado. But if the Prince were to become the public face of dissent, the platform needed careful preparation.

The Ambassador settled gratefully into the remaining armchair, filled glass in hand. He was tired; he saw that, until a moment before, he himself had been a topic of discussion. In an effort to lighten the atmosphere, he turned politely to the Sikh. 'How did you get involved? And why?'

The man rubbed his injured thigh. 'It wasn't a sudden conversion, if that's what you're asking. A number of things. It's hard to talk about it without sounding pompous or self-righteous.'

'The most self-righteous noises come from the likes of Graf von Richthofen and Sir Robin Butler-Armstrong,' Marius remarked. 'Go on.'

'My brother, first. Ten years ago. He had three daughters and wanted a son. They decided to go the whole hog. He and my sister-in-law badgered everybody in sight until they got a permit for a top-grade NT. Which, of course, we're not ourselves. And personally, I have no desire to be. My own children are – normal.'

Strether waited. He wondered if he could guess what was coming.

'When the baby was born, he was the most adorable infant you ever saw. No question about that! His mother was ecstatic. Only, forgive me if this seems strange to you, he was almost white. Quite different from his parents. Don't misunderstand me, he was obviously their son – his bone structure, the shape of his head are exactly like my brother's. He's a sweet kid and the apple of his parents' eye. Smarter than anyone else in the family – that's what they requested. But the skin colour, to me, was an insult.'

'Did his parents think so?'

'I could never get them to admit it. I'm the eldest, and the strictest in the faith. I've seen that as my role in the family. When I took my brother on one side and asked him whether a white child was what he ordered, he became a bit evasive. I admit I shouted at him – we were estranged for a while. But my guess is no. It was as much a surprise to them as to me.'

'It must have made you uneasy?' Strether had become an inquisitor, but he sensed that Spartacus needed to talk if trust between the three men was to be established.

'I can't put into words exactly what it did to me, seeing that child like an incubus in our midst. But what can it mean? Is somebody trying to eliminate some of our racial characteristics? Why shouldn't we be coloured?'

Marius snorted. 'My parents demanded that I shouldn't look Japanese. In their view that would have been a disadvantage in Europe. But at least that was their choice.'

The Sikh glanced quizzically at the Prince and did not respond to the point. Instead he continued, 'That raised my hackles. The whole system had lost, for me, the benefit of the doubt. Whenever we were told that the government knew best, I suspected the opposite, that the politicians were operating entirely in their own interests.' ('That used to be a widespread belief,' Marius interjected, with a hint of his old cynicism.) 'No, I'd been happy with the rubric. And if their interests and ours coincided, it didn't matter. But what happens if they start wanting something for themselves and not for the rest of us? What then?'

'It used to be money. Or mistresses. Or nubile boys. Nothing new about that,' Marius chuckled.

'But power over our genes? That's a power only God should have. I began to see oddities at every turn. Repeat copies, for example – they're supposed to be illegal, but apart from insignificant details, they're everywhere. Sports personalities – the star footballers conform to only four main types, we're losing natural variation. The rules of the game were altered to suit them – they're fast but have no stamina, so matches were shortened. Young actors and actresses: their faces have precise symmetry, because that's what we humans perceive as beauty. Skin colour – goes without saying. And far too many of the workforce in a place like Milton Keynes look as if they're multiple twins. It gets hair-raising here at times, I tell you.'

Some of the examples were familiar to his listeners. 'But you came back abruptly, didn't you, from your last posting? Did something happen in particular?'

'I served at Kashi, on the border. Horrible dump. One of my duties was to supervise the guarding of the prison.'

Strether sat up sharply. He reached for the bottle and refilled both their glasses. For a few moments Spartacus described the site; his listeners let him proceed without mentioning that they had also been there, rather more recently than the Sikh himself.

'Two elements – I'll describe them briefly. The politicals was one. I hadn't realised, idiot that I was, that a society like the Union might incarcerate citizens for their political beliefs. I'd swallowed whole the line that

the convicts were untouchables, wicked men, urban
guerrillas or some such. It was true that they'd been
caught, mostly, up to no good, though chunks of evidence were planted, I am now convinced. You don't
think DNA can be faked? Sure it can, especially when
the expert witness is a high-up NT. I wasn't supposed to
fraternise with inmates, so I pretended to my superiors
I was trying to get them to recant. They filled me in on
the genetic programme and got me to see that it wasn't
haphazard but a great plan – a huge, evil conspiracy.
We had plenty of time to chat – most of them were lifers.
They weren't going anywhere, not least because of the
PKU.'

'Ah,' came the measured response. Strether felt it wise
not to reveal too much of what he had already heard.
'Can you get hold of a monograph on how that works? It
intrigues me.'

Spartacus tilted his glass. 'No problem. It's simple, but
effective. A convicted man is given a radioactive concoc-
tion that destroys his body's ability to produce a certain
enzyme: PAH is the name, though I can't tell you what it
stands for. He has no say, of course – politicals lose their
civil rights under the code. He becomes PAH-deficient
from there on. Then the prisoner's daily diet includes the
necessary pharmaceuticals. If he tries to escape, his gut
can't cope. Ordinary protein lodges in the brain and starts
to poison him.'

Strether needed to clarify. 'They put something in the
water?'

'No. That would affect everybody. A pinch of green
powder in the politicals' food. That's enough. Kept under
lock and key – only the Commandant has access.'

'You know,' Marius mused, 'I don't recall this was ever

agreed in Parliament. I doubt if either House would find it easy to pass such legislation.'

'They would if they had to. But you're the master mind on that, Prince. If you wanted to change the law in secret, there must be ways?' The Sikh's voice was sombre.

'Yes. Executive action, for a start. I bet it's buried in some sub-clause of a prisoners' welfare bill from years ago. Is that why you quit?'

'Partly. I found that disgusting. Then one of the prisoners died.'

'Was he beaten up?'

'No, nothing like that. He got an infection and developed septicaemia. His whole system collapsed. The authorities made half-hearted efforts to save him, to no avail. But I'd got to like him and I was upset. I made inquiries. I discovered that they'd been removing a kidney. As a donation.'

'I'm not sure I follow,' Marius frowned.

'Think about it. We have artificial organs, we can grow disease-free tissue in culture. Perfect matches, or engineered to match. That's what the genetic programme should be doing, not churning out little white clones. But the best transplant is still a person-to-person living donor. And I'm damned sure he was not a willing participant.'

'Why do you say that?'

'He'd have told me. We had become – quite close.'

Strether felt his head begin to swim, whether from the alcohol or from the avalanche of extraordinary information he could not tell. He passed his hand over his eyes. After a pause Spartacus continued, 'I had to be careful. But soon afterwards his sister contacted me in secret. She was in touch with Solidarity. By then I was seething. I was so angry I was putting myself at risk as well as my

informants. Soon after, when I was involved in an accident, I was medivacked out and wangled a year's leave.
I've devoted myself full time to the movement ever since.'

For a moment no one spoke. Then Strether asked, 'You
said you have to return. Do you mean that?'

Spartacus's shoulders sagged. 'My family think I'm off
on a spying trip and my unit think I'm recovering from a
multiple fracture of the thigh-bone. The endless decep-
tions are getting me down. But the Prince is the leader
now. He will decide.'

Marius half smiled. He offered round the rest of the
bottle but opted out himself. Strether glanced at him and
could almost read his thoughts.

The day had been arduous; the journey they had made
may have started at entrance 7-14 of the underground car
park, but it was unclear where it would end. Yet for
Marius the effect was obviously liberating; he had come
into an inheritance that must fill him with fearful anticipation, but also fitted his nature. He should not rush.
There was too much to think about, and too much knowledge to absorb. Not least, the Ambassador reflected, there
was the nagging requirement for the Prince to burrow
into his own background, to discover who he really was.
Far too many others seemed to know more than he did.

The visitors rose and Marius pulled on his jacket. He
brushed it with his hand; it still carried the stains of the
tunnels. 'You will show us a more convenient exit, I
hope?'

The three men smiled at each other. 'Certainly, Prince.
This way.'

Marius paused at the door. 'I suppose I ought to have
some sort of codename too. Any ideas?'

The Sikh laughed softly. 'If you announce yourself in

the next few weeks it won't be necessary. But there was another prince who was not what he seemed. What would be your reaction to – "Moses"?'

Strether should have been concentrating. On his desk lay the tidal wave of files that had swamped it two days before as he had left for Milton Keynes. Its volume had doubled; more items carried the red 'Urgent' sticker. The ten-page diary required his immediate approval. A working dinner tomorrow required a seating list; the chef's menu deadline was noon. *Now*. The afternoon was filled by a Packer Television plc seminar where he was to speak on foreign service broadcasting – tedious, but he could not wriggle out of it. And he was expected at Buckingham Palace for supper with the King, another invitation that could be neither refused nor deferred.

He rifled half-heartedly through the folders. It amazed him how, when virtually everything could be generated by electronic means, and children were taught to use the computer before they could walk, so much still ended up with archaic technology. A previous incumbent had once erased every file on the hard disk by mistake; the office now insisted on paper, which could not be made to vanish at the touch of a button. In a truly up-to-date society, Strether grumbled to himself, printers would be illegal. That view did not seem to have found favour in the Foreign Service. They were not satisfied unless they had a signature – equally old-fashioned and far easier to forge than DNA testing – on a sheet of A4.

The diary was depressing. So many dinners, with so many hideously boring guests at the embassy, the Residence and elsewhere. Mostly other diplomats, whose

tinny superficialities jarred, especially after his recent
terrifying adventures – which he had not yet dared share
with anyone. So few hours for himself, or for the neces-
saries of life: riding on the Heath, a discreet dalliance at
the Toy Shop, a quiet night in with one of those classic
books nestling by his bed. He longed to try Salman
Rushdie or the searing prose of Jackie Collins's later
works. The twentieth-century literary canon repaid the
effort, though it would take his full tour of duty to plough
through *Ulysses*. Or he could start on Solzhenitsyn. But
not if he were out gallivanting past midnight every night;
youngsters like Matt Brewer could cope, but not him.

Where was Matt? Come to that, where was everybody?
His coffee had not arrived at ten as usual. Engrossed, he
had barely noticed, but the phone had been silent for
over half an hour. Usually his office was a buzz of activity with staff and secretaries traipsing in and out. He
pressed the bell, which sounded in the outer room, but
there was no response.

Maybe they'd had trouble getting in today because of
the tube strike. Some suburbs had had electricity cuts as
well, so perhaps wake-up alarms had not gone off or vehicle batteries had died. Strether considered: maybe these
events were not entirely coincidental. He recalled a comment of Spartacus's. Perhaps Solidarity or some other
underground movement lay behind them. The fact that
virtually no information was available strengthened that
possibility. A natural disaster – a tornado, or a lightning
strike damaging pylons, say – would have been widely
reported on TV and vidnews. Deliberate acts of sabotage,
on the other hand, were bound to be downplayed.

Since that fateful visit to the tunnels the world had
gone topsy-turvy for the Ambassador. Had it really been

only forty-eight hours before? In every way he had lost his innocence. He no longer believed that there was much to admire in the European system. Something was rotten in the state of Denmark, and England, and France and several other regions too; and above all in the uppermost echelons, among those unelected apparatchiks who, as he had suspected and as Marius had hinted months ago in Brussels, were the driving force behind the entire operation.

But that loss was also a profound gain. He was no longer so naïve. For months he had been criminally slow on the uptake. That made him ashamed. He had been dazzled. His own essentially open nature led him largely to accept what he was told, and had shielded him from the callousness and cruelty of much of what he encountered. But now, the arrogance of the leading castes towards those they ruled, and their determination to keep the rest, the lower classes, ever more firmly in their place, angered his democratic soul. To him, leadership depended on the informed support of the masses, not on their stupefaction by physical and worldly well-being. The elimination of poverty and misery had been the goal of respectable statesmen since time immemorial, but once it had been securely achieved, surely more noble aims could take their place. Instead in the Union they were being ignored entirely.

He had lost Lisa. In moments of solitude he pondered how serious he had been about her. It had not been a casual affair, not to him. She had awakened in his heart that latent regard for women and pleasure in their company that he had buried on the death of his wife. Some men, released from the anguish of that dreadful time, would have turned in relief quite speedily to other women, but not Bill Strether. After a while, as the pain of bereavement slowly diminished but nothing positive surfaced to replace it, he had believed he would never fall in love again, or feel any powerful attraction for a woman: both lust and love had seemed beyond him, at any rate emotionally.

Then he had loved Lisa, and had felt her slip from his grasp. As he had watched her with Marius he had felt helpless, and old, and envious. Of their youth and beauty – for they were, whatever might be feared for their future, a handsome and well-matched couple. He recalled an ancient Chinese explanation of true love: that on conception certain souls are twinned, so that for the remainder of its life each twin seeks the other, and can find happiness only when they are at last united. He had felt thus about his wife. It didn't rule out another romance, but in his mature years he knew he would be expecting something altogether less dramatic. Indeed, he had this cause above all to be grateful to Lisa, despite losing her: she had made him start searching once more.

Marty was a different animal entirely. For a start, she earned her living as, bluntly, a prostitute. Mesmerising though she was, he could hardly go parading with her in polite company. She would be a raucous and bizarre intruder at diplomatic dinners. The entertaining vision of her spectacular entrance made him chuckle, but also squirm with embarrassment. Her gorgeous flesh would excite ribald comment, though she could probably cope with that better than most – as had the original Marilyn. But to American eyes she was, as a clone and a toy, an example of everything wrong about the programme. She epitomised the *fin-de-siècle* decadence of Europe to a degree that could not be explained away.

He could well imagine that outside the artificial world of the Toy Shop she would get fed up with endless inquiries and snide remarks. He wondered what she was like beyond her own environment. At what point would she be out of her depth? The question gave him pause for thought.

For Marty, Strether felt a vivid, somewhat dazed affection mixed with straightforward lust. It had begun as a contractual arrangement; she was paid to be available, and friendly. At first he had experienced some guilt, but this had evaporated under her tender solicitude. Only faint stirrings of responsibility for her had surfaced, at any rate while Lisa dominated the frame. Indeed, Marty might resent any interference. Unlike many good-time girls she seemed comfortable with her profession and would defend it vigorously. Although she had had no choice about it, her upbringing had fitted her to take a justifiable pride in her job. Over the years the Toy Shop management must have been superb foster-parents. Marty was easily the best adjusted person he had met, with little guile but an endless ability to make a man feel special amid a solid dollop of her own self-esteem. And, increasingly, in Lisa's wake, she was a pal.

He was daydreaming, but to what purpose he was unsure. Marty did have worries. Probably they were groundless – but, then, he'd once believed that about the whole caboodle. An appointment with Marty after the palace that evening, however, if it could be fixed, would be a delight to look forward to all day. He could marvel aloud with her about his trip down the tunnels. Her responses would be grounded in sound common sense. He consoled himself that he valued Marty's worldly wisdom as much as her fabulous bosom. He pushed the buttons on the vidphone and waited.

Nothing. The line was dead.

Strether got up and went to the door. Nobody was about in the outer office. Bewildered and mildly alarmed, he trotted down the main stairs. Near the front entrance he heard a commotion. Several employees, girls and men, were in the hallway, with two burly police officers in blue municipal uniforms.

'Your Excellency,' one of the staffers said. 'Sir. We have some bad news.'

One of the young women burst into tears. Her wailing rose to a high keening and she was comforted by an older woman, who led her gently to a nearby chair. Her sobs filled the air – 'Oh dear, it's awful. Oh! Oh!' The others present shuffled their feet and blew their noses but were unable to meet his eyes.

The policemen looked from one to another, unsure whether to address him. Strether squared his shoulders. 'What's the matter?'

The senior officer stepped forward. 'Sir? Sergeant Carter from the Met. Sorry for the intrusion but the phone lines are down round here. The engineers are working on it.'

'I'd be grateful if you'd get on with it, Sergeant. What's the problem?' Strether was aware he sounded impatient.

'D'you have staffers by name Matthew Brewer and Dircon Cameron?'

'Yes, indeed. Two of my best young men.'

'Then, sir, I'm afraid we must ask if you could come down to identify them.'

'Come down? Where? What have they done?'

The sergeant ignored the last query. 'To the morgue, sir. I'm afraid they're dead.'

Strether pulled the officer out of earshot of the weeping girl. 'Dead? What on earth? Where? When?'

The sergeant glanced back. His voice dropped to a hoarse whisper. 'I'm sorry, sir, but that's why we need you. Their bodies were found early this morning by a refuse collector. They'd been dumped. They appear to have been murdered. I'm afraid they've been –' He stopped.

'You'd better tell me, Sergeant, before I get there,' Strether growled.

'The corpses have been mutilated, sir. Cut in pieces and trussed up. Have you any idea where they might have been last night?'

Winston Kerry grinned in delight. Eureka!

The screen before him was filled with a scatter of tiny lettering and numbers. He scrolled down, sheet after sheet. Just for fun he kept his finger pressed on the down cursor. For several minutes the sheets continued. The last page came to an end with a question: *Return? Retry? Print?*

He was about to press *Print* then hesitated. This material was dynamite. Not that it would mean much to the average browser. The fact that elaborate damage was being waged on the most delicate of chromosomes was detectable only by a handful of aficionados like himself. But buried in this heap of hieroglyphs was the originator – not just Lisa. Her ID number, 89004567-LEP, he recognised. He wondered to whom the other numbers referred, though it was a fair guess that 87567400-JDC might be James Churchill, the Director.

He downloaded the material on to his own hard disk,

then exited from the Edinburgh matrix, carefully wiping any traces of his own electronic fingerprints. The caution that had stored back-up files physically separate from Milton Keynes had also offered a security weakness. While access had been firmly barred to the home system, the other had had the easiest of locks to pick. It had been particularly useful to have filched the ID number of a selected top-ranking parent who had recently ordered an IQ-enhanced baby. A Mr Dainty, though the child would be anything but. It was the equivalent of a master key. Access to that ID had not been denied.

The question was, what to do with the material. First, a copy; he slipped a minidisk into the port, formatted and labelled it. Barely two centimetres across – easy to lose, but easy to hide. Then he realised, with a groan, that he would need to translate it. That would take hours. He would do it on the minidisk – then, even if his own machine were compromised, he could claim that he had not understood the significance of the information. He could play dumb if he had to.

Dates, locations, times. That bit was easy. ID numbers, some known, others he would probably never know – who was JSL? Or JM? Or WJH? These turned up several times, especially after February when Lisa had begun to lose her files. Perhaps they were other workers at Porton Down, or high-up officials. He doubted the latter, somehow; they would work at arm's length. He might never find out. The code numbers for the chromosomal locations: that required him to look up his own abbreviated manuals, stored elsewhere on his computer. The alterations began with familiar sequences, then veered off. One element repeated itself thirty or forty times. He took that to be the deliberate manipulation which had caused Lisa such grief. Somebody wanted to make absolutely certain that the twist occurred at site 21q, though in variations so subtle only an expert would spot it. Whoever was playing this game knew their stuff.

By early afternoon Winston was satisfied, yet his brain was still racing. He sat back and cogitated. Combinations of letters and numerals flashed through his mind: one in particular nagged at him. Lisa had had a further concern. She had mentioned to him the puzzle of PKU, the possibility of some form of chemical handcuffs used on convicts. That would be nothing to do with Porton Down. The Prison Service, however, might be able to tell him more. Maybe a delicate tiptoe through the Edinburgh complex would be illuminating there, too.

In the greenish light of the monitor Winston's straining eyes flickered. The first break-in to the back-up files had been tricky and had needed all his ingenuity. The second time it was a cinch. He typed in *Prison Service*. Asked to choose between a dozen names including Group 4, Rottweiler, Texas Inc and the Justice Ministry he was stumped for a moment, then shifted instead to locations. He wished he'd asked Lisa for more details. He switched to *Find* and typed in *PKU*. The computer buzzed and demanded an ID. With a shrug, Winston tried the putative father's. It worked again. Whoever that was, he was worth knowing.

An hour later the work was complete. Winston, his face grim, signed off and put his machine into hibernation. The minidisk nestled in his hand. No bigger than a piece of chocolate. That gave him an idea.

*

The King, Strether discovered, was in an excited mood. The main dining room was a-glitter with the best porcelain and silver; candles were lit in freshly polished silver candelabra. Some thirty important personages, most of whom Strether recognised, were ranged on four sides of the rectangular table. It meant that the two footmen had to work overtime.

As the dessert was served the King tapped a wine glass. The tinkle brought a degree of order, though at the far end of the table private conversations continued in muted tones over the profiteroles. He had called together various friends, King William said, to pick their brains. The century was drawing to its close, so the New Year festivities would have a special flavour. His own role would be central. What did they think about a spectacular fireworks display over the Thames? A masked ball? A hologrammatic presentation of the 1999 Dome, so derided until it had been blown away, so lamented thereafter? Bingo played on the face of the moon?

The mention of the moon brought the Ambassador down to earth with a crunch. He recalled the day spent shopping with Matt Brewer, and how thrilled the young man had been at reserving a ticket on the space trip. The boy's eager, honest face flashed into his mind. He would have to visit the shop again, and cancel the reservation – or possibly, since the staffer had grieving family, try to retrieve it for someone else's pleasure. As a memorial, at least.

It had been impossible to eat. Indeed, he had seriously contemplated backing out of the occasion until he reflected that the King would have been hurt and offended. For what Strether had seen at the morgue had been revolting, though luckily he had been obliged to do little more than view the heads.

The slashes across Matt's stone-white cheeks looked more like claw-marks than anything inflicted by a human. The gash that had severed Dirk's cranium from the torso had been a knife-wound, but done with such ferocity that centimetres of sliced flesh had been exposed in a single cut. Dirk's eyes had been gouged out; the bleeding around the sockets indicated that he had not been dead at the time. Matt's features were not so mutilated, but when the morgue officer, Dr Cornwell, had begun to describe what had been done to the body Strether had quickly stopped her. What he didn't hear would hurt less, he had mumbled hurriedly.

Some faint whiff of indifference on the part of the investigating officer had made him pay closer attention. Instead of assuring him that the perpetrators of this wicked and horrific crime would be pursued with all the wiles at their command, the senior inspector seemed to imply that this kind of gross violence was nothing new. Strether, clutching a handkerchief to his mouth and fighting nausea, had contained his temper and begun to ask pointed questions.

The answers enraged him further, but introduced a loud note of alarm. The police officer casually informed him that it was known that the young men had frequented the Toy Shop and had made illicit arrangements with a couple of the women employed there. At least, he had added, the boys had assumed they were the same women. Perhaps they weren't. Such injuries were not atypical of contacts of this kind.

Strether had wished more than anything that Marty had been around to help him translate the police officer's elliptical comments. As time ticked on to the moment he had to leave for the palace, he tried a frontal attack.

'So you're giving me to understand that these two young men may have believed they were out for the night with a pair of girlfriends, but it could have been look-alikes? That they couldn't tell?'

The police officer shrugged. 'If they're identical, nobody could.'

'So you must know who we're talking about?'

Another shrug. 'Could be tricky to prove. Identical DNA, you know. Could be a score or more the same.'

Strether remembered Lisa's rebuttal of the clone argument. 'Not acceptable in a court of law?' he persisted, his spirits sinking.

'Difficult. Doesn't give them immunity, of course.'

Strether felt his brow darken. 'Wait a minute. You're not levelling with me. If you think you know who they are, why aren't they simply arrested? Incarcerated? Kept out of harm's way? Destroyed, even?'

The police officer blinked twice. 'We're talking about human beings, y'know. Can't just go around arresting people. Gotta have some evidence.'

'There's something going on.' Strether wondered whether to bluster or pull rank. 'Look, I shall be seeing the Prime Minister tonight. At supper with the King. Shall I raise the matter with him? Would that be a good idea?'

To his surprise the police officer hardly reacted, apart from a slight tilt to the mouth. 'Prime Minister? That'd be rich. King's okay, innocent as the day he was tipped out of the test-tube. Sir Lyndon, though. Hardly innocent. But not guilty either.'

And he had refused to say any more, other than to reassure the by now thoroughly bewildered Strether that the matter was in the best hands and would be fully investigated.

As he had left, he had noticed Dr Cornwell watching him, her face impassive.

Across the table the capillaried cheeks of the Prime Minister had taken on the puce tinge that signified a six course meal eaten and a superb wine imbibed. The Ambassador had sat mostly silent, his plate untouched. At last his reticence was noticed.

'I am so sorry, Your Majesty,' Strether responded formally. The royal innocent commanded a duty of courtesy, if nothing else. He dropped his voice to spare the King. 'I had to view the bodies this morning of two of my finest young men. They had been involved in liaisons with women from a club called the Toy Shop. It appears something might have gone dreadfully wrong. All very sordid, I'm afraid.'

As he spoke he stared directly into the florid face of the Prime Minister.

He had his reward. The fleshy mouth dropped open and a gobbet of chocolate pudding dropped out. For a moment Strether thought Sir Lyndon might be choking, as the politician reached for a napkin and pressed it noisily to his face.

But how could the Prime Minister be caught up in such a horrible business?

'They were handsome young men,' Sir Lyndon muttered at last.

'How do you know?' Strether instantly demanded.

Sir Lyndon took a gulp of wine. In the vicinity the conversation had stilled to a buzz. The Prime Minister waved his napkin in a vague arc. 'Met them in your embassy. Must have. The red-haired one – bit wild, wasn't he? Didn't know the other.'

The King was looking cross that his celebratory schemes were being forgotten. 'I say, Strether,' he called down the table, 'do be a good fellow. What's your President planning to do on New Year's Day? We don't want to appear copycats, do we?'

Copycats? The Ambassador pulled himself together with a massive effort. His men had died. He sensed that if he examined the dreadful episode carefully enough he might figure out how, and why. And why the police had failed to convince him of their concern; and in what manner the belching corpulence of the Prime Minister opposite was involved. He took a deep breath.

'I suspect, Your Majesty,' he answered slowly, 'that, given half a chance, Mr Kennedy would take the day off and go to the moon. It would strike him as sufficiently surreal. In fact, if it's within my power, I shall ensure that he does.'

Chapter Eighteen

By the time Marius arrived at his mother's apartment he was tired and dishevelled. The disruptions to public transport were enough to drive a man spare, but the hour spent stuck in a stationary express near Luton had been useful for much-needed reflection. The intensive briefings at Milton Keynes had left him reeling. At the same time he felt exhilarated. It was as if a newly discovered will had been read out to him, outlining a rich but unexpected inheritance.

Unexpected, and undeserved. The mantle that Spartacus and Solidarity members wished to lay upon his shoulders demanded strength and qualities of character that Marius sincerely doubted he had. He had not been brought up to leadership. On the contrary, his background imposed restrictions on ambition: a Prince was supposed to behave graciously, be a witty and charming companion, mix easily with strangers of every race and style, and generally not be too thrusting. He wasn't expected to demonstrate erudition, have original ideas or flaunt his looks or contacts. He was *royal*, first and foremost; and his nobility, however insignificant, conferred on him mostly duties. *Noblesse oblige*.

Yet if anything convinced him that Winston was correct and that he wasn't what – or who – he had always assumed, it was the vivid excitement in his breast at his new prospects. Somebody in his lineage had liked to lead, had relished responsibility and the exercise of power. It might well have been a forgotten prince or king; with a shrug, Marius accepted that he would be disappointed should he discover he had no royal blood whatsoever. Maybe that made him a snob; if so, he could live with that.

The details Spartacus had given him remained sketchy. He had referred to similar groups on the continent yet had been unforthcoming about their numbers. Communication was difficult and an open invitation to spies. Face-to-face contacts were necessarily limited; Marius wondered which of his many acquaintances he would eventually discover to be conspirators like himself. Who were the leaders in the various regions? Where were the gaps? Might it be worthwhile to arrange an event – a royal birthday party, perhaps – to which the key figures could be invited, in all innocence? Was there a sign – a lop-sided handshake, a way of styling the hair or wiping the nose – which could be developed in secret, so that they could know each other without discovery?

He felt keenly the obligations of leadership. He must put his own stamp on the organisation, and quickly. Its amateurish enthusiasm must be converted into practical action as quickly as possible and new recruits obtained. He began to consider possible names, then resolutely put the issue from his mind. His errand tonight was of a different order. It was his own name with which he was concerned.

It was late. Princess Io might have retired. Yet the most intimate of conversations between mother and son was in the offing. Her formidable Highness might, in such circumstances, momentarily drop her guard.

Marius had not devoted much introspection to his mother over the years, though he had assiduously, and with pleasure, observed the courtesies. As a child he had been closer to his father, the vague, shallow man with craggy good looks who had regaled him with sagas of Hungarian knights, princesses, heroes and deeds of derring-do. Mostly the Hungarians had won the battle but lost the war. Their bouts of self-rule over the centuries had been brief. Their magnificently Gothic Parliament on the Danube was a ridiculous copy of the Palace of Westminster, but its renovation had been paid for with Communist gold. After flirting with a restored monarchy, the expense and pointlessness of it had brought peaceful abolition after a plebiscite. By then the republic was a confirmed member of the Union, its independence seceded for ever. And Marius, still a boy, had learned from his father the manners of an exile, who being neither rich nor poor must ensure he is eternally welcome.

The Princess was by far the tougher personality of the marriage. Marius smiled to himself as he spoke into the voice recognition grille at her door. On her arrival in Budapest she had been already an *arriviste*, a tiny, exotic humming-bird of a woman who had captivated his father. Her delicate appearance was utterly deceptive: beneath the fragile exterior Princess Io was forged of tempered steel.

The two, mother and son, had developed an easy relationship of mutual respect and affection. It dawned on the Prince, however, that when his mother died she would leave a black hole in his life – greater than his father had. Given her age, that date could not be postponed for ever. He felt slightly ashamed, not for thinking about her demise but for not having dwelt on it before: it meant he had to hurry, if he wanted to know her better and to love her properly. Family mattered. Especially now that he might be starting a family of his own. If Lisa had meant the words she had thrown at him in the bunker; if she would have him.

The catch clicked open and he entered. The fragrance of lily-of-the-valley, fresh and oddly girlish, filled the warm air. A high voice called from the elevated platform of her boudoir. 'Marius? Darling boy. So late. Come up and talk to me.'

Marius pottered about for a moment. 'Can I get you something? No? May I help myself?' With a large vodka and ice he climbed the thickly carpeted stairs and seated himself on a stool at the bedside.

She was propped up in bed, her hands frail on the rose-pink counterpane, the cashmere bedjacket modestly tied at the thin neck with pink ribbons to match. Glossy magazines, still produced for wealthy women, were scattered about. The wall vidscreen flickered, the sound turned down.

'I can't tell you what was on,' she murmured, though he had not inquired as he bent to kiss her cheek. 'Some romantic movie. Melanie Streisand, I think. I gave up trying to improve my taste in my twenties, dear. Don't look so disapproving.'

The Prince sipped his drink and smiled. 'I am not. Your style is a source of constant wonder and delight, Mother.' He paused, then added softly, 'If you were not here I should miss you dreadfully. I have realised that you have been a far more positive influence on me than I have ever given you credit for.'

'Merciful Lord. What can I say? Thank you, Marius.' The old lady's eyes grew misty.

'No, I mean it. I will spend a little more time with you, if I may. I have neglected you, and I am sorry.'

'Now you're talking poppycock,' the Princess said sharply. 'What's up? What have you really come for – at this strange hour, too?'

Marius swirled the drink in his glass then took a gulp. He paused while the vodka burned his throat. 'Mother, I think I have found my future wife. I believe we will make our lives together.' He waved away his mother's rapid litany of congratulations and queries. 'You have met her. Dr Lisa Pasteur. She was at that lunch on the terrace of the Commons.'

'An attractive young woman, I recall,' his mother said diplomatically. 'Wasn't she a scientist? Heavens, Marius, you're going to marry a bluestocking! Is she a commoner? Is that wise?'

Marius relaxed with a chuckle. 'I feared for a second you were about to ask whether I couldn't find anything better, Mother,' he answered. 'Lisa is splendid. A true help-meet, and a lovely woman.'

The Princess fixed him with a stare. 'There's more. I can feel it. You didn't come here solely to tell me that, or you would have come together.'

Marius let a quietness descend. Then he spoke. 'Yes. If Lisa and I are to have children then there is something I must ask you.'

The old lady composed her face and folded her hands, one over the other, on the counterpane. One finger, as if independent of its owner, twiddled a ring. 'Go on.'

'Mother, who am I?'

'What? Do you want me to recite the royal lineages of Europe – and of Japan, come to that? What do you mean?'

'I think you know what I mean. I am not – I am not the person whose DNA printout I received on my eleventh birthday, am I?'

The silence sang and was tangible. Marius held his breath, as if to move an iota would crush the unblinking china doll of his mother into pieces. He tried again.

'Don't tell me it's nonsense, Mother. I'm sure of this, at least – that I'm not who everyone says I am. It doesn't seem to matter as much as I thought it would. But what I need to be told – for practical reasons if nothing else – is this: if I'm not Prince Marius, son of ex-King Hendrick of Hungary and Princess Io of the Japanese royal family, then who the hell am I?'

Her head rocked slowly from side to side. 'No, no,' she appeared to be saying, but Marius could barely catch the sound. He rose and stood over the old woman, his expression grave.

'Am I at least royal? Or a foundling off the street?'

Her hand rose and shook, as if wafting away ghosts that threatened to enter the room. Then the trembling fingers indicated to him that he should sit.

'*Who told you?*' came in a cracked whisper.

'Nobody.' Marius made his voice matter-of-fact. 'Not for certain, anyway. But my printout and my looks and character don't match – I've had expert opinion on that. It's okay, Mother, don't get upset. I am exploring my new self and quite like what I find. But please, won't you tell me? Whose son am I?'

'I can't answer that for sure.' The Princess spoke so low he had to strain to catch the words. 'You had been ordered. To be the next king. To rule in our palace, the Budavari Palota. It was the year 2059. I chose to carry you myself — I so wanted my own baby. I had a maid, a Romanian girl, a bit gypsy-looking but sweet-natured. She and I were pregnant at the same time. Then I lost mine, at twenty weeks.'

She opened her eyes wide. 'Do you understand how devastating that is, to lose a child? A living, breathing creature who has kicked and swelled inside you? No, of course you can't grasp it. Only another woman would. I was devastated. Hysterical. Suicidal. I wanted to jump off the Chain Bridge. I wept enough tears to fill the Danube by myself. Then Ilona — the girl — came to the rescue.'

Marius sat very still, hiding even the movement of the drink's surface. The old lady's febrile hands seemed to be doing the talking, fluttering like little birds about her face and body.

'She offered me her baby when it was born. A son, a fine healthy child. Black-haired, like me, quick and bright — all the birth signs were excellent. She would help me care for him, and would be delighted to see him brought up a prince. We squared it with the doctors — an expensive business. But when we left Hungary she decided to go back to her own village. To give us the best chance, she said, our son especially. We were stateless refugees, of course. Perhaps she felt we had no prospects, but I cannot think ill of her. She wrote for a while, then contact ceased.'

'Might she still be alive?'

'No. She died. When you were about twenty, I think.'

It was not the end of the story. Marius drank the remainder of the vodka. 'And who was the father?'

His mother sighed, a soft exhalation, as if her soul

hovered on her thin lips. She twisted her head and gazed at Marius.

'She would never say. But the older you get, darling boy, the more you resemble . . . physically, at least – the man I married.'

'*The King?* My father?'

'Ah, yes. Your father.' A faint smile lingered on her features and those delicate fingers touched her wedding-ring. Then she looked full at the Prince, her eyes luminous as he had never before seen them.

'I did not pry. I was in no fit state to do so – and I was so happy to have this beautiful little boy put into my arms. You have always made me happy, Marius. And proud. You are not about to start making me weep, are you?'

'Oh, *Mother*,' he answered, and bent his head over the bed and buried his face in the perfumed counterpane. But she did weep, and so did he, and they spoke together of the dead and the living, deep into the darkest hours of the night.

To Ambassador Strether, by personal courier, from the Office of the President of the United States. Your messages received and understood. We are testing the surviving boat people for PKU condition, according to your last communication. The remains of the dead are also under investigation. Coastguards have been issued with a supply of intravenous PAH for emergency treatment – we do not know yet if it works. Your query about lost kidneys is confirmed; two of the dead had had a kidney surgically removed, one had only half a pancreas. We have no further data at this time. Not all

*the arrivals were tattooed – perhaps it is only cer-
tain prisoners. All those still alive have been offered
refugee status and that will be the practice from
here on. Under wraps for the moment. Thank you
for your efforts.*

There was a postscript, handwritten:

'*I've sent personal condolences to the Brewer and
Cameron families. Terrible business. Is it connected,
do you think? What a mess. Take care. JFK.*'

Strether stared at the flimsy paper then pushed it
away. He ran his hand through his hair. It was thinning,
goddamn it. Less than a year spent surrounded by the
economic and scientific miracles of the European Union,
and the heavy fair hair of which he had been somewhat
vain was the first bastion to fall, the most visible evidence of the strains he worked under, though not the
only one.

Several members of the embassy staff were off ill, too.
One through stress, a close friend of the two murdered
boys. Two, irritatingly, with colds and flu-like symptoms;
Strether wondered whether the mild infections might be
linked to the rubbish which piled up in the streets near
their homes. Had the garbage collectors' strike taken
effect near the embassy he might have been tempted to
pull strings with his underground comrades to have it
removed. But the strikes were sporadic, and the junk
would vanish as quickly as it appeared; and he could not
be sure that every episode emanated from Solidarity.
Since the clearance operation was linked to additional
overtime payments for the operatives it might be nothing

to do with political protest. In the confusion, without reliable news media, it was increasingly difficult to identify the truth.

The news, or rather the lack of it, frustrated and alarmed him. With thousands of channels digitalised around the world it should be possible to pick up some scraps of unbiased information. CNN reported fires and floods throughout the world but shied away from interviewing controversial politicians. The other English-speaking networks produced game shows and soaps, but seemed unaware of what genuine news values might be. The BBC still existed, though in an etiolated form; 'public service broadcasting' had come to mean putting out whatever government departments required, which suited both sides. The citizens' modern distaste for interrogatory questioning, linked with high approval ratings for the administration over the years, had made many journalists redundant. The remainder had learned their lesson and taken courses in what used to be called spin-doctoring. Or they had sought employment with the commercial operators who made clear that their customers came first; entertainment, not brain-exercise, was required.

Strether suspected that it was more than a simple change in taste, compared, say, to the twentieth century. Then, many people had been dissatisfied and distrustful of governments. The press had responded by putting presidents in the dock; reputations could be made or destroyed (and rightly) at the flick of an eyebrow. Once governments in Europe had learned how to provide more effectively for their voters' physical and emotional needs – and to convince them in advance that such was exactly what they wanted – elections had become predictable, and the media utterly bland and non-confrontational. Since the channels fed off each other anyway, and little fresh 'news' was allowed to reach the airwaves, the similarity of output was hardly surprising. Even the local version of CNN was mostly about the beautiful hotels in which it could be viewed.

It suited the audience. It suited everybody. Maybe that acquiescent tendency Winston had alluded to had been brought in subtly on other genetic introductions over the decades without anyone noticing. A contented people – who could complain? If pap thrived on the wall-screens, who objected? Nobody, except lunatic outsiders like himself. Even he, he had to admit, had scarcely been an avid follower of analytical documentaries prior to his entry into politics. Only in their absence had he realised what was missing.

He was certain, however, that he was now under systematic observation. In itself that was nothing remarkable, though it was disconcerting. The ubiquitous cameras squinted endlessly at him, as they did at everyone. Only in the embassy, and in Winston's cubicle, where by some trickery the clerk seemed to have disabled his, and in the underground car park where neglect left the eye riveted on the entrance, had he felt briefly free. As a foreign national, albeit from a supposedly friendly nation, he took for granted some curiosity about his contacts. Surveillance was a habit even in free countries – FBI files of a century before were a *Who's Who* of show business and literary celebrities, many of whom were so open about their leanings that the Feds had been wasting their time; a perusal of their published *œuvres* would have sufficed. But Strether was a diplomat and should have been protected from intrusion. Or perhaps, given his clandestine activities, he had simply grown more aware of what had been there before.

The vidphone he had long treated as an open line; the ragged calls from protest cells continued, but less frequently, perhaps because Solidarity did not need to use it with him. It was a constant precaution to consider whether private conversation was being taped – but, then, he was broadly circumspect in his speech. What had become far more painful were the faces at gatherings and in the street.

When he entered a room, a reception at another embassy, for example, faces turned away. First their bland whiteness was there, tinged with mild interest in the newcomer, then it wasn't. Instead, the backs of well-barbered necks above dark tunics were presented resolutely to him. He was not ignored entirely – nothing as obvious as that. But by such signals he understood that he was not privy to the inner circles of the Union. Other European diplomats airily promised invitations for private suppers that never materialised. The King had required his presence, along with two dozen others, solely to test a package of personal fantasies for the End of the Century celebrations. He was being quietly but rigidly isolated.

Yet other faces – one or two – would slide out from behind pillars, or stare openly at him: a barman here, a security guard there, a receptionist, her blonde hair in ringlets, her blue eyes piercing. At times he wondered if he was being trailed, or whether somebody prying on him was warning others up ahead. Living cold eyes followed him. It was unsettling. And was probably intended to be: it was his nerves they were after.

It was almost a compliment. He was seen as a threat, albeit, surely, a small one. What could one man do? He

led no military. He was the advocate of no secret philosophy; his position precluded any such involvement.
Knowing what Marius was up to – and approving of it,
indeed, having willed him on – was not the same as
active membership. It was not his job to undermine the
Union; nor did he wish to see Europe weakened. If that
happened it would work mainly to the benefit of the
enemies of the free world.

Change, however, was desperately needed, the quicker
the better. The enemies were not merely at the gate, they
were close by and in the highest places. Again Strether
ran his fingers over his pate and swore at the fine hairs
that sprinkled his palm. Stress was making him literally
tear his hair out. The Énarchy, the senior NTs, they did
not lose their hair, though the fashion was to trim it close
to the scalp to give a disciplined, ascetic style. They did
not see themselves as enemies of society. On the contrary: given a chance no doubt they'd have declared
themselves its saviours, and would claim that future generations would praise them. And that was unarguable:
for those future generations would be their own creation,
and would probably be thoroughly programmed to praise
those who had begot them.

Strether shivered. He hated what he knew. He would a
million times rather not have uncovered the sinister
trends in the programme, never have visited Milton
Keynes. An idiot would make a better fist of the role of
Ambassador of the USA.

His Bible-bashing compatriots flitted through his
mind, squawking platitudes at him, like so many fat
crows in those black gowns that flapped about their well-
stuffed forms. They were in control at home and regarded
scientific progress as the devil's work. They would say he

should not have tasted of the fruit of the tree of knowledge: his unease, and the danger he found himself in,
were the price he must pay.

Danger? That had not properly occurred to him before.
Was he himself in serious danger? Might somebody try to
dispose of him? Scare him, yes. Panic him into abandoning his post, or at any rate into no longer pursuing his
inquiries with the same tenacity. But it was too late for
that. He had bitten deeply into the forbidden fruit and it
tasted foul. And further ahead the harvest of the coming
century would ooze poison. Unless it could be destroyed.

He half rose in his seat. He would do all he could. He
would utilise every bit of influence at his command, and
whatever modest power was available to him. He had
warned his President. If necessary he would go public
and utter words of outright condemnation, in the name of
thinking citizens everywhere. He would become a rally-
ing point for intelligent and effective criticism.

Across the room his image in the mirror caught his
eye and he subsided, sighing. A greying, balding cattleman with middle-aged spread, who at the first challenge
had lost his girlfriend to a younger man, would be leading no crusade. That was not his task: that was for the
likes of Marius, Lisa, Spartacus and the rest, whoever
they were.

But they had his support, and he would do his best. He
could not say better than that.

The Army and Navy Club had been moved from its regal
headquarters in Pall Mall soon after the Hyde Park under-
pass had become irremediably flooded. The committee,
old buffers to the last, had delayed the decision until the

river water was seeping through the stone walls; an alternative, a small dock for river taxis, had been interminably
discussed, though few members ever travelled other than
by private car. Eventually sounder counsels prevailed,
though downright hostility to the left-wing nuances of
Hampstead had resulted in a transfer to the edge of
Richmond Park. Here, it was felt, a retired general might
doze off the excesses of lunch within sight of green trees,
much as his predecessors had in days of yore.

Colonel Thompson and his guest, the Prime Minister,
were not sleeping. Had they been tempted, the stern gaze
of the Duke of Wellington, in a gloomy life-size portrait
opposite, would have kept them at full attention. The
Iron Duke's haughty manner and aristocratic bearing were
of particular significance to the Colonel, as his own
genetic blueprint included references to the Wellesleys. It
was like sitting at the feet of Grandpa, he mused. The
reflection gave him confidence.

'Just coffee, if you don't mind,' he said. They were
seated in the deep, buttoned armchairs of the lounge, the
sole occupants. Buried in the basement was the famous
smoking room, which at this hour would be fuggy and
full. He had considered whether to offer his guest the
opportunity of a visit, but his objective was business, not
amusement.

Sir Lyndon Everidge accepted a large port. 'Quinto do
Noval 2067,' he murmured appreciatively. 'A rare drop.
Legend has it that a few cases were found in the basement
of Number Ten when it was moved from old Parliament
Square. Didn't last long.'

The Colonel smiled grimly. That didn't surprise him.
The invitation was plain: he could join the serried ranks
of metropolitan butterballs any time he chose. Life in the

city was soft and seductive. The indulgence grated; he itched to return to active duty – even Kashi and the desert were sweeter than this.

'I need my responsibilities here spelled out, sir. I've read my instructions, of course. But I thought' – he indicated the plush furnishings, the Wilton carpet, the gilt-framed portraits of past heroes – 'it might be easier to talk in salubrious surroundings.'

Sir Lyndon puffed out his cheeks as if exhaling a cigar. He may wish he were downstairs, but that's too bad, Thompson reflected silently. He had seen the Prime Minister over-indulge on numerous occasions during his stint at Buckingham Palace but had not taken much notice. Now, however, he began to examine the man more carefully, with a growing sense of dislike, though it was hard for the moment to put his finger on why.

'We are facing grave difficulties, I will not conceal that from you,' the Prime Minister said, in a low voice. He looked around furtively to confirm they had the lounge to themselves. 'You will have seen the disruption – may have experienced it yourself. We think several groups may be operating independently, though we've infiltrated only two, the main ones, naturally – the rest are insignificant.' He outlined to the Colonel the current state of play, but without names.

'I see,' the Colonel responded, in a tone that implied he didn't. 'But surely these are matters for the security services. The Union Bureau of Investigation, Interpol, the like. They're the specialists. And the domestic police. Where does the Army come in?'

'You remember your orders. To provide support in cases of civil unrest.' Everidge took another gulp of port.

His lips were wetly red, his eyes pink-veined but hooded
and alert.

'Oh, emergency fire trucks and the like – you want us
to run the fire engines, man the railway stations if there
are strikes, is that it? My men won't take kindly to strike-
breaking, sir. I must put that on record.'

'They'll do as they're told,' the Prime Minister
retorted. 'You'll have the back-up of private security services – Rottweiler are training up fresh guys now. Good
Lord, Colonel, there has to be somebody who'll remain
loyal to the civilian authorities.'

Thompson's face became a mask. 'Thank you for
making that clear, sir. If that's the sum total of what we're
required to do, I'm sure we can manage.'

'It isn't. You've been stuck out at the back of beyond,
haven't you? Been cut off from the gossip. I'm afraid that's
pretty obvious, Colonel.'

Thompson bridled but kept his mouth shut. He began
to formulate in his mind exactly why he found this
important man so offensive.

The Prime Minister leaned forward confidentially. 'We
think there may be a rebellion of some sort. Open confrontation in the streets. And that's where your units will
come in. If it happens – God forbid, but it might, they're
fool enough – then it'll have to be suppressed pretty
quickly. That way we can keep news of it under wraps.
But not if it drags on for days or weeks.'

'So let me get this right.' The Colonel lifted his coffee
cup, sipped and put it down, setting it precisely in its
saucer. 'I may have to instruct my men to open fire on
their fellow citizens?'

'You might.' The Prime Minister nodded vigorously.
'And clean up the mess, pronto. Those fire engines of

yours – the Green Goddesses – will come in handy. Wash
the evidence away. Everything squeaky clean the morning after. On the other hand, it may never happen, in
which case you can resume active duty. Or I can fix up
something cushier: old Morrison the MD Perm Sec is
looking for a senior desk officer. Might suit you down to
the ground, Colonel. Either way, I shouldn't worry about
it.'

Thompson exhaled and sat back. 'I'd rather use the
machines as water cannon, sir,' he said gruffly. 'That way
nobody'd get hurt. Then you could arrest the perpetrators
and put them on trial for sedition, or some such charge.'

'And give 'em a chance to spout their propaganda from
the witness box? Not bloody likely.' The Prime Minister
glanced at the Colonel. 'You look a bit peaky. You all
right? I was advised to choose you because I was told
you're a proper soldier, loyal, brave, that sort of thing.
You've got the stomach for it.'

'I have been well-trained, yes,' Thompson replied,
holding his temper in tow. He fixed the Prime Minister
with an icy stare. 'The whole point is to get rid of any
objectors, once and for all? And leave no traces.'

'More or less – as if it had never occurred. Got it now?'

Bill Strether paid off the electric taxi with a feeling akin
to relief. He was sufficiently a regular at the Toy Shop
not to have to brave the fire-eaters at the entrance; now
he could step discreetly up to door seven and press a
bell, to be admitted with a gracious 'Good evening,
Ambassador.' It made life tolerable in the midst of all the
pressures. At least Marty did not seem to mind the receding hairline.

Once he had no longer felt encumbered by the link to Lisa, something within had been liberated. It was not just sex, though that was magical. It was also the sheer pleasure of conversation with Marty, a woman close to his own age, whose untutored intelligence was the mirror of his own and whose practical nature was impatient with introspection. With her, he did not feel excluded or inferior or helpless. She was, by contrast, the most normal person he met in any week and he relished her company. Even if it was becoming a very expensive pastime.

On the visit after the murders his step had had no bounce. Marty had spotted his sombre mood immediately, had swiftly summoned up drinks and canapés, and drawn the curtains against the raucous show in the main hall. He sat down heavily on the *chaise-longue*, fully clothed, a glass in his hand while she hovered, her exquisite face full of concern. She seemed unusually edgy.

After a few gentle preliminaries he embarked on the task he had set himself, to question Marty closely about his staffers and their toys. To begin with she demurred, glancing about as if fearful that, despite her assurances, the box might be bugged. He reminded her that she had issued a veiled warning.

'You said the boys shouldn't meet them outside,' he repeated. 'Is that company policy, or was there more to it?'

Marty shook her glorious platinum head. She was dressed in the white silk robe trimmed with fur, his favourite. 'Rumour has it somebody's been playing about with the material,' she said quietly. She tilted her eyes towards the ceiling, once, as if to alert him. He did not look up. 'New clones. But without the quality control. Too young, inbred.'

'You're all inbred, with respect, Marty. I don't mean that as a criticism.' This time the champagne was untouched, its fizz ignored. He found he was hungry and absentmindedly nibbled a square of toast smothered in caviare.

She did not respond to his comment. Once more she glanced at the chandelier, then came and knelt beside him so that her cheek rested on his knee. That way he had to bend to hear her.

'Bill, they're weird. Lovely to look at, but warped. They have a taste for the – corporeal.' Her voice was very low.

'You've lost me. What do you mean?'

A soft sigh came from her. 'They like it hot and nasty. Like to draw blood.'

Strether's eyes opened wide. 'I didn't think my boys were into that.'

'You've no idea what they were into. A couple of spiked drinks and they'd be hollering for more. That suits the other customers fine.'

'What other customers? What on earth are you talking about?' Strether peered round in alarm.

'No. Not here. That's the whole point. It can't take place here, only outside. And only if some dumb clucks like those handsome boys of yours set up private assignations.'

'My staffers did that?' Strether remembered the rising total on his credit cards following visits to the Toy Shop. Like the Japanese geisha house on which it was based, it was not for the impecunious. The boys may have found it cheaper outside. 'You may be right. I don't rule it out. What then?'

'They could find themselves in a room in a specially selected hotel, with a big mirror.'

Strether frowned. Marty was beginning to behave as if

she were frightened. One hand clutched her gown about her, the other kept wandering to her mouth as if to hide her words. 'You mentioned other customers. Where do they come in?'

She let the words sink in. 'It's a two-way mirror, Bill.'

'The other customers – they're *watching*?'

She shrugged unhappily. 'They pay big money for it. Has to be good-looking guys, so yours were ideal. The girls are gorgeous too – at least, outwardly. Real toys won't do it. It degrades our profession. We're class. Partying is one thing, as many as you like, we have well-appointed large rooms here. But drooling over some half-doped fellah beaten red raw? No. That's out.'

'So who watches?'

'You'd be surprised.' He was, but as much at the brusqueness of her tone. She could not be persuaded to offer any names but rubbed one forearm repeatedly, agitatedly over the other as if feeling bonds on her wrists.

Then Strether put to her the query that had been in his mind since his trip to the morgue. 'It can go too far? It can go wrong?'

There was a silence, the more dreadful for its length. Then Marty's eyes rounded and she put her thumb in her mouth, in what must have been a childhood gesture. It made her appear, despite the bleached hair, the beauty spot, the silk gown, about six years old. Her voice was faraway, high and weak.

'Of course. All sex games can. Especially when one partner keeps pushing for more.'

'Might they have died – there and then?'

'Maybe.'

'While somebody watched? The other paying customers?'

Marty suddenly looked up, her face set hard. 'Stop that, Bill. You don't want to know. You are treading on dangerous ground. Use your brains – there will be no arrests. Except of you, if you go delving around too much.'

She rose in some agitation and left him. After she had gone, he sat quietly in the perfumed booth until his heart had stopped pounding. The caviare tasted sour in his mouth. For courage he drained the glass of flat champagne. Then he pressed the intercom button and begged her to return.

When she stood hesitantly at the entrance, he grabbed her hand, pulled her inside and shut the door. 'I'm sorry,' he hissed in a hoarse whisper. 'I shouldn't have forced my troubles on you like that. But it can't be allowed to continue.'

Her face was sad; although the glossy lipstick was freshly applied, he suspected she had been crying. 'Nothing you can do, Bill,' she murmured, in a wooden voice so unlike the breathy gurgle he adored. 'You'd need a full investigation and, believe me, that's not going to happen.'

'Is the Prime Minister involved?'

'Christ almighty. *Don't ask.*'

The fact that she had not reacted in horrified indignation gave him more clues than he had bargained for.

'The toys die sometimes, Bill,' she continued, in that same sad, low voice. 'Some of the punters prefer to see a woman hurt. Perhaps I shouldn't be bothered by it: they're not proper toys. And they're so crazy, one or two of them, that a bit of genetic therapy is overdue. But then they couldn't perform.'

'Ah!' Strether banged his fist furiously against the wall

and left an indentation in the red velvet. 'What kinda world is this, Marty? Live snuff shows attended by the biggest names in the land? Who don't mind if a victim dies in front of their eyes?'

'They are paying for it,' Marty answered dully. 'It is a world they created. It is a world *you* created. With respect.'

He stopped then, overcome by her distress. He took her hand and drew her towards him. She came limply, without resistance, without guile or coquetry. And she rested her shimmering head on his shoulder for a long time.

Marius and Lisa strolled arm in arm back to her London apartment, breathing in the cool evening air. Starlings whistled and jostled for position under the eaves. Window-boxes with night-scented stock and nicotiana filled their passage with perfume. The hibiscus trees sighed in the last stirrings of the breeze as their day-old flowers gently faded, ready to fall during the night. Above hummed the last 'copters; far overhead hung the white vapour trail of a fastjet heading for its home airport. Even the cameras attached to the street lamps seemed half asleep, mainly ignoring their passage.

'I love this hour,' Lisa said. 'Everyone, everything, curling up to rest. That was a marvellous dinner, Marius. Am I to grow accustomed to meals of that standard, or do you want me to learn how to cook?'

It was astonishing how easily they had slipped into good-natured teasing. Not yet entirely comfortable with each other, conscious of how much each had yet to learn of the other, it gave both Lisa and Marius immense fun to make suggestions in a half jesting fashion, to test the ground, and to sway and give way. This is how new lovers learn to accommodate each other. It was as if their union had been in their stars, years before they had met, even as the Prince had played the field and joked that he would never settle down. Even while Lisa was sleeping with his friend the Ambassador.

'Whichever you prefer.' Marius smiled down at her. The street lights had begun to dim; it was past midnight. Her face upturned to his was mystical and bluish, the moonlight giving her skin an ethereal sheen. 'Perhaps I should express shock, though whether at the implication that you can't cook, or the inference that you, a professional upper-caste NT woman, might be willing to learn, I can't judge.'

'It might be useful,' Lisa offered gravely, 'if things went wrong and we had to go into hiding.'

His pace slowed. 'You have a point. Our lives may change more than we realise.'

They walked on quietly, talking of the events of the last few days. 'I will have to go and see the Prime Minister, I suppose,' Marius told her. 'I don't relish the prospect. What am I to say? That I'm part of the gang which is causing so much disruption? That'd do me – and the cause – the world of good. I don't think.'

'You don't need to mention that,' Lisa replied. 'As a member of the House of Lords you can raise any issues with him which bother you. Like PKU for prisoners. Like the very existence of political prisoners, and the denials. The invention of forensic evidence against dissidents – Spartacus can probably provide chapter and verse. Human rights issues – that'd do for starters.'

It occurred to neither to query the degree of news control, for they had never known anything else. But Marius saw at once that a face-to-face meeting might warn off the Prime Minister from considering any trumped-up charges against himself. Whether the Prince became known in public as a member of Solidarity or not, his position was bound to be precarious. He tried another tack. 'Should I lead on the missing files at Porton Down, and our fears that material is getting into the wrong hands? Mutated, deliberately? It's not too fanciful that somebody is trying to create a new breed, is it?'

'Or, at any rate, that they're taking advantage of mistakes further up the line,' Lisa corrected him. 'That seems more probable to me. My brain can't take in that anyone might set about subverting the human race under the pretence of improving it.'

'Come on. That's been your whole life.' The moment he had said the words Marius could have bitten out his tongue. His hand flew to his mouth. He stood stock-still and faced her. 'Heavens. I didn't mean that. Oh, Lisa, forgive me.'

But she squeezed his hand and walked on. 'Don't apologise. You're right. And I'm now convinced: I cannot work there any longer. My resignation is written and will be handed in tomorrow.' She laughed softly. 'I feel quite composed about it. Given our multifarious activities, Marius, if I don't resign I shall get the sack. Or find that my clearance has vanished completely and I can't get into my own office.'

'So what will you do? You're not the type to stay at home all day, or spend your afternoons drinking tea with my mother.'

'I should be able to get a lecturing post quite easily. And there are other possibilities.'

'Such as?'

She swung his hand up and down, clasping it tight.

The idea had been in her mind since before Marius, before Bill. But this was the moment to say it. 'I dunno. Having babies, maybe?'

He put his arms around her waist and whirled her round and round, her feet off the ground and kicking helplessly, until the two of them were breathless and laughing. A passing cyclist nearly cannoned into them and shouted a rebuke. As he wobbled away, the Prince held her hands and spoke anxiously.

'You sure? Remember, I'm not an NT. I told you what my mother said – or as much as she would say. I'm a mongrel, sweetheart. A jumbled mixture.'

'We are all rather more random than any Porton Down scientist would willingly admit. Nobody can avoid some spontaneous regeneration. And mongrels tend to be healthy.' She was teasing him and he relaxed, a little.

'But we can buy sperm, if you prefer – we can buy whatever you want.'

'Don't be *silly*. It's you I love, and your babies I want, if you'll allow me. We don't have to mess about applying for a permit. We can pay the school and college fees ourselves – or the children can win scholarships. We must surely be smart enough, genetically speaking, for that to be an option.'

That might be thinking much too far ahead, the Prince countered. But in this joyous mood, excited and exultant, then sober and meditative, they rounded the corner, which brought them to the front of the apartment block. Here they had to pick their way between bags of rubbish: the strike had been quite effective in the neighbourhood. A brown rat scuttled away at their approach. Lisa wrinkled her nose at the smell.

Her mind had returned to her laboratory. 'I will copy

as many of my files as I can tomorrow before I go to see Dr Churchill. And I have to discuss it with Winston – I'm afraid my quitting will put more pressure on him to stay. We do need a records clerk, somebody on the inside, to keep tabs on the data, and to track any further misapplications.'

Marius nodded. They had arrived at the door of the building: more garbage littered the steps. He shoved one bag out of the way with his foot and it split, its sludgy contents spilling decomposing vegetation on to the masonry. 'Yuk. I suppose this is one way to make a point. Actually I don't think these strikers are ours – this is a bit of private enterprise. The refuse men'll charge the municipality through the nose to clear it while protesting their innocence.'

Gingerly he lifted a couple of intact bags to clear a path and wiped his hands on a handkerchief. Then he squatted down.

'This blue one's labelled. That's your number, Lisa. Were you expecting anything?'

'No. Not like that, anyway. Should we take it inside?' She looked doubtful.

'Best not. It could be something stinking, though why on earth would it be addressed to you here? Well, we won't find out unless we open it. Here, I have a pocket knife. I was a Union Pioneer as a teenager.'

He was still chattering inconsequentially as his blade cut the string. The bag fell open. He reached for the bottom edge of the plastic, tipped it and shook it. Out rolled a hard, round black object, which gleamed stickily in the moon's pale light. The two of them eyed it in bewilderment. Marius touched it gingerly with his toe and it rolled over.

Then Lisa began to scream.

The object had been alive, and not so long before. What lay before them, its eyes bulging, its mouth wide open, the fleshy lips lolling out, was the severed head of Winston Kerry, who was a records clerk no more.

Chapter Nineteen

'I won't. I can't.'

The Sikh's face was grave. 'You must, Prince. I am sorry if I have misled you. It is the only way.'

'But it's *wrong*. My God, we castigate the regime for the cruel and crazy things they do. They have no respect for human values whatsoever. We should not – dare not – operate the same way. It would undermine our own position. It would destroy us.'

The two men were in the Milton Keynes bunker, Spartacus slumped in his battered chair, his face a furious scowl, Marius pacing about agitatedly. A powerbook winked on the untidy desk, phones rang in another office. It was hot: somebody had left the lights on through the night. Burning the midnight oil.

'I used to think the same myself. Those are fine principles, Prince,' the Sikh growled, 'fine principles – but where do they get us? The Énarchy goes from strength to strength; the Prime Minister, their chosen puppet, will win the next election with a solid majority; the Prime Minister in waiting is virtually a mirror image, with identical slogans and philosophy. Meanwhile, our supporters are being butchered. Most citizens couldn't give a damn either way. What alternative is there?'

'Plenty of alternatives to direct action,' Marius answered grimly. 'You know my view. You may have changed your tune, but I haven't. We have to kick-start the democratic process – we can't rule ourselves out of it entirely. And the data gathering must continue, if we are ever to convince the outside world.'

'*It's not enough.*' Spartacus caught and held Marius's gaze, until the Prince broke away with an expletive. 'Forgive me, Prince. You are our leader now. But a few extra computer files and a speech in the House of Lords aren't going to make a scrap of difference. That'd suit the authorities. It would identify the dissenters nicely. You, in other words. They'd simply take a step back and secure their activities more tightly. And eliminate the upstream sources of information.'

'Winston, you mean. And people like him.'

Spartacus did not need to respond. Both had been present as the severed head had been buried in the garden of the Stony Stratford cottage, with Martin, Winston's partner, bent double in grief, his tearstained face more eloquent than words. They had tried to ignore the police officer who paused at the gate. The body had not been found.

'Poor bugger. And a brave man.' Marius drew himself up. 'No direct action. Not yet. I still think we can make headway. With confrontation, by speaking to them direct. If the people in charge realise somebody's on to their little game, they may well attempt to conceal it, as you say. Or they may decide the game's not worth the candle. It's a warning. And it's an essential part of tackling them. Head on.'

'You have something in mind, Prince? Or *Moses*, rather?' Heavy sarcasm curdled the voice.

Marius sighed. 'I don't have much choice, I guess,' he answered sombrely. 'I have to see Lyndon Everidge. I've known him for years. He probably assumes I'm still one of them. He may not be aware of what's going on.'

'He's in on it. He has to be. You're wasting your time.'

'Maybe. Anyway, I have to try. I *have* to. We've had too many deaths already. I don't want any more. Understood?'

Spartacus paused, then shrugged. His brows, which had knitted together in a single angry slash across his forehead, separated. The debate was abandoned.

'Well, if you must. We have prepared an information pack for him – details of crimes on record, and a few about which we can drop hints. To put him on his mettle.'

He rose and reached for a blue file-box on the cabinet behind. The contents seemed to satisfy him and he closed the box with a click.

'You'll be familiar with most of what's inside, Prince. And I will bet you a dozen hot dinners, so is the Prime Minister.'

Marius stomped away, muttering furiously to himself. The Maglev back to the metropolis arrived quickly and he climbed on board. As the vehicle lifted effortlessly on its linear-induction motors and hummed to high speed he forced himself to relax.

The countryside beyond simmered in autumnal heat. The fields were brown and covered in stubble which was being ploughed in; burning and chemical eradication, the older methods of clearance, were both strictly forbidden. Winter wheat would be drilled as soon as possible. The few agricultural operatives visible wore cartwheel straw hats and wraparound shades against the glare. One burly man sat astride his trundling twenty-metre plough and rubbed sunblock on to his exposed arms.

Marius sipped a fizzy drink and brooded. Was he being too wise for his own good, and for the cause? Or too naïve, or too cowardly? The possibility made him shrink back. An ill wind was blowing: it smelled of trouble and made him angry and fearful.

He tossed his head impatiently. Across the gangway, a heavy-set man with cropped sandy hair raised his eyelids, no more than a flicker, then returned to his powerbook. Marius's own lay open but unseen on the table top before him, next to the file-box with his drink and an uneaten orange.

The appeal had to be made to the Prime Minister. Of course it did: Solidarity could not emerge into the light as anti-government revolutionaries unless every legitimate avenue had been explored. And it did not sit well with his role as an elected politician – even if merely in the House of Lords – to ignore these time-honoured processes. And yet, try as he might, he could not so easily parry the Sikh's points.

He had dismissed Spartacus's arguments too readily. The diplomat in him was attracted to compromise; the soldier in the Sikh possibly too tempted by a more militant approach.

Those initial discussions had been misleading. Spartacus had implied that the organisation was resolutely against militancy. Perhaps it had been meant sincerely – the sentiments had certainly been expressed

with some warmth. The performance, genuine or otherwise, had been for the Prince's benefit also: he would
never have accepted the leadership of a mission committed to lethal means. The death of Winston had affected
everyone in the Bunker, the Sikh more than most. But
that was no explanation. It could only be an excuse to air
opinions suppressed before, but which had since gained
greater respectability. Faced with murder, murder became
a weapon. Retaliation might bring safety. Or it might
make everything fiendishly worse.

Had there been some jealousy? Despite his courtesy, a
jaggedness had lurked behind the Sikh's eyes as he had
out-stared Marius. The blatancy of the challenge, its inso-
lent undertone had made the Prince uncomfortable. The
Sikh must have been in the inner cabal that had decided
to approach him. Spartacus must have agreed: at his sen-
iority, he would undoubtedly have had a veto. But it was
not beyond imagination that the man might have
dreamed the choice would fall on himself. Unfortunately
for him, the idea was preposterous. Ranjit Singh
Mahwala, with his squat muscled shoulders and beetle
brows and brown skin, was not about to lead a protest
movement centred in western Europe. Nor could he be its
public face, not while tall blond NTs walked the earth,
their etiolated physique the badge of authority everywhere.

But that glint in those black eyes, that flash of annoyance and sarcasm, had indicated more than rivalry. It had
suggested a taste for violence.

Was violence the only answer? And if so, in what
form? One thing was clear, at least to Marius: with limited numbers, many of whom were, as far as he knew,
inexperienced civilians, an armed revolt was out of the

question. They would be slaughtered, and their comrades
with them.

Marius saw that his hands were shaking and he held
them clasped out of sight. He had others to think of now,
not least Lisa. Time might be short. The legal bonds with
her must be tied as soon as possible; he badly needed to
call her his wife.

He had no doubt, once he let his mind focus on it, that
men like Sir Robin Butler-Armstrong, archetypal ice-cool
bureaucrats, answerable only to themselves, would be
utterly ruthless. Spartacus's misgivings had to be met by
a far more vigorous approach than simply chatting to the
Prime Minister. In that the soldier was absolutely right.

Marius cursed himself for his limpness, and his own
dearth of military experience. His preference for talk
came in part from fear; his courage had never been tested.
It did not take courage to sit through endless diplomatic
dinners or put parliamentary questions in the politest
terms to an elderly Lord Chancellor on a sleepy
Wednesday afternoon. The prospect of open conflict, of
laser guns and warfare, of spilled brains and screams of
agony, made his stomach turn over.

The terror was not merely on others' behalf, but on
his own. He might tell himself that he would behave
bravely, and if necessary, ultimately, die with dignity for
a cause he believed in. He might *tell* himself that, but his
palms went clammy. He was *scared.* He would admit it to
no one but himself – and maybe Lisa. Since he had never
been tried, there was no way of knowing: and every gram
of his being strained for gentler, peaceable ways of settling the matter. Not violence. Not pain.

Moses, they wanted to call him. How totally inappro-
priate. The original Moses had indeed returned to the

palace where he had been raised, and upbraided Pharaoh. And been laughed at, his mission rendered a joke. He had led a collection of freed slaves out of bondage and had been pursued by the wrathful King – Marius smiled to himself. He could not quite see why. Pharaoh might have done better to wave the rabble goodbye with a kindly gesture. Rather the way he himself would probably be fobbed off by Sir Lyndon Everidge.

Another image assailed him. Another peaceable man, who had felt Himself called, but who had begged the caller to take the burden from Him. Only in fasting and prayer at Golgotha had He come to accept his fate. Marius wriggled shamefacedly. He was not about to compare himself with Christ. But the dilemma Christ had faced – the growing and terrifying obligation, the awful knowledge that the burden was unavoidable and that he had no choice but to accept whatever mayhem lay ahead – that the Prince could grasp. It made his heart skip a beat, then refuse to resume a normal rhythm.

As a distraction he played with his powerbook, scrolling up and down among the thousands of titles available. The flat plastic machine was his constant companion, as it was everyone else's. He could download from satellite a hundred TV or radio channels or a movie or tape. He could read any of tens of thousands of books, depending on which library he subscribed to.

The title on the screen was enticing. Christabel Bielenberg, *The Past is Myself.* The synopsis outlined events in the mid-twentieth century. Her husband, a Hamburg lawyer, had been a friend of the officers who had plotted to kill Hitler in July 1944. Bielenberg was promptly interned in Ravensbrück concentration camp. His British-born wife, niece of Lord Beaverbrook, had volunteered to be interrogated herself. *We know nothing of politics*, she insisted guilelessly. *We are ignorant of plots.* Hour after hour she stuck to the line. Their stories tallied and he was released. Marius punched a few buttons and read on.

The bomb had been placed in an attaché case which the plotters, trusted cronies of the Führer, brought into a conference room and left behind. It exploded; four men were killed but its target was only slightly injured. Revenge was swift and extreme. Even as the conspirators announced that Hitler was dead, he was having them arrested. They perished after torture, strung up with piano wire. Their slow deaths were filmed for the Führer's enjoyment.

I know nothing of plots, Marius mused to himself. I can hardly claim to be ignorant of politics. I've no idea whether I could cope with interrogation, let alone torture. I would be hopeless when it came to priming a bomb. Then he stopped short. Was that the ultimate? Did Spartacus harbour secret thoughts of an assassination? Surely not. It was unthinkable.

Marius swallowed. This was murky business. Given their frame of mind, and the hatred of the Énarques in the wake of Winston's decapitation – and the unwavering distrust of some of Solidarity's leftist members for his own background and moderation – he would not put it past some of the group, the hotheads, to try it.

He would not put it past a few of them to place a bomb in his case without telling him. The most effective assassin might be the man kept in the dark. And who might, in the aftermath, be regarded as expendable. Who might, in fact, have been brought in as a temporary measure: a conduit, a means of murder.

If murder were on the agenda, it might not be in the hands of a remote sniper taking a pot-shot during an official parade. It might be far closer to home. He would have to tread delicately. Some wouldn't care if he, Prince Marius, went up in a puff of smoke.

His face grim, he switched off the powerbook and stared out of the window. The sandy-haired man nearby blinked once and settled back for a doze. Marius did not see the sun slide across the man's cufflinks. Old-fashioned and heavy, they would reveal on close examination the head of a slavering dog.

Lisa ran her fingernail over the thin rod implanted under the skin of her inner upper arm. It had been freshly inserted soon after meeting Strether. So strong was her desire then for a fresh sexual partner, so prompt her response to his hints, that contraception had been the necessary consequence. Since it was anathema to become pregnant and her physical signs showed positive fertility, a slow release implant had been the obvious answer.

Other women had their Fallopian tubes tied, or resorted to devices. In some areas of eastern Europe disease pockets survived and condoms were advised. Other women and those with children might donate their unwanted ovaries and unripe eggs. But Lisa had always felt instinctively that the day would come when those ova would be useful. And, selfish or otherwise, her own had a uniqueness she wished to preserve.

She had decided against a lifetime hormone implant. Those were aimed not at contraception but at preventing osteoporosis. Lisa pitied those women, and some men, who in the previous century had entered advanced age with crumbling bones, hip joints that could not bear their weight, ribs that cracked at a cough. As neck vertebrae disintegrated and upper backs rounded into humps, the change in appearance was stark. 'Old people' used to look different. But not any more.

Those supplements granted not only skeletal strength but gave elastic skin and sexual potency well into the users' nineties and beyond – or until whatever birthday the senior picked to opt out. Some never stopped. At third- and fourth-age entertainments, hoary gents with cochlear and penile transplants and oestrogen-plump women on their third face-lift would jiggle gaily to 2020's musical favourites. Their great-grandchildren would pretend that it didn't happen, as if the elderly were another species. But since what flowed through their veins was a cocktail of chemicals as close to the original as possible, nature herself had conceded defeat. Each year a new record was broken. The oldest new mother on the planet, certified and garlanded, was 102.

The barriers were forever being expanded. Genetic manipulation meant that nobody need endure the degradations of ageing ever again. She could be proud of the part she had played. The programme had banished misery and suffering on a cosmic scale.

But she was with the programme no more. The computer links had been blocked. She could no longer tap into the network that had been her *raison d'être*. Oddly enough, it did not bother her much, not since another passion had supplanted it: to support Marius, and help him reintroduce to the system those values of public service that had once so inspired her. If Solidarity were successful, some day she might return.

But by then, she would be a mother. *A mother*. With a

swift movement, she rummaged in her first-aid kit, found the tiny sealed scalpel, and nicked the translucent skin covering the end of the hormone rod. A drop of blood oozed, as if in warning.

It meant pregnancy. Was she ready for it? With its risks, both to herself and the unborn – as yet unconceived – child? A swollen belly, breasts popping with milk, veins varicosing in her legs, repeated nausea, back pain, a slowing down of her brain patterns to cow-like complicity? What if it went wrong? An ectopic pregnancy – or the agony of endometriosis? Eclampsia, when her blood pressure might go berserk and kill them both? The dangers were horrifyingly vivid, not least to one who moved in circles where viviparous pregnancy was seen as wildly irresponsible. And in a world with elevated mutation rates, it could mean a handicapped child. She might carry a monster.

Then there was birth. Lisa moaned softly and clutched at her abdomen. Caesarians were available – more than two-thirds of all natural births were performed by nurse-surgeons, so common was it. The babies were unmarked and less traumatised. But if she were to nurture a baby herself for forty weeks, it would seem like cheating. She needed to *feel* the moment when they became two separate individuals. Even if she might die, as women once did, in the process.

Every shred of common sense advised that a couple apply for a licence and go through the proper procedure. Since Marius was in the records as an NT, and of royal lineage, she could not realistically foresee any hitches. The baby would be born, in due course, a year or two from the application date, as perfect as any offspring could be.

NTs did not have 'natural' births. The notion would have been met with embarrassed disdain. Lower-caste citizens did, but then, they could not help themselves. Once they became more prosperous, the biggest consumer product they expected was a licence and a surrogate, whether mechanical or human. They'd deliberate for hours, then, in effect, buy a baby, with a warranty as to looks, talents and future prospects. They could even request a money-back assurance that its adolescence would be trouble-free.

But that was not what she wanted. She wanted one special infant. Marius's child, even though its progenitors were unknown. It might be mad, or carry recessive genes. It might be deceptive or disloyal. Given his background, that was distinctly likely. Or was it? She chided herself. A man's personality did not derive from a sheet of computer printout: it could be judged from his behaviour. Marius was no mystery.

Every fibre of her being told her not to wait. What the Prince was engaged in was perilous. He might be captured. And if a search revealed that his genetic record was a sham, he would be refused access to any modern reproductive facility.

Lisa's hand strayed again to her abdomen and she rubbed her flat belly thoughtfully. '*I* have a reproductive facility,' she said out loud. 'Functional, if not very modern.'

It was settled. She pressed her thumb at the end of the implant furthest from the incision. The flexible silvery rod three centimetres long, streaked with red, slid out. It emerged painlessly, like a splinter. Its expulsion brought an unfamiliar elation.

She caught sight of herself in the holograph mirror.

She made the image laugh and tilt its head. The tiny ear-rings winked and glowed.

'And now, Marius,' she murmured to her own face, with a smile, 'we will find out what you and I can do.'

'Yeah, well, we thought a bit of liaison would do no harm,' Kowalsky said affably. He chose the second largest leather chair, parked himself solidly in it and put his booted feet up on the Colonel's desk. His leather Rottweiler jacket was slung lazily over his lap. A faint whiff of dog excreta filled the air from the soles of the scuffed boots.

'More'n our job's worth, innit,' Finkelstein agreed, and occupied the biggest chair. His uniform, smarter than Kowalsky's, had acquired another star on each shoulder. He shifted so that his host could not avoid seeing the badges of rank. The Colonel had not invited them to sit, which in his view was bad manners with fellow combatants. Or blokes who were likely to be fellow combatants in the next few weeks. If not sooner.

'Whatcha got in that cupboard?' Kowalsky nodded towards a likely-looking fixture. 'Got any whisky? I'm thirsty, after coming all that way.'

Mike Thompson moved to the cupboard and found a bottle of Johnnie Walker and two glasses which he pushed silently in the direction of Rottweiler Security Services.

'Not joining us?' Finkelstein asked. The Colonel might be a stuffy oaf who went too much by the book, and had carved on his stony moniker a distaste for non-NT side-kicks, but an effort to be matey had to be made.

The Colonel shook his head. 'Not when I'm on duty, gentlemen.'

'Gentlemen! That's rich.' Kowalsky drained half his glass.

'You might prefer to say that I like to shoot straight.' The Colonel did not blink.

'Yeah. Got it. But we won't have to shoot all that straight. As long as we hit 'em and put 'em down. And nobody much'll be shooting back.'

'You sure? Armed insurrections are no picnic. I've seen them at the border.'

'What – them Chinese? Yeah, but they were soldiers, really. Trained and armed. Only dressed as peasants. Leastways, that's what I read. Well, this lot'll be *real* peasants.'

Mike Thompson decided not to discuss the finer points of who exactly had been raggedly dressed and why they had been waving relatively new and shiny laser machine guns, which they obviously knew how to use. The incident, a year or two before, had been suppressed with the minimum of fire-power on his side; those had been his orders. Something about his two official visitors in their Rottweiler navy blue fatigues suggested that the rules in this current civil dispute might be different.

'My instinct, for what it's worth,' he said smoothly, 'is to keep any demonstrators under control by means that will not cause lasting damage. We should not create martyrs, or fresh grievances. If we meet force with minimum force, they will eventually get fed up and stop. Especially if the authorities can meet some of their demands.'

Kowalsky's face darkened. 'Now look,' he grunted, 'don't you get in the way of us doing our jobs. Whatever your – what's it – your *scruples* might be. You might be some high-falutin' NT type, but we've got work to do. Don't want none of your nonsense. Anyway, there's our bonuses.'

'Bonuses? What will you get bonuses for?'

'Bodies. Dead, preferably. Or so we've been told.' Kowalsky tapped the side of his nose and winked.

'My objective,' said the Colonel coldly, 'is to ensure that nobody gets killed. Not least, my men. Or yours,' he added, almost as an afterthought.

'You don't need to worry about our boys. Got some special recruits.' Finkelstein smiled proudly. 'A new corps. Specially selected.'

'To do what?' The Colonel could not prevent his voice rising in alarm.

'To do what they're told, and no messing. To do their jobs properly, like you're supposed to as well.'

'And what exactly are they trained to do? Kill innocent people?'

The two guards exchanged glances. Kowalsky reached for the bottle to refill their glasses and snickered softly.

'In a manner of speaking. Doesn't seem to bother them. And, by God, if we tried to stop 'em, I wouldn't like to get in their way.'

''Sright,' his companion agreed, but without the swagger. 'When they're in the mood, they'd slice us in two. An' you, Colonel. An' anybody that crossed their path.'

The delivery boy whistled and chewed, his hands full. An unusual trip, this one. He wondered if the parcel would be opened in his presence. That was not as important, however, as his tip. If the lady remembered this time.

It had taken several minutes hard ringing on the intercom bell to arouse Lisa. With a shake of the head she came to from a doze, and wondered idly whether the cow-like state had already started. She ordered the voice-activated camera to *Show*, and stared in puzzlement at the youth in a pale blue tunic and pillbox hat standing on her doorstep, his jaws working rhythmically.

'Gotta sign for it, miss,' the boy said. The sun on his shoulder braid gave him the appearance of a toy martinet. 'I brought them flowers. Didya like them?'

Lisa came drowsily to the door and opened it. 'Oh; yes, very much. Is it more flowers?' She dug into her pockets for a euro coin. Would one be enough? If this were another gift from Marius then two might be better.

It was a large scarlet box decked out in red and gold ribbon. She handed over the coins and, intrigued, carried the box upstairs.

Then caution kicked in. The memory of what they had found on the doorstep in London: the murder of Winston, her close associate and a key member of her team, had shaken her rigid. Especially as it was she who had tasked him to investigate and if possible corroborate her misgivings about the programme. And the PKU. And the prisoners. She had made him a target. Though if Winston had managed to find anything useful, he had died with it. He had presumably been stopped before he could make much progress or send any of it on.

The cursory examination to which she had been able to subject the severed head suggested that he had been crudely tortured. Burn marks from some simple electrical prod, or a lighted cigarette, had disfigured the face and a hole had been burned right through one cheek. It was almost a blessing that no other remains had been found with more gruesome evidence. If he had suffered, it was she who was guilty.

But why? Lisa, born and raised an NT and servant of

the state, still found it incredible that she might be under suspicion for any nefarious activity. Surely visiting the tunnels without notice and thus inadvertently making contact with Solidarity had not been sufficient to trigger a manhunt. Her record to date was unimpeachable. It took a fevered imagination to conclude that she, Dr Lisa Pasteur, an apolitical scientist, was any kind of threat to society. Nevertheless, like Strether and Marius, she acted with the utmost care. The phone was not private and she had detected signs that her e-mails had been read. And now this parcel.

She set the red box carefully on the table before her. The boy had also handed over a small envelope: old-style technology for a romantic old-fashioned way of giving presents. On the front was a traditional design of inter-twined flowers, with 'For You' in embossed cursive script. Yet the address was formal: Dr Lisa Pasteur. That could not be Marius.

Inside was a simple piece of plain card. '*A token of my esteem. W.*' was all it said. But the handwriting she recognised. It was without doubt Winston's.

She sat upright. Had he been forced to write it under duress? She held up the card to the light; the writing was as she had always known it, scribbled in the margins of printouts, tiny and surprisingly neat for such a loose-limbed guy.

The box was tied with the ribbon only; there did not appear to be any other form of seal. Holding her breath in case – in case what? It exploded? Why would anyone do that? With brow furrowed in resolution, Lisa untied the ribbon and waited.

Nothing happened.

Heart pounding, she touched the edges, right and left,

with her fingertips, careful not to disturb the box itself. Very gently, hardly daring to breathe, she lifted the lid, holding it so lightly, clear of the box.

There was no explosion; the contents did not scatter themselves in her face with an almighty bang. She let her breath go. She would live another day.

Inside, nestling in crisp red tissue and golden cups, wrapped individually in coloured tinsel foil, sat two dozen chocolates – even the strange number was the old order. The printed guide indicated that the biggest, the one in the middle, was a walnut whip. Her favourite, and prized all the more as a rarely indulged treat.

She picked it up and began to unwrap the foil. Then she stopped again. Poisoned? Was that a possibility? There was only one way to check. From the kitchen she fetched a table knife, a pair of tongs and a plate. Then, with a sudden thought, she ordered the intercom and the internal cameras to switch themselves off for half an hour, as she might if she wanted to make love or have a bath.

Once more in privacy she placed the chocolate on the plate, removed the foil entirely with the tongs. Then held it at arm's length and gingerly began to slice right through the centre. She was unsure what she was looking for. An ampoule of aggregated cyanide, still the quickest way to kill, was not inconceivable.

The knife hit something metallic and stopped. Lisa dropped both knife and tongs and recoiled, shaking from head to toe. For a moment she stared at the messy heap of cream, nuts and broken chocolate on the plate. The base had been sliced through horizontally – not by her, but by whoever had tampered with it originally. In fact, looking closer, it was apparent that the base was not chocolate at all; rather, it was the hard object that had stopped the knife in its downward track.

With the tongs, extremely carefully, a gram at a time, she pushed the cream to one side and tentatively held up the object, twisting it this way and that, to catch the light. Then she took it to the sink, and washed it clean. As she did so, a broad grin broke out on her face.

'Winston, you darling,' she whispered. For now she held in the palm of her hand a minidisk with Winston's reference number clearly printed in his own writing. And she did not need to put it in the computer to guess what information it would contain.

Strether rang again. He allowed his irritation to enter his voice.

'Whaddya mean, she's fully booked? When I spoke to her last week she was complaining that clients were dropping off a bit. She fretted about not having enough. That's why I hoped to make a multiple booking. She can't be busy for ten weeks ahead, surely?'

The face on the vidphone was not the slimy moustachioed individual who had greeted him originally. It was older, and thick-set, wearing not a smartly cut tunic but some kind of navy uniform. It mouthed back platitudes at him, and asked whether he wouldn't like another Marilyn, a younger version, or somebody else entirely – Grace Kelly, since he appeared to like mid-twentieth-century blondes, or Zsa Zsa Gabor or Jayne Mansfield if he preferred the busty type? They were free that evening, and several of the other dates he had specified.

'No,' said Strether grimly. He twiddled the knobs on

the monitor, but the picture remained resolutely out of focus as if on purpose. 'I want Marilyn Six – I know that's her official title. Otherwise known as Marty.'

'Otherwise known as Marilyn Monroe, sir. They don't have nicknames. That item is not available. The management of the Toy Shop has authorised me to apologise, especially to such an excellent customer as yourself, Mr Strether. Would you like to try Brigitte Bardot? Special offer, half price: a new model, to introduce her to the paying public. Fresh from the nursery. Superb value for money.'

'I don't want a Brigitte Bardot, fresh or shop-soiled, thank you very much,' Strether shouted angrily at the vidphone. The picture broke up into jagged lines as if in distress before reforming into the passive shape of the man in uniform. Strether was shocked and offended by the mention of his name: Toy Shop transactions were normally done by membership number only. He could feel his bile rise, through both frustration and anxiety. For once he would allow himself to sound exactly as he felt. 'Anyway, if you're not the management, who are you?'

'Me, sir?'

'Yes, you.' Strether was conscious that his rudeness was probably counter-productive and not typical of the diplomatic corps, but he was past caring.

'I am security, sir. Rottweiler SS Incorporated. We've been appointed to the contract at the Toy Shop and other establishments in the same group. I'd have thought, given the sad incidents involving your staff, Ambassador, you'd have been pleased to hear that. It's our responsibility to keep an eye on things from here on.'

Strether sat back, his mouth dropping open. 'My staffers? What do you know about that?'

'Nothing significant, sir.' The man's face was a blank mask. 'The investigation is proceeding, that's all I have here on file.'

'I'll bet,' Strether muttered furiously to himself, and ignored the man's 'Beg pardon?'

'Look,' Strether continued after a moment's frosty silence, 'we're getting nowhere. I still want to book Marty, and as soon and as often as possible. Are you telling me I can't, period?'

'No, sir, not at all. But she's busy right now, and for every one of the dates you mentioned. Got some important clients. Keeping her occupied.'

'*I'm* an important client,' Strether ground between his teeth, 'damn you. Can you put me through to her? At least I can leave a message.'

There was a pause. The guard's face seemed to set rigid, as if he had been well briefed to deal with impatience. Then he shook his head slowly and appeared to reach for the off button. 'I have explained, sir. None of the Toys takes private clients. That particular model is not available. And especially not to you.'

And with that the picture vanished. Strether tried to redial but the number was unobtainable. He banged his fist on the desk till his wrist hurt. Only then, as he stared at the screen with its default picture of scudding innocent clouds across a blue sky, did he ponder what had been said.

And then he thought again of Marty, and began to feel frightened.

Chapter Twenty

In the hazy November sunshine the metallic clunk of hammering rang loud and clear. Around New Parliament Square ranks of temporary seats were being busily erected. Brawny operatives in identical dungarees, their eyes shaded from the light, strained and sweated like so many worker ants, tools dangling from their belts and scaffolding poles balanced on their shoulders. Their efforts were watched lazily by a troop of grizzled guardsmen in Tudor-pattern cherry-red uniforms.

Satellite dishes had already been installed in one corner of the greensward and a terrestrial aerial some twenty metres high was under test. Flags had been hoisted from supports painted white and gold in time-hallowed tradition. Overhead cameras were being serviced, extra ones fitted. More workmen swayed precariously on elevated platforms near the Palace of Westminster archway. In their arms were broad blue banners proclaiming a triple hurrah of welcome: to King William, to the new parliamentary session he would shortly open, and (for good measure and to save a few euros) to the new century too.

Sir Lyndon Everidge leaned out of the window, puffing at a fat cigar. With a sigh of regret, he stubbed out the remainder against the stone sill, threw the stub expertly into a distant drainage hole, exhaled and shut the casement.

'Aren't you worried that they'll see you smoking?' Marius asked, curious. 'The Prime Minister is supposed to keep the laws of the land, especially in this building.'

'Ye-es, well,' the Prime Minister commented laconically, 'I'm getting past that stage. Can't do it indoors or we'd set the screaming banshees off – and I mean the smoke detectors, not the lady members. But nobody'd credit it anyway. I'd claim they'd seen another geezer and set up an inquiry. Standard practice.' He winked towards the surveillance camera in the corner of the room. 'The day may dawn, old chap, when the fact that a man smokes will be regarded as irrelevant when it comes to whether or not he can fulfil his office. But we're some way off that at present.'

'I suppose,' Marius murmured, 'you can claim the benefit of the doubt. A well-known figure like you.'

'The trick is to act not guilty,' the Prime Minister expanded. 'Look supreme, and you'll be supreme. What brings most politicians down isn't what they *do*, it's the beaten expression on their mugs when they're found out. The media scent a wounded victim and go for him. Or her. Me, I don't give a damn, and it shows.'

He motioned Marius to a leather armchair that looked as if it had seen better days. Like the King's home, the Palace was a trifle shabby; little money was wasted on it. The Prime Minister settled his ample self in a smarter winged chair with the crowned portcullis stamped in gold behind his head. His back was turned squarely to the

moving eye, which trained itself instead on Marius. The
sound of a military band in practice floated in through
the open window. The humidor, disguised as a ministe-
rial red box, lay open on the table next to a powerbook.
The Prime Minister held up the key. 'You sure you won't
take one with you? Best Cuban, very rare.'

'No, thanks.' Despite his ominous errand, Marius
found himself in mild collusion with the Prime Minister.
As he had remarked to Spartacus, he had known Sir
Lyndon much of his life. In years gone by they had travelled together on official delegations, and Marius, no
aesthete, had warmed to the ebullience and drive of the
older man. On a tedious trip Sir Lyndon was wonder-
fully entertaining. They were nominally members of the
same party: when he paid attention to a party whip,
Marius tended to go through the lobbies with the Prime
Minister's friends – though which parts of the manifesto
attracted him and which repelled, he had not been wont
to say. Until now.

Next to the humidor was the blue file-box Solidarity
had prepared. It had no identifying labels. Marius pushed
it politely towards the Prime Minister.

'I asked to see you, Lyndon, because a number of
people have expressed to me grave concerns about the
direction of policy. As an elected member of the Lords, I
felt it my duty to raise these problems with you. I'm sure,
once you understand the implications, that you will take
steps to put matters right.'

The Prime Minister planted his elbows firmly on the
table. The shiny fabric of his suit stretched across his
broad shoulders and slid back from his thick wrists. A
jewelled antique Rolex glittered. He put his fingers
together like the roof of a house. 'Go on.'

Marius kept his voice light. The moment for indignation or aggression would come soon enough. He was
conscious that a rapid pulse at his throat could reveal
his nerves, and wondered fleetingly whether the camera
was sufficiently digitalised to spot it. He plunged in.
'Well, first of all, a range of issues that are normally met
with denial. I take it we can talk freely, man to man?'

The Prime Minister nodded gravely. 'Of course. What
issues? Such as?'

'Political prisoners, for a start. We aren't supposed to
have any in the European Union. But we do. And they're
incarcerated in outlandish places so that escape is difficult, though some manage it and end up as boat people
on the shores of America. Where it has become apparent
that we are breaking every ethical code in the Union.'

'Good Lord,' was the reply. Everidge made a great
show of tapping into his powerbook. 'I'm not sure I have
details on this. Go on.'

Marius had not paused for breath. 'They are subjected
to chemical handcuffs – they can survive only if they
don't attempt to escape. There's a paper about it in here.'
He tapped the blue box. 'And what are we doing with
political prisoners anyhow? This is a free society according to every law ever written. The evidence against them
is manufactured and planted. Some are distinguished
men, NTs of the highest caste.'

'But still criminals, my dear Prince,' the Prime
Minister intoned gravely, 'dedicated to overthrowing
legitimate authority.'

'I doubt it. They have important criticisms to make.
And whatever, that's no excuse for treating them like farm
animals. For spare parts surgery. Without their consent.
Do you know about that? What are the surgeons thinking

of? That is frightful, horrible.' He enlarged on the forbidden practice, hardly daring to believe it himself.

'Really?' The Prime Minister diligently made a note in the powerbook. 'I will have that matter investigated. Anything else?'

Marius felt his mouth go dry. The camera was aimed straight at him and started whirring slightly, as if a double film were being recorded. He dug deep for his courage and pointed a finger. 'Plenty. I witnessed a shoot-out in July. I saw a police officer killed by a high-powered laser weapon. Yet nothing appeared in the press – no report of the incident or the death. A complete blackout. And no analysis of why the protest was staged –'

'My dear fellow! Have you never heard of the oxygen of publicity? We cannot allow such topics air-time.'

'– nothing about tube strikes, or electricity failures, or rubbish pile-ups. Other deaths have been ignored. Murders are occurring which are not being properly investigated.'

'Ah, yes. July the fourth. You were with Ambassador Strether.' It emerged as an accusation.

'It was US Independence Day. A big event,' Marius retorted. He wanted to wag his finger again but saw that it was shaking. 'Anyway, what was going on? Why don't you find out what they want, and put an end to these confrontations? And bring the murderers to justice, from both sides.'

'Oh, we will, we will, Prince.' The Prime Minister's eyes gleamed. 'All in good time. Don't you worry about that.'

A shiver ran up and down Marius's spine. 'The place for dissent is here, in Parliament,' he persisted. 'Especially on these human rights questions. In proper open debate. Or, failing that, in the press.'

'But if few dissenting voices are raised in public, maybe that's because nobody dissents,' the Prime Minister remarked coolly.

'You know that's not true.'

'I do? And what else, pray, am I supposed to know?' The odour of cigar wafted from the Prime Minister's clothes as he leaned menacingly forward, hands still clasped. 'I get the feeling you haven't finished, Prince. Tell me, are you on medication? You don't look well.'

Marius's mind raced. His hands felt clammy and he dropped them below the table. This interview might be terminated abruptly; he did not have much time. 'The genetic programme. You should be worried sick about it. Not simply the trivial stuff we see daily, the three-eared dogs, the clones produced for our amusement. Sorry to use — *that word*, but it's time we stopped the euphemisms. It's an appalling misuse of science. Though I suppose some foolishness was inevitable, if people are given so much choice.'

The Prime Minister shrugged. 'I thought you liked free choice, Prince. Or is it only if *you* are choosing?'

Now Marius let his voice rise in anger. He was panting slightly; as he spoke he cursed himself inwardly for having been so foolish, so complaisant, for so long.

'More than that. The facilities at Porton Down have been hijacked. It's the premier state laboratory in Europe, the heart of our efforts to improve the human condition. It's supposed to be tightly supervised, monitored to stringent ethical standards. That used to be the case, but no more.' Behind the door to the corridor he could hear voices, low and concerned. The brass handle began to turn.

'I should be most surprised if that were the case,' the

Prime Minister replied formally. 'The trivial stuff, as you call it, is done privately under licence. Not a government function. But the Porton Down operation is covered by criminal law, and anybody interfering risks the strongest retribution. What exactly are the – ah – miscreants trying to do, in your view?'

'Wicked things. Altered codes are slipped in, by executive command – from on high. Skin colour is lightened. Docility is increased. Defects are left in, like colour blindness, without any discussion – who decided that? Parental choice enshrined by law is being eroded – the parents don't know what they're getting and, increasingly, it isn't what they've ordered. This seems to be widespread practice.'

The Prime Minister nodded, but his chin lifted slightly as he glanced at the door. The handle stopped moving. 'Ah, yes. A little over-enthusiasm by some junior clerks. Though I confess it's not a bad idea. Parents are seldom the best judges.'

Marius charged on, his mind registering the other's lack of perturbation. 'And – somebody's trying to grow a violent gene. Live rejects have been spotted, appallingly deformed. Secret clear-outs at night, like unwanted garbage – that's being denied, too. Files have vanished, access is barred. Experimentation is taking place far beyond protocols. And someone's given orders to enhance certain IQs and lower the rest.'

The Prime Minister laughed softly. 'So what? That's not a bad idea either.'

Marius rocked back in his armchair in astonishment, his breath coming in quick gasps. '*Not a bad idea?*'

'That's obvious. It'd benefit our children – the upper caste – and make the Union far easier to govern. My own son-in-law ordered such an enhanced child recently. An IQ of a hundred and seventy. Delivered last week. A baby boy. Delightful little fellow.' A half-smile played around the Prime Minister's heavy jowls. 'I see you don't know everything, my dear chap. Have they told you about the acceleration project?'

'I'm listening.' Marius pursed his lips. He hunched his shoulders against the surveillance, as if his tunic would give him cover. Outside, the band was exploring a repertoire of marches from the glory days of the British Empire. Ceremonial taste had not advanced much in two hundred years.

'Ah, yes. A splendid development, for which, in due modesty, I can take some credit. You know how most alterations are not effective till the child is grown? We've tried gene therapy in adults and, apart from one or two isolated conditions, it hasn't worked. The graft doesn't hold, the material reverts. So we've had to do it with embryos then wait twenty years or so till the citizen could emerge into society. But not any more.'

Sir Lyndon Everidge's florid face was creased in smiles. Marius was stunned into silence. The ball seemed to have passed into the Prime Minister's court.

'The director of Porton Down,' Everidge continued, 'discovered that, provided some growth is still under way, new grafts will take. The latest possible age for boys is fifteen. So if, say, we want to improve character, we won't have to wait a generation. We can start with youngsters of school age, and have 'em on stream within five years.'

'So, let me get this straight,' said Marius slowly. The fear, the shock of what he was hearing, the stuffy room and the sour smell of over-aged tobacco were combining to make him feel quite nauseous. 'If you wanted to increase their intelligence, you could do it virtually at once?'

The Prime Minister unclasped his hands and waggled one to and fro. The grin on his face stretched from ear to ear. A childhood corner of Marius's hot mind recalled the last line of the limerick: '*the smile on the face of the tiger*'. 'More or less. Not overnight, naturally. Not everything, yet. And it's still experimental.'

'And if you wanted to make them more stupid, and at the same time more belligerent, you could do that, too?'

The Prime Minister's eyes widened innocently. 'We could, I suppose. Never thought about it.'

'I don't believe you,' Marius said bitterly. He half rose, and held on to the table to steady himself. 'It makes my skin crawl. You've been in power too long. But be careful. Human beings are not that easily manufactured. They have wills of their own. That makes them highly unpredictable.'

'No, really? How do you figure that?'

The tension and rivalry sang viciously between them. It came to Marius with blazing certainty that the Prime Minister might not simply throw him out but could have him arrested at any juncture, and would not hesitate to do so. 'Think, man, for God's sake,' Marius rushed on urgently. 'They may be psychopathic. No normal feelings. Like paedophiles or child murderers. They couldn't help it, but they could become uncontrollable. If that's what you're breeding, it's insane.'

'Like dogs,' the Prime Minister added.

'What?'

'I said, like dogs. A better example than paedophiles – we wouldn't try to create *them*. But dogs: well, savage canines were all the rage in my father's youth. Rottweilers, pit-bulls, dobermans. The inbreeding that went on! They couldn't give birth normally and would kill their owners. Had to be destroyed, whole breeds. If that's what you suspect, dear Prince, do set your mind at rest. Extra work has indeed been commissioned to improve the fighting qualities of our soldiers, and civilian guards. But we can rely on their obedience. That's inbred too.'

'Obedient to whom?'

'To the state, of course. To elected and appointed authority. They take an oath. And they're genetically programmed *not to break it.*' The Prime Minister clapped his hands together and looked mightily pleased with himself.

The book he had read on the Maglev came back vividly to the Prince. His voice dropped to a whisper. 'Like the German hierarchy. The colonels, the field-marshals. They took an oath to the state and could not break it. So Hitler lived.'

'And, if I remember my history, they died. The renegades, that is.'

For a long moment a dreadful silence filled the room. The band had moved on; the hammering had come to a halt. Then the sound of marching boots scrunched below the window. The Prime Minister rose and motioned the Prince to join him. Reluctantly Marius complied; he had no choice. The two men gazed out at the sunny scene below.

'See? They're going to check the basement for bombs.' The Prime Minister pointed. 'Beefeaters, with docile dogs. Bit of pomp and circumstance. Relic of Guy Fawkes's time. More of your renegades.' He seized

Marius's sleeve and tugged to emphasise his words, his face thrust close. 'Don't you join the rebels, Prince. We have them taped. Infiltrated – oh, *yes*. We know what they're up to before they do. Why should you care? Just as long as you're one of us.'

The gaudily dressed guards disappeared into an underground tunnel, their sinewy animals straining at the leash, tongues lolling. Slowly Marius and the Prime Minister straightened and walked back into the room. The interview was over.

Sir Lyndon Everidge swung Marius round to face the unmanned camera, then grasped him warmly by the hand and slipped his other arm round the younger man's shoulders. His eyes, a few centimetres from Marius's, were red-veined, the irises palely blue. Gently but firmly the Prince was propelled towards the exit.

Marius shook off the enfolding embrace and tried one last time. He was beginning to hyperventilate; his words tumbled out jerkily, as if from a computer whose memory was fragmenting. 'I am troubled, sir. Not just the genetic industry. Hijacked. Whole of the Union – being taken over. Énarques in charge – unelected. Apparatchiks. Plus their clones. News suppression, no debate. Bland acceptance. Terrifying. Driving me crazy.'

'Now don't bother yourself any further, my dear chap.' They had reached the door, which opened noiselessly at their approach. A microscopic flicker suggested that they had also been watched through a peephole. Yet when the door was wide open no one was visible. 'You *are* one of us. So is your beautiful fiancée. Why bother about the little people? Why trouble yourself about rights for terrorists? Leave that to the fanatics. They'll get their comeuppance. Our aims are far wider. Our legacy to our children. A clean healthy world, the human race free of suffering and poverty. Who could ask for more?'

The door closed firmly behind him and Sir Lyndon strolled off, whistling, in the opposite direction. Marius was left, shaking, in the empty echoing corridor. As he shambled down the steps and outside, he knew the answer to the Prime Minister's taunts. 'You don't care about any of that, you evil bastard. But I do. I want a society in which the little people matter. Even prisoners,' he whispered brokenly to himself. 'Where choice exists. Consent is sought. Opportunity exists for everyone. The press never rest. And this ancient Parliament isn't a bloody fancy-dress show, but *works*.'

He felt a dreadful shame, matched by a burning sensation in his gut. His next words he said aloud, to the curious glances of passers-by.

'A society free from fear. In which the élite are the servants. Not the masters.'

He was no longer ambivalent. He would play the jester no more, or go along with the pretence. It had been too damned easy to assume that governments were on the side of the angels, that those arrested were obviously guilty, that the state was doing them a kindness in apprehending them and protecting its electors to boot. Trials might be held in open court, lawyers might be well known and erudite. But the whole system was rotten to the core, all the worse for its sugar coating. The stench filled his nostrils.

Marius found himself leaning against an ancient wall, its stones warm to the touch. His breathing came rapid and shallow. His heart hammered inside his ribs; his temples throbbed, stars flashed and danced before his eyes. Had it been high summer with a blazing sun, he might have suspected a touch of heatstroke. The smell of the Cuban cigars returned and he retched.

He struggled to regain control. That old urbane superficiality might have enabled him to hide the truth from himself, but it had also been a useful carapace. He glanced fearfully over his shoulder. In *there* he had been too vulnerable – too unguarded. That had been immensely foolish.

Such cynicism. Such a blatant invitation to join the conspiracy – but the *wrong one*. By contrast with the Énarchy and their friends – of whom, it was now obvious, Sir Lyndon was one – the efforts of Solidarity seemed childish and hopelessly outclassed. Spartacus had been correct all along; the Prime Minister was firmly in the other camp. What made Marius groan was the open invitation to himself to stay with that same élite; an appeal to the worst, laziest, casual elements of his personality. Lord, how superficial he must have seemed, especially to the rebels. He banged his fist against the wall in frustration. And Solidarity wanted him as a leader?

But that decision had been taken. Whatever his personal hesitation about his suitability, he had accepted. He would not let them down.

On the journey into London he had faced up to his own fear. Then, it had been the fear of the unknown, of which the most significant ingredient was his own untried courage. That anxiety no longer detained him; in a crisis, he felt he could act with as much bravery as any man.

His judgement, however, was another matter. So far, it had been proved hopeless at every turn. That lack could be excused by a shortage of information, or of experience in moving in the undergrowth, but he could hardly claim not to know these men. Indeed, it was he who had insisted on the verbal confrontation with the Prime Minister. And it had been a miserable failure. Except to confirm the nightmare, that the top NTs were abrogating to themselves a gross power that could turn them and their class into unassailable tyrants.

Did they know he was not 'one of us'? Winston had reckoned so; the data, or rather the mismatch of data and fact, had not been difficult to find, once the search had been made. Then had the invitation to stay put been genuine? He suspected it had. It would suit the Énarchy and the upper castes to keep their ranks intact, not to have him openly defect. No news was good news. And they'd prefer to keep his status a secret. Apart from anything else, the infiltration into their caste of a complete outsider would take some explaining.

That offered a faint beam of hope, long term, if his defection became a public matter. The question might be raised in some thoughtful quarters as to whether, if a mongrel non-NT could rise to high office with his lack of reformed genes going unnoticed, the expense and expansion of Porton Down were really so essential. Sooner or later there had to be a backlash. Those without the funds for enhancement would demand entry for themselves to the higher grades of the civil service. It had been like that once, when open competition was the norm. It could be that way again. If anybody wanted it.

But the programme existed precisely because everyone wanted *that*. Anyone hostile or suspicious – and some ultra-religious sects in Europe did take their cue from the United States – was not forced to make use of it; but their numbers were few. Like hand cream and garden pesticides,

like cosmetics and hair tints, like face-lifts and Maglevs
and air-conditioning, the clamour for consumer goods
was overwhelming. What was first rare and prized
became a luxury, then a necessity. The damage, the
resources diverted and wasted, were discounted. By def-
inition, scientific advance was progress.

The Prime Minister had been arrogance personified. In
his mouth, the official justifications were like maggots.
*'Our aims are far wider. Our legacy to our children. A
clean world, a society free of suffering and poverty. Who
could ask for more?'* But governments throughout the
ages had touted such sentiments. Wise or incompetent,
democratic and despotic. Empty words, unless made
wholesome by good practice.

The fact that the main genetic programme had been
under official control for over half a century was trotted
out to allay all fears. *Pro bono publico.* Why not? What
could go wrong, if an intelligent cadre exercised responsibility, honourable souls with the highest motives?

Everything. Marius groaned and shook his head, as if
to clear the desperate worries that shrieked at each other
in his brain. He had been blind. But seeing was horrible.

The enormity of his own position began to dawn. If an
appeal to the Prime Minister was indeed seed cast on
barren ground, what next? If Spartacus's assessment were
to be trusted – and he had been spot on so far – what followed was violence. Not on the part of the evilly bred
guards, or the dumb soldiers, but on his own.

And if the PM's claim about infiltration was even
partly accurate, then he might be seized and dragged off
at any moment.

A shadow fell across his feet. All pretence at sophistication abandoned, Marius crouched, his back to the wall,

in utter terror. His mind juggled about randomly, independent of any tug of logical thought. Some fundamental instinct made him scrabble inside his tunic pocket. His security clearance at the entrance had been, as was usual for Hon. Members, perfunctory. That had its advantages.

An electric vehicle of outlandish design, a mid-twentieth century tail-finned Dodge, had halted at the kerb. The tinted back window opened and a head poked out.

'Thought I'd find you around here,' Bill Strether called. 'Want a lift? Did it go well?'

The back door opened and Marius, dazed but relieved, stumbled into the cool interior. The car glided smoothly away, heading west.

'Your lovely wife-to-be,' Strether said, carefully. 'Lisa. Had a call from her. She told me where you were so I came past on the off-chance. Any joy?'

Marius shook his head. Slowly he slumped back into the creased leather seat, his eyes half closed. At the corner of his mouth a line of spittle showed; he found a tissue and wiped his lips, as if to rid himself of a dreadful taste. Then he reached inside his jacket and took out the small, hard object from his breast pocket.

'I should have used this on him,' he whispered hoarsely. 'Maybe I should use it on myself.'

Strether peeped then recoiled with a spluttered oath. On the Prince's lap, held loosely in his hand but with the safety off, was an object he had seen before: the Prince's silvery personal gun.

Colonel Mike Thompson switched off his powerbook and closed it. He needed to think, but not to communicate his thoughts to anyone. You never could tell with any kind of electronic equipment; it was too darned simple for some-one within reach to hack into, even − with the latest gadgets − from an apparently safe distance.

'God grant me the strength to change what must be changed, the courage to leave what needs no change, and the wisdom to know the difference,' he remarked to him-self, but his craggy face, its desert tan bleached by the months spent in the city, had a sardonic cast. He was seated at a plain wooden desk in his office. He searched in the drawers and found dusty sheets of paper and some ballpoint pens and pencils. The pens were dried out but one of the pencils had a workable point. He began to make a list.

The office was peaceful, situated on the inner court-yard of the Ministry of Defence. A grade three room, he had been told as the key was handed over, a cut above the usual accommodation. That concession probably impressed the bearer of the news, an ancient doorkeeper in a grubby green tunic, more than himself. Its décor did not interest him; the faded prints on the walls, of bewigged heroes posed against a background of swirling battlegrounds, clutching the reins of wild-maned white stallions, were as unreal as if they had depicted Martians − though the kind of warfare they waged, in which politics, greed and ambition were the driving forces, was much the same as his contemporaries'. The main difference was in the weaponry, its fire power, its accuracy. And the type of soldiers they led.

Or was that so? When Blücher's Prussian cohorts marched on to the field at Waterloo and saved the day, Wellington had been predictably grateful. He had reviewed his own troops at dawn. 'I do not know what

effect these men will have upon the enemy,' he is
reported to have said, 'but by God they frighten me.'

Mike Thompson was certain he could trust his own
units, particularly those who had served with him in the
desert and elsewhere. They were seasoned campaigners;
regular soldiers, professionals who had chosen the military as a career. Conscription was still common in border
regions, but only for the reserves. Like himself the officers
were NTs, but he had inculcated in them a questioning,
liberal attitude. It made him more comfortable, gave them
self-respect, encouraged initiative, and was superb for
morale. In his units there were no sex scandals, no courts
martial, no bullying or stupid drunkenness or drugs. Gays
and lesbians served with distinction; men and women
worked side by side with focused concentration on the
task in hand. He would not tolerate or condone bad
behaviour and neither did his subordinates. They knew,
as did he, that readiness was all. Nor were they the only
such units in the Eurocorps: his brother and sister officers, the French, Spanish and Germans especially,
schooled alongside him at Sandhurst, operated in much
the same manner. The knowledge eased his mind now, as
he pushed himself to consider the strange, apparently
unconnected pages he had downloaded on to his powerbook and their implications.

He made a pencilled list.

1. *Kerry file. Worked for Porton Down. Hacked into
   Edinburgh. Used pass-name 'Dainty'. Prime
   Minister's grandson. Did he know? What was he
   chasing?*
2. *Brewer/Cameron file. Worked at American
   embassy. Mutilated bodies found in garbage. Into*

> *S/M? Friends say not. Were they chasing some-*
>   *thing? No leads.*
> 3. *Rottweiler. Links to? Who owns this company?*
>   *PM v. keen on their use. Why?*
> 4. *Acceleration project. PM sent out circular about*
>   *this – limited access. What's he trying to acceler-*
>   *ate?*

'There are links between you lot,' he muttered. 'I'm sure of it. But what?' He peered more closely then drew a circle round four words. Two were the same. *PM. PM. Prime Minister.*

'Surely not.' Colonel Thompson did not believe in luck, or in coincidence. Just because three out of the four revolved somehow around the Prime Minister, it didn't mean that the fourth did too. On the other hand, nothing was impossible.

Could the Prime Minister have been involved in some way in the death of the young Americans? He reopened the powerbook and used his ID to scroll through the official file. The inquiry seemed to have stalled at an early stage. That suggested a speedy decision not to track down the killers or to publish the exact nature of the outrage. Or maybe somebody knew already and preferred the information kept under wraps.

'He's an old rogue and I wouldn't trust him further than I could throw him,' Thompson growled. Ministry gossip placed others in the administration on a higher mental plane. His own contacts with Everidge, first at the Palace where he had been a largely silent and indifferent observer, later ostensibly for briefing, had made a poor impression. In his estimation the man, whatever enhanced genes he might possess, did not have the intellect or twisted vision to develop a plot for himself. Somebody else, another NT, was behind all this. But it had to be a senior figure with whom the Prime Minister was intimate, and who was both subtle and powerful enough to bend the PM's will to his own. If not one man, then a bevy of them.

They had to be civilians. The grapevine of the military was extraordinarily effective; had a coup been planned by anyone wearing a Eurocorps uniform, it would have been noticed and excised very firmly indeed. Too many European regions had painful memories of tanks in their main squares, of flame-throwers directed at their own unarmed citizens. The interregnum in the West, when royal families had been replaced by quasi-elected presidents backed by martial law, was still spoken of in hushed tones. Loyalty to due authority had been drummed into the military ever since, but tempered by a shrewd awareness of the quality and style of those holding high office. 'Following orders' was no longer in law a defence for mistakes. Whenever due process was at risk, the hairs rose on the back of Mike Thompson's neck. And they were rising now.

4. *Acceleration project. PM sent out circular about this – limited access. What's he trying to accelerate?*

'I don't know the answer to that, but it's the key.' Thompson leaned back in his chair and sucked his teeth, his brow furrowed in thought. There had been no official announcements, but the Prime Minister had been overheard at a ministry reception boastfully outlining it to Morrison, the Defence Permanent Secretary, whose

manner had been one of intense concentration. Sir Robin
Butler-Armstrong had hovered nearby, looking
inscrutable. The Colonel had caught only scraps of the
conversation. As he had sidled closer the subject had
been changed. That alone intrigued him.

He reached for the vidphone, flicked it on and set the
scrambler. In a moment he had been connected to the
number he wanted.

A pretty blonde receptionist smiled at him. 'Porton
Down Laboratories, Miranda speaking. How may I help
you?'

The greeting sounded so old-fashioned that Thompson
had to stop himself laughing at her. Most switchboards
were automatic and simply requested the name of the
person required in a flat, tinny tone.

'Professor Churchill's office, please.'

In a moment the Professor appeared and identified
himself. Below his face on Thompson's screen appeared
the lettering *Source: Porton Down*. At his end, Churchill
would know only that the caller was from the Ministry of
Defence in London.

'My name is Colonel Mike Thompson. I work for Mr
Morrison, the Permanent Secretary here. He wants me to
get more background on the acceleration project the
Prime Minister was telling him about. Could you fill me
in, please?'

'This.'

Lisa held up the tiny metallic object with a wide smile.
The amber earrings swung and twinkled in the afternoon
light. It seemed to Strether, seated on the sofa in her
London apartment, that everything in it was brown or

gold, pure ancient colours, earthy and warm. Those
honey-flecked eyes of hers were alive with pleasure. Her
dark hair, brushed and loose, swung about the nape of her
neck; her cheeks were flushed. Her shirt and the narrow
trousers were a pale khaki shade which flattered her.

He felt his soul sigh; she had a bloom about her, something new and womanly. It came achingly to him then, as
he observed her, so excited and queenly, how much he
had lost when she followed Marius out into the hangar.
She was more than a remarkable woman: she had been
the woman he loved. And still did, though never again as
a lover.

'It's a minidisk,' she explained. 'A back-up. We used to
use them a lot when systems were less reliable. It has
everything we need – chapter and verse.'

She pointed to the chocolates. The elaborate box was
nearly empty, with silver and red foil scrunched up
inside. 'Only one person was privy to that secret vice. I
hadn't even told you, Marius. And that's how Winston
got the material out.'

Marius was seated on a low chair on the opposite side
of the room. He brushed a hand wearily over his hair. To
Strether he appeared exhausted, though after some per-
suasion the silvery gun had been returned to its hidden
inner pocket.

The Prince's voice was barely more than a croak.
'What do you propose to do with it, Lisa? You can't leave
it lying around.'

'Absolutely. But we have our own diplomatic bag sitting right here.' The potential insult made her giggle.
She laid a hand on Strether's shoulder. 'I'm sorry, Bill. I
didn't mean it like that. But you will work with us, won't
you?'

Mistily, the Ambassador recalled those minutes in the dimly lit hangar when, voyeur-like, he had observed Lisa and the Prince together. She had been arguing furiously with him, pleading, haranguing him. Marius had tried to disengage himself and had protested his unsuitability for the role she and others wished to foist on him. Given the waves of despair that seemed now to emanate from his slumped figure, perhaps he had been right first time.

But on that occasion, Strether recalled forcefully, as he had felt slip through his fingers a future with the slim woman who now half bounced, half danced about the living space, he had made a promise. That, loving them both, he would help them in whatever way he could.

'It seems to me,' he suggested quietly, 'that we have to remove that disk to safe-keeping in the United States of America, pronto. You can leave that to me. We can analyse the material, publish excerpts, and ensure, through CNN and elsewhere, that the news is spread world-wide. That should stop the Énarchy in their tracks, make 'em think twice. At least, those who are attempting to take the Union into a minefield.'

'What they're up to is madness,' came from Marius in a low growl. 'You see bits, then when you put the whole picture together you're appalled. I wish we'd never started on this genetic programme game.'

'No, Marius, you can't say that. It's done such a lot of good,' Lisa began, but he waved away her objections with a dismissive hand.

'I haven't benefited from it. Neither has Bill here. Nor Winston, who slaved away to get us this disk and paid for it with his life, poor sod. Nobody's shoved our chromosomes about and told us at the microscopic stage to do this or that. We're different, and it's a blessing somebody is.'

His speech had an edge of belligerence and anger. Lisa put a restraining hand on his arm, and spoke more calmly. 'Your abilities occurred naturally. Don't you want everyone else to have the same chance?'

'Oh, don't, Lisa. There's no black or white about this. Nature does a pretty good job on her own, you know.' He started to bite a fingernail, a new habit, until her eyes caught him in sweet reproof.

'Yes,' she smiled, 'I do know.' And she circled her hand on her belly, then her face broke into a delighted, girlish grin. Her eyes were for Marius alone: Strether felt completely superfluous, yet privileged to be allowed to stay. 'And you will too, soon.'

'You're talking in riddles, Lisa. What do you mean?'

'I'm pregnant.'

The Prince jumped up in astonishment. 'You are?' His face was a tumble of emotions; Strether recognised panic, then doubt, then wonder. 'But I thought – I mean, you said you were safe!'

Strether smothered a chuckle. She had been so in charge, the Lisa he once knew, in the embassy, on 4 July, upstairs in the private room as dusk fell outside. If this young woman was pregnant, there was only one explanation. It was because she intended it.

As Marius floundered Strether rose and, in as avuncular a fashion as he could manage, held Lisa's hands clasped in his own. 'My warmest congratulations, dear girl,' he boomed, and kissed her on both cheeks.

'Oh, my God,' was all Marius could offer for some minutes, then 'Oh, my God' several times more. Then he whooped with animal joy, swept her into his embrace and held her, then walked her round so he could look at her, shyly as if she were a precious work of art instead of a robustly healthy young female. At last he stopped, his expression a daze mingled with pride and happiness.

'I've never touched a pregnant woman before. What happens now? Will you be okay? Will it –?'

'The midwifery manuals say so. I looked them up – fascinating stuff. I'm supposed to feel sick when I wake for a couple of months, then we should start noticing the bump. And it will start to kick around sixteen weeks.' All this was delivered matter-of-factly, though Lisa could not keep a shaky tremor entirely out of her voice.

'It?' Strether murmured. 'Boy or girl? What do you think?'

The putative parents stopped their gyrations. Lisa laughed. 'Goodness, I haven't a clue. And no way of finding out. Unless I go to a non-NT clinic. That'd be an adventure in itself.'

'Does it matter?' said Strether. 'You'd welcome it, boy or girl, wouldn't you?'

'Of course it matters,' Lisa said instantly. 'Some genetic defects are carried by male gametes only . . .' She stopped dead and her hand flew to her mouth. 'Oh, heavens, I can't talk like that any more. We'll never know. That checking and cleansing should have been done already. It's a bit late.' She became crestfallen. 'And I was so damned thrilled at getting into this interesting state.'

Strether pushed home his advantage. 'But, Lisa, it might be better this way. You wouldn't terminate. Not if you're the person I think you are. My wife and I were never lucky, but we'd have been grateful for whatever bundle of creation came to us. The baby will be strong and fit, boy or girl. But even if it had any problem, you would love it dearly.'

She gazed at him, her eyes enormous. 'What do you mean?'

'It will be your baby. Yours and Marius's. Untouched by human hand, unseen by human eye. Until your little boy – or girl – is born and placed in your arms. And you will adore him for the rest of your lives, whatever he is. Blond or dark, blue-eyed or brown, tall or small, whatever, he'll be a unique production with no copies, no blueprint. Except what you already have in the two of you. And to me, I must say, that's a magnificent combination.'

And Strether took their hands, and held them tightly, and could say no more, though his heart was full to bursting with the realisation of what might have been: his child, his own, a son. But then he let them go, as Marius and Lisa clung together, their bodies entwined, with the tiny life to come pulsing and growing between them.

'Bill? Bill, you there? Oh, Christ, it's the bloody answerphone. Where the hell is he? Bill, sweetheart, if you're listening to this, please push the Accept button. I gotta talk to you, urgent. For Christ's sake. Answer me – I can't leave the number. Bill, you know who this is. You tried to get hold of me at the club but they wouldn't put you through. I've been taken off the rota. Terrible things are happening down here. Bill – you there? For the love of God, pick up the phone . . .'

The DNA detector in the metal binding had registered its main target twice. Minute flakes of skin, a hair, droplets of breath were all it needed. But its processes were more intricate, the inadvertently revengeful fruit of a dead soul: that of the murdered records clerk. But not until the DNA of a second target was present, with both men in the vicinity, was the fuse to be activated.

The bomb used a refined form of Semtex. An anonymous blob no larger than a fingernail could be disguised as a piece of chewing-gum or, in this case, as a scrap of blu-tack apparently left over from a previous use, stuck inside a file-box.

A blue file-box which, at the split-second of ignition as the second man entered the room, was sitting neglected on a chair in the corner of Sir Lyndon Everidge's office in the House of Commons.

Chapter Twenty-one

Lisa and Marius clung together. She was shaking, her arms bent double before her body, her eyes wide with terror. He grasped her by the elbows tightly to steady her and stared closely into her face.

'We have no choice. Get packed. Fast as you can.'

'What's happened – and why us? You've done nothing wrong.'

'No, I don't think so either, but it won't stop them. They'll grab it as an excuse. They'll round up everyone. Get cracking – just what we can carry, mind. Do you have your passport?'

'Passport? No. Why would I need a passport? It's in Porton Down. I only use it for scientific conferences. Where are we going?'

'Not sure. But we can't stay here.'

With leaden movements Lisa started to open cupboards and drawers and pulled out a suitcase. Suddenly Marius slumped down on the bed.

'Oh, my dearest. You ask what's happened. I haven't the faintest idea. How did that bomb get planted? Who else in Solidarity could gain access to the House of Commons – to

Lyndon Everidge's own office? Is there an insider? Maybe it was another group. Nobody's claimed responsibility. I was there myself only a few hours before . . .'

'Maybe it was you,' Lisa said, without thinking, clothes clutched in a jumble to her breast like protective armour. Marius seized her arm and whirled her round.

'What did you say?'

'You were there. You just said so. Maybe it was you. The best courier is one who isn't aware he's carrying something. Did you take anything with you? Leave anything behind?'

Years of travelling as a small boy returned to Marius, who lifted the pile of garments from her and began methodically to place them in the suitcase. He thought hard before answering. 'No, not that I'm aware of. Only some papers for the Prime Minister. I shouldn't think he glanced at them twice.'

Their eyes met. 'Oh, Lord. That's it. Timed to explode after I left.'

Lisa's voice was toneless and almost devoid of emotion. 'Could have been more sophisticated than that – some detector fuses can sniff their targets. They can wait till the right people are in the neighbourhood. Then they'll go off. Not before.'

'How do you know?'

She shrugged. 'I heard Winston talk about it once. He said the problem was to get the explosives close enough to the chosen victim.'

'Which they managed. Spectacularly. Three people blown to pieces – the cleaner in the corridor outside, the junior secretary and Sir Robin.'

'Sir Robin must have been the one for whom the bomb was primed. His DNA would be on record at Porton Down from his visits. The others were probably accidental: in the wrong place at the wrong time, I suppose.' Lisa frowned. 'Not that that's any excuse. I worked with Winston all those years. I never thought he had murder in him.'

'Maybe no one realised how much he hated the system. And what it did to him.'

'That's no excuse either. Not in my view.' She stood quietly, her hands loose at the sides. The glow Strether had noted had vanished, replaced by a dull listlessness.

Marius wanted to agree with her, but any chivalrous sentiments had been destroyed for ever during the altercation with Everidge. Rather than argue he stroked her face tenderly. 'The Prime Minister escaped. I'm not sure whether that pleases me or not.'

'Goodness knows why he was spared.' A mild animation returned; now, she moved round the room quickly, almost throwing items into the open case until it overflowed. 'Charmed life, that man. Maybe it was aimed at his DNA too and he was simply on the other side of the room.'

'Like Hitler.'

'What?'

'Nothing.'

She stood, hands on hips, contemplating the packing. 'Will that do?'

He tidied the top layer and closed the clasp. He tested its weight then, with shoulders humped and head bowed, turned towards the door. 'Let's go.'

'Where to?' She picked up her tunic, carried his. It would be sunny outside. Elsewhere, it might be much colder.

'I don't know, Lisa. God help us, I wish I did.'

*

Maxwell Packer ran a finger round the close-fitting neck of his tunic. Black, a silk and linen mixture, suitable for a solemn day, though a trifle warm for the studio. He stood bolt upright at his desk, another well-manicured finger-nail poised over the *Off* button.

'Lady Butler-Armstrong,' he was saying, in a voice oiled with sympathy, 'I do totally understand. Normally, of course, I would do what you wish. Far better to keep these tragedies private. Nobody's business. Absolutely.'

His finger hovered; a closer examination would have detected impatience on his taut features. On the vid-phone the old lady's mouth was contorted in distress. At Packer's end the sound was lowered so that only a squawky burble emerged. He nodded gravely.

'We do, Lady Butler-Armstrong. We can usually reassure the authorities that troublesome incidents are not highlighted. It is in no one's interests to do so. Far better to ignore them. Keeps the peace, avoids alarm. Viewers prefer it, I quite agree. But these are not normal times. In this case I regret – difficult to deny – big explosion – such a public place . . .'

The producer stuck his head round the door anxiously. If the station owner really did want to make the opening announcement for the flagship programme he had only forty seconds to take his place before the camera. Packer grimaced. He was still speaking as he pressed the control.

'I apologise. Sincerely. A tribute programme. Then that's it. Goodbye.'

The red light over the automatic camera winked. Packer slid noiselessly into the seat, adjusted the desk microphone and furrowed his brow. It took him back to his early days as a tyro reporter on local television in Australia. He had bought that station, and others, and had kept on buying until his empire's annual turnover now exceeded fifty billion euros. Those Hong Kong and Malaccas backers had been generous. His friends in high places had been hugely supportive; he had reciprocated whenever possible, with a broadcast entertainment and sport service second to none. But, despite those pleas for a complete blackout, this was rare news, which made his pulse race. Moreover, the ten-second slots in the commercial break had been sold for a quarter of a million euros each; an opportunity not to be missed.

Packer's pale eyes narrowed on the rolling autocue. He had written the script himself. Behind him swelled the sullen boom of the Death March from *Saul*; the usual credits with their plinkety signature tune had been abandoned for this special edition.

'*Good evening. Welcome to* Speak to the World, *your nightly news and reviews round-up. This is – Maxwell Packer.*' He let the enormity of that name sink in, then pulled down the sides of his mouth and shook his head slightly. As a young trainee he had seen videos of Dan Rather and Sir David Frost: it was a style worthy of imitation.

'*Barely twenty-four hours has passed since the bomb outrage at Westminster. Later in the programme we bring you live interviews with the relatives of the tragic victims, who'll tell us how they are feeling now, and with the police chief charged with catching the perpetrators of this monstrous crime. Here in the studio our political correspondent, Harold Docherty, will be assessing the life and career of the murdered head of the home civil service, Sir Robin Butler-Armstrong. May he rest in peace. We have exclusive footage from inside the damaged room, showing where the ceiling fell in and trapped the*

survivors including Prime Minister Sir Lyndon Everidge,
who I hope will be well enough for me to talk to. But now,
ladies and gentlemen, viewers, I beg you all to join me in
a moment of prayer . . .'

Strether's vidphone had been a battleground the entire
afternoon. Anxious not to lose any transmissions he had
grabbed a double-user connection from a nearby office
and had been taping anything that showed, even the
scrappy emergency bursts that interrupted more sedate
items. It seemed wiser for the moment to remain in
Accept mode and listen to everything, rather than try to
send any messages himself. In any case, he was as yet
unsure what line to take, other than to express condolences to the families. With the scrambler and filter both
switched off in order not to interfere with any fainter
fragments, normality intervened bizarrely from time to
time with junk mail and invitations to dinners and semi-
nars. It made his head reel.

'*Ambassador Strether and two guests are invited to a*
preview of the spring collections at Saks Fifth Avenue,
Thatcher Square, SW1 . . .'

'*Christmas shopping by computer! All your require-*
ments at the push of a button, delivered direct to your
door! Ten euros off your first order . . .'

'*Mayday – Mayday – Solidarity – all friends please –*
help us – our headquarters are being raided – troops of the
First Division, Eurocorps – unauthorised entry – Rottweiler
SS in attendance – arresting everyone – our situation is
desperate – Mayday, Mayday – assistance needed –'

'*Ambassador, scramble your phone please. Incoming*
message from the Secretary of State . . .'

'We appeal to our friends – for God's sake don't abandon us – Mayday, Mayday –'

'Bill I have to speak to you – Bill – please –'

The last voice was female and sounded strange and wobbly, almost but not quite unrecognisable and nothing like the breathy drawl he had learned to adore. Quickly he pressed *Transmit* but she had gone. Cursing his slowness he leaped to the door and yelled down the corridor.

'Somebody come help monitor these contacts! Keep all lines open! People are trying to get through. It's mayhem in here. What the fuck's going on?'

A young woman staffer trotted down the hallway, paper in hand. Strether recalled her tearstained face in the downstairs hall when Matt and Dirk had been killed. 'Sir, it's under control. But a message is arriving for you direct on the scrambled phone.'

She handed the paper to him with a slight smile. 'The operator said he couldn't get through to you because your girlfriend was on the line. Sir.' She paused while Strether read the message, which he then showed to her without a word. She tilted her head, and abandoned the coquetry. 'I'll go see if there's any more, sir.'

Back in his own office the vidscreen was a virulent oblong of zizzing lines, black and white, rainbow flashes. Then a face he knew, a blue turban, wild hollow eyes.

'This is Spartacus. To all allies and supporters. Mayday, Mayday. We are under attack –'

A burst of – what? – machine-gun fire, or a laser gun which, at short range, sounded much the same, and a noise of shattering glass. The image blipped from the screen. Strether swore, twiddled knobs, crashed his fist down on the table. But the monitor had gone blank.

He waited, panting, an artery thrumming in his

temple. Then the emptiness resolved itself into blue skies, trees laden with blossom and mood music.

'*New improved Levi's – made from genetically modified cotton with natural in-built colour, environmentally friendly, no toxic dyes, no waste. Available in your size, William Strether. Call this number now . . .*'

The expletive he used surprised even himself. Then he examined the flimsy pink paper on which the staffer had printed out the scrambled message from State.

'*The uprising to be monitored with the greatest care. No public statements. Explosions reported in central Paris, Berlin, Prague – small-scale, sporadic but coordinated. Satellites show street action in Gdansk and Warsaw. Troop movements around Brussels but quiet. Use your own judgement about asylum seekers . . .*'

Spartacus had said little about continental contacts. In fact, Spartacus had said precious little, it transpired, on anything except what suited him. Though the Sikh's sincerity was not in question, his tactics were distinctly devious and had probably served the cause ill. With a sinking sensation at the pit of his stomach Strether realised that the Prince equally might have been kept in the dark.

The Ambassador ran to the elderly television in the corner of the room and set it to CNN. The picture was fuzzy; someone was trying to jam the broadcast and almost succeeding. But the commentary was loud and clear and appeared to be coming from Hamburg where part of the waterfront was alight.

The girl hurried in with another pink sheet, tapping briefly on the door as she entered. 'I thought you'd like this straight away, sir,' she added. He read it, and passed a heavy hand over his brow.

'*You should know that the last of the boat people has just died here. Whatever was done to them, it's not reversible. Take all care.*'

He turned to the young woman. 'Anyone knocks on our door asking for help, we let them in. Anyone. Understood?'

Instantly she was the consummate professional. 'Consider it done. And, sir –'

'Yes?' He was impatient and upset.

'That'll be a popular move here. The best response by far. Thank you.'

Sir Lyndon hitched the sling higher over his shoulder and forced himself not to wince. He had insisted on being fully dressed for his first appearance since his discharge from hospital. The television makeup made his skin feel sticky, but it concealed the minor lacerations and mini-dressings. When he had been found under the rubble, his head covered in gore, the paramedic had screamed; survival at first had seemed unlikely.

Across the interview table sat his old crony and drinking partner Max Packer, looking disgustingly spruce and sober in trim black. For nobody else – *nobody* – would the Prime Minister have given a live interview. The favour would have to be returned, sooner or later: a plum job for a grand-daughter, perhaps, or an adulatory documentary on governmental achievements on the eve of the election. The producer, a slim youth, treated his proprietor with due awe and flitted about like a fussy sparrow. Everidge's shoulder ached viciously. But the interview had to be done, as Packer had urged, in order to reassure the nation.

'The injuries,' Packer empathised. He motioned at the sling. 'Prime Minister. You have been seriously hurt.'

'No, no, nothing much. I'm made of sterner stuff,' the Prime Minister responded, then regretted it; that might imply that those who had died were not. Then it came to him that the Permanent Secretary was gone for ever; no more would the bastard be around to taunt him with that beady gaze, those thin lips, that air of infinite superiority. Sir Lyndon permitted himself the ghost of a smile. 'Of course, Sir Robin was a lot older,' he continued smoothly. 'Not as robust. But his passing is a great loss.'

Packer's warning blink suggested that the remark had been a mite too offhand. 'A great, great loss,' Everidge repeated, eyes downcast. 'A state funeral. Tuesday.'

'Of course,' Packer picked up. 'And will you be declaring a state of emergency?'

'No. What for?' Everidge allowed himself to sound astonished, though the areas to be covered had been settled in advance. 'Some lunatic flings a bomb and the whole panoply of state grinds to a halt? We carry on. The work of government continues without a pause, without rest. Dissident elements are being rounded up as we speak. Fair trial, and all that. Justice will be done.'

'So it's business as usual, Prime Minister?'

Everidge grunted a Churchillian affirmative. Packer posed several more anodyne questions, and the interview was rounded off neatly with a light handshake. With a sigh of relief Everidge heaved himself to his feet, balancing his weight on his knuckles.

'Congratulations on a near escape,' Packer added, as the camera indicator went out. He moved forward as if to pat the injured hero on the arm. At Everidge's glower he backed off. 'You'll take a quiet couple of days, though, surely?'

'Yes. Suppose so. Gotta show respect,' the Prime Minister mumbled. He suddenly felt faint and gratefully accepted the handful of paper tissues offered by an assistant to clean his face. The orange pan-stick he wiped off was spotted with scabs.

Then he lightened. 'But I'm going out for a quick drink tonight. In fact, I may have more than one. I really feel like a blinder, y'know?'

'Yes,' agreed Maxwell Packer. He eased himself out of the black tunic while mentally calculating, and with some satisfaction, how much the interview, syndicated round the globe, would earn Packer Television plc in the next few weeks. Those Far Eastern shareholders would be delighted. 'I know exactly how you feel. Life is a bitch. You enjoy yourself, Lyndon. You deserve it.'

After the chaos upstairs Peter, the embassy chauffeur, decided to make himself scarce. A former Army reservist who regarded himself as an uncomplicated patriot, he had nevertheless become fond of his American employers, and particularly of the Ambassador. To him, Bill Strether exhibited some of the best qualities, including an old-fashioned consideration towards his staff that had been sadly lacking in those Whitehall circles of his previous employment. It was a pity Mr Strether had given up that attractive dark-haired scientist lady. Repeated visits to the Toy Shop instead did not meet with the chauffeur's wholehearted approval.

He took refuge in his lair, down in the cool basement surrounded by cars and tidy workbenches. He put the kettle on and made tea, the traditional way in a warmed pot, and sipped it appreciatively. The comforting smell of ancient grease and oil, of machinery, rubber and leather filled his nostrils. He tinkered with the veteran petrol-driven Mercedes, running his fingers lovingly over the aluminium engine casing which gleamed whistle-clean in the halogen light. It remained here because nobody wanted it; the booming market for such antiques was in China, but it would have been an economic crime, as well as environmental vandalism, to have let it go to them.

The afternoon wore on. The radio on the workbench droned quietly in the background, brief news clips interspersed with solemn music, but he paid no attention. He whistled through his teeth as he checked that the two electric vehicles were fully charged. With so much trouble on the streets – and in his opinion it could take weeks before everything settled down – his role was to ensure that whenever the Ambassador or his staff needed personal transport it was ready for them in an instant, especially if the recent disruptions to the public services continued.

Peter did not grieve for Sir Robin or the other victims, whom he did not know, but he was sorry the Prime Minister had been spared. The word among the government car pool drivers was that Sir Lyndon was a corrupt and sleazy individual; conversations in the back of vehicles, and his spluttered comments when alone afterwards, suggested he let it be thought he was no genius and easily manipulated. Instead, however, the man was at the core of any devious activity. The Prime Minister was a nasty bag of tricks and the world would have been a pleasanter place without him.

Peter had no knowledge about the explosions. It didn't matter much; the protesters could not be successful. Dissidents might rail, but if the voters at large were content then nothing would change. The urban proletariat, men and women he met in pubs, cared mainly whether their teams won on Saturday and took chances only in betting shops with slow horses. The more affluent occupants of suburbs and villages had too much to lose. Their prosperity made them greedy for more, and unwilling to put it at risk. For them, disorder was a pain. It was a viewpoint he understood.

Nothing would come of it. To Peter, a straightforward if wary cynicism about the latest events was wisest. Plus a quiet determination to stay out of harm's way.

His eye was distracted. He gazed around, puzzled. A slight twitching movement came from one corner of the garage. Rats, probably, or other vermin. They'd have to get a cat. He focused briefly but it had gone. He shrugged, fetched liquid polish and a cloth and began to rub down the chrome facings on the Dodge.

That twitch again. His heart began to thump. Access from the street down a narrow alley at the back of the embassy was possible, if you knew how, or stumbled on it by accident. A drunk had been found down here once, badly shaken by falling down the stairs. A stray dog had slipped through the grating. What could it be this time?

The chauffeur was as capable of bravery as the next person, but he was not mad. Breathing hard, he ran on tiptoe back to his workbench and snatched up a flashlight and a crowbar.

The heap in the corner moved again and a groan seemed to come from it. The chauffeur bent over it and shone the flashlight cautiously. A grubby bundle of clothes, scarlet silk and feathers, oddly incongruous, showed up in the yellow circle of light. Another groan came from the depths of the clothing, which began to shudder. A leg jerked out, barefoot and blackened with dirt.

A woman's leg. With a streak of blood down the calf.

Peter dropped the crowbar and jumped to the intercom.

'Security? Security. In the garage. Something – a person. Is there a paramedic on call? Yes. Bring him too. Somebody's down here. I think she's hurt – badly hurt. Hurry it up, won't you?'

'He's in there, Colonel.'

'Have you searched him?'

'Thoroughly.' The adjutant's demeanour was grave. He stripped off the thin plastic gloves and threw them in a bin.

Colonel Mike Thompson hunched his shoulders, his hands clasped behind his back. He felt disoriented and uneasy. Beyond his window the collection compound in the MoD courtyard was filling up. Out of the corner of an eye he could see slumped figures, male and a few females, some in huddles, others weeping or conversing angrily. His own men were on duty to guard them; the Rottweilers, unoccupied and frustrated, had been ordered merely to stand by. They did not like it.

The recent arrival of his Azeri adjutant Neimat Vezirov was a consolation. The young officer had obtained a transfer from the desert to be at his side. That kind of loyalty would give anyone a surge of confidence. Thompson tapped a file. 'And you reckon this mob were behind the Westminster bomb?'

Vezirov glanced over his shoulder. From a room along a corridor came the noise of singing: deep, raucous male voices, raised in unison. In that room, its door ajar, were slumped five Rottweiler guards in their distinctive navy fatigues. He spoke quietly.

'We tried fingerprints. That worked. Everybody forgets about old technology. But that lot' – he jerked his head – 'they'd use even older methods. They'd love to lift this chap and beat him senseless. We pulled rank and got him first. But we can't keep them at bay for ever. And our bunny hasn't given us any names. Yet.'

'Some bunny.' Thompson's face was grim. 'We have to co-operate with them. Top level instructions – give all assistance necessary to civilian units.'

'But, Colonel –' Vezirov stopped. His voice was clipped; despite his excellent English the auto-translator was plugged in and switched on. It was as if the lieutenant did not quite trust himself to believe what he was hearing in the unaccustomed milieu of civil disorder.

'I know. I don't like it either.'

'There's something not right about them,' the adjutant persisted, in a low murmur. 'Heaven knows, sir, I don't like terrorists. It's not warfare as I understand it. But those new guards give me the creeps. They are not normal.'

'Some of them are. Their captains – I quite like Finkelstein. In his better moments.'

'When he's sober. He's been drinking a lot lately. Maybe he doesn't like the new recruits any more than we do.'

Colonel Thompson sighed. 'Stop that. We have a job to do. Our suspect has to be interrogated. His name sounds familiar – I think he may have served with one of my units some while ago. To be honest, I hope not. And I agree with you. I'd much rather we do it than let them get at him.'

'They like cutting things,' the lieutenant brooded. 'I found a cat in there the other day. Or rather, the remains of a cat. But it was still alive.'

'I said *stop it*.' The Colonel's voice rose sharply above the singing. He gathered up his powerbook, a file and a swagger stick. On second thoughts, he reached inside the desk drawer for the sheet of paper he had scribbled over, folded it and put it in his breast pocket. Then he checked his holster: the safety was off. 'Come on.'

Spartacus stood as the two men entered, his hand-cuffed hands held in front of him, pumping up and down. In a hectoring tone he began what was apparently a prepared speech: 'I demand my rights under the Geneva Convention. I am held illegally as a prisoner-of-war . . .' Then as the small windowless room filled with the authoritative bulk of the Colonel, he gaped in confusion.

'Colonel Thompson – sir? What are you doing here?'

'Captain Mahwala, isn't it?' Thompson consulted his powerbook coolly. He motioned to his prisoner to sit then took the chair on the opposite side of the table. The adjutant closed the door and positioned himself across it like a barricade. 'I think the question is, what are *you* doing here?'

Spartacus opened and shut his mouth but said nothing.

The Colonel put the swagger stick on the table, then his elbows, and folded his big hands together. Slowly he crunched first one finger then another till the joints cracked like pistol shots.

'I am here to question you, Captain Mahwala, about your involvement in terrorist action. To be precise, the assassination attempt at the House of Commons. What do you know about it?'

'I am not obliged to say anything,' Spartacus replied formally, but it was clear that his resolve was wilting under the cold, steely gaze of his former superior. Patches of sweat appeared under his arms. Suddenly he burst out, 'You should not be supporting them. You, of all men – I thought you had some humanity about you. What they're up to is dreadful, terrible. They are destroying the very fabric of society . . .'

The Colonel waited till the mini-tirade petered out. Then he rotated his shoulders, deliberately, as if bored.

'Are they? I thought that was *your* intention – Spartacus. That is your codename, isn't it? Now I don't want to waste any time, Captain. We already have a great deal of solid intelligence. Your group has been penetrated for some months. We know, for example, that whereas you used to be the leader, someone else more recently has been entrusted with that crown of thorns. Who is it?'

Spartacus was sullen. 'If you have inside information, you don't need me to tell you.'

'But I do need you to admit it, and to turn King's evidence against him,' the Colonel responded silkily. It came to him that he secretly enjoyed the interrogation process, the battle of minds so akin to poker or chess; and provided he performed well, the excesses on offer next door could be avoided. A cackle of wild laughter came from that direction, and the crunch of boots on the floor.

'Never.' Spartacus tried to fold his arms across his chest but the handcuffs defeated him. He stared belligerently at the Colonel. 'We tried to kill the Prime Minister and the Permanent Secretary together. Oh, it can only be a gesture – others will step forward to take their place.

But such a spectacular act could not be glossed over. It has to be reported. The conspiracy of silence will have been broken. The media might start asking questions. And the voters might be interested in some genuine answers.'

'And who gave you the right?' Thompson mocked. 'And by such means? Does your Guru Nandra give you permission? Is it written in your holy books?'

'Sikhs are warriors.' Spartacus held himself proudly. 'We are not afraid to fight, and die.'

'Oh, fine.' The Colonel leaned forward and played with the swagger stick, rolling it under his fingertips, lightly, back and forth. 'The targets you attacked yesterday were not soldiers. They were elderly men. Sir Robin, whom you killed, was over ninety. That was not an act of bravery, Captain. It was a piece of sheer cowardice.'

'No. It takes more courage to stand against the wicked. To advance and be counted. To separate oneself from the common herd. Those men have been leading the Union to disaster. You can make your racist comments, Colonel Thompson; they don't worry me. You have thrown in your lot with the forces of evil. They have conspired to put my people to the bottom of the dung heap. To bar the top jobs to everyone except their own offspring. They use prisoners as a source of farmed organs – do you know about that? They manufacture evidence to put dissidents into gulags and concentration camps. They . . .'

He continued for several minutes in this vein, his voice rising to a rapid whine. The adjutant began to look unhappy and shuffled his feet, while the Colonel sat impassively, grunting occasionally but making no attempt to interrupt.

Then Spartacus seemed to waver. 'I don't have to tell

you any of this,' he muttered. 'And you'll cook up charges against me, anyway. I personally am finished – I know I shan't see my family again. But it is for them that I am doing this.'

The Colonel placed both hands on the table, palms down, as if he wished to push himself away from his victim. His voice was level but with an edge of menace. 'I am not a racist, Captain. But I need you to grasp this, and quickly. If you don't assist us now, in this relatively civilised setting – not just with details to fill in a few gaps, but with your pledge to help put behind bars the leader you call Moses – then other methods are at our disposal.' He tapped the swagger stick on the table, once, twice.

'You do not frighten me. And I will not betray my friends and comrades.'

Colonel Thompson sighed. 'You will. I tell you, MI5 used to calculate that a captive had done his duty if he could hold out against torture for forty-eight hours. Then he would break – any man, or woman. But by then other operatives had been warned and gone into hiding. You, my friend, should not assume that you are any different.'

'You torture prisoners. Yes, I should have expected that,' Spartacus said bitterly. 'But if you make too good a job of it, I wouldn't be able to speak for you as a witness anyway. So I am ready. I would prefer to die.'

The door banged open. On the threshold stood two of the Rottweilers, their faces shiny with liquor. One held a bottle of whisky in one hand and a thonged bull-whip in the other. Their wrists were strapped with studded leather bracelets; their upper arms bulged with muscle. Tattoos festooned every square inch of revealed flesh, replete with fanged dogs and bloodcurdling epithets.

Behind shuffled Finkelstein, who peered over their shoulders then slipped away. Kowalsky was nowhere to be seen.

'You've had him long enough, Colonel,' one of the guards growled. 'It's our turn now. Give him here.'

'I haven't quite finished.' The Colonel's voice was calm but his mouth was hard. He had remained seated and motioned to Spartacus to do the same. Under the table his right hand slid to his holster. 'Five minutes.'

The guards grumbled, argued with each other, handed round the bottle then reluctantly slouched out. But they left the door wide open.

Thompson leaned forward. 'You see?' he hissed. 'I can't save you if you won't help me. If this is to go to open trial, I must put together a court case. You are our prize witness. You must do this.'

'No.' The Sikh's face was set.

The corridor had gone quiet; a commotion outside in the yard heralded the arrival of more detainees who were providing sport for the drunken guards. Spartacus's eyes darted past his captors to the open doorway. All in a flash he seemed to make up his mind. With a yelp he jumped up, knocking over his chair. Then he put his handcuffed hands under the table, and with a desperate heave threw it over. The edge caught Thompson in the gut and winded him; he staggered and nearly fell. As the adjutant, uncertain who to attend to, knelt to the Colonel's aid, Spartacus seized his opportunity. He hurdled over the fallen chair and ran.

'Stop him!' the Colonel yelled, and pulled out his laser gun. But the prisoner was already at the doorway and, without a backward glance, sprinting into the corridor.

'No!' Thompson staggered after him, holding his left

side. It felt as if a rib might be broken, but his thoughts were with his quarry. What had Vesirov called him jocularly, not half an hour before? A bunny? Some rabbit – trying to escape, and running straight towards the waiting pack.

The Colonel held himself upright, the weapon in his hand, and took a bead at the flying Sikh's back. 'Colonel?' came the troubled voice of his adjutant, who scrambled out behind him.

At the far end, silhouetted in the dim light of a dirty window, the two Rottweilers reappeared. Broad grins broke out on both sweaty faces. They took their stance, legs planted wide apart, rocking on their heels. One passed the bottle to the other, then flexed the bull-whip. The fugitive skittered to a halt, handcuffed arms flailing.

'Captain,' Thompson called out. 'Captain. This way.'

As Spartacus spun about in panic and faced him, the Colonel took aim. It was hardly necessary. The man was no more than ten metres away.

Careful aim. And fired, twice.

A flash of deadly light blazed from the muzzle of the gun and blasted a scorched hole in the Sikh's shirt, just over his heart. A dark red mark appeared and oozed slowly for several seconds as his legs crumpled. His eyes widened, a rattle sounded in his throat.

He was dead before his body hit the ground.

The Rottweilers ran up, but were kept at bay by the weapon. The acrid smell of singed flesh filled the air. 'Whatcha do that for?' one demanded angrily and prodded the Colonel's arm with the bull-whip. 'We were going to have some sport.'

'Sorry to disappoint you.' The Colonel did not holster his gun but nudged the limp corpse with his toe. 'Get rid of it. Preferably in one piece. And no reports, d'you hear?'

It was twenty minutes later, back in the restored interrogation room as the Colonel submitted to a pressure bandage administered by his nervous adjutant, that the Azeri at last ventured a low comment.

'You should have aimed at one of those guards. Sir.'

Thompson snorted. 'Plenty more where they came from, Lieutenant. There are hard choices in this life.'

'Sir ? You meant to . . . ?'

'Think about it. One was an escapee. The others are in His Majesty's service.' The adjutant's anxious face became a bronze mask. Thompson brooded in silence, then spoke in a low voice, as if to himself. 'They can't hurt him now. And we got out of him everything – legitimate.'

He rose and lifted his left arm, gingerly, then patted his side.

'Believe me. I had to make a decision. I shot the man I wanted.'

Strether took the white towel, wrung it out in the tepid water and placed it, folded, on her forehead. Then he sat, hands loose between his knees, and looked at her.

They had cleaned her up as well as possible and, at the Ambassador's insistence, taken her to the spare bed in his room, upstairs in the little-used private quarters. Were she to be rushed to hospital, he reasoned, he could not guarantee her safety.

The bedside lamp hid the extent of her injuries. A cursory examination had revealed two broken fingers and a great deal of hideous bruising. She had been beaten up with a brutal thoroughness. The lovely face was swollen, purple in places, with one eye closed into a slit. One temple had been sliced open with a razor; the cut was now firmly taped. It would heal, with a scar needing plastic surgery. The platinum hair was matted, some torn out at the roots. Her pulse was shallow and fast but her blood pressure was close to normal. That suggested, unless he were mistaken, that there was no major internal damage. What she needed most was protection, and rest.

The eyelids flickered. One blackened eye stayed firmly shut, but the other opened a fraction.

He pressed forward. 'Marty?' he said. 'Can you hear me?'

She shrank back from him, fearful. He grabbed the light and twisted the stem so that it shone on his own face. 'It's me, Bill. Bill Strether.'

A slow hiss came from between the cracked lips. 'Bill?'

'Yes, sweetheart. You're safe. In the embassy. Nobody can get you here.'

'I'm thirsty. So thirsty.'

He offered the straw of the water bottle and she drank greedily. Tenderly he wiped the dribble from her chin.

'Bill? What time is it?'

'Time? Nearly twenty-two hours. We found you this afternoon. You've been asleep almost since then.'

'Oh, yeah. I remember.' She seemed to smile a little. Her hand emerged jerkily from under the bedclothes and he let it lie in his. The splints on the broken fingers were unfamiliar and ghostly in the dim light. 'Found the back door to your garage. Knew you wouldn't mind.'

'Stay as long as you like. Who's been doing this to you?'

'Dunno exactly. They didn't give their names. And I didn't ask.'

'But you must have some idea.'

She paused and seemed to be dozing. Then her voice came again, a mumble so low he had to bend to hear it. 'Something to do with the bomb. I'd seen one of them with the Prime Minister. A bodyguard. And some of his pals. Wanted to know about you.'

'Me?'

'Yeah. They figured, since you were a customer, I might have something incriminating. Don't worry, I couldn't have given them anything useful if I'd tried. The girls helped me get away. The other Marilyns.'

He touched her strapped fingers with infinite gentleness. 'I can't believe they did this to you. What did they want to know?'

She lifted the hand and waved away the inquiry. 'Later. Maybe. After midnight.'

'Why? What's going to happen at midnight?'

'Uh-huh.'

She had closed her eyes again and would say no more.

At midnight, however, he armed himself with a stiff bourbon and went back into her room. The bedside light was on and her eyes were fixed on the clock on the dresser. As it pinged for the hour, she smiled again, and tiredly patted the side of the bed. 'It's done. I hope.'

He seated himself and helped her with the water flask. 'What's done? What kinda mystery is this?'

Marty snickered softly. 'That Prime Minister. He went to the Toy Shop tonight. Another snuff party was booked. They wanted me to join in but I refused. But the toys had had enough. Him and his monsters.'

She lifted her head, gazed at the clock, then let herself

fall back on the pillows. 'Yes, it's done. I can feel it. At the midnight hour.'

'What is it? You can tell me now,' Strether urged.

It took her an age to reply.

'When he gets drunk, and starts yelling for more. If he was into S&M for himself he could have as much as he liked. No shortage of volunteers to knock *him* about. But no, he wants to watch while other people get torn. Stark naked, tied up with straps and chains. Bleeding from every orifice. Not tonight. Not tonight.'

'My God, Marty. What do you mean?'

'I mean that we toys, we clones, we worthless drones, we did something good for once. We finished a job that your Solidarity friends bungled. Been planning it for weeks – we'd had our fill, up to here. After all, nobody knew who was going to be next for the snuff box. Especially the older ones – it could have been anybody.'

Her face suddenly hardened, in a manner he had never seen before and never wished to see again.

'Sir Lyndon, Sir bloody Lyndon. He's the one hanging by the skin of his shoulder blades from the ceiling with his balls stuffed in his mouth. He's dead meat right now, Bill. He's the victim tonight.'

She sighed, restless in the bed. 'Oh, Bill. It's finished here. It's finished.'

It was dark. Strether awoke with a jump from his self-imposed vigil in the armchair by Marty's bed. She was sleeping peacefully, mouth slightly open. The swellings were slightly worse but the bleeding had stopped. He could see a chipped tooth; they must have smashed her full in that alabaster face, tried to destroy her glorious beauty.

His neck was painfully stiff and he stretched gingerly. Then he realised what had woken him and leaped to his feet.

The girl staffer was standing hesitantly at the door, her hand on the outside knob, silhouetted against the landing light. She was dressed in a pink towelling robe and, he noted with vague surprise, fluffy mules on her feet. Her hair was tousled and piled in a topknot. Phrases came into his mind, bland reassurances, but one glance at her stricken expression stopped him in his tracks.

'I'm sorry to bother you, sir. You should be getting some rest. But we've just found another woman, this time on the front doorstep. I've taken the liberty of bringing her indoors. I believe it's someone you know.'

'Yes? Who is it?' Strether shook his fuddled head to clear it of sleep.

'We think it's Dr Pasteur, sir. She's in a hysterical state. And she's alone.'

Chapter Twenty-two

It was four a.m. The night was dark, a reminder that the winter solstice and the shortest day were not far off. In the courtyard slumbering figures huddled together under blankets. The silence was punctured by men muttering in their sleep; others wailed or snored. The sentry in his blue box on the far side of the compound had his feet up on a chair, arms folded loosely across his chest and his head lolling slightly. Somewhere a lone bird began to sing, then thought better of it and settled back in its nest to sleep on.

Prince Marius Vronsky sat slumped at the table in the interrogation room. In deference to his status he had not been handcuffed and had been brought in via a back door. His tunic was dishevelled and stained, and a lock of hair fell across his forehead. He seemed dazed, though there were no marks on him. He also posed, as far as Colonel Mike Thompson was concerned, the biggest problem of his career.

The Colonel nudged his adjutant; the two moved to leave the room and shut the door behind them. Mike Thompson's face was grey with fatigue. The savage pain in his side had been controlled with an injection but he wheezed noticeably as he breathed. There would be no more running after fugitives for a while. Nor was he in any shape to resist the Rottweilers, should they choose to come for this prisoner. Not that they were much threat, at least before daybreak.

'Colonel, you should rest.' Vezirov touched his arm anxiously.

'It's not important. And I don't want any more blood on my carpet. You're a fine officer, Neimat, but I don't think that bunch of murderous lunatics would take much notice of you.'

The Lieutenant bit his lip and refrained from observing that the most recent murder he had witnessed had been carried out by the Colonel himself. He glanced down at his feet and wished he hadn't. A thin black trail led from the doorway into the darkness – evidence that a body, still bleeding, had been dragged away.

'Where did you say the Prince was picked up?'

'At the airport, sir. They were trying to leave. They'd been spotted on the high-speed rail link – everyone was being scrutinised. But we wanted to know where they were headed, so we waited.'

'And where did they try to go?'

The adjutant shrugged. 'They didn't seem to have any particular destination in mind, sir. Miami was what they asked for, but it also happened to be the next flight outside Europe on the board. My guess is they would have gone anywhere, just to get out.'

'It comes to something,' the Colonel mused, 'when a peer of the realm, a man of princely blood, wants to flee the Union by the fastest means possible.'

'Sir.' The young Azeri's face was a studied blank.

'She got away – the woman companion?'

'It is unclear – she's not in custody. She wasn't the key person. The warrant was out for him.'

'We have to be careful what we say, I think.' The Colonel walked away down the corridor, slowly, then looked down and tapped his foot. The Lieutenant saw that he too had noticed the blood trail, with much the same reaction of shame and revulsion.

Thompson walked back and eyed his young assistant. 'We are élite corps, you and I,' he said softly. 'We are not thugs, but we are brought to this. Your family, Neimat. What sort of people are they?'

'I'm told my great-grandfather was First Secretary of the Azerbaijani Communist Party a century ago, sir,' the young man answered. 'When Gorbachev was still alive. The family joke is that he was also the last Secretary, since the Party collapsed soon after. But I don't have the details.'

'I trace my ancestry back to the Wellesleys, to Wellington himself,' the Colonel murmured. 'He would have taken a dim view of such disorder. Though in his day as Prime Minister, the mob's fury was frequently directed at him. I gather our own esteemed Prime Minister was on television?'

'Yes, sir. He looked – ah – a bit battered.' The two men laughed.

'Serve the bugger right. He's been up to no good, of that I am quite sure.' The Colonel absent-mindedly patted his breast pocket where the folded sheet of paper nestled. 'When everything has calmed down, I intend to get to the bottom of this. Several of my superiors will be interested. Apart from any other considerations, we can't sit twiddling our thumbs while those – those *mutants* down

the corridor take over. Or none of us will sleep soundly in
our beds.'

'Some of the younger Eurocorps officers . . .' The adjutant hesitated.

'Go on, Lieutenant. I am listening.'

'We have been disturbed at – at the turn of events, sir.
Naturally we have all taken the pledge to uphold the
Union, its laws and codes.' Vezirov paused, as if searching for words. His accent had become more clipped and
formal. 'But there is deep concern at recent – distortions.
I did not entirely believe it before, but after what I've witnessed I do now. Power-hungry men are misusing their
positions. For their own ends.'

'Is that why you requested a transfer?'

'Partly. I could do nothing in the back of beyond in
Kashi. But also, sir – because of you.'

'I'm flattered. And duly grateful. Only you'd probably
be safer on the frontier at the moment than here.' The
Colonel half smiled ruefully and pressed the adjutant's
arm.

'No, sir, you don't understand. If there is to be change –
if we are to find a better way forward – you are one of
those who can initiate it, and insist it be carried through.'

'Me? Good Lord. No, no. I'm nowhere near senior
enough.'

'Maybe not. But it's a practical question – who is the
most suitable? You're one of the most experienced and
respected commanders, sir. You can carry the Army with
you. And if you're convinced, you can convince others.
You have that talent.'

Colonel Mike Thompson stared hard into the face of
his young assistant, but the Azeri did not flinch. Then the
Colonel turned away and studied the flaky paint of the

closed door, as if the answers were written on it in invisible ink. The muscles in his cheek clenched and did not
relax. It was a full minute before he spoke again.

'Well, Lieutenant, what are we to do with him?'

The Azeri's hand slipped to his holster and he adjusted
his laser gun to sit more easily. 'He was armed when he
was caught, sir. But he's an NT, so it would be difficult.'

'Ah, yes. We can dispose of one type of corpse but not
another. Not so readily, anyway. But the Prince is also a
well-placed person, is he not? Elected to Parliament, a
kinsman of the King. The highest caste of NT, a friend of
the famous. So I return to this question. What was he
doing, getting mixed up with Solidarity and protesters
and conspiracies to blow up the government?'

'Maybe he thought it was the only course of action,
sir,' the adjutant said stubbornly.

The Colonel swore under his breath. 'Don't go putting
ideas into my head, sonny,' he said brusquely. Then he
grasped the doorknob and went inside.

The adjutant made to follow but was politely but
firmly left in the corridor, with instructions to keep any
intruders well away.

Inside, for what seemed an age, the interrogation continued. Vezirov could not make out what was being said,
except that for much of the time it was conducted in low
urgent tones, the words and phrases indistinguishable.
He could hear the Colonel moving about – or, at least, he
assumed it was the Colonel; the prisoner had seemed
almost moribund in his defeat. After the first hour the
Colonel emerged and disappeared, to return with a jug of
water and two cups in his hands, chewing painkillers.
The door banged closed after him. Only once were voices
raised, when the Azeri heard the name 'Spartacus' and a

furious altercation ensued, which continued several minutes. It was succeeded by a heavy silence, punctuated by the sound of the Colonel's footfalls as he paced, up and down, in the tiny room.

Down the corridor, light was beginning to filter through the grimy window. In the courtyard, bodies were stirring. A dog barked. A bell rang somewhere, and was greeted with a sleepy oath. The Lieutenant checked his watch and tapped softly at the door.

It opened a crack and the Colonel's bleary eye above unshaven jowls peered out.

'What is it, Lieutenant?'

'Sir, it's five forty. The new shift will be coming on soon.'

The Colonel's head dropped on to his chest in thought. Behind him Vezirov could glimpse the prisoner, slumped in his chair in much the same position as he had been hours earlier. The jug was empty, and so was the brandy bottle at its side. 'Thank you. Could you please find out whether anyone is on duty at the moment – down there?'

Vezirov trotted off and returned quickly.

'No, sir. Not yet.'

'Right. Then bring my Jeep round the back.' He rubbed his chin tiredly. 'And I could do with my razor. Though I don't suppose anyone will notice, not at present.'

Shortly after, the Colonel, shaved and in a fresh shirt, with his adjutant, laser weapon at the ready, might have been observed walking purposefully out of an unlit back entrance of the Ministry of Defence into a waiting military vehicle. Its cover was up and a colonel's flag had been attached to the bonnet. Its dipped headlights barely broke through the winter gloom. Between them, hands cuffed behind his back, was a scruffy individual in what might once have been a designer suit. The prisoner's head was down and he seemed demoralised to the point of stupor. He had to be shoved into the back of the Jeep and fastened into his seat-belt. The Colonel slid cautiously into the passenger seat in front. He winced and touched his side. The vehicle moved swiftly away from the kerb.

'Where to, sir?' Vezirov asked.

The Colonel waited till they were out of sight of the ministry. The journey would not be straightforward; the streets near the Palace of Westminster were littered with broken glass, as if further demonstrations had taken place, yet the city was eerily empty, as though a self-imposed curfew was in place. A drain had burst on one corner and was gushing spouts of brown water into the air; it was unattended. Street lamps were out down several thoroughfares, cameras smashed. A minibus, the kind used for transporting Rottweilers, was on its side in New Parliament Square, unoccupied, its tyres and interior scorched and still faintly smouldering. There was nobody to be seen.

'Turn left and follow this road for about five kilometres,' Thompson ordered. 'Steady. We don't want to attract any attention.'

The figure in the back stirred. 'Where are you taking me?' he asked hoarsely. 'If you're going to dispose of me, I'd rather it be somewhere – public. Not some quiet spot where you can dump the body and no more said.'

'We don't go in for summary executions in the Union, Prince.' The Colonel twisted round to address his captive direct, but could manage only half-way. 'It's six o'clock. Can we get the news on the radio?'

The adjutant spoke clearly, 'Radio, channel fourteen. News, please,' and the machine switched itself on.

The funereal dirge did not surprise them; it had been playing monotonously in continuity gaps since the explosion. What came next made them all sit up with a jerk. The Jeep skittered across the road until Vezirov regained control and slowed.

'*Good morning. Here is the news. Prime Minister Sir Lyndon Everidge and two of his bodyguards have been found dead in London. It is believed they may have been victims of a further assassination attempt following the blast at Westminster which killed the Permanent Secretary of the civil service, Sir Robin Butler-Armstrong and two others on Monday. Tributes have been paid . . .*'

'Take a right here,' Thompson ordered. Vezirov drove the Jeep at a crawl and they listened carefully to the broadcast, the Colonel with his teeth gritted, half snorting in discomfort. He addressed the grey-faced Prince roughly. 'Your mob again, was it?'

'Not as far as I'm aware. But then, as I kept telling you, I know hardly anything.'

The Colonel grunted. He squinted out of the windscreen. 'Okay, left, then to the end of the block. Stop.'

Three minutes later, the Jeep disappeared rapidly round the corner, squealing on two wheels. It contained only two men, both in Army uniforms, and with stony expressions on their faces. It headed in the direction of Eurocorps headquarters, out of town near Bracknell.

And Marius, alone and shabby on the sidewalk, gazed up into the pale dawn light and rubbed his sunken cheeks with his free hands in disbelief. It took him a long time to grasp where he was, but eventually, somewhat timidly, he climbed the steps and pressed the intercom buzzer.

A female voice answered.

'American embassy. Good morning. Can I help you?'

Epilogue

Seven years later, Kremmling, Colorado

'Darling, haven't you finished yet?'

He waved her away. 'Nearly. I just wanted to check this through. Then they can take it with them and read it on the fastjet. Won't be a minute.'

She pouted. 'Lunch has been ready an hour. We're all starving.'

'Let them get started. I'll be down shortly.'

As the swirl of her silken patio pants disappeared across the tiled floor, he smiled contentedly to himself, pressed *Scroll* and found the passage in his diary he had been seeking.

The wedding. He had conducted it himself, as he was entitled to do under US law, in Air Force One several kilometres high above the Atlantic. The Prince and his Princess, still exhausted, she a little weepy, he withdrawn and unusually quiet, but both refreshed after making use of the shower and kitchen facilities on board, had stood side by side, leaning tiredly on each other as they exchanged vows. He had urged that they sleep on it first, but neither had had the capacity to rest. Not until long after disembarkation, the completion of formalities and President Kennedy's welcome to the USA.

The rings had been his wedding gift. On the grass lawn outside he could see them still on their fingers, glinting gold in the sun, fashioned from the ores found in the red ochre hills in the distance. The man's had had to be made smaller to fit the Prince, but that came afterwards, when they were at peace. The woman's had fitted exactly, and he had felt his heart skip a beat as he slipped it on Lisa's finger. In doing so he laid a much-loved ghost gently to rest, even as he handed his first European love over to her husband. For it had been his dead wife's, and the Prince's had been his own.

The terrible days of the failed uprising and its bloody aftermath had taken its toll. Infiltration meant that names were known; over five hundred had been arrested, Marius among them, but few had escaped or been seen again. It would have been excusable had either of them, alerted to the emotional turmoil ahead, suggested backing off from the commitment of marriage. But although he had put the issue privately to each, neither Lisa nor Marius wished to wait. They had been steadfast. And he had been proud to officiate, and to make their union a reality.

Yet it had done them much good, Strether reasoned, to have begun their married lives in a new country. Most of all, their child had been born in an environment where natural conception and birth were the accepted norm. Instead of second-class facilities with non-NTs, the finest medical arrangements were on hand. Both pregnancy and birth had been free of incident, though to the young parents it was a most wondrous journey. And that was true of Strether himself, the boy's godfather, despite all the many calves he had eased into the daylight before he had ventured into the hazardous labyrinths of international politics.

The child had cemented their bond, all three, had become a symbol to them of new life, of hope. And of the urgent and absolute need to consider the future. No more could Marius act insouciant and pretend that tomorrow would take care of itself. No longer could Lisa retreat into scientific literature and talk as if wisdom came from a downloaded hard disk. Both had had to explore feelings they barely knew existed; both had learned, slowly and with many stumbles at first, how to trust to inarticulate instincts and emotions. To the Ambassador they resembled intrepid travellers in a freshly discovered and unmapped continent. Which, indeed, both were.

The news from Europe continued to be patchy and disturbing. Strether had badgered CNN and the main news channels into taking a greater interest, pointing out (this, he found, worked) that if the front line in Europe weakened, the USA would be exposed to aggressive challenge from further east. It was no coincidence that his successor at the Court of St James was a noted military man from West Point. The possibility that USA servicemen and women might again have to spill blood on foreign shores did galvanise public opinion, but unfortunately the effect was largely negative. 'A plague on all their houses' was a frequent reaction. The Americas slid towards being more isolationist than ever.

With the help of the State Department, Winston's minidisk had been transcribed, the material analysed and disseminated. A series of in-depth reports had been produced for public service broadcasting channels and repeated on numerous occasions, but there was scant evidence that the revelations were making much impact at the highest levels in Europe itself, where it mattered most.

So the Prince had become a tireless campaigner, travelling throughout the hemisphere and further afield, outlining what ailed the Union and how it might be rectified, even while declaring himself keen to end his exile as soon as possible. But the regimes in London and Brussels had deemed it best to ignore him and the other voices that spoke out. Rather, the focus of debate had continued to be in the USA itself, where fundamentalist opposition to genetic programmes intensified. No wonder the Prince was determined to go home.

Lisa too, Strether knew, was restless, and it grieved him. Stateside she was much in demand on the lecture circuit describing and denouncing the worst excesses of chromosomal intervention. On the other hand, the main employment she had been consistently offered in America – and it had been lucrative – was in the numerous private IVF clinics. There, she had explained to him in disgust, she would be expected in secret to 'augment' embryos before implantation, and to train technicians, also in secret, how to do it skilfully. In other words, to carry out exactly the kinds of enhancement that she herself now found so distasteful and which were banned by federal law. Apart from the absence of official approval, the main differences, it transpired, were that Americans desired more trivial modifications than Europeans: permanent slimness, delayed ageing and the high cheekbones suitable for television were the primary requests. And, for the females, naturally shiny hair, a straight nose turning up at the end, bigger breasts and

Miss America legs. The male children were to be invested with untrammelled ambition, particularly to make money. Enhanced brain-power was not, on the whole, in demand. When Strether, in defence of his countrymen, suggested that that indicated satisfaction with what they'd got, Lisa gave him a withering look and did not respond.

With some difficulty information had been obtained about other, minor, changes. Porton Down had been temporarily closed when financial irregularities had been uncovered; Director James Churchill had been prosecuted, but charges were eventually dropped and he took early retirement. It reopened soon after with another NT in his post, pale-eyed if marginally younger, but otherwise so similar in appearance and philosophy that, Lisa declared dispiritedly, there had been no point in the hiatus.

Other clinics continued busy and more had been licensed. Packer International had become a prime mover in the business and, it appeared, held the main patents on the acceleration project. It might be some while before their deliberate creation, virtually overnight, of world-beating footballers and other super-talented sports stars would produce a backlash: but not, she expected, a clampdown, just more of the same in other commercial hands. In the modern Union, competition was touted as a fairer means of control than regulation. As for Rottweiler SS – which had dismissed some guards, and disciplined others – the firm had amalgamated with Group 4, Securicor and the Ministry of Justice Inc. The multinational company was quoted on a dozen stock exchanges, but the identity of its main backers remained a mystery.

The young family had disappeared from Strether's line
of sight. They would be sitting down under the trees at
the white ironwork tables, plumping up cushions for the
child and helping themselves to the food. Strether chuckled. They had been reluctant at first to eat either beef or
lamb, until he pretended to be offended; on their return
to Europe they would probably cause offence in their
turn enthusing about their newly acquired tastes.

And to Europe they would soon be going. Although it
was, of course, with Strether's blessing, it was also with
his profound regret. A great deal of heart-searching,
debating late into the night with both Lisa and Marius,
together and separately, had occurred. But the Prince had
been asked – been begged, indeed – to take a post in a
fresh administration in London, a 'ministry of all the talents' being put together by Prime Minister Bretherton.

Strether could not quite see which subtle distinguishing marks from its predecessors gave it such worth that
the Prince was willing to consider serving in it; but
Marius had murmured about shake-ups, and had mentioned a former colonel, a Michael Thompson who was to
be Minister of Defence, and who had pledged to secure
improvements. Several transatlantic vidphone calls with
this soldier, conducted for hours in the middle of the
American night, had set minds at rest, at least partially. It
was no trap: the man was sincere, though how effective
he might be remained to be seen.

An amnesty for political prisoners was to be declared
as a mark of goodwill, so the Prince himself would be
unmolested. The camps on the border were to be closed
down. A 'Truth and Reconciliation' tribunal was proposed, on the lines of one in South Africa many years
before, that might jog consciences and memories. Several

other named non-NTs were to be Ministers, including two blacks. As Marius explained it to Strether, it was a challenge he felt he could not refuse. Especially as he had 'come out' as a non-NT, and had some pride in his new-found notoriety.

Had the dam broken? Would it be possible in future for non-NTs to assume their place at the highest levels of society, by merit alone? Might their own child one day grow up to be Prime Minister? Some parts of Europe had not found that difficult – Germany, for example, or Spain. But the French were adamant. They had created ÉNA in the first place, and still argued that its graduates alone should take the top three grades at the Commission. Their answer was to clone ÉNA itself, to seed mini-establishments in other regions. That had gone down well in Poland and Russia, where there was still a hankering for officials with labels, licentiates and built-in superiority. The English, to Strether's mind, were the nation least amenable to fresh ideas. They were snobs, and preferred their upper classes entirely composed of insiders. The old school tie, they called it. And they still spoke as if they could tell the rest of the world what to do.

Strether slipped a minidisk into the port and ordered the machine to *Copy*. Marius could use it in his powerbook, and would have it as a record of amazing and terrifying events, but also as proof, if needed, of the complicity of certain NTs in attempts to subvert the Union to their own ends. Given that their close relatives were in jobs throughout the higher echelons of the Union, there was no assurance that it could not happen again. Indeed, a live conspiracy still flickered in the eastern regions, where democracy was a newer introduction. The civil guards there had an uncanny resemblance to those

Rottweilers sacked in the West. And since nobody had
been executed, presumably the violent gene pool was still
lurking and available. To Strether, it was the strongest
argument in favour of capital punishment he could imagine.

If disaster were to be averted in future the best weapon
was knowledge. Awareness of what *could* go wrong,
allied with general vigilance, might prevent a recurrence.
That, and a more finely developed ethical sense than had
been apparent in the Union for decades to date.

'You can't tell science to quit,' Strether murmured to
himself. 'You wouldn't want to. But you can learn how to
use it, limit it, even harness it to moral attitudes.'

He paused, then shook his head at the conundrum. At
moments like this he regretted that his education, such as
it was, had leaned more to the practicalities of animal
husbandry and not at all to Bertrand Russell, Kant or
Aristotle.

'That's exactly what they were doing – using science.
Perhaps Lisa was right when she says it's not the scientists' fault. The thirst for knowledge is never slaked –
they can never call it a day. Discoveries make possible
choices that once were fantasy, or accident, or the gift of
God. The researchers don't say *how* to choose – that's not
their job. It is the responsibility of each of us to make
those choices. To use our free will, but not selfishly. And
to try to remain human beings in the process.'

From beyond the window came the sound of happy
laughter. Ah, that they would stay, and let today last till
eternity. But they could not.

'I suppose,' he said wistfully to himself, 'you need to
have the moral values embedded in society to begin with.
You need to see human beings as ends in themselves, as

valuable, however crooked or bent or disabled or incomplete. That takes some doing, because we all warm to beauty and shrink from the imperfect. But if we can break our own prejudices, everything else will follow.'

His wife reappeared, the pucker on her brow deeper and more genuine than before. He slipped the minidisk into a protector and instructed the machine to switch itself off. Then he stood and gazed at her in rapture.

She was not bent or incomplete. She was utterly lovely, still. The scar on her temple had healed without a trace. The split lips, the swollen eyes, were a forgotten nightmare. The magnificent figure was as breathtaking as before, the creamy flesh billowed splendidly over the silvery lace of her low-cut sweater. The trim ankles, the painted toes in their sling-back shoes, the confidence, the easy sexuality: all were voluptuously on show. The white-blonde hair was worn longer than in her working days, but suited her, framing the face and eyes with a soft, feminine grace. Best of all, as she had lost her gauntness, that heart-stopping smile had returned, and the highlighted spot by her lip was more entrancing than ever.

'D'you know, darling,' he murmured, as he slipped an arm round her waist, 'I agree with Arthur Miller. I prefer you a little plump.'

His wife pinched his cheek. 'You always did,' she answered playfully.

And Ambassador Lambert W. Strether the Fourth and his wife Marilyn Six, otherwise known as Marty, with a surname of her own for the first time in her life, descended the staircase hand in hand, and went out to eat a farewell lunch with their guests.